TALE
OF THE
HEART
QUEEN

TALE OF THE HEART QUEEN

NISHA J. TULI

FOREVER

New York Boston

Forever
Hachette Book Group
1290 Avenue of the Americas, New York, NY 10104
read-forever.com
@readforeverpub

First Edition: November 2024

Forever is an imprint of Grand Central Publishing. The Forever name and logo are registered trademarks of Hachette Book Group, Inc.

The publisher is not responsible for websites (or their content) that are not owned by the publisher.

The Hachette Speakers Bureau provides a wide range of authors for speaking events. To find out more, go to hachettespeakersbureau.com or email HachetteSpeakers@hbgusa.com.

Forever books may be purchased in bulk for business, educational, or promotional use. For information, please contact your local bookseller or the Hachette Book Group Special Markets Department at special.markets@hbgusa.com.

Library of Congress Cataloging-in-Publication Data

Names: Tuli, Nisha J., author.
Title: Tale of the heart queen / Nisha J. Tuli.
Description: First edition. | New York : Forever, 2024. | Series: Artefacts of Ouranos; book 4
Identifiers: LCCN 2024023666 | ISBN 9781538767696 (trade paperback) | ISBN 9781538767702 (ebook)
Subjects: LCGFT: Fantasy fiction. | Novels.
Classification: LCC PR9199.4.T8347 T35 2024 | DDC 813/.6—dc23/eng/20240524
LC record available at https://lccn.loc.gov/2024023666

ISBNs: 9781538767696 (Trade paperback); 9781538767702 (ebook)

Printed in the United States of America

LSC-C

Printing 3, 2025

*To everyone who's waiting for their rainbow
at the end of the storm.*

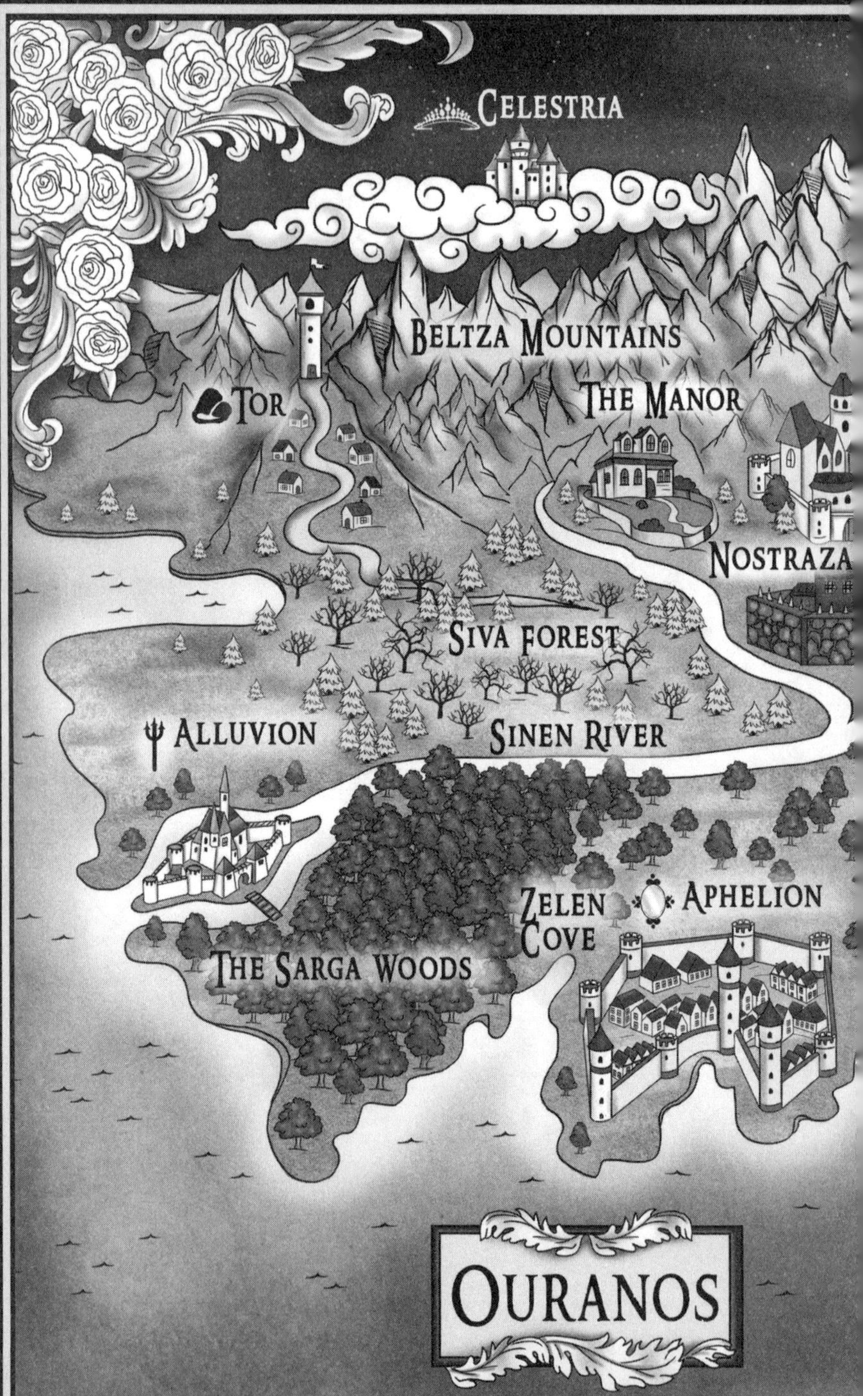

CELESTRIA

BELTZA MOUNTAINS

THE MANOR

TOR

NOSTRAZA

SIVA FOREST

ALLUVION

SINEN RIVER

ZELEN COVE

APHELION

THE SARGA WOODS

OURANOS

THE AURORA

THE VOID

CINTA
WILDS

THE VIOLET FOREST

QUEENDOM
OF HEART

THE WOODLANDS

W   N   E
     S

Author's Note

Dear Readers,

I'm so excited to welcome you back to Ouranos one more time for the conclusion of this series that has taken over and changed my life. I know I left you on a bit of a rough note at the end of *Fate of the Sun King*, and I'm very sorry, but you're about to see why and how it all comes together now.

Tale of the Heart Queen was the hardest book I've tackled yet. (I think I said that last time, but finishing up a series turns out to be more challenging than it looks.) It's also the longest book I've ever written, but we had a lot of things to accomplish ... as you'll see.

I wrote every single word with the goal and hope that you'll love this series until the very last page. I know I did, and I'm very happy with the ending I gave them all.

Lor goes on her wildest adventure yet, so hold on to your hats because this will be a ride.

Listed below are the content warnings for this final installment of the Artefacts of Ouranos. Thank you for coming on this journey with me.

I promised you all a happy ending . . . so here it is.

Love,

Nisha

<u>Content Warnings:</u> You'll find the same themes and topics as the previous books in the series, including mentions of past abuse, both sexual and physical. There are mentions of trauma, suicide ideation, alcohol abuse, nonconsensual touching, and child abuse. There is also mention of pregnancy and its possible complications, though everything turns out fine.

The dogs are safe. Nothing happens or ever will happen to the dogs. They're both very good girls.

Chapter 1

LOR

My heart lives outside of my body now, bleeding out on the hard-packed earth where I kneel on the unforgiving ground.

Sobbing, I cling to Nadir, pressing my ear to his chest, willing his heart to beat. It remains silent and inert, like wood charred by wildfires, drained of life and slowly crackling to ash.

My ribbons of my dense crimson magic pump through his limbs, grasping at nothing but the yawning emptiness in his chest. It's no use. My grip slips and stutters, and I struggle to cling to the shreds of his spirit draining into the soil.

If I keep pushing myself, I risk losing control of my healing magic and sliding into the electric threads of my lightning, causing even more damage.

It's hard to believe I could make this any worse.

I scream. I cry. I let every tear fall. I plead to the skies. I beg the goddess to save him. I bargain with the heavens. I offer up my soul in exchange for his life. I will do anything.

My vision blurs at the corners, and my stomach roils, bile basting the back of my throat. Sweat beads on my forehead as my surroundings tilt on an axis. My cries vibrate through every nerve, assaulting my ears and the tiny hairs covering my arms and the back of my neck. My skin hurts. My hair hurts. The pain in my chest feels like I'm being manipulated by giant hands, twisting my body at opposite angles until I'm nearly torn in half.

Distantly, my mind registers that Rion and his army are still close. Though we're hidden from view, I need to stay aware. Soon enough, they'll wake up under my dome of lightning unless I managed to kill them too. But something tells me it won't be that easy to finally rid myself of the Aurora King.

He has the ark of Heart in his possession. Until a few days ago, I'd never heard of it, but it belongs to me. And I want it back. Something tells me I *need* it back.

I recall the way it looked as it landed in my outstretched hands. What the Empyrium shared with me in the Evanescence. *Virulence.* That black glittering stone I looked upon so many times when I stared at the Aurora Keep from the Hollow, vowing to tear it apart.

Are the arks made of the same substance?

The memory of Rion's choking black magic filters into my turbulent thoughts. What shadowed power flows in his veins? What forces has the Aurora King been toying with? Is *that* what all of this has been about?

The Lord of the Underworld was the first Aurora King of the Second Age. He used virulence to attempt to destroy Zerra, and now Rion has his hands on the ark of Heart. Does he intend to destroy me with it? But why? Or am I only a step on a ladder to some other purpose?

Does Rion *know* that he sleeps in a bed surrounded by dark magic?

Could virulence bring Nadir back? I'd crawl into the very heart of the Beltza Mountains on my hands and knees if that's what it took.

"Nadir," I sob into him, soaking his shirt with my snot and tears. "I'm sorry. I'm so sorry."

I did this. I was reckless and impulsive, failing to consider who might be close when I unleashed. Rion and his guards had to pay for touching me again.

Thank you for telling me where she would be.

Rion's words come back to me with the diamond-hard clarity of honed steel.

But I refuse to believe them. If Nadir gave me up, he had a reason. He had no choice. He would never have done so willingly. After everything we've been through, I have to believe that. I handed him my trust, and I refuse to waver at the first test.

I fist the fabric of Nadir's tunic as I wail, wondering how I'm supposed to go on. How can I possibly exist without him?

My magic fizzes under my skin, pulling towards him like fingers seeking a drop of moisture in a desert. It's that same formidable tug I always felt before we finally admitted who we were to one another. Does it feel his loss, too?

No one's heart has broken into as many pieces as mine. No number exists high enough to count these shards pushing under my skin. I am bereft. Tossed in the waves of a sea with no bottom where I'll sink and sink for eternity.

My mate. *I killed my mate.*

"Help!" I scream as though anyone could make this stop being real. My stomach lurches, and my pulse pounds inside my skull, chipping away at its brittle walls. "Take me too," I whisper. I can't go on knowing *I* did this to him.

My heart lives outside of me now, exposed and raw for the world to witness the monster I've become.

I cry, and I cry until my soul melts out of my chest and my limbs drain of every emotion and feeling, leaving me numb and hollow and broken.

CHAPTER 2

"Oh, do stop your blubbering," comes a sharp voice, shocking me into choked silence. My head snaps up to find we're no longer in the forest where I dragged Nadir. "It's so very...phlegmy."

We're in a massive round room, the floor made of a shiny material that might be marble, except it's one continuous slab with no discernible breaks. Windows surround us, filtering in soft white light that seems to almost hum. I feel it more than I hear it with the barest vibration in the backs of my teeth.

Though this isn't the same room where I met the Empyrium, premonition tells me I'm back in the Evanescence, but I can't tell if that's a good thing or a bad thing.

Given my luck lately, it's probably a terrible fucking thing.

Before me stands a woman wearing a silvery dress that dusts

the floor in light, airy folds. Her bronzed arms are bare, and her blonde hair curls almost to her waist, crowned with a silver circlet framing her lovely, heart-shaped face. A pair of piercing aquamarine eyes stare down at me with cool detachment.

She seems familiar, and it takes me a moment to place her. She's the former Aphelion queen who failed to help her people and was "volunteered" to become a god.

"Zerra," I whisper, and she tips her head, looking down at me like I'm dung smeared on the heel of her shoe.

"You called me." She gracefully spreads her arms with her palms turned up. "So here I am."

I search my surroundings for the Empyrium and their strange shifting body of many people, but there appears to be only the three of us in the room.

"*This* is the male you're so attached to," Zerra says with a sniff as she elegantly sinks to her heels and assesses him from head to toe. It takes a moment to process those words. Does she know who I am? Who Nadir is?

I reach out and grab her slender wrist. She feels as delicate as a bird, but the air around her is perfumed with the stench of chaos, and I would do well not to underestimate her.

"Can you help him?" I ask as she snatches it away.

She's a god. Surely if anyone can fix this, then it's her.

"Please. I screwed up. I lost control of my magic, and I . . ."

Zerra's nostrils flare before she pushes herself to stand and takes two careful steps back, putting distance between us.

"I can help him," she says matter-of-factly, as though she hasn't just offered me a lifeline woven of glittering golden thread.

"Thank you," I say, prepared to lay down my own life or whatever else she demands. "Please. I'll do anything if you can help him."

Zerra's mouth twists up into a smile that sets me on edge.

"Yes. That you will, Lor."

I blink, again noting the ominous bite of her beauty and waiting for whatever condition she's about to attach to my future. *Our* future. I squeeze Nadir, hoping he knows I'm doing everything I can to fix this.

"What?" I finally ask while she continues staring at me with that same haughty look. "He's not breathing. Hurry up. What do you want?"

She waves a hand. "Don't worry. As long as he's with me, he's in a suspended state. He'll be fine once I choose to revive him. It will be like you never killed him at all."

Those words loosen the bolt screwed inside my chest, but it can't be that easy. I'm confident I have many bridges yet to cross before this is over. I cling to him tighter, feeling how cold he's grown already and how the color has leached from his skin. I run a thumb over the arch of his dark brow, my fingers caressing his cheek as my eyes burn with tears. When I look back at Zerra, she's watching us, a crease denting the space between her brilliant blue eyes.

"What will make you choose to revive him?" I ask, gritting my teeth with impatience.

She clasps her hands at her waist and slowly paces a few steps left and then right before turning back. With my heart wedged in my throat, I clamp down on the urge to scream at her to hurry the fuck up.

"The arks," she says after a few moments as a few pieces shift into place.

"The arks. Cloris Payne told us about them."

"*High Priestess Cloris*," she says. "You will respect her position and address her as is her station."

I roll my neck because otherwise I'll roll my eyes. I'll respect Cloris fucking Payne when pigs grow unicorn horns.

"Fine. *High Priestess Cloris* told me."

Zerra tips her chin as if that pleases her. But only a little. Her entire demeanor speaks to something that resembles a mortal-shaped sneer. This is the goddess who controls our lives? This small, petty woman?

"I don't have the ark of Heart if that's what you're after."

"All in due time," she says.

I'm choosing not to think too hard about what that means, because for now, Nadir is the only thing that matters.

"The Alluvion King has an ark in his possession," Zerra says.

I sigh, feeling pressure build in my temples, already knowing where *this* is going.

"I want you to retrieve it for me," she says.

"Of course you do. And then you'll bring him back?"

She presses her lips together and nods.

"Then I'll bring him back."

"What if I can't find it?"

She wrinkles her nose and tips her head in a smooth feline movement. "Then your mate will die."

At those words, my chest squeezes like my ribs are tied together with thick iron chains.

"Bring him back now," I plead. "He can help me find it. And if we can't, we'll find another way to repay you. You have my word."

Zerra paces a few more steps in the other direction, taking her time. I get the sense she wants to make me squirm, and I do my best to control my temper. She's the only hope I have right now, and I have to remain on her good side.

If she has one.

Just from this single interaction and my brief window into her past, I suspect the good side of this High Fae queen-turned-goddess was set on fire and burned to ash a long time ago.

"No," she says. "I don't care for that idea."

"But Nadir knows more about the rulers and their kingdoms than I do," I say. "He'll be a much better asset in aiding me. I'll find it much quicker."

I try modulating my voice into something that resembles confidence when my insides are liquefying into a raw pool of regret.

"And have you two plotting against me?" she asks. My forehead furrows as I think about the last thing the Empyrium said to me. They want to replace Zerra... and that's when their final words come barreling back with the force of a tidal wave.

A queen without a queendom.

They want me for the job. I think.

Does Zerra know that? Am I now a threat to her?

Suspicion burns up the back of my neck. What are the odds Zerra found me only moments later? Surely the Empyrium wouldn't have told her? And if they did, *why*?

I shake my head, pretending I have no clue. "I don't know what that means. Why would we plot against you?"

I don't want this role. It's the last thing I want, just like the original rulers who also refused this fate. They wanted to return home and help their people recover from the disasters plaguing their lands. That's what I want. I want to return to Heart and take my place where I'm sure I belong.

I ignore the tiny, chastising voice in my head telling me that maybe that has never actually been my destiny, even if it's what I want.

But one problem at a time, I guess.

Should I tell her I don't intend to replace her? Would she believe me? What if she doesn't know about any of this, and I'd just be revealing everything to her?

"We wouldn't do that," I say. "I don't even know *how* we'd do that."

She makes a noise that suggests she doesn't believe me.

"These are my conditions. You will travel to Alluvion, ingratiate yourself with Cyan, and find out where his ark is hiding."

"That's it?" I ask, hope spiraling in my chest. That I can do.

"No, that's not *it*," she bites out like I'm literally the stupidest person she's ever met. "Then you're going to steal it for me."

I hold in another weary sigh that threatens to topple this entire room. Everyone wants something from me. Rion. Atlas. Cloris. And now...this goddess who seems like kind of a bitch. But worse than that, she seems dangerous. A knifepoint dangling over my head.

"And then you'll bring Nadir back to life?"

"Yes," she says. "Decide. I grow weary of this conversation. I can just as easily let him die right now. It truly doesn't matter to me."

She says the words casually, but they taste like a lie.

The Empyrium described the great lengths she went to retrieve the arks in the past. She wouldn't have done any of that if they didn't matter. She tore apart Ouranos trying to root them out, and now she intends to search for them again.

Why does she think I'll succeed where her priestesses failed? Why is she asking *me*? Did she see an opportunity when I called for her, knowing she could use Nadir as leverage? Or is all of this a coincidence?

Does any of it matter right now when his life is on the line?

"Where will Nadir be while I'm in Alluvion?"

"Right here with me," Zerra says. "Were you expecting a parade for him?"

The bitter taste of anger flashes in the back of my throat. "I just need to know he'll be safe."

She rolls her eyes. "You really don't have much choice, dear Lor. Either accept my offer or I'll send you back to Ouranos, and you can see how you manage on your own. But he'll be gone. Understand that."

I could be walking into her trap if she *does* know of the Empyrium's plans, and I have no idea if she'll keep her word, but I'm also aware that I have little currency to offer. If I don't try, then Nadir will die for sure.

She waves her hand over his body like he's a fallen log blocking her path. How can a goddess be so callous? I remind myself that she was a spoiled young queen who was forced into this role. She is no benevolent spirit, as we've all been led to believe. She never lived up to the potential the Empyrium saw in her. This might be all she knows.

"Fine," I say through gritted teeth. It's a fool's mission, but I'll do anything to save my mate.

And really, how bad could this be?

I rub a hand down my face.

When did I get so good at kidding myself?

"I thought you'd say that," she says with a simpering smile. "You have five days."

"What? That's not enough time!"

But a second later, my surroundings blink out in a flash of white light, and I find myself lying facedown on a warm patch of sand, a strong wind tossing my hair and tugging at my clothing.

I cough the grit out of my mouth as I roll over to find an expanse of crystal-blue ocean filling the horizon. Sitting up, I scan my surroundings and realize Zerra must have dropped me in Alluvion.

At least she did me this favor. She must really want that ark.

"That bitch," I say, wiping sand from my mouth, but the effort only deposits more fine grains onto my tongue. I try to spit them out, but more wedge between my teeth and in my throat.

I wince at the ache in every joint and muscle. Between the fight and the chase inside the Sun Palace, trying to heal Nadir, and the emotional weight of losing my mate, I feel like I've been filled with a thousand pounds of lead.

My quest stands in the distance. A shimmering palace made of what looks like sea glass sits on the shore, glistening in the sun—the Alluvion King's home.

I stare at it, wondering how to approach this. Walk up and announce myself? Tell Cyan who I am? Would he believe me? And if he does, will he welcome me or vilify me for my grandmother's actions? Maybe he'll try to use me like everyone else. Can I trust my secrets with him? Do the rulers of Ouranos know the heir of Heart has surfaced?

I stumble to my feet, dusting sand off my golden Sun Palace livery. I think of Nadir in his black clothes and how he refused to wear the uniform during our mission to the Mirror. A sob cracks in my chest, and I hold my hand against it as though I could stop my heart from leaking out and bleeding through my ribs. But I have to keep it together for his sake.

I attempt to straighten my wrinkled clothes and finger comb the tangles out of my hair. I rub my face as if that might do something to make me more presentable. I must look like something the ocean vomited onto the shore.

"You couldn't have given me something clean to wear?!" I shout at the sky, but I'm met with only belligerent silence.

Zerra's probably watching me, loving every moment of this.

"Fucking gods," I mumble to myself as I pick my way through the soft sand that's already filling my boots, chafing my skin.

I remember the beaches of Aphelion and the day I was dangled on a rope over the water. I've decided I hate beaches and sand and maybe the ocean, too, as pretty as it is. This one's probably also filled with deadly, flesh-eating creatures.

I pull off my boots and then curse when the hot sand instantly burns my feet.

Yes, I fucking hate the beach.

Loathe it, in fact.

I move quickly, attempting to find relief from this cursed stretch of blazing sand.

Finally, a stone pathway appears, winding towards the palace. In the distance, I make out a pair of guards flanking an entrance.

It feels as though I have no choice but to walk up and introduce myself. I could try to find a way to sneak in, perhaps get a job as a servant like Willow in Aphelion, but the clock is ticking on an impossible timeline, and I only have five days. This will require directness.

I make my way up the path. The stones are warm, but at least they don't singe my feet. When I'm in view of the gate, I stop, again trying to smooth down my hair to make myself appear somewhat like the queen I apparently am. I'm sure it's hopeless, though.

I consider putting my boots back on, but my feet are covered in sand, and the idea is deeply unappealing.

So I straighten my shoulders, trying to radiate confidence.

Fake it until you make it, they say.

I have a feeling I'm about to become the world's biggest imposter.

I blow out a breath and then march towards the gate with my boots dangling from my hand and my chin held high, clinging to the promise of my certain failure.

CHAPTER 3

ALLUVION—THE CRYSTAL PALACE

I limp my way up the path as the Alluvion guards eye me with understandable suspicion. They wear light clothing—swaths of blue fabric slung across their broad chests, leaving slivers of exposed sun-kissed skin, and knee-length skirts draped around their hips. Silver shoulder plates, vambraces, and shin guards complete their armor.

They each hold a spear in one hand and wear a sword strapped to their back. My lightning magic buzzes under my skin, and I'd have no problem dispatching these two obstacles, but I don't want to make that sort of entrance. Cyan will never trust me with the ark's location if I go around maiming his guards without provocation.

The palace glints in the sun, reflecting so brightly its brilliance sears my retinas. The guards wear shields over their eyes made from pairs of oval-shaped lenses, obviously meant to protect from the glare.

When I'm a few feet away, I stop. We eye each other as they look at me and then beyond as if trying to determine where I've come from. Fair question because there's nothing behind me but miles of empty sand and ocean. It makes me wonder why guards protect this entrance, but I guess that's neither here nor there. Maybe Cyan is the paranoid type.

"Hi," I say, waving like an idiot as they stare at me wordlessly. I drop my hand, suddenly nervous, as heat pricks up the back of my neck that has nothing to do with the temperature.

"I am here to see your king."

Oh, very smooth, Lor. That'll convince them. I attempt to infuse some authority and poise into my posture, but I've clearly failed as the guard on the left stares at me like I've grown another head.

"Now," I add, hoping it makes me sound sufficiently bossy. That's what a queen would do, right?

The guard narrows his striking blue eyes.

"Who are you?" he asks.

"I'm..." What do I say? I can't just blurt out that I'm the Heart Queen. First, who'll believe me? Second, too many people in Ouranos view my family in a less than favorable light. I'm just as likely to be gutted with a stake and left for the vultures as offered the welcome mat.

"I'm Serce's granddaughter," I say, hoping that's vague but

also specific enough. I wait for some sign these words mean something to this pair.

"Who is that?" the guard on the right asks. "And why should we care?"

I blow out a breath and scratch the back of my scalp.

"Please. Will you just go and tell your king that? He'll know what it means."

The guard scoffs. "Run along, sweetheart, unless you want to spend a night in His Majesty's dungeon."

"Just for asking a question?"

"For disturbing the peace."

I make a show of looking at the empty space around us, at the deserted beach where not a single other soul is present, and then raise an eyebrow with a pointed look.

He clears his throat. "Nevertheless. No one demands an audience with the king."

"I'm not demanding. I'm asking. Very politely."

The guard sighs and shakes his head before he exchanges a look with his companion.

"Very well," the first guard says. "Follow me."

"Really?" I say, hardly daring to believe my luck. This still doesn't guarantee Cyan will see me, but at least it's progress. "I mean . . . yes, okay. Good. Take me to your king." I throw my shoulders back again, trying to pretend I belong here.

He starts to roll his eyes but catches himself like the well-trained soldier he is. He opens the dark blue door made of some kind of shimmering material and gestures me ahead.

"Walk directly in front of me and don't touch anything," he

says. I nod, lifting my hand in promise before I'm ushered into the palace's cool interior. I blink as my eyes adjust to the shift. Though high windows let in plenty of light, it's an abrupt change from the blazing reflections outside.

The watery blue tiles are cool on my feet, and I wince at the sensation of a reverse burn against my sweltering soles. I lift the hair on the back of my neck, attempting to expose it to a lick of cool air, savoring a break from the beating sun.

"Walk," the guard says before we march down a hallway towards a large chamber through an arched doorway. As we near the end, he calls out, "Halt."

He brushes past me. "Stay there."

Two more guards flank the entrance. One male and one female, both stiff with attention. My escort exchanges a few words with the High Fae female in a low voice that I strain to hear. She casts a look at me and then back before jerking her chin.

The first guard then passes me by and walks in the direction we came, shaking his head as though I've ruined his entire day.

"It was nice meeting you too," I call to his retreating back.

Not surprisingly, he doesn't respond or acknowledge my existence.

"Come with me," the female guard says as I turn to face her.

She has deep olive skin, her nose and cheeks covered in a dusting of brown freckles, likely garnered from hours in the sun. Her brown hair is tied in a high braided ponytail that accentuates the hard lines of her face, and her dark green eyes flash with anger. I can't tell if it's because of me or because she's just having one of those days.

I'm led through the palace and its winding halls, hearing the crash of the ocean in the distance. Otherwise, it's quiet here, no one passing us as we walk. The woman stares straight ahead as she marches at a brisk pace.

We pass high windows made of stained glass in various shades of blue and green and walls embedded with the fossils of seashells and sea life, all dusted with sparkling silver. As we head down another long hall, I see more guards waiting at the end.

We approach them, and the woman says, "Take her."

Before I have a chance to react, two enormous male High Fae wearing Alluvion armor seize me roughly by each arm.

"What are you doing?" I ask as a door swings open and they drag me through. "I demand to see your king!"

The female guard walks ahead of us and calls over her shoulder. "You were told you'd be sent to the dungeons if you insisted on bothering the guards."

"What?" I say, realization dawning on me. That bastard tricked me into following him inside, and I did so like a gullible little duckling.

My magic sparks under my skin, begging to be released. All it would take is a flick, and all three would be dead. But who else would I kill?

My heart stutters in my chest when I think of Nadir's lifeless face on the ground. Of the way it felt when his heart stopped and the screams ripped from my throat. I don't think

I can face that again—even if these Fae are all strangers intent on locking me up.

My hands ball into fists as the guards force me to walk-stumble down a set of winding stairs.

They're just doing their job. I've been granted immense power at the tips of my fingers, and I've discovered the hard way that I need to learn how to use it responsibly. I can't just go around blasting away everyone who pisses me off.

A previous Lor might have done that, but I'm trying to be a better person.

Besides, I'm inside the palace at least. I'll find a way to convince them to grant me an audience with Cyan, though I'm painfully aware that spending any time in the dungeon means fewer days I have to save Nadir.

Inhaling a deep breath, I will my nerves to settle. I have to keep a clear head. I won't do him any favors if I panic and mess this up. I need to earn Cyan's trust. My insides war with the need to think logically while my heart flakes away bit by bit. I've always been a master of compartmentalizing my emotions, but even I have my limits.

Finally, we reach the bottom of the staircase, and the female guard leads us past a row of cells, some already occupied and some sitting empty, until she comes to a stop and points.

I'm shoved inside by the guards with such force that I trip and drop my boots, still clutched in one of my hands. Someone kicks them in after me, and the door clangs shut before the lock clicks into place.

"Let me out of here!" I shout, grabbing the bars and shaking them. "I didn't do anything wrong!"

The female guard stands at the bars, and it's then I notice the ornateness of her armor—it's similar to the men's behind her, but detailed scrollwork marks her shoulders and vambraces, suggesting she's someone of higher rank. Stacked with lean muscle, she looks like she could kick my ass using just her pinky finger.

There's also something familiar about her, but I can't figure out what.

"You'll be quiet," the woman says with such vehement authority that I do, in fact, go very quiet. "*Serce's* granddaughter is not welcome here."

The coldness in her eyes sets the hairs on the back of my neck at attention. *Shit.* Maybe that was the wrong hand to play.

But who is this woman, and how did she know my grandmother?

"I don't know what vile scheme brought you here, but the *only* reason I'm allowing you to live is so His Majesty can question you first."

Then she scans me from head to toe, her eyes narrowing ever so slightly with an implied threat, before she turns on her heel.

"Come," she says to the guards before they all disappear, leaving me alone in my cell as Zerra's clock *tick tick ticks* over my head.

CHAPTER 4

GABRIEL

APHELION—THE SUN PALACE

My sword dangles from my hand, the tip dragging over the pavement with a dry scrape. It feels like it weighs a hundred pounds. Maybe a thousand. I step over a body, barely noticing it, my legs heavy and leaden, and make my way towards the palace.

I stare at the carnage, the air singed with smoke and ashes. And death. So much death. More than I ever imagined and so much more than I ever hoped.

When I concocted the plan to reveal Tyr to the world, I knew it would break us. I knew it would stir up ancient grudges and shake the foundations of our existence, but I hoped it wouldn't be this bad.

What a naive asshole I was.

The sky is finally lightening after an endless day and night of fighting. Red bleeds into the sunrise, mimicking the blood that runs along the streets.

Gods, I fucked this all up.

Running a hand through my hair, I feel my fingers tangle in the knotted strands sticky with sweat and blood, and Zerra only knows what else.

Everyone finally saw the truth. Tyr is alive, and Atlas is a fraud.

I've lived with this secret for so many years, but its release doesn't feel as light as I expected. Now I stand burdened with something entirely new and unfamiliar.

Tyr is alive, but he isn't *present*. And Atlas is a traitor. He has always been a traitor.

He cursed me as they took him away, screaming and hurling accusations of my betrayal. I tried to drag up an ounce of sympathy for what I'd done. I've condemned him to an inevitable fate, but will this be where it ends? I've lived in Atlas's shadow for so long, a victim of his ambition and his cruelty, but I'm not sure if I have the strength to face what comes next. There's a punishment for traitors in Aphelion. The rules are clear. And for what reason would anyone want to show him leniency? I'm just hoping I'm not the one forced to make that call.

My only consolation is that I got Tyr to safety before the

fighting became unmanageable. I'm not exactly sure what precipitated the eruption. Tensions were high, and people were angry and confused, but I don't know what single entity triggered the match that lit the fuse. It probably wasn't only one thing. It was a thousand tiny moments, each one pulsing with blood and fury and betrayal, crackling with dry sparks until the wildfire could no longer be contained.

My toe catches on a piece of paper. A torn poster with Atlas's face on it. I lean down and pick it up, staring at his likeness. The crimes against the low fae are listed in bright red ink. Not only had he sequestered them to The Umbra, refusing to meet their demands or even hear them out, but he'd never had the authority to do *any* of this.

It all became too much.

Thunder rolls overhead, dark grey clouds tumbling over one another. A gust of wind tears the paper from my hand, and I watch it toss in the air like the final leaf falling in winter. It feels like an omen.

The gilded Sun Palace stands muted against the dull sky.

I wonder if it will ever sparkle the same way again.

I scan my surroundings, searching for my brothers. I spy their wings in the distance, their shoulders hunched. Drex and Syran guard Atlas in the dungeons while we all attempt to make sense of everything.

My gaze wanders to the palace and the shattered throne room ceiling. The dome that once looked over Aphelion is gone, every single piece obliterated into dust.

That awesome show of power might have been the spark that ignited the chaos. When those red bolts of lightning filled the sky, it shook something loose that had been squeezed tight for far too long. *Lor.* She got to the Mirror. But what happened to her? The fact that I haven't seen her yet sits like a rock in my stomach, and I ask myself why I care at all.

Somewhere along the way, I started to care, and I know that's dangerous. Caring always leads to disappointment. I've learned that the hard way, far too many times to count. But I recognize the good in her. She is brave and strong and loyal. She approached those barbaric Trials head-on and never faltered. Even I'm not too much of a cynic not to respect that.

She'd give the people of Heart the queen they finally deserve.

I shake my head and run a hand down my face. Shit, when did I get so sentimental?

Sighing, I limp towards the palace gates hanging askew from their hinges, my knee twisting with each step. I don't remember how I injured it, but it's enough to hamper my movement, sending jolts up to my hip.

Small fires burn all over the place, rubble coats the street, and ash drifts from the sky, dusting everything with death. What a fucking mess.

My thoughts of Lor wander to her family and to Nadir, who is also missing. Mael and Lor's brother, whose name I can't remember—Tyler?—have been helping around the palace, attempting to subdue the riots and bring order to the chaos.

Her sister—who I am sure now was Apricia's maid who looked so familiar—hasn't been around, and I hope she got to safety.

They were obviously trying to find a way into the palace,

and I have to admire their cunning, though masquerading as Apricia's maid was a lot to ask. Maybe they were spying on me too. I can't really blame them for that. I have so many secrets.

Had. Now everything has been exposed.

I inhale deeply, wincing at the ache in my lungs. When Tyr finally released me from Atlas's commands, it felt like drawing a proper breath for the first time in a hundred years. Still, it was short relief because . . . well, look at this place. I've just exchanged one set of problems for another.

Slowly, I approach the palace doors, dreading what I'll find inside.

The nobles had no choice but to fight back, some with magic, leaving the scarred evidence on the walls and floors. The mobs didn't care who they hurt. They only cared for blood. They only cared about making the High Fae hurt. And there are plenty here who deserve every bit of their vengeance.

Inside the palace, I find a scene of destruction: rugs torn up, mirrors smashed, broken glass crackling under my steps, blood covering the walls. I'd expected as much. I just hope Tyr is still safe. I'll check on him in a moment, but first, I must deal with something.

As my Fae healing catches up with me, my steps become more sure while I proceed through the halls, relieved to find the palace unscathed the deeper I move. I pass my fair share of bodies and avert my eyes—not because the sight of death bothers me, but because I'm not ready to face it yet.

When I reach the entrance of the dungeons, I find it unguarded, and my senses prickle with alarm. Entering the dim stairwell, I circle down into the depths. It's too quiet.

When I arrive at the bottom, everything breathes with the silence of stone. I hear nothing, not even the soft murmurs or the occasional whimpers of the inmates.

I lift my sword, pointing it towards the darkness, noting every door stands open and every cell stands empty. Did the rebels come down here to break out their friends? Moving along the narrow corridor, I sense there's more to this eerie dread swirling in my gut. What if they saw Atlas and tore him to shreds? My feelings for him are complicated, but I would never wish him that.

I continue walking, staring into each empty cell, then reach the end as my breath stalls in my chest. A neatly folded golden jacket lies on the floor in the middle of a cell. On top of it sits an ornamental gold crown, like an offering.

Not an offering. A signal. The immutable evidence that Atlas was here and now . . . he isn't. I recognize the crown and jacket he wore during the presentation when I tore apart my home.

I swing around, wondering how he escaped, then bile surges up the back of my throat.

Drex and Syran, the warders I assigned to guard Atlas, hang suspended to the wall, iron pins shoved through their white wings, and long gashes slit across their throats. Gold blood drips down their feathers, and crimson stains their gilded armor, their heads hanging, and their bodies limp.

And Atlas . . .

That fucking traitor is gone.

CHAPTER 5

LOR

ALLUVION—THE CRYSTAL PALACE

I sit in my cell and wait. I've considered a thousand options to extricate myself from this stone box, but none of them make sense. Sure, I could use my magic to blast a hole through the wall, but I need to earn Cyan's trust. The ark isn't just lying around for anyone to find, and I'll have to talk—or trick—him into revealing its location.

I've already lost an entire day languishing in this prison, and I try not to think about Nadir's pallid face, but I see it every time I close my eyes. The way he appeared, teetering on the razor-fine edge of saving. Is he awake? Does he know what happened? Does he think I left him with Zerra?

My heart squeezes with a physical pain that makes my bones feel too tight. I stare at the ring he gave me for my birthday and remember the promise of forever he made with it. I clutch my chest at the thought of losing him. I can't do this. I *can't* lose him. I just found him. I suck a deep breath in and then let it out, trying not to spiral into a pit heaped with regrets and self-loathing.

Left alone with my thoughts, I also can't stop thinking about everyone back in Aphelion. My brother and sister. Amya. Mael. Even Gabriel. Gods, how I wish I could see them all. Wrap them in my arms and make sure they're safe.

For the rest of the day, the only people who visit are tight-lipped guards, who drop off minimal amounts of water and some kind of thin fish stew swimming with tentacled morsels I don't recognize before they disappear, pretending I don't exist. A congealed bowl sits near my feet, abandoned after I sniffed it and nearly went cross-eyed.

"Please!" I scream with my hands gripped around the bars. "I need to see the king!"

I haven't quite worked out what I'll say should he grant me an audience, but I'm banking on the "everyone hates Rion" card and hope that he, too, has no love for the Aurora King. I'll tell him part of the truth—that Rion captured me, and I escaped, but then I got lost, and that's how I ended up on his doorstep.

It's close enough to the truth to be believable. I hope.

"Please!" I scream. "Please!"

Is anyone listening? Maybe that female soldier with the fancy armor. She looked important and like someone who makes decisions about prisoners. She said the king would question me, but it seems like she's forgotten about me.

Or maybe she hasn't forgotten at all.

The way she hissed when she told me Serce's granddaughter isn't welcome here felt... personal? I recall the blistering rage in her eyes, and she might actually be using her time considering the best and most excruciating way to dice up my organs and string my head up onto a pike.

"Please! Someone!"

"Shut the fuck up!" shouts another inhabitant from his cell. "I'm trying to sleep!"

"Rude," I say, and then I start shouting again.

Eventually, my voice gives out, and I slump against the stone wall as I slide to the floor, watching the sun set through the tiny high window. I *can't* stay in here any longer waiting for Cyan to receive me. I crawl over to the bars and press my face between them, trying to gauge the number of prisoners trapped down here.

I didn't want to resort to this, but it's time to blow a hole through this dungeon. However, I refuse to hurt anyone in the process. If I listen carefully, I can hear the ocean's thunder through the thick stone and decide the back wall makes the most sense.

Footsteps sound from the distance, echoing through the space. It's time for what passes for dinner around here, I guess. I scramble back and curl up into a ball, uninterested in their slop, even though my stomach twists with hunger.

Once the guards leave, I'll escape. Once I'm free, I'll find another way to enter the palace. It means I won't find the ark through diplomatic means, but at least I'll be out of here and can start strategizing a new plan.

I scrunch my eyes as the steps approach but realize I don't hear the sounds of carelessly dropped trays of food. Instead, the footsteps stop outside my cell, and my eyes peel open.

"I've been told you've been making quite the ruckus," comes a deep voice.

There stands Cyan, the Alluvion King. I remember during the Sun Queen ball when he sat on his glass throne in an insouciant pose, possibly wishing he was anywhere but that over-the-top party masquerading as a glittering backdrop for the Tributes' deaths.

That made two of us. Three if you count Nadir.

His skin is so pale it's nearly blue, and a long fall of indigo hair covers his bare, sculpted shoulders. He wears nothing on his top half, showing off the planes of a chiseled stomach and chest, along with fitted shorts made of thin white material clinging to his thick thighs. Dark blue eyes peer at me with a mixture of curiosity and, maybe, a touch of amusement.

"Your Majesty," I say, pushing the tangle of hair from my face. "I've been wanting to speak with you."

I use the wall as leverage as I push myself to stand. I've barely slept or eaten for days, and my limbs tremble with hollow exhaustion.

"So you've made clear," Cyan says as he scans me from head to toe. Next to him is the same female guard who threw me in here, standing curiously close to her king while giving me that same scathing look. "Please call me Cyan."

"Why?" I ask, instantly on alert at this show of camaraderie.

"Did you not tell my guards that you are Serce's grand-daughter?"

The female guard scowls and then spits on the floor, her eyes darkening with rage. I frown at her before swinging my gaze to Cyan.

"I did. I was hoping that would get your attention."

"So it's true?" Cyan asks.

"It's true—" interrupts the female guard, her voice laced with poison. "Look at her."

Cyan raises a hand. "Linden, please. Allow the girl to speak."

Linden bristles, sealing her lips shut like they're rusted hinges, but not before she pins me with another caustic look that attempts to melt me into the floor. I make a mental note to keep my distance.

"I am Serce's granddaughter," I say and hold my breath.

Cyan squints, attempting to assess me through the dimness of the dungeon. Maybe he should consider adding a few more lights. Perhaps a pallet to sleep on and food that doesn't taste like sweaty socks spiced with rotting garbage.

He shakes his head.

"I don't see it," he says, lifting a hand to scratch his chin.

"Excuse me?" I reply.

"I see your grandfather," he says, and that makes me blink.

Linden's olive skin turns bright red. She's squeezing her lips together so hard, I'm surprised she hasn't sliced them off with her teeth.

"Yes," I breathe. "I am also Wolf's granddaughter."

Something about those words hangs in the air, like a smoke signal curling against a blue sky on a clear day.

"I'll kill her!" Linden says, finally losing control of her emotions as she draws the blade from her hip.

"You will not," Cyan says, lifting a hand and looking down at her with a pointed glare. "At least not until we understand why she's here."

Cyan turns back to me with a gleam in his eyes, and I swallow down my nervousness. Maybe revealing who I am was a mistake. But how else was I supposed to get close to him? At least he finally showed up and I wasn't forced to resort to more drastic measures.

"Open it," Cyan says to a guard who waits in the shadows. "I won't restrain you," he says, addressing me. "Provided you're willing to cooperate as my guest."

He presses a large hand to his pale, carved chest and gives me the same pointed look.

"Sure," I say. "I didn't come here to cause trouble."

I mean ... that's sort of true.

Any trouble I'm here to cause is completely against my will. So that counts, right?

The guard opens my cell door, and then Cyan and Linden turn as the king beckons me to follow. I do as he says as two more guards bring up our rear.

Guest, indeed.

We head up the same stairs I was dragged down earlier. Cyan and Linden speak in low voices, their bodies still weirdly close, his hand resting on her lower back, but I can't parse out their conversation.

When we enter the brightly lit palace, Cyan stops to address me. "Come, dinner is waiting."

He says it cordially as if I truly am an invited guest, but I'm not about to forget how he told Linden that she couldn't kill me for *now*.

I eye him with suspicion, but his half-cocked smile doesn't waver. Linden, on the other hand, keeps throwing me looks as dirty as the water we used to clean the sheets in Nostraza.

"Okay," I say before he nods and then continues walking, his bare feet quiet against the smooth floors.

We pass through a set of arched glass doors out onto a large balcony with a white pergola decorated with strips of sheer white fabric blowing in the breeze. The ocean stretches before us, crystal blue and sparkling. The sea in Aphelion had been stunning, but there's something extra about this ocean. A technicolor quality in the hue and the way the waves roll over one another like I'm watching a painting spring to life.

In the middle of the balcony is a long white table covered in white dishes filled with an array of colorful food.

Cyan takes his seat at the far end while Linden sits to his left.

"Ah, you're here," comes a breezy voice, and a moment later, another High Fae female approaches. Her skin is a deep, rich brown and her hair is a long fall of turquoise curls. She's wearing a sheer blue robe that molds to her body—I can see her dark nipples through the fabric—and a small pair of white bottoms on her lower half. As she walks, the slit in her robe reveals a length of her smooth leg that shimmers in the light.

"Anemone," Cyan says to the woman, his tone warm. "Come have dinner with us. Our guest has arrived."

She stops, places a hand on her hip, and scans me up and

down. "So this is her?" she asks. There's no menace in her expression, but there is something calculated in it.

"Yes," Linden says, gritting her teeth. "This is the filth that dared to darken our doorstep."

"I'm sorry," I say, finally having enough of her attitude. "What exactly is your problem with me? I know we haven't met before."

Linden's green eyes flash, a snarl ripping from her throat.

"Linden," Anemone chides. "Let's not be rude to our guest."

Anemone then moves down the length of the table, dragging her fingertips along the surface until she reaches Cyan and drops into his lap. Immediately, his hand finds her bare thigh.

"I will not deign to have dinner with *her*," Linden hisses.

"What did I do?" I demand, officially sick of this shit.

"Lor," Cyan says, his tone light. "I think it's time you are properly introduced to my second-in-command."

"Okay?"

"Linden is the former princess of The Woodlands, and I believe that makes her ... your great-aunt."

CHAPTER 6

O h. *Ohhhh.*

It takes a moment to fully process Cyan's words. Linden, with her brown hair and green eyes, looks nothing like the residents of Alluvion. Everyone else has silvery or blue hair and eyes that range from nearly white to charcoal to navy.

I look at her more closely, and there I see the resemblance to Cedar, the Woodlands King, in the slope of her nose and the bow of her lips.

"She *killed* my brother," Linden spits with enough venom to burn a hole in the floor.

"I had nothing to do with that," I say, feeling the desire to defend myself. "That was hundreds of years before I was born."

Linden takes a step towards me, and I scuttle back. I could

pretend I'm not afraid of her, but I'm ready to fold like a cheap paper fan. Meanwhile, she looks prepared to tip me into a pot and then enjoy me with a nice glass of wine. Or maybe a goblet sloshing with my blood, her chin dripping with my soul.

"Your entire family is responsible," she hisses. "She tricked him. Used him. And then *destroyed* him."

I open my mouth to respond, but I don't know what to say. That might all be true. It might not be. Everyone accuses my grandmother for what happened, but how much of a role did Wolf play in their downfall? It's curious that everyone blames her.

"I'm sorry," I say because I *am* sorry. I'm sorry for everything that happened. That I never had the chance to know them. That we spent our lives in hiding. I'm sorry for every single day and every person Serce hurt, even if I wasn't directly responsible for any of it.

"Linden," Cyan says, interrupting our tense exchange. "You can't blame the girl for Serce's mistakes."

"I can," Linden says, whipping around to face him. "I will."

Cyan presses his mouth together as his nose flares. "Come and sit," he says, patting the table next to him. "Have something to drink."

Linden grunts but drops into the seat next to him. Holding an ornate crystal decanter, Anemone leans across and fills a glass that she hands to Linden. Linden then drains the entire thing before slamming the glass on the table hard enough to nearly crack it.

The table, I mean. The glass is toast.

"Another," she barks as she grabs a new glass, and Anemone

fills this one too. Cyan takes Linden's hand and squeezes it before he flips it over and places a soft kiss on her palm. No one else blinks at the intimate gesture between the king and his army commander.

After Linden destroys another stiff drink, everyone's gaze falls on me. I swallow as the silence stretches awkwardly. I wasn't expecting the red carpet upon my arrival, but I also wasn't prepared to be accused of a litany of crimes I never committed.

I remember when I voiced these fears to Nadir and he said no one would hold me accountable for what my grandmother had done. I'm not happy to prove him wrong. I should probably get used to this, though perhaps Linden has more right to feel this way than most.

Anemone rises from her place on Cyan's lap and moves to the chair on his other side. Not wanting to be anywhere near Linden, who's still staring at me like she's trying to decide which part of me to stab first, I move around the table to take the empty seat next to Anemone.

Cyan sits back and regards me with an amused twinkle in his eyes. "A wise choice."

He gestures around the table. "You've met Linden. Please let me introduce you to Anemone."

"Hi," I say, already preferring her over my great aunt.

"Why don't you tell us a little about yourself," Cyan says. "Lor, is it?"

"How do you know that?" I ask.

He leans forward and clasps his large hands on the table. "Do you think you've been moving through Ouranos undetected? Rumors have been spreading."

"What rumors?"

He shrugs a broad shoulder. "Atlas stole you from Nostraza, where you've lived for most of your life. And Rion wants you for some reason I'm still trying to puzzle out."

"How do you know all that?" I ask. "When we were in The Woodlands, Cedar had no idea what had become of us."

Linden slams a hand on the table, making me jump.

"Do not speak my family's name," she growls. "My brother did not allow you into his home!"

My indignation flares, and I lean towards her, baring my teeth. "Yes. He did. He welcomed us into his home and let us eat his food and sleep in his beds. He invited us to attend the Winter Ball." I pause, wanting these next words to sting. "He let me hold the Woodlands Staff."

Linden hisses like a venomous snake twisting around my ankles. "Liar."

I roll my eyes. "Why would I lie about that?"

"You must have some angle." Linden stops and then glares. "What did you do with it? Why would he let you touch it?"

"Because it's my family, too," I say. "And I asked nicely."

Linden does not care for that answer or that reminder because, if it's possible, her expression turns even more toxic. Given how welcoming Cedar and Elswyth were, I guess we got off easy. I'm grateful Cedar didn't blame me for Wolf's death, too.

"Who is 'us'?" Linden asks.

"Me and my brother," I reply, and then inwardly grimace. She's really going to lose her shit when she finds out Tristan is the Woodlands Primary. With the way she's behaving, I kind of hope I'm there when she does. Maybe I should wrap up this gift with razors and barbed wire and hand it to her.

"There are two of you?" she snarls.

"Yes," I say with a glare, deciding to leave Willow out of this for the moment. "Your brother welcomed us as family. If you aren't inclined to do the same, then I can't force you, but stop looking at me like that and *stop* threatening me."

Linden glares for another few seconds before she takes another drink and then faces away. So it's to be pointedly ignoring me then. Fine, I can live with that.

"Why don't we eat?" Cyan suggests. He waves a hand, and a gaggle of servants materializes to fill our plates—some human and some low fae.

The low fae are of a type I've never seen before, with pale blue-and-green skin that shimmers like pearls. Some have gills on their necks, and others have patches of scales. Many of them have long blue-and-green hair, while some have hair that almost resembles beaded crystal strands.

I try not to stare, but they're beautiful.

They move about the table, ladling food onto our plates and bowls. A thick cream soup bobs with clams and pieces of fresh raw fish that are so bright and colorful they look like jewels.

Once the servants have finished, they bow, leaving us alone once again. My gaze follows them, and apparently my interest doesn't go unnoticed because a moment later, Cyan cuts through my thoughts. "Is there some problem with my staff?" he asks.

"Do low fae hold only positions of service here?" I ask, remembering what Nadir told me about Alluvion and how their laws don't oppress the low fae.

Cyan arches an eyebrow. "I see you've been spending time around Erevan."

I blink. How does Cyan know the rebellion leader in Aphelion?

"Yes, but I can think for myself, thanks."

"Erevan lived here with us for a time," Cyan says, answering my unasked question.

"So this is where he got his ideas?" I ask.

"In part," he says. "He told me he could never return to his home and look at it the same."

"He's been stirring up a rebellion in Aphelion," I say.

"I've heard as much. Tell me what's going on," Cyan says. "Reports have been coming in, but I can't parse out what is truth and what is fabrication. While you're at it, why don't you tell me what you're doing here? And where you've been hiding all this time?" He raises a hand. "The truth would be nice."

I take a few moments to gather myself, doing what I do best. Curving around truths to make my lies seem as believable as possible without revealing too much of myself. One day I'll be able to meet someone new and just be honest, but today is not that day.

"I was in Aphelion because I'm trying to locate the Heart Crown," I say, deciding not to mention the ark lest I arouse his suspicion.

I *had* the Heart Crown, but I dropped it when the Mirror tossed me the ark. Then Rion appeared, and now it could be anywhere between the Sun Palace and the Beltza Mountains. Maybe someone found it? Maybe Willow or Tristan? Gods, I hope they're okay.

"Why in Aphelion?" Cyan asks. "What would it be doing there?"

"I need to back up a little," I say. "There are many pieces to this story. We grew up in the Violet Forest under the secrecy and protection of the Woodlands King."

Linden bristles across from me, but she holds her tongue as I take a deep breath and prepare to live the pain of my history yet again. I don't mention Nadir during my narrative either. That feels like a secret I need to keep for now.

When I'm done, Cyan studies me as if trying to decide whether I'm telling the truth. I don't really care if he believes me, at least in so much as I can find the ark and get the fuck out of here.

"You went to Heart," Cyan says. "My scouts reported a skirmish near the castle not long ago."

"I did," I say, deciding that information is safe enough. "Rion found me there and tried to recapture me, but I managed to escape."

"So resourceful, aren't you, Heart Queen?" Cyan says with a smirk.

A loud bang startles us all. Linden is back to her storm cloud presence, her fist against the table where she just smashed it. She stands up, her chair tipping over in her haste. "Do not utter those words in my presence. The Heart Queen is dead. As she should be."

Cyan smiles at Linden, not the least bit affected by her hostility.

"Oh, Linden, come here."

He gently snags her wrist, tugging her closer before wrapping an arm around her hips and kissing the bare skin of her stomach. She doesn't move, her posture rigid.

"Are you all a . . . unit?" I ask, gesturing between them.

"You could say that," Cyan says.

"So who are you going to bond with? Atlas told me you'd been searching for a partner for a long time. Can you bond with more than one person?"

The question slips out, and it's clear this is a touchy subject as their eyes all meet and then look away.

"Who are you?" I ask Anemone. "What's your story?"

"You do ask a lot of questions, don't you?" she replies.

"It seems you all are asking the most."

"Hmm," Anemone answers. "I am a citizen of Alluvion who caught the king's eye."

She exchanges a warm look with the king, and I believe that part of her story, but something about her claim doesn't sit right. I scrutinize her as she tucks a piece of hair back from her face. Then I notice that her roots are black like they've grown out, and it almost seems like her hair has been dyed teal to mimic the people of Alluvion's. But why?

"Tell us what happened in Aphelion," Linden interrupts, clearly trying to change the subject, which feels a little obvious. They're clearly hiding something.

It's the first time my great-aunt has deigned to address me with anything but accusations and hostility, but I'm not chalking this up to any kind of win just yet. She just wants information.

"There are rumors of a battle," Cyan says. "That things went poorly for the king during the bonding ceremonies."

"A battle?" I ask. I've been so focused on returning to Nadir that I haven't had time to digest everything that went down in Aphelion. I have no idea what happened after Nadir and I entered the palace. Gabriel revealed the truth about Tyr, and then what? I just hope Tristan and Willow are safe.

"Yes," Cyan says. "Apparently, it turned quite violent."

He peers at me, and his suspicions are growing by the minute.

"Did you not just say that's where you came from?" he asks. "Surely you know this already?"

"Yes. No. I mean . . . yes, I was there, but—" I stop and take a deep breath as my lies and half-truths start to topple over each other. "Let me explain."

"Please," Cyan says, his patience clearly wearing thin. I've stumbled into his life with a lot of wild stories, and he doesn't even know yet that I'm here to steal from him. If I'm not careful, he'll sniff out my true purpose, and then I'm well and truly fucked. "Enlighten us."

I tell them more about my mission in Aphelion and what happened with Gabriel and Tyr, giving them enough details to make my stories sound plausible.

"Tyr lives?" Cyan asks, sitting up, the incredulity in his voice obvious. "That's impossible."

I shrug. I can't be sure the man Gabriel presented to Aphelion is, in fact, the true king, but everyone else seemed to believe it.

"And then what happened?" Cyan asks.

"I'm not sure. You know as much as I do at this point." I toy with the fork on the table, flipping it over and over. "Why weren't you there? Were you not invited?"

Cyan nods and sits back. "I declined my invitation. I had things that kept me here."

"I see," I answer when it appears he has no intentions of explaining any further.

"What does the Aurora King want with you?" Anemone asks.

"I don't know that either." It's partly the truth. I recall the details of what Cloris shared with me and Nadir. She revealed our location to the Aurora King, and he sought us out, but what was his goal? I had always assumed he wanted to keep us close and contained, but the way he's been chasing me across the continent suggests it's something more. We know he wanted the ark, but for what purpose?

I fall silent as their expressions all turn solemn. There's technically nothing *false* in my story. But my words are edged with emotion that even these three have to sense. I don't want to reveal my vulnerabilities before them, but I also need them to lower their guards. To trust me somewhat.

Cyan is the next to speak, his tone a little less flippant and with a bit more reverence.

"So what happened when you got to the Mirror?" he asks, picking up the thread of my earlier tale.

"I never got the chance to reach it," I lie. Again.

I cannot reveal anything that truly happened in that throne room. I've never been able to trust anyone beyond the safety of my family, and that has never changed. "Rion was in Aphelion, and he found me. He overpowered me and then captured me. I passed out and woke up somewhere in the forest. I used my magic to blast them all away, and then I ran, ending up here."

I take a long sip of my wine. Reliving those events feels like losing Nadir all over again, and it's everything I can do not to choke on the thick knot of my grief. I'm putting on a great show here, and they can't know how desperate I am. That would ruin everything.

Everyone is quiet for a few seconds, lost in their thoughts.

"That is quite a story," Cyan says a few moments later.

"Yes," I say. It sure is.

His eyebrows pinch together as he bites the inside of his cheek. "Well, then you must stay as my guest for a few days. To recover," he adds. "And perhaps we can get to know one another. A king and a queen of Ouranos's realms. You're practically family."

His gaze slides to Linden, who growls under her breath.

"I'd like that," I say, hoping it sounds like I mean it. My plan is to get the fuck out of here as soon as I can, but I'll have to pretend if I want to find out where the ark is.

He raises a glass and waits for the rest to do the same.

"To new beginnings," he says and takes a drink.

I follow suit, watching his face, wondering if he believed a single word I just said.

CHAPTER 7

NADIR

E verything fucking hurts. I inhale a long, deep breath through my nose as a wave of pain crests into every cell, squeezing my ribs until my bones feel on the verge of collapse.

What's wrong with me? My eyelids are weighed down, and my limbs feel like they're filled with lead. Why am I lying on the ground, and why does it feel like stone?

More breaths. In and out. In and out.

In through my nose and out through my mouth.

I'm no stranger to pain. I've fought in wars. I've sustained injuries that would kill a human and nearly kill a Fae. I've been cleaved with knives and swords and been stitched together more times than I can count. But this feels like pain turned inside out. I want to curl into a ball and die.

In and out. In and out.

More deep breaths as I attempt to sort through a haze of turbid thoughts.

What's the last thing I remember? *Lor.* My father captured us. There was that strange black smoke, but that was not his magic. That was something else.

I remember a flash of red light, and I remember flying a long distance before my heart seized in my chest.

And then what? Nothing. Just darkness.

Why can't I move, and where the fuck is Lor?

She left me. My father made it seem like I'd helped him, and like an idiot, I stood there and said nothing. I'd been too stunned to move. She has to know I would never have given her up to that monster, but everyone in her life has betrayed her. Why should she think I'm any different? It took everything for her to learn to trust me, and then my father wiped it away in one sweep.

But I *am* different. I would travel into the darkest pits of the Underworld to save her, and she knows that. Right? But where is she now? Does my father have her? Is he hurting her?

Why can't I *move*? I'd cry if I had the strength.

Agony ruptures through my bones with every serrated breath. I hold perfectly still, hoping to ease my pain as I listen to my surroundings.

Where am I? Are we back in The Aurora? Why can't I open my eyes?

A cool breeze ghosts over my skin, loosening some of the

tension in my muscles. Something warms my bare feet—what happened to my boots? It feels like sunlight, though I can't say why exactly.

So I'm not in The Aurora, then. Somewhere else.

I wiggle my fingers, trying to stretch them out, and even that hurts, pain radiating up my arms as I groan.

There's a soft rustle of fabric near my head, and I scrunch my eyes together before I will them open. The effort is monumental. Staggering. I tow up my lids, dragging them open like pulling up a corroded anchor from the bottom of a frozen sea.

The world before me is a blur of colors, everything smearing together into a shapeless blot. I blink, nearly losing the will to open them again. I repeat the process over and over until they eventually become like well-oiled hinges, and my vision slowly crystallizes into coherence.

Above me are clouds. I think? Or maybe it's a ceiling painted with clouds. The blue sky curves in an unnatural way, like I'm trapped inside a bubble.

Next, I move my arms and my legs, wincing at the buzz of pain that lances from my fingers to my shoulders. A movement from the corner of my eye summons my attention, and slowly, I twist my neck to be met with a pair of bronzed toes, the nails painted with creamy white, and the feet they're attached to covered with a fall of soft white fabric.

Lor? My mind forms the word, but my mouth doesn't move. My tongue is like faded canvas—dry and rough and thick and not much use. The feet move out of my vision, and I sense them walking around me as they circle to my other side. Once again, I perform a colossal feat by swerving my head to follow.

This time, the person bends down, balancing on their toes. A woman, who I've never seen before, stares at me. She's beautiful, with golden blonde hair and bronzed skin framing a pair of striking aquamarine eyes. I want to ask who she is, but the organ inside my mouth sits limply, so I moan. It's not all that dignified, but it's all I can muster.

The woman tips her head and then tuts. Something about it irritates me, though I can't really explain that either. Her expression isn't one of pity or worry but instead of cold curiosity, which fires a warning in the back of my head. Who is this? Is she working with my father? I'm reminded of the sunlight and reason that can't be it. He would have taken me back to The Aurora if he'd gotten the chance.

"You are in *rough* shape," the woman says. Her voice is musical and beautiful, but if I listen carefully, I swear I can hear venom licking through each syllable. "Your mate really didn't care at all about your well-being, did she? She just used her magic and"—the woman holds out a hand and springs her fingers out—"poof."

My mate.

The taste and scent of Lor overcomes my dulled senses. Everything about her paints a picture in my mind. Those deep, dark eyes that see right into me. That soft skin and that mouth she uses to make my skin shiver with a kiss but also to cut me down a peg every chance she gets. I don't know how long it's been since I've seen her, but I miss her like a burn singeing a hole straight through my chest. I wish I could speak or sit up or do anything but lie here like a lump of fucking nothing.

The woman tips forward, landing on her hands and knees.

She crawls towards me and presses her ear to my chest. All I can do is peer down, helpless to resist or protect myself. She remains there for a few long seconds before she sits back up, settling on her heels.

"It seems your heart is beating normally again. Lucky that."

My heart? What does she mean *again*? Why are my thoughts so jumbled?

The woman hovers over me and smiles. "Don't worry. I'll take care of you. That so-called mate of yours doesn't deserve you, does she? But don't you worry—Zerra will give you everything you need."

Zerra? What? She places a hand in the center of my chest, and my skin crawls at the contact. I want to tell her to stop fucking touching me, but I can't make the words come out.

I blink and feel my eyebrows pulling together.

She shuffles closer and leans down, pressing her lips against mine. I make a sound that's somewhere between surprise and protest, trying to move away, but she holds me in place with her cold hands pressed against either side of my face. There's nothing passionate about the kiss. Just the press of lips against mine.

"Hmm," she says with a sound of satisfaction before she pulls away. "Yes, I can see why she was so fond of you. You're very pretty. Just like he was."

I try to shake my head. None of this is making any sense. Why is she referring to Lor in the past tense? *What* is happening?

Zerra pushes herself up again and then pads around to my other side. I hear the murmur of low voices and the drip of water. A cool, wet cloth lands on my forehead, covering my eyes. I try to shake it away, but I'm too weak.

A finger digs into my bottom lip and pulls it down, making me groan. A moment later, something cold drips on my tongue and slides down, soothing my raw throat. I swallow it because at least I can manage that.

"Next time you wake up, you'll feel much better," she says, and her hand—I think it's hers—caresses my cheek before, once again, everything goes black.

CHAPTER 8

LOR

Linden continues to glare at me throughout dinner, alternating between stony silence and the occasional verbal jab to remind me she doesn't buy a word of my shit. I had expected this. I knew there would be people who wouldn't forgive or forget my grandmother's mistakes. That doesn't mean it doesn't sting.

Dinner feels like it lasts forever, but mercifully, I'm finally escorted through the Crystal Palace by Linden and Cyan, who flank me on either side. While Cyan has been hospitable, it's obvious he doesn't trust me. I should commend him for his instincts, except this is very inconvenient for me.

Open windows set high in the walls let in the crisp ocean air and the sound of waves crashing against the shore. The hallways made of rippling glass tiles, marble, and paint feels almost like we're walking underwater.

We pass through a tall arch and into a massive oval room. At one end sit two thrones made of the same glassy material as the palace. Surrounding them are dozens of small tide pools cut right into the marble floor. They churn with small creatures, bioluminescent stones, colorful plants, and waving tendrils of translucent seaweed.

But what really catches my attention sits at the far end of the room. A massive aquarium stretched across a wide arch opens to the outside. The curved glass wall towers at least three times my height and is filled with multi-hued schools of fish—most of which I've never seen before—along with orange and red flowers and waving plants that shift lazily in a current.

In the center sits a massive branching piece of shimmering white coral, reaching almost to the vessel's height.

This can be only one thing.

The Alluvion Coral and this kingdom's Artefact.

Cyan and Linden have stopped walking, watching me as I stare at the Coral.

"It's beautiful," I breathe.

It shimmers in the water like the rarest pearl, surrounded by waltzing fish.

"Thank you," Cyan says.

"May I take a closer look?" He purses his lips together. I think he's about to refuse but must decide it's a harmless enough request because he nods. I move towards it, my bare feet soft against the marble floors.

An idea is already forming in my head. Three different Artefacts have spoken to me now. I don't know why or what makes them do so, but the Coral might have the information I'm seeking. What if it knows where the ark is?

As I draw closer, I sense its presence. It has an energy that draws me in. Is it calling to me? Does it want to speak with me too?

The tank opens to the sky, with the back half perched on a cliff. Due to the perspective, I can't tell how far it stretches. I place a hand on the glass, flattening my palm against it.

"Can you hear me?" I whisper softly under my breath, conscious of Cyan and Linden watching me. I can't give them any more reasons to suspect I'm up to something.

"Hello?" I try to cast the message through my thoughts.

I wait for it to answer—it always seems to take a few moments before they notice me—but it remains silent. I need to get closer and touch it. But how am I supposed to do that when it's surrounded by water?

"It's Lor. Will you talk to me too? I spoke with your . . . friends."

"What are you doing?" Linden demands, coming up next to me. "Why are you whispering?"

I jump at the intrusion and whip my hand away.

"I wasn't whispering," I say.

"You were," she replies, still not buying my shit.

I shrug. "Sometimes I talk to myself. I don't even notice I'm doing it."

Linden glares at me, and I do my best to look innocent.

"Linden," Cyan says, his tone bordering on threadbare, as though he's tiring of her attitude as well. "I think we can allow the girl her thoughts."

Linden shoots a look at the king, her eyebrow arching, clearly wanting to disagree, but she lets it lie.

"Come," she says. Then she starts marching away. When I don't immediately follow, she stops and pins me with a dark look over her shoulder. I cast one more glance at the Alluvion Coral, cycling through a hundred ideas of how I might access it before following her pointed footsteps through the palace.

I'm escorted to a gorgeous room that contrasts vividly with my prison cell. Maybe I should be grateful they're not making me sleep down there, at least.

After Cyan bids me goodnight and Linden threatens to feed me to the sharks, I'm left alone, though she informs me two guards are stationed outside. Great. I'll have to earn enough trust to be allowed free movement around the palace. Or I'll have to deal with the guards in a possibly messy way.

My room overlooks the ocean, reflecting under the light of the moon. It expands as far as I can see, and I clutch the diaphanous white curtains and breathe out a sigh laden with anxiety and exhaustion. I've lost an entire day already, and I can practically feel the tick of the clock vibrating under my skin, echoing in my ears like a hammer striking glass. The Coral. I need to find a way to talk to the Coral.

Can you hear me? I ask in my head. *Nadir. Are you there? Are you okay? I miss you. I love you.*

We had so little time to explore the possibilities of our mate bond. Does he need to be close to hear me? In the same room?

I'm assuming he *does* need to be alive, and I try not to let his silence add to my worries. Zerra promised she'd keep him safe while I carried out her unreasonable task. While I have no actual reason to trust her, I also don't have much choice.

My gaze wanders behind me to the giant silver bed covered with white sheets and blue pillows. It looks so inviting, but I'm not sure I'll be able to sleep. My stomach is twisted into too many knots.

I can't stop worrying about Nadir, and also Tristan and Willow. What did Cyan mean when he said a riot broke out? How can I be doing this again, wondering if they've survived while I've been stolen away to another kingdom?

Next thing I know, Cyan will surprise me and tell me I'm here competing to be his bonded partner. But he seems to already have his hands full in that department.

I strip out of my dirty clothes—I can't believe they ate dinner with me in this state—and pad into the bathroom, where I take a hot shower and wash my hair for the first time in days.

It feels like a lifetime ago when I stood in Aphelion's throne room and felt all that power coursing through me. I stare at my hand, watching the water sluice between my fingers. They curl into a fist and then open again as I try to channel out a small slip of magic.

Sparks of red lightning dance between my fingertips, and I grit my teeth as it surges through my limbs, cresting into a torrent. A moment later, the shower's glass walls shatter as magic blasts from my fingertips, rendering the entire thing into razor-sharp fragments.

Shouts rise from the bedroom, and two guards burst

through the door, their gazes falling on the broken glass and then me. It's at that moment we all realize I'm completely naked, and I use my hands to cover myself as they both direct their eyes to the floor.

"Sorry," one of them says. "Are you all right, my lady?"

No. I'm not fucking all right. I finally have my magic back, but I can barely use it. It's like a cannon blasting through parchment. All or nothing. What am I supposed to do with this?

"Can you get me a towel?" I ask, trying to sound dignified without much luck.

One of the guards shuffles to the side, keeping his gaze averted as he retrieves one from the hanging rack. Then he approaches me with his eyes still on his feet and holds it out towards me like a shield.

When he's close enough, I snatch it from his hands and wrap myself up. But my feet are bare, and we're surrounded by broken glass. The guard looks at the floor and then up at me.

"Would you like me to carry you?" he asks rather reluctantly.

Gods, this is humiliating. "Yes," I say. "But keep your hands where I can see them."

He raises them in surrender like he has no intention of dishonoring me, and then he scoops me up and carries me across the room. To his credit, he's an absolute gentleman, and once we clear the doorway, he deposits me gently onto the carpet.

My bedroom is now full of people, including a cleaning staff who've arrived to sweep up my mess. Cyan appears in the doorway with Linden and Anemone in tow—they're all barely dressed—and I'm pretty sure I've just interrupted something.

"What happened?" Cyan asks with genuine concern. "Are you all right?"

"Yes," I say. The glass left a few small cuts on my arms and legs, but they'll heal quickly, and other than my wounded pride, I'm fine. "I'll be okay."

"What were you doing?" Linden asks, understandably suspicious. I just tore apart an entire bathroom and can't really claim I was up to nothing. I'll have to come clean. Ha. Pun intended.

"I was practicing my magic," I say, hating that I have to reveal any measure of vulnerability to them.

Cyan raises an eyebrow. "You have no control over it?"

"I'm . . . I've got some."

"Why?"

It's a fair question.

I look around the room, conscious of the guards and staff moving in and out. None of the others seem the least bit bothered that we're all half-dressed.

"Could we talk about this later?" I ask, hoping to buy myself some time to come up with a story that isn't completely the truth but sounds good enough. "I'm really very tired."

Cyan's eyes darken, but he doesn't argue. "Very well. We'll get you a new room."

"Thank you," I say as he rattles off instructions to one of his staff. Then I'm escorted to a new suite similar to the one I just destroyed. Cyan, Linden, and Anemone follow me, and I turn to face them, still clutching the towel around me.

"Tomorrow, you will be explaining why you just blew a hole in my palace," Cyan says pleasantly enough, though the underlying threat is obvious. "Until then, please rest up. I'll see you in the morning."

I nod, not trusting myself to speak. When they all leave, I close the door behind me and lean against it.

A moment later, there's a knock, and I swing it open to find a servant.

"I thought you might need these," she says, handing over a pile of white cotton balanced in her arms.

"Thank you," I say gratefully before she curtsies and scurries away. When she's gone, I drop my towel and pull on the soft white pajamas, which include loose pants and a sleeveless top. It feels good to be in fresh clothing and it has the effect of clearing my head a little.

Pacing the length of the room, I consider my next move. I need to speak to the Coral. It seems like my best chance. Heading for the door, I twist the knob, hoping for a late night visit. But I'm greeted by the presence of the two guards Linden promised.

"You are to remain in your room until morning," one says, folding his thick arms.

I squeeze the door handle, but this isn't really a surprise. Getting to the Artefact won't be that easy.

"Fine," I say, slamming the door.

For now I'm stuck and tired enough that maybe I'll be able to sleep. I pull back the covers and slip under them, tucking them up to my waist. Once I've had some rest, maybe I'll be able to think clearly enough to come up with a plan.

Then I open my hand and stare at it. I've spent so many years craving my magic, but I've forgotten what to do with it.

I miss Willow and Tristan, and I wish they were here with me to sort this out. Tristan controlled his magic so easily. Why am I so bad at this? Willow would know what to say to make me feel better.

And Nadir. I would give anything to feel his arms around me. To slide into my feelings for him and pretend nothing else exists. He would help me, too. He's the only one who's ever been able to coax anything from my magic, and I'm sure he'd know how to help understand this.

With my other hand, I clutch at my chest, my breath pinching with loneliness. Once again, I'm alone in a strange bed in a strange palace, being asked to risk my life to save the ones I love.

Pressure wells in my eyes until tears start to fall. I wipe them away, but more replace them, so I let myself go, sobbing into my pillow until I cry myself into a lonely, troubled sleep.

Chapter 9

PRINCE RION

Rion stood in front of the mirror, smoothing the lapel on his black jacket, wishing this day into oblivion. He'd been such a fool to sleep with that woman, but she'd been attractive and embarrassingly flirtatious, clearly eager to bed him.

Rachel had been giving him the cold shoulder again after he'd canceled another dinner when a skirmish had occurred along the kingdom's southern border. She didn't understand the pressure he was under and how much The Aurora needed his firm hand.

He'd wanted to make her jealous that night. Make her pay for her lack of . . . attention.

But then Meora had fallen pregnant. She must have bewitched him into the entire scheme, intent on joining him on his throne. His father was this close to dying from the Withering, and Rion was only biding his time, waiting for the inevitable.

He'd spent years acting in King Garnet's stead, conquering territories in the name of The Aurora, but without the crown on his head, he could do only so much. Once his father was gone, he'd expand The Aurora's army, redirecting funds towards training new recruits. He knew the Heart Queen, Daedra, was plotting against him and the other rulers were speaking of allying to overthrow his kingdom. If Rion wanted to secure The Aurora as the leading power in Ouranos, being its king only in name wasn't enough.

He'd been so close to getting everything—his crown with Rachel at his side.

And then he'd fucked it up.

He'd tried to make Meora go away, but that damn Torch wanted the baby, and now he would become a father and partner, responsible for two people he had no interest in protecting.

"You don't have to go through with this," Rachel said.

She lounged in the corner, looking like every fantasy he'd ever had. Round curves and lush lips made for sin. Violet eyes and hair so dark it drank the light. She wasn't just beautiful. She was clever and cunning. He could talk with her for hours about nothing and everything, her mind as challenging as a riddle that held him utterly captive.

"You know I do," Rion said, tugging on the cuffs of his jacket. "I'll lose my position as Primary and lose my crown."

Rachel remained silent, and he looked over. He saw the hurt and disappointment in her eyes, but if she really loved him, she'd never ask him to choose. He *did* love her, but how could he possibly be expected to give up what he'd been coveting for over five hundred years?

If he walked away now, Meora would remain here, raising the child until it was old enough to take the throne and Rion's legacy would become a memory. It was another option. One he would never take.

"Okay," she said, and he didn't miss the shine in her eyes as she turned her gaze to the window, staring out at the snowy landscape.

For a moment, he considered leaving with her. What would it be like to give up everything and hand over power to a child he'd never met? Live with Rachel somewhere deep in the mountains where they might have children of their own. They could lead a simple and quiet life without these burdens.

But the idyllic picture with the woman he loved, body and soul, wasn't enough. He was choosing his crown over his heart. That was what he'd always done and what he would do now. Though he'd considered his options, weighing each side with careful scrutiny, he'd always known on which side he'd fall.

Rion crossed the room and dropped to a knee, sliding his hands up Rachel's thighs, feeling the warmth of her skin through the thin fabric of her dress.

"Don't be angry with me," he said, and she turned to look at him with a sharp gaze. What he saw in her eyes was a turbulent mix of so many things, most of which he could guess.

"I had to fall in love with a future king," she said softly, almost wistfully, already speaking of him in the past.

"I'm sorry," he said. "You know that I can't control who the Torch chooses."

She shook her head. The problem was that she didn't understand this need to rule and wear that crown. She hadn't been born into the weight and expectations of royalty. "I know that, Rion. But *you* are making this choice. You are choosing yourself over me."

The words hurt, as they were meant to, but not enough to alter his course. Walking away from that crown would ultimately hurt more. He knew himself well enough to understand that. It was true. He *was* choosing himself.

"I'm sorry you feel that way," he replied, and she closed her eyes as she inhaled a deep breath. He considered asking if she'd be interested in one last kiss for old times' sake, but he had a hunch he knew the answer.

A knock came at the door, followed by a muffled "Your Highness, they're ready for you."

Their time was at an end, anyway. They both looked over and then back at each other.

"I guess this is it then," he said.

"I guess," she replied.

"What will you do?"

"Before it's over, I will be gone."

"Where?" He couldn't help wondering.

"You would ask me that?" she demanded with an arch of her brow.

"You'll be provided for," he said. "You have an open line of credit for whatever you need. Just write to my accountants."

She nodded. "Yes, Rion. You're buying me off. I understand perfectly."

"Rachel..."

"Don't," she said, lifting a hand. "I don't want to hear any more of your excuses. Bond to that woman. Take your fucking crown. I hope it keeps you warm."

The firm set of her jaw told him she was done with this conversation. She'd always been very stubborn.

"Very well," he said, attempting that last kiss. She turned her face so he was met with only the curve of her smooth brown cheek. He paused and then pressed his lips to it, allowing them to linger for a moment. She held completely still, blinking as he pulled away.

"Goodbye," he said, receiving no response as he stood and headed for the door. He opened it and looked back, but she continued staring out the window, pretending he was no longer there.

Then he dipped his head and entered the hall, where a group of soldiers waited. They surrounded him, forming four corners, as they led him through the palace towards the throne room. The wide doors stood open, revealing a space already filled with hundreds of nobles who had arrived for the occasion.

Garnet, the Aurora King, sat hunched on his throne, his shoulders bent and his head hanging limply. His once robust frame had shrunk, his skin stretching over angled, protruding bones. Shadows darkened his eyes, and his hair, once thick and black like Rion's, had been leached of its color, trailing in thin wisps of near white.

Garnet had been taken by the Withering decades ago, yet he still lingered, clinging to this shallow excuse for life. Rion couldn't understand why he wouldn't just descend and put himself out of his misery.

He entered the room and stopped, surveying the crowd. He would convince his father to descend or find some way to bend the rules of the Torch. He was done waiting, and this bonding made the matter even more urgent. Without the ascension, this bonding was worth less than nothing. While he *would* come into his full power, all it really did was leash him to a woman—a family—for which he felt nothing.

A path ran through the center of the crowd. As he strode down it, he couldn't help but feel he was headed for the gallows, heads bowing as he passed. He rolled his neck, trying to dispel the pinch between his shoulders. This was the decision he'd made, and now he'd live with the consequences. There was no other choice.

At the front of the room, his father and mother watched over the proceedings. They were thrilled about their first grandchild, but they wouldn't have much time to spend with the baby—not if he had his way.

Meora, that *woman*, already waited at the front of the room, and he did everything he could to control the curl of his lip. It wasn't that she wasn't beautiful—that's what had drawn him to her in the first place—it was that she was baseborn. Nothing but a lower-class woman who worked in a school. How she had even garnered an invitation to the same event was still a mystery, and he was sure it had been part of her plan to trap him. She must have talked someone into it. Planned the entire thing from the very start.

Her hand rested on her stomach, visible with the first indication that she was with child. He looked at it and then up at her doe eyes swirling with fear. She'd had the gall to entrap him, and now she was learning he wouldn't simply be had. Now she would suffer for what she'd done.

"Your Highness," she squeaked, dipping into a curtsy. Rion nodded, saying nothing as he took his place next to her before the Torch suspended in its bracket between his parents.

In front of them stood another woman—a High Priestess.

They didn't actually need her for this, but these messengers of Zerra liked to insert themselves into the happenings of Ouranos and somehow arrive on the eve of anything important. Rion glared at her, and she gave them both a beatific smile as though she were the one in charge. He didn't like these women. They always wanted something, and they made his skin crawl.

Maybe once he was king, he'd ban them from The Aurora entirely.

"Welcome," the priestess said. "Today, we celebrate the bonding of two High Fae who hold destiny in their hands."

She smiled at Rion and Meora, but he'd never felt less like returning it. He stared at his soon-to-be bonded partner as the High Priestess began the ceremony, willing Meora to stop existing. As the priestess droned on, he shifted from foot to foot, wishing they'd just get this over with.

But then, something else curled in the back of his mind. Something softer and lower.

Rion.

Another voice. He blinked, looking around him.

Everyone watched the priestess, their eyes glued to her as she waved her arms.

Rion.

Once more, he looked around the room, but it was obvious that no one else had heard it. If Rion didn't know any better, he could have sworn it was coming from the Torch, but it was too soon. He was not a king yet.

The orange flame in its mouth flickered and sparked as the priestess continued enjoying the sound of her own voice.

Rion listened intently.

When nothing else happened, he shook his head, trying to focus on the proceedings. He must have imagined it. He was under a lot of strain.

Finally, the priestess was done speaking and she stepped aside, a hand sweeping towards the Artefact.

The Torch sparked, the flames turning green, then purple, then blue.

Rion stared at Meora unblinking, seeing the future stretching before him, uncertainty paving every step of his path.

But the pieces had been set. It was time.

Chapter 10

Lor

I t's hard to tell how long I've been sleeping when I awake. Grit scrapes my eyes, and my head pounds in a steady rhythm, making the room twist.

A tray covered with fruit sits on the table near the bed. My stomach grumbles, and I heave myself up, hobbling on aching legs. It appears fresh enough, so I nibble on a piece of something I don't recognize. It's vibrant yellow with a sweet but slightly sour flavor. A knock at the door precedes the entrance of a low fae servant. She has long white hair and shimmery blue skin covered in scales.

"Hi," I say. "Who are you?"

"I'm Pressia," she replies, dipping into a curtsy. She's wearing translucent white scraps of fabric strategically covering her unmentionable bits. Probably the type of thing that makes swimming easier.

"How long have I been asleep?"

"Since yesterday, my lady," she says, with a confused look.

I breathe out a shaky sigh. I was worried about being so exhausted that I'd sleep for a week. I have three and a half days left and I have to find a way to talk to the Coral. It may not know where the ark is, but it seems like the best place to begin my hunt.

It's then I notice the dress hanging from Pressia's arm. When she catches my stare, she holds it up.

"You're to dress for lunch with His Majesty," she says, and I suppress a groan, thinking about our dinner last night. But the Coral may not know the ark's location and I might need a backup plan. Which means getting closer to Cyan, so I'll have to make nice. A talent that has never been high on my list of strengths.

Pressia waits while I shower, managing to avoid rendering it into a pile of glass. I also need to deal with the issue of my rampant magic, but for now, I'll resist the urge to use it. Maybe once I get my hands on the ark, I'll be forced to blow a hole in the side of the palace and run. Though, I remain uncomfortably aware of who I might hurt in the process.

When I'm clean, Pressia tends to my hair and makeup. While I'm still not used to having these tasks performed, I have so much on my mind that I allow myself to settle into it. My thoughts churn as she tugs and brushes and dusts me from head to toe. Then she helps me into the dress, which resembles a slightly more modest version of the one she's wearing, though it still leaves my stomach, my shoulders, and a decent amount of cleavage exposed.

My first thought is to wonder what Nadir might think of this outfit before my throat chokes with a torrent of repressed emotions.

Pressia notices. "What's wrong, my lady? Is the dress not to your liking?"

I shake my head. "It's fine. Sorry. This is about something else."

I try again to call him with my mind, closing my eyes and hoping, *hoping*, something will happen.

Nadir. Can you hear me?

No answer.

Because he's dead.

I killed him, and if I don't get moving, I'll never see him again. Even if I find the ark, my far-fetched odds are stacked against me like oily, unscalable bricks.

Pressia's answer is a skeptical look, and I'm tempted to explain that I have much bigger issues to contend with than worrying about my stupid dress, but that wouldn't be fair.

Another knock at the door summons our attention, and Pressia walks over to open it.

Cyan enters the room, still shirtless and wearing pants made of a soft, dark blue suede that melds to his strong thighs. A low-slung belt wraps around his hips, glittering with an array of colorful jewels. His long hair hangs down, and his feet are bare. Everyone's feet are bare, including mine. I'd think this is a ruse to keep me vulnerable, but I have a feeling it has more to do with the environment. What need is there for shoes when your world is the beach and the ocean?

"I've come to escort you to lunch," Cyan says, his eyes roaming over me. Something about the expression on his face sends an itchy warning up the back of my neck.

"Why?" I ask, narrowing my eyes, and he places a hand on his chest, giving me a hurt look that lacks the flavor of authenticity.

"You are my special guest, Lor. It's the least I can do."

I narrow my eyes further, positive he's full of it, but what else can I do but go along with this?

"Please say you'll join us," he says with a smile that feels as genuine as leather made from papier-mâché.

"Fine," I say, and he nods.

"Perfect. They're waiting."

"Who's waiting?"

"You'll see."

I don't care for that answer, and I make my displeasure known with another narrowing of my eyes, but it fails to make an impression. "Come along."

We pass the guards standing outside my room and march down marble halls covered in white tile striated with hints of blue and gold and silver. Floor-to-ceiling arched windows line every available space, making it almost feel like we're outside. Most are devoid of glass, covered with a network of lattices constructed of blue pearl carved into whorls meant to look like rolling waves. The effect is magnificent.

As we pad through the wide halls, I wonder where we are

in relation to the throne room and the tank with the Alluvion Coral. Can I sneak in there tonight? How can I convince Cyan I'm not a threat and dispense with my guard?

"How are you feeling?" Cyan asks as we walk. "That was quite an impressive display last night."

"Sorry about your bathroom. I didn't mean to destroy your palace."

He waves a hand as if it's of no consequence. "It's fine. This place has been through worse."

I nod, and we continue walking. I can practically hear the questions he must be screaming in his mind. It's very suspicious that I have so little control over my magic. I know that's not normal for a High Fae of my age. Even if I hadn't just come into my full power, I should have more control.

Cyan opens his mouth to speak, but I don't want to answer whatever comes out of it, so I deflect his questions with one of my own. I hate always lying about everything, but I've spent so many years hiding who I am that the truth feels impossible. As long as no one knows too much, they can't use it against me.

"So what's with you and my aunt and Anemone? Doesn't that get complicated?"

Okay. That wasn't really what I was planning to say. Foot, meet mouth.

Cyan's eyebrow arches as he gives me a cool look. I can't tell if my question angers him or if he sees right through my pathetic attempts to hold on to my secrets.

"That's perhaps a discussion for another day, Lor," he says in a way that sounds like he's speaking with a child who just asked where babies come from.

"Right," I say. "Sorry." I am sorry because that was kind of rude.

Cyan doesn't reply as we round another corner and are greeted by a set of translucent crystal doors embedded with a design of pearlescent shells. He hauls one open and then ushers me inside. We enter a room that serves as a library and study, with shelves lining the walls and a large white table in the center.

I take two steps and then freeze, recognizing the two visitors seated at the table.

"No," I say, and back up. This is an ambush. I've been tricked.

Cyan circles his large hand around my arm and holds me in place.

"Come, Lor," he says. "When they heard you were here, they just had to meet you."

"Heard?" I ask.

"Well, I sent a message. They'd just returned home from the chaos in Aphelion."

I glare at Cyan and then at D'Arcy, the queen of Celestria, and Bronte, the queen of Tor, who are both eyeing me with a curious mixture of intrigue and distrust.

The Star Queen, with her pale skin, long silver hair, and eyes so dark they're inky puddles, is draped in a silvery dress that looks like it's been literally sewn from moonlight.

Bronte is the Star Queen's complete opposite with her dark, gleaming skin, and waist-length hair that's also silver but in an entirely different way. It's like iron and layered with streaks of black, like she was chipped from the heart of a mountain rather than scooped from a falling star.

She wears a set of grey leathers that look soft and supple and obviously designed for ease of movement. She's the epitome of a warrior queen if I ever saw one, and I already love her. Even if she's looking like she wants to pick me up and toss me over the balcony. It's a love borne of admiration, not warmth.

"What's going on?" I ask as Cyan drags me towards the table. I voice my protest, but I'm surrounded by royalty, by three of the most powerful people in Ouranos, and I'm still the wild girl they stole from Nostraza and stuffed into a golden dress.

"We just wanted to say hello," Bronte says, sitting forward, scrutinizing me from head to toe. Despite her fierce exterior, I see a softness reflected in her eyes. "Is what Cyan says true? Are you really Serce's granddaughter?"

I nod. The secrets I've kept for so long have been spooling apart for months now. Pieces of cotton teasing away on the tips of thorny branches. There was no keeping the lid on this. Do I even want to? If my goal is truly to reclaim my legacy, that task is impossible without proclaiming the truth out loud for everyone to hear. Whatever happens, this was always inevitable. At some point, the mask had to come off.

"It's true," I say, a tight stitch releasing in my chest at the admission.

"And where have you been all this time?" Bronte asks.

With a sigh borne of an exhaustion that has nothing to do with a lack of sleep, I run through the same abbreviated version of events I gave to Cyan. I've retold this story so many times now that I should have it tattooed on my forehead. I understand why everyone is curious, but is this all I'll ever be?

When I'm finished speaking, everyone watches me in silence. I can't tell what they're thinking from their expressions. I look around, hoping for something to drink. When I spot a bar cart on the far side of the room covered in bottles filled with various colored liquors, I don't bother asking. I stand up and pour myself something from a decanter of pale, bluish liquid. As I toss it back, it burns down my throat with a mixture of bitter and sweet.

"Help yourself," Cyan says wryly, and I shoot him a glare.

"Manners would have suggested you offer us all a drink to begin with."

"It's barely noon," he answers, and I snort before I pour myself another glass.

Like I give a shit.

"You reek of The Aurora," D'Arcy says a moment later, staring at me as uneasiness burns over my scalp.

"What?" I manage to squeak out. Why is she smelling me?

"Your story, while a truly thrilling tale, appears to be missing a few key details. Tell me why you smell of the Aurora King." She tips her head and offers me a sly look. "Or perhaps not its king, but rather one of his children? The prince? The princess?"

"As I already explained, I spent half my life there. Why shouldn't I bear its taint?"

D'Arcy rises from her seat, all elegance and lithe movement, and strides towards me like she's floating over the floor. She stops and sniffs, her nose burying into the curve of my throat in a move that is definitely crossing many personal boundaries.

"What the fuck?" I exclaim, jumping back. "Has no one ever taught you about consent?"

"She's mated to someone," D'Arcy says, facing the other two rulers. "The bond hasn't been completed, but they've mated."

"Excuse me," I say, backing away and bumping into the bar cart before I slide left to put some distance between us. "*That* is none of your business."

"Except it is," D'Arcy says, closing in on me. "If you're lying to us."

"I don't owe you anything."

"That's true," Cyan says. "But you are here in my kingdom out of my goodwill. I have no desire to harbor liars under my roof."

I press my mouth together. I have only three days left to find the ark, and I can't get myself thrown out of here before I do.

"Fine," I say. "When I left Aphelion, I didn't escape on my own. The Aurora Prince took me."

"Why?" Cyan asks.

"Because he was under his father's orders to return me to Nostraza."

Okay, that's not the entire truth, but what's another white lie on top of this snow-covered mountain I'm building?

"And then what?" Bronte asks. I remember Nadir saying something about Tor being somewhat allied to The Aurora. How friendly are they?

I clutch my glass between my hands with my back pressed to one of the shelves.

"And then we realized we had a connection."

"Your mate is the Aurora Prince," D'Arcy says, and something moves behind her eyes.

"Yes," I whisper, emotion twisting in my chest. *Is. Was.*

"Where is he now?" Cyan asks.

"He's dead." A collective intake of breath swirls around the room.

Tears fill my eyes. I don't have to pretend any of this.

"Liar," D'Arcy says. "If your mate were dead, it wouldn't be possible to have this conversation with us."

I blink at her words. "What does that mean?"

"I mean, if your mate had died, you'd be a broken mess of nothing." She pins me with an unsettling look, dark remorse flitting across her expression. "Believe me. I know what it's like."

I'm so thrown off that it takes me a moment to process what she's saying.

"You lost your mate," I say.

My words come out strangled because I *know*. I know what she means. I feel this cavernous space in my chest where Nadir has been carved out of me.

D'Arcy tips her chin, and Bronte and Cyan exchange a look. Something tells me this isn't information she offers up willingly or often. "It was a long time ago. But yes, I did."

I remember Nadir telling me she's had seven different partners, and I wonder if that's how she's filled the void of losing her mate.

But now they're all looking at me curiously, and I've just been caught in yet another lie.

My eyes narrow, and I lift my chin, trying to salvage this.

"Perhaps some of us are just stronger." I issue the words as a challenge, hoping to force her to back down, but I'm dealing with an ancient queen who radiates power. She scoffs, and something about that raises my ire.

"Don't be ridiculous," she says, hissing at me. "This isn't about what you can and cannot endure. When someone's mate dies, the one left behind succumbs to the worst sickness you can possibly imagine. Pain and agony like you can't even comprehend. I spent months screaming and wailing, wishing to die. There are entire weeks of blackness I don't even remember, my mind and body were so broken. It took years to fully heal, and even now, centuries later, I will never be the same."

She's leaning towards me now, her cool demeanor siphoned into a rigid slab of steel. "So do not presume to turn your nose up at me, thinking you're somehow immune to the worst fate a Fae can endure, *girl*."

The way she twists the last word tells me I've yet to earn her respect, and while I want to snap back at her, I decide that sometimes I can take the higher road. It's clear I've just scratched open a festering wound with my carelessness. But then another thought occurs to me. If I'm okay, then does that mean Nadir is actually . . . alive? A light tweaks in my chest.

"What? What is that?" Bronte asks, far too observant for my liking. "Why are you suddenly happy?"

"I'm not," I say defensively, trying to smooth my face into a different expression.

"You're keeping many things from us," Cyan says. "First your magic, and now this."

"What about her magic?" D'Arcy asks, her voice sharp as a needle.

"Nothing. My magic is fine," I say.

At the same moment Cyan declares, "She has no control over it."

My face heats as both women's gazes turn to me, fire burning in their eyes.

"Why don't you have control over your magic?" Bronte demands. "And why are you lying to us about your mate?"

The wheels in my head accelerate into high gear as I attempt to devise a plausible explanation for any of this. The truth is, I don't have one.

"I can't tell you," I say, and *that* is sort of the truth.

"Can't or won't?" Cyan asks.

"Does it matter?" I ask. "Know that I'm not here to cause you any harm. Atlas tried to bond with me and use my magic, and the Aurora King is after me for some reason I've never understood. All I know is I need to keep out of their way and try to get back to what's left of my family."

The words flow out of me in a rush, and I hope it's enough to convince them to let this go, even if they don't entirely trust me. It's not a complete lie. I don't mean them any direct harm, but I very much intend to steal from the king, who's staring at me as though he's trying to figure out what to make of me. Maybe it's wrong, and maybe I'm a terrible person for putting my needs and desires ahead of his, but if it comes down to some stupid piece of rock or Nadir, I won't hesitate to make that choice.

"I suppose not," Cyan eventually says. "But you understand I can't just let you walk out of here?"

"Why not?" I croak.

"Because you've been lying to me, Heart Queen. And I want to know why."

"I can't tell you anything else."

"So you've made clear."

"What happens now?"

"You'll remain here as my guest."

"Your guest or your prisoner?"

"You'll have some freedom of movement around the palace." He sits back and folds his hands over his bare stomach, daring me to argue.

I straighten my shoulders and lift my chin, trying not to panic.

Three days. Three days. Three days.

"How long do you plan to keep me here?"

Cyan shrugs. "I haven't figured that out yet."

"Will you send word to Aphelion that I'm here, at least? My brother and sister will worry about me." And hopefully they, along with Mael and Amya, will figure out a way to get me out of here. I just hope it's not too late.

"Sister?" he asks, his gaze narrowing. "I thought you said you had a brother?"

Shit. I forgot I hadn't told them about Willow. Too many things are happening, and I can't keep all of my lies straight. I wince and then hiss out a stream of air.

"Oh, yeah. We have a sister, too. She didn't come to The Woodlands with us, though."

Cyan shakes his head, and I notice D'Arcy and Bronte share a look.

"I *will* find out what you're hiding, Heart Queen. And if I deem you a danger to me or my kingdom, there will be consequences," he says.

"Got it," I answer because I'm not sure how else to respond. I believe him. He turns away, but I grab his arm.

"That message to Aphelion? Please?"

"I'll consider it."

I dip my chin, partly grateful that he seems to be a decent king but also annoyed that he's keeping me against my will. Though if our situations were reversed, I'd probably do the same.

Before placing the glass still in my hand on the table, I clasp my hands in front of me. "Then return me to my room."

"What about lunch?" Cyan asks and I repress a polluted laugh. Sure, sitting here being grilled by these three for another hour sounds like my ideal afternoon.

"I'm not hungry."

Cyan and the others all exchange looks before he sighs and stands, walking over to stop before me. I look up into his deep blue eyes, hoping he can't read the truth on my face. Maybe I approached this entire situation the wrong way and should have been honest with him. But sometimes I wonder if I even know *how* to tell the truth anymore.

"Very well. Let's go," he says before gesturing for me to walk. I nod at the two queens.

"It was so nice to meet you."

Neither responds as I pass their seats, heading for the door.

As Cyan escorts me through the palace, we cross through the throne room again.

The Coral sits in its massive tank, and I eye it desperately, wondering how I'll access it. I'm an adequate swimmer, but I have no idea what else lurks inside that tank. With those high, smooth walls, I'm not sure how I'd even get in there.

As we round the curve, I notice a male High Fae standing on the other side. He's clutching a notebook and stares up at the Coral intently before scribbling in it.

"Who's that?" I ask.

"Bain," Cyan says, his tone clipped like he doesn't want to answer me.

"What's he doing?"

Bain looks up and nods at Cyan, who then presses a hand to his chest and bows at the waist before straightening up.

"He's monitoring the Coral," Cyan says before gesturing for me to follow.

"Monitoring it?" I ask as I scramble to keep up.

"He's the Artefact's caretaker."

"Caretaker?"

He glares at me. "Are you just repeating everything I say?"

"Fine, don't tell me," I grumble as I cast another look over my shoulder. I wish I could stay with the Coral, but I'm worried showing too much interest will further raise Cyan's suspicions.

Tonight, I'll come up with a plan. I'm resourceful. I've gotten myself out of tighter jams. Unfortunately, I can't think of anything right now. Pain builds in my temple, and I massage it, willing down the nausea swirling in my gut.

I have three more days to get my hands on the ark.

Three more days until Nadir is lost to me forever.

I can't let that happen. I will *not* let that happen.

So help me—I will raze this entire fucking palace to the ground if I must.

CHAPTER 11

GABRIEL

APHELION—THE SUN PALACE

I stare around the empty cell in disbelief. At the neatly folded clothes sitting on the floor like they're mocking me. I can almost smell Atlas and the taint he's left behind.

I avoid looking too closely at the worst horror in this dungeon, but there's no shying away from it. The drip of blood fills the silence, hitting the stones and echoing off the cell's damp corners, which means Atlas can't have gone far.

I should do something. Call for help. Summon every guard in Aphelion to hunt him down. But I can't seem to make myself move. I'm frozen to the floor, stuck in the churning darkness of time. The load I've been carrying for a century finally catches up with me. My chest tightens and my limbs ache, becoming physical manifestations of every hurt my king— *former* king—has inflicted upon me, Tyr, and my brothers.

Finally, I coax my gaze up, bearing witness to the warders' lifeless bodies and their sagging wings. I stare at Drex's fingertips, watching a line of blood slide down his hand and land on the floor. It makes almost no sound, but I flinch like someone set off a cannon.

How did Atlas overpower them? Warders have special protection against Aphelion magic. We aren't completely immune to it, but its effects are limited. Atlas's magic isn't the destructive sort, anyway. That's what so much of this has been about.

He must have caught them by surprise. Used his intimate knowledge of their weaknesses to trick them. Or he had help. Which means I'll have to add rooting out anyone loyal to him to my growing list of chores.

Blood stains the front of the warders' armor, and I force myself to acknowledge the wound sliced through the shimmering tattoo on Syran's throat—that binding mark imprinted on our skin that made us all prisoners.

One of the few rules governing the kings and queens of Aphelion is their oath to protect their warders. Given the complicated nature of our relationship, they are sworn to never lay a hand on our bodies. Atlas has already broken that rule many times, but murder goes beyond anything I thought him capable of.

How could Atlas do this? After the decades that they've served him. Lied for him and kept his secrets. *How* could Atlas do this? I've long questioned Atlas's weak moral compass, but I shake my head, wondering why I had any faith left in him at all.

I still bear the scars of his torture. We all do. Why do I keep giving him the benefit of the doubt? *Because I never wanted any of this to be true.*

Finally, I look around, searching for clues about how he escaped or where he might have fled. Or maybe I'm stalling because the longer I stand here, the longer until I have to make the decision that's squatting on my chest like a stone.

I bend down and pick up a feather that's floated to the ground, one side smeared with golden blood. I haven't cried in years, but tears press the back of my throat.

With a heavy sigh, I close my eyes and attempt to sift the pieces of myself into something that resembles a man who has any idea what to do next.

My feet carry me back up the stairs, an unwilling passenger on this ride, where I emerge to find Jareth and Rhyle, two more of my brothers. Their eyes widen as I emerge from the dungeon, clearly sensing my distress.

"What's wrong?" Jareth asks, looking beyond me into the darkness of the stairwell.

"He's gone," I say. "He killed Drex and Syran, and then he fucking ran." The words bruise my ears with the sagging weight of their impossibility.

Immediately, they both head for the stairs, but I call out. "Don't. There's nothing to be gained by seeing them. What he did was...unforgivable. We must focus on finding him and bringing him to justice. I'll send someone down and remove the bodies and give them their due, but I can't face it right now. I need a moment."

My brothers exchange a wary glance, and I push between them, marching down the hall. I didn't even realize my sword was still in my hand. Suddenly, it feels like it's welded to the floor, and I toss it to the side with an abrupt clatter.

Jareth and Rhyle shuffle quietly behind me, probably wondering if I'm losing my mind.

"Where are the others?" I ask, looking over my shoulder.

"They're with Tyr in Atlas's study—I mean . . . Tyr's study." I hear the uncertainty in his voice.

None of us were prepared to navigate this new reality.

Looking forward, I nearly halt at the presence of two figures now directly in my path. A low, impatient grumble rattles in my throat at the sight of Mael and that brother of Lor's. *Trevor?*

"Get out of my way," I say, already knowing I don't have the patience for whatever this is. They attempt to stand their ground, but my stride never wavers, and they're forced to step out of my way.

"Where are you going?" Mael asks as I brush past. "We have to do something about Nadir and Lor."

I ignore him as I continue down the hall. I have no idea what happened to Nadir and Lor, and it's not that I'm not worried about them, but I have bigger problems to deal with right now.

"Gabriel!" Mael calls, but I still don't stop. A moment later, I hear two more sets of footsteps join alongside my brothers'. Storming through the palace, everyone leaps out of my way.

I'm like a thundercloud rolling through a picnic on a sunny day, scattering food and lemonade.

When we reach the king's study, I slam open the door with enough force to crack it. This room is Tyr's now. A sharp breath pierces my chest because everything is different.

Inside the room, I find the other warders along with Erevan, Amya, Hylene, and the lady's maid who's actually Lor's sister Willow. Apricia sits sniffling in a chair, dabbing her eyes with a tissue. I'd almost forgotten she existed.

"Rion took Nadir and Lor," Mael says to me at the same moment I declare, "Atlas is gone."

Everyone in the room goes still, our gazes meeting.

"We need soldiers to go after them," Mael says.

"The abduction of your prince and his girlfriend are matters for The Aurora, not Aphelion," I bark and spin around, pointing to my brothers.

"Atlas killed Drex and Syran and has escaped. We have to find him."

"We'll leave immediately," Jareth says.

"Just us," I say. "Any more, and he'll sense us coming."

"You can't leave," Erevan says to me. "We need you here." His gaze slides to Tyr, who sits in a chair staring straight ahead into nothing. Gods, he's right. I can't leave him alone like this after what I've done. I run a hand down my face.

"Then you go," I say to my brothers. The more of us there are together, the less effective Atlas's magic is against us. They'll be only seven without Drex and Syran, but it will have to be enough.

"What about the king?" Rhyle asks, and it takes me several seconds to realize he's talking about Tyr.

"I'll protect him." There's a certainty in my words, and I know they don't doubt me, but these are perilous times.

"Okay," Jareth says, though I can tell he doesn't like the idea of leaving Tyr's side. We exchange another look and then they turn to leave, but I call out. "Wait."

Approaching Tyr, I drop to one knee. He stares at me, his ashen hair hanging in his eyes as I carefully lift one of his hands, touching the arcturite cuff that circles his brittle wrist. Reaching under my collar, I pull out a thin gold chain dangling with a small pin. Inserting it into a small hole on the side of the cuff, I press down, and it pops off. Then I open the second cuff, followed by the one around his throat. As I stare at Tyr's pale, bared skin, my ribs expand with relief from this burden I've been carrying for a century.

His eyes widen as I pull the chain from around my neck and gather the cuffs in my hands.

"Never again," I declare. "I will never let these things touch you again."

He nods, his expression vacant, and I hope that's a promise I can keep. I walk over to Jareth and hand him the cuffs and the key.

"Put these on Atlas when you find him."

Our gazes lock together. This breaks every vow we ever swore to protect the Sun King. It goes against everything we were bred and trained to do. But Atlas has never been the Sun King, and we've all been living nothing but a lie.

It was Atlas who first broke the king's vow to protect us, and the old rules have no meaning here anymore.

"Go," I say. "Before he gets any further."

Jareth tips his head, and the remaining warders leave the room. A moment later, a knock comes at the door and a palace guard enters, carrying a bag in his hand.

"We found this in the throne room, Captain," he says, handing it to me. "I thought you'd want to take a look."

I open it, staring at the contents in disbelief.

"What is it?" Amya asks as I reach in and pull out a glittering silver crown with a blood-red stone set into the center.

"Is this what I think it is?" I ask, looking up.

"The Heart Crown," Amya breathes.

"Lor must have dropped it," Willow says, bringing a trembling hand to her throat.

Lor's brother snatches it from my hand. "We have to go after her!"

"Go ahead," I say.

"We need your help."

"Then find someone else. I need my soldiers here."

"Gabriel," Amya says, standing up. "You have to understand this is about something bigger. We need your help, and so does Ouranos."

"I don't know what that means."

Amya exchanges a look with Mael and then tells me everything about Lor. About who she is. *What* she is. I knew she was the heir of Heart, but I was definitely missing some key details.

"So you see," Amya says, "my father wants her for something, but we don't know what, and given his ambitions, I'm afraid that if he gets his hands on her, it will have consequences for everyone. This is not just The Aurora's problem anymore."

I let out a weary sigh, looking at Tyr, but he doesn't answer. I'm not sure he's even listening.

"Lor is a queen?" comes a voice from the corner. Apricia has stopped crying and is now staring at everyone. "*Lor* is the Heart Queen? That's who I was competing with? What chance did any of us have!"

Everyone in the room stares at her like she's sprouted weeds from her ears, and she at least has the sense to look abashed at her narcissistic outburst. I'll also have to figure out what to do with her. She *cannot* remain here.

I open my mouth and shake my head. "Is that really relevant right now?"

"What happens to me?" she demands. "I was supposed to be queen of Aphelion until *she* ruined it for me."

"Oh, shut up," Willow says, and the look on Apricia's face is almost worth everything that's happened. "I have never met anyone so utterly childish and self-absorbed. Do you honestly think any of this is about you right now?"

Apricia's mouth gapes like a fish, and I almost start laughing in spite of everything.

"How dare you!" Apricia says, finally finding her tongue. "What are you even doing in here? You're supposed to be tending to my bonding suite!"

"What bonding?" Willow snaps, and now she might be my favorite person in the room.

"Willow," Amya says before lifting her hands. "Actually . . . never mind. Keep going. I'm enjoying this."

Willow smiles. "I think my point has been made."

"Everyone stop," Mael says, holding out his hands. "Please. We need to go after them, but we can't do it alone."

"I don't know what you want from me," I say. "I need my soldiers here. We're in the middle of a riot, our traitor king is on the loose, and our forces were already stretched thin before all of this."

Mael is a soldier, too, and I know he understands what I'm saying.

"Then we're going alone," says the brother. *Thomas?*

"Us against the Aurora King? He's going to tear us apart."

"I'm gaining better control of my magic," he says, but Mael remains unconvinced. I don't blame him. Rion is a formidable foe, and these four are hardly a match.

"I'm coming too," Amya says.

"Do you think we can actually stop him?" Mael asks.

"No, but we have to try. For Nadir."

Nadir might be a bit of an ass sometimes, but it's obvious from Amya and Mael's pained expressions that these two love him.

"We'll try to pick up their trail," Lor's brother says. *Timothy?* "We have to go after them."

Everyone looks to me again, and I want to help. I do. But my hands are tied.

"Then let's go," Mael says. He claps me on the shoulder and squeezes it gently in what I understand is a gesture of forgiveness.

"Good luck," I say, meaning it.

CHAPTER 12

LOR

ALLUVION—THE CRYSTAL PALACE

After I'm returned to my room, I pace back and forth, trying to formulate a plan. The ocean roars outside, and it's almost soothing, but too many things are happening in my head.

I think about what D'Arcy said regarding mate sickness. This has to mean Nadir's alive, right? It's the feeblest glimmer of hope, but I'm clinging to this mote of dust with all of my might. I felt him die. I felt his heart stop and his skin grow cold under my touch. But he's in the Evanescence, and maybe that's holding the sickness at bay, or maybe, just maybe, I didn't permanently kill my mate.

Closing my eyes, I try to speak to Nadir, screaming in my head as loud as I can.

Nadir. Are you okay?

Can you hear me? I'm so sorry. Answer me!

But again, I'm met with nothing but silence.

I cry out in frustration, gripping my forehead as I pace back and forth. The image of the Coral sitting in the center of the throne room pulses in my thoughts. I can't keep dwelling on things I can't change. What I need to do is find the ark and save my mate. That's what he needs from me right now, and I can't fall apart.

So what do I do? Ask to see Cyan again? What would I give for my reason? He won't believe me if I claim I just want to spend time with him. That would be absurd. Besides, he's a king and probably has duties to attend to. Then a thought occurs to me. What if the Coral's caretaker is the key? Maybe *he'll* talk to me.

Storming over to the door, I fling it open. My two muscled guards wait outside, all gleaming and sun-kissed, their hands planted on their hips like they mean business.

"Hi," I say. "How are you?"

"We're here to keep an eye on you," one says. Not what I asked, but I guess we're bypassing the small-talk thing.

"Oh. That's nice. It's good to have such strong, handsome guards." I wink, and the one on the left frowns.

"Is there something in your eye?" he asks.

Right. I suck at flirting.

"What are your names?" I ask.

"I'm North, and this is West." The first points to his companion.

"Cute."

That earns me an even deeper scowl.

"Is there something you want?"

I consider the question. How much harm might there be in asking to visit the throne room? I worry it will get back to Cyan, but I don't see I have any other choice.

"I'd like to go for a walk."

"We're to escort you everywhere," North says. Or maybe it's West.

"Yeah, I figured that. How about the throne room?"

"Why?"

"Do I need a reason?"

My response earns me another glare.

"I'd love to take a closer look at the Alluvion Coral. It's very pretty."

West's eyebrows draw together, and I twirl a lock of my hair, trying to make it seem like I'm just a silly girl who likes shiny things. They appear to fall for it and, without another word, step back and gesture for me to walk.

We pass through the same wide blue-and-white corridors, my bare soles slapping the tile. Somehow, my escorts walk silently and not like they have flippers attached to their feet.

We enter the throne room, and I suck in a breath of relief to find Bain still peering through the glass, staring up at the Coral. West and North take up positions against the wall and I give them a little wave before I approach. Busy scribbling something into his notebook, he doesn't notice until I'm nearly upon him.

Bain regards me with surprise. I wonder if he recognizes me from earlier. He has the same dark blue eyes common around here, with silvery blue hair cropped around his pointed ears. He also has the same pale, almost blue skin as Cyan.

"Hi," I say, attempting to snatch a peek at what he's writing.

"Hello luv," he says. "Have you come to pay your respects to Coral?"

Sure. Respects.

"Oh, totally," I say. "It's . . . great."

He nods with a beaming smile. "She. *She's* truly a magnificent being."

"She?" I ask. I've never heard a gender ascribed to any of the Artefacts. I guess most people don't know the spirits of the former kings and queens of Ouranos inhabit them.

"Oh, I've always imagined her as a woman with all those curves and lithe limbs," he says, clutching his book to his chest.

That's . . . a very strange thing to say.

"Don't you agree?" he asks, looking at me expectantly.

"Sure," I agree, because why not? "Very . . . ladylike."

He nods and then proceeds to continue writing.

"What's in the notebook?"

"Oh, these are my recordings of her form," he says. "She's a living thing. She shifts and changes in the water, growing new branches while others break off. It's all part of her life cycle and what makes her so special."

It's like he's in love with the thing. I watch as he stares up at Coral with adoration.

Maybe I can use this to my advantage.

North and West stand against the wall on the far side of the room, vigilant but giving me space. They probably wish I'd return to my room, but I guess they're stuck babysitting me no matter where I am.

"Your name is Bain, right?"

"It is."

"I'm Lor," I say, pressing my hand against the glass. "She does seem very special. But maybe not as special as the Mirror."

"The Mirror," Bain sputters. "That hideous thing? It's all flash and artifice. No, my Coral here is an organic creation of sublime beauty."

"*Your* Coral?"

He smiles and nods. "My Coral."

"Have you . . . ever spoken to her?" I ask.

His eyes widen before his face turns sad. "Alas, I am not the king, and she will not speak to me."

"That's a shame," I say as I wander towards the other side of the tank, out of North and West's view, hoping Bain will follow. When he does, I weigh the odds of revealing my hand. I turn around to face him and then crook a finger. "I have a secret about the Artefacts. About Coral."

Like a fish being reeled in on a line, he approaches me.

"What is it?"

I stretch onto my tiptoes and make a show of whispering in his ear. "They talk to me."

He gives me a skeptical look. I can tell he doesn't want to believe me, though he desperately wants it to be true.

"They do?"

I nod and then once again place my hand on the glass, dragging my fingers as I continue my way around the circumference.

"Could you speak with Coral?" he asks.

"I think I could," I say in a coy voice. "But I'd need to touch her."

Bain looks at me and then at the Artefact. "No one but me and the king are allowed to touch her."

"Why are you permitted to do so?"

"To clean and polish her," he said. "Otherwise, she loses her shine."

"Who are you?" I ask, wondering why Cyan has entrusted Bain with this task.

"I'm the king's father," he says, surprising me, though it does explain Cyan's earlier bow of reverence.

"You weren't the king?"

"Oh no, that was my brother. I don't have the right constitution for ruling. Coral chose Cyan to follow him."

"And he lets you clean Coral?" I ask, feeling terrible for how I'm about to take advantage of this poor man's delusions.

"Yes," he says proudly.

"How do you do it? Do you get in the water?"

"Sometimes," he says. "But that doesn't get her as clean as I like. There's a mechanism that drains the tank so I can do the job right."

Perfect.

"Can I do that?" I ask, and Bain shakes his head.

"Oh no. That is forbidden. Only I'm sanctioned as her caretaker."

I drag in a breath, hating that I'm doing this.

"But you wanted to hear what she has to say, right?"

His eyes widen, and he whispers, "I do."

"So help me, and I'll talk to her for you."

He looks behind him, but no one is within earshot. West and North remain on the far side of the tank, where I can make out their blurred, watery forms through the glass.

"We'd have to do it at night when no one else is around," Bain says, lowering his voice.

"Okay—tonight. I'll meet you here at midnight."

His eyes flick to Coral and then back to me. I reach out and grab his wrist. "I can give her any message you want."

"You really can talk to her?" he asks.

"I can. I've already spoken with the Mirror, the Torch, and the Staff." I expect him to ask me what they said, and I'm already trying to think of a lie, but it's clear he only has eyes for Coral because he brushes past it.

He touches the glass and then peers down at me, hope swirling in his eyes.

"I can't tonight," he says, and I'm about to argue when he adds, "But tomorrow. Midnight."

Slowly, I blow out a breath and nod. That's another day lost, but I'm already pushing my luck.

"See you then," I say, and then approach North and West, asking to be returned to my room. I say nothing to my escorts as I slam the door on their faces.

Immediately, I proceed across the room and exit onto the balcony. It dangles over a cliff, the churning ocean below filled with an inconvenient array of sharp, jagged rocks. This was obviously intentional. I peer over the edge, wondering if

I could survive the drop. I'm not sure what I'm capable of now that I'm in my High Fae form.

Leaning out as far as I can, I scan the side of the palace. I'm about four stories up from where Coral's massive tank juts out from the back of the castle.

How do I get down there without anyone noticing me?

The wind blows my hair, and I stare out at the water. There's nothing but ocean and sky stretching in front of me. If I lean forward, I can see the city of Alluvion to the north. Even from this distance, I can make out a path of destruction along the coastline—smashed city walls, piles of debris littering the beach, dead sea life, and plants. I remember the conversation I overheard in Aphelion about this. More evidence of the magic's loss of control.

I stare at my hand, considering my own magic. If things go sideways in the throne room tomorrow, I might need to use it for a quick escape. But the idea of killing innocent people makes cold sweat break out on my forehead. I don't want to fear my magic, and I need it, but I killed the most important person in my world with it.

Scanning the horizon, I hold my hand over the water and concentrate on filtering out a small bit of magic. It buzzes under my skin, wrapping around my fingers and up my arm. With my breath held, I attempt to direct it towards the rocks below, but it takes only a moment before my control slips and magic slams out of me, filling the sky with a flickering curtain of crimson lightning.

It's so vast it engulfs the horizon, stretching across my vision. It flows out of me in a rush, pulling on my veins like they'll tear straight out of my skin. I scream as it gushes from my hand, an inferno, a raging torrent. I try to call it back, but it's stronger than me. A loud crash draws my attention as a portion of the cliff below starts to crack.

It's enough to shock my magic, cutting it off abruptly as the cliff pops apart and a giant piece cleaves off. I watch it dive in slow motion, crashing into the sea, water droplets splashing high enough to reach where I stand.

It takes a moment for the chaos to settle, and when it does, I stand waiting, wondering if anyone noticed. When the door to my room remains shut, I breathe a sigh of relief. Hopefully, the sound of the waves and the wind covered that up. And no one saw the entire sky turn red. My magic seems to be getting stronger since I left Aphelion, and I need to be more careful.

If I get caught tomorrow, I'll have to decide if I want to risk using it.

Heading inside, I search my room for something I can use to access the throne room.

"Aha!" I cry out when I open a closet full of linens. It's not a great plan, but it's not the worst. I heave the lot out and dump them on the ground.

Immediately, I set to work ripping them up, attempting to be as quiet as possible. I begin tying them together to start forming a rope. Over the next several hours, whenever a knock signals a meal delivery, I leap up to answer it after shoving the evidence of my escape under the bed.

By noon on the following day, I've assembled a rope that I hope is long enough to serve my purpose. Another knock comes at my door.

"We have lunch for you," comes a deep male voice. I look around at the disaster that surrounds me.

"I'm not hungry," I call as my stomach grumbles. I don't want to open that door. There's too much to hide now—tiny threads and fibers cling to my hair and clothes, as well as the carpet and furniture. "Actually, I'm not feeling well. Please see to it that no one disturbs me until morning."

"Very well," North or West says.

If everything goes as planned, I'll be long gone with the ark by the time the sun rises. Tonight, I'll talk to Coral and get Nadir back. If she doesn't know where the ark is then I'll be almost out of time and back to square one.

I can't let that happen.

She *has* to know.

CHAPTER 13

NADIR

THE EVANESCENCE—ZERRA'S PALACE

When I open my eyes again, I'm lying on something soft. A bed? Or maybe a cloud? My body aches, but it's not the same bone-deep pain I remember the last time I opened my eyes. I blink, and the world slowly morphs into focus. Above me is an ornate carved ceiling made of a creamy material resembling vanilla ice cream.

Gods, I could go for some of that.

"Oh, you're awake," trills a melodious voice, and once again, the woman from last time comes into view. *Zerra.*

The Zerra?

"How are you feeling?" She purses her lips and creases her

forehead like she's exceedingly concerned about my well-being. Her hand lands on the center of my chest, and that's when I realize I'm naked with nothing but a sheet covering me from the waist down. Her skin is like ice, and I attempt to shrug off her touch while covering myself.

Though every movement hurts like a bitch, I'm relieved to find I *can* move again.

"Now, now, don't go straining yourself," Zerra says. "It's nothing I haven't seen before." She slides her hand lower, stopping at my navel, her fingers dipping a little too low to be innocent. "In fact, it's nothing I didn't see when my ladies bathed you." Her eyes flick down and then back up. "And it was *very* impressive."

Oh, good gods. Did she just compliment my cock? I'm way too fucked-up for this. Also, I don't want her touching me. Objectively, she's a beautiful woman, but something about her makes my skin crawl.

"Who are you?" I say, though my voice is a croaked whisper and my vocal cords ache with the effort. I need to hear her say it again because, surely, I heard her wrong.

"I'm Zerra," she answers and then blinks as if daring me to argue. Is she telling me the truth, or is she crazy? Or maybe the problem is me?

"Where am I?"

"You're in the Evanescence," she says, setting off a wail of alarm bells in my head. I'm skeptical, but the light and the air and mood in this place feel otherworldly and distant. It *feels* like I'm somewhere lost in another dimension or another world. I can't explain it, but a shiver climbs over my scalp, confirming what I already suspected. We're definitely not in Ouranos anymore.

"Am I ... dead?"

If I am, then I don't technically belong here. I never ascended to the Aurora throne. The Evanescence is reserved only for kings and queens—not princes who didn't quite make the cut.

If they don't find themselves banished to the Underworld for their misdeeds, most people—fae and humans alike—just cease to exist, their souls floating in the ether until they're claimed by another body to do it all over again. Or at least that's the theory. Fae live so long that we don't tend to give much thought to the afterlife.

"Not in the way you mean," she answers, "but you aren't really alive right now either."

"What ... does that mean?"

"Ohh," she coos. "Don't trouble yourself with such deep thoughts. You're still recovering and need rest to build up your strength."

No, I don't like that answer. Either I've been captured by a lunatic or I really am lying in a bed in the Evanescence. It's hard to decide which is less disturbing.

I struggle to sit up, but she places a hand on my shoulder and easily forces me back. I'm as strong as a baby bird.

"Ah ah," she scolds. "You're staying here until you have some rest. I remember how you land dwellers require sleep. So inconvenient. Don't worry—when you become mine, we'll do away with such trifling needs. Being a demigod has its issues, but there are many perks, too."

I'm having trouble forming coherent thoughts, but did she just say "demigod" and "mine"? More alarm bells ring in my head, pinging around the inside of my skull like sharp iron burrs.

"Come," Zerra says. "Dinner is ready, and we mustn't be late."

She grabs my wrist and tugs, dragging me into a seated position. My head spins, my vision tipping sideways. What happened to insisting I lie down and rest?

Once my mind clears, I use the opportunity to take stock of my surroundings. I'm in a large oval room covered in cream rugs, surrounded by cream walls decorated with a pattern that might be clouds. Long windows surround us like we're inside a tower. Beyond the windows, I see only pale mist and wispy clouds against a light blue sky.

The Evanescence.

This . . . cannot be.

And yet, somehow, I know it's true.

"Here are some clothes for you."

Zerra lays out a pair of white pants and a shirt at the foot of the bed.

"I'll just wait while you dress."

She drops into a chair and props an elbow on the table next to it, blinking at me with her bright blue eyes. I lift the hem of the sheet covering my lap, and yep, I'm completely naked. I try not to think too hard about how I got this way. Zerra's a god, surely she wouldn't—

Except she's watching me like she's preparing for a show.

"Could you leave?" I ask. "I'm not wearing anything underneath."

She smiles with a raw mania carved into the lines of her face.

"Like I said, nothing I haven't already seen." She then gives me an exaggerated wink that I think is supposed to be sexy or cute, but it's neither. It just makes me shudder.

"Yeah, well. I'm awake now and would prefer the dignity of dressing without an audience," I say, trying to keep the growl out of my voice. Something tells me it'll be best to remain on her good side and keep my temper. Not exactly my strongest quality.

Her smile drops into a pout. "Oh, you're no fun," she says, toying with the bow at her neckline. It's then I finally take a proper look. She's wearing a sheer robe, and I catch the hint of her bare breasts and pink nipples through the material. What the fuck is happening here?

"I could show you mine in exchange." She tugs on the silk, and her robe slips open, revealing her perfect round breasts and flat stomach. Thankfully, she's wearing panties, but they're so small they can barely be called that. Wildly uncomfortable, I look away.

"No, thank you," I say. "That isn't necessary."

I hear her moving, and I look over, careful to keep my eyes glued to her face. She stands in front of me with her hands on her hips, and then she taps my nose. I try not to flinch.

"Very well," she says in a tired voice. "I'll allow you your modesty for now. I'll see it all soon enough."

Then she turns and saunters across the room. When she opens the door, all I see beyond it is more of the same misty sky.

"Call for a servant when you're ready," she says.

When she's gone, I wait for several seconds. Then I slip out of bed and tug on the pants. They're loose and light and made of the softest material I've ever felt. The shirt drapes over me, hanging low in the front, exposing my chest.

I figure I have a few minutes before she starts to wonder where I am, so I explore the room. What I see outside the windows troubles me in more ways than I can count. There's nothing but a blank expanse of swirling mist interspersed with the occasional cloud spreading in every direction. We're not in any sort of building that I can discern.

I'm in the fucking Evanescence, and whatever doubts I have about that are erased in this moment. This is impossible. What am I doing here?

I rub my chest as a dull ache flares under my ribs. As I move about the room, my limbs and joints creak with the stiffness of disuse. What happened to me after we were taken from Aphelion?

I open the drawers and closets but find little but clothing and a few books.

I stare at the door Zerra vacated. My intuition suggests she wants something from me. Obviously sex from the way she is behaving, but what did she mean about being hers? A demigod. What does *that* mean?

I have to find Lor. What happened to *her*?

But I appear to be stuck here and realize the only answers I'll get are from the goddess herself. I run a hand down my face and take a deep breath before I open the door. I'm met with nothing in front of me. Just the same empty sky. Peering down, there's more nothing. What would happen if I stepped off this edge?

"Hello?" I call, and immediately, a High Fae female appears so suddenly, I jump. She's wearing a long purple dress, and her thick red braid hangs over her shoulder while gentle curls frame her face.

"Are you ready for dinner?" she asks, staring at me with a blank expression. Not really, but I nod.

"Very well. Then follow me."

She turns, and as she walks away, a shimmering pathway forms beneath her feet—transparent like glass. When I don't immediately follow, she stops and peers over a slender shoulder.

"Come. I assure you that it's perfectly safe." Her voice is devoid of emotion, spoken with an airiness that suggests she's not all here.

Then she continues walking, and I have no choice but to follow. Carefully, I step out onto the pathway. I'm not afraid of heights—I can fly, after all—but the uncertainty of my surroundings is throwing me off balance.

Just in case, I spin up my magic to generate my wings, but nothing happens. My magic is blocked. Is Zerra doing that? I try not to worry about the fact she holds that sort of control over me.

Placing one foot in front of the other, I follow the woman down the path until another building materializes before us. Made of creamy stone, it hovers in the air like my room, with windows on all sides.

We arrive at a set of double doors, and my escort flings them open.

"Her Majesty awaits you." She clasps her hands in front of her and bows her head.

"Majesty? Is she a queen?"

"Of this place, yes."

I peer at the doorway before I brace myself and enter another oval room rendered in hues of creamy white. In the center sits a large dining table groaning with food including colorful desserts and drinks as elaborate as art.

Zerra waits at the end, still wearing her sheer robe, hanging open to show off her . . . assets. My lip curls with distaste.

This is vile. And quite frankly, freaking me the fuck out.

"Feel free to tie that up," I say, gesturing to her body. "I'm not interested in whatever you're offering."

Her smile is sly as she sits back and crosses one smooth leg over the other, picking up her wine and taking a long sip. She eyes me up and down, her gaze lingering around my hips, sending a frosty chill trickling down my back.

"Where's Lor?" I demand. "Why am I here?"

"Lor?" Zerra says with a breathy laugh. "That silly girl?" The way she says it makes me want to commit an act of violence. Maybe upend this whole table, food and dishes and all. Except that seems too mild a reaction.

I want to splatter blood on these walls.

She stands up and slowly prowls towards me. Still, I keep my gaze on her face. I don't know what game she's playing, but I have no interest in it. Even if I weren't already in love with Lor, this woman reminds me far too much of a snake slithering through oily grass.

Zerra stops in front of me, and the triumphant look on her face suggests she's about to deliver a crushing blow.

And that she's planning to enjoy it.

The last coherent moments with Lor come crashing back to me in a memory that sinks in my stomach like a stone. My father thanking me for helping him and telling him where to find her. But he was lying. Trying to rip us apart. But what if she believed him?

The last thing I remember is a bright red flash. Lor's magic? I dig further into my memory. I hear her voice, and I hear her crying. What happened?

Zerra watches me with a simpering smile as I meet her gaze.

"Did you just figure it out?" she asks, and though I'm not entirely sure what she means yet, my ribs seize with fear.

"You're here because of your *mate*. She's the one who killed you."

CHAPTER 14

LOR

ALLUVION—THE CRYSTAL PALACE

That night, a storm rolls in. I sit on my bed, watching lightning streak across the sky and listening to water crash upon the rocks. Wind howls through the castle, like ghosts slipping through the cracks.

This feels like something unnatural. Something conjured from magic. More evidence of the land suffering and Zerra weakening, but I'm still not sure what any of it really means.

It also complicates things for me. I had planned to wait in my room until just before midnight, reasoning that most of the palace would be asleep. But the ferocity of this phenomenon means everyone is on alert. With any luck, they'll be too focused to pay much attention to me, but I'm praying this doesn't mean Bain will stand me up. By the time the sun rises tomorrow, it will be my final day to save Nadir.

An oily green bubble expands in my stomach at the thought. I thought I died already when I lost him once, but losing him again would turn me from a violent scream into a whisper.

When it's close to midnight, I scoot off the bed as silently as possible and drag out the long rope made of sheets. Due to the rain and thunder, I probably don't need to bother with stealth. It's drowning out everything, even my thoughts, which is helpful because I might crack in two if I think too hard about any of this.

I'm wearing light grey leggings and a turquoise sleeveless top I dug out of the closet that stretches with my movements. I'm opting for bare feet since I couldn't find anything to offer me a proper grip.

Balling the rope under one arm, I tiptoe across the room and ease open the door to my balcony. Wind and rain gust through my hair and clothing. It's been three seconds, and I'm already soaked.

After dropping the mass on the floor, I dig out one end and secure it to the railing, my hands slick. One thing I learned from my father is how to tie a knot that becomes tighter with pressure. It's a random memory that surfaced at the most useful time possible. I ignore the tears that blur my eyes because this is a stupid thing to cry over and I really don't have time right now.

Once I've secured the sheet rope, I lean over the railing, looking down as rain drips into my eyes. Despite the tempest, the light in Coral's tank glows softly against the night. I toss the rope over the edge and watch as it tumbles down, hoping I made it long enough. I breathe a sigh of relief when it hits the lower level with a thump.

Everything is wet and slippery, but I push myself up to straddle the railing, gripping it so tightly my hands ache. I quickly glance back at the door, but it's inconceivable that they could hear anything over this ruckus.

Turning back, I study the churning water and jagged rocks as my stomach lurches. A loud clap of thunder booms across the sky, nearly causing me to lose my balance. My vision spins with vertigo as a cold sweat breaks out at the back of my neck.

Leaning forward, I grab my makeshift rope and heave myself off the side, clinging to it with all my strength. Using the knots I tied along its length, I ease myself down slowly, passing darkened windows and praying no one turns on a lamp to find me dangling outside their window like a fool.

Rain lashes against me, the wind buffeting me from side to side. My rope sways like a pendulum as my stomach climbs up my throat. I grip it with my hands and feet, the wet fabric starting to chafe my skin.

This reminds me all too much of the Trials, dangling on a rope over an ocean of sea monsters or maybe hugging to that narrow beam during the gauntlet, nearly falling to my death.

I shake it off. I have things to accomplish.

I don't have time to indulge in my trauma.

Maybe I'll have that luxury when this is over, but not today. Nadir needs me.

Mercifully, I go unnoticed as I shimmy to the bottom and drop onto the puddled balcony with a slap. Once I'm safely standing, I peer over the edge again, thankful I didn't end up as food for the churning ocean.

The balcony sits off a small room lined with bookshelves, and I tiptoe across it and ease the door open, leaving a trail of wet footprints. I wipe them on a rug near the door before I poke my head into the quiet hallway, looking left and right, scanning for guards. If I'd had more time, I would have made an effort to understand the details of Cyan's security, but the clock on Nadir's life is winding down and this is yet another luxury I can't afford.

Thankfully, they seem occupied with the storm, so maybe it did me a favor.

Recognizing the hall as the same one we walked down previously, I turn left and set off perched on my tiptoes so I don't make a sound. Even with the storm's cacophony, the instinct to keep quiet is impossible to ignore.

I pray again that Bain keeps up his end of our meeting.

I enter the throne room to find everything cast in a soft blue glow from the massive water tank. The air is still, suggesting some type of barrier must be in place to keep the wind and rain out.

My breath expands with relief when I see Bain staring up at Coral with his hands clasped behind his back.

I scurry towards him, and he turns at my approach.

"Lor," he says warmly, giving me a kind smile, and guilt twists in my chest. But I won't hurt him or anyone else. I just need to talk to Coral. Surely that isn't a crime. I ignore the reproving voice reminding me that I also plan to rob Cyan if I get the information I need.

"Hi," I say. "We ready?"

Bain's eyebrows furrow. "You're sure you can talk to her?"

"I'm sure," I say.

I'm not completely sure, but he doesn't need to know that.

He scans me up and down, his eyebrows crumpling.

"Why are you wet?"

He didn't ask who I was earlier, which is curious. He had to have seen West and North trailing me. He saw me with Cyan. Either he doesn't care, or he's oblivious. If it's the second, I probably should keep my current not-so-trusting relationship with his son to myself.

"Just went for a walk," I say, tugging a dripping piece of hair out of my eyes.

"In this weather?"

"Got caught in it. Had to run back."

"So late?"

Gods. How many questions is he going to ask?

"Was killing some time before our meeting. Should we talk to Coral now?"

He nods, a light sparking in his eyes at my deflection. He really wants this, and I am a terrible person for taking advantage of his hope.

"Come with me."

He turns, and we make our way around until we reach a door. Bain swings it open, revealing a curved glass tunnel that burrows into the center of the tank.

He gestures for me to follow. It feels like I'm walking straight through the ocean, thanks to the surrounding wall of fish and sea life teeming with color.

We walk towards another door, and then Bain stops, pulling a key from his pocket. He inserts the end into an ornate keyhole and then twists. With a soft whoosh, the water around Coral swirls and churns into a cyclone before it drains away.

When the water is gone, Bain opens the second door and I enter the massive chamber formed by a high wall of rippling waves.

"Can I touch it?" I ask, staring at the water, and Bain nods. "Yes."

I thrust my hand through the surface, marveling at how it remains upright. At once, a dark shape charges towards me, and I scream, yanking my fingers away, just as it comes to an abrupt halt.

"But I wouldn't," Bain adds, and I scowl.

Floating on the other side is the same type of creature Atlas used in the trivia challenge. The same mottled blue skin and nest of black hair and sharp, very sharp teeth. It snarls at me as I stare at it with my wet hand clutched to my chest. I think of how I punched its friend when I rescued Marici and hope these things can't gossip with one another across the miles.

"Can it get to us?" I ask, eyeing it warily.

"*She* cannot," Bain says pointedly. "But don't worry, she's mostly harmless."

I snort out a laugh. It's very obvious she is *not* harmless.

I keep the creature in my peripheral vision. She's staring at me like she desperately wants a bite. Then I head towards Bain, hiding behind him like a shield.

Finally, I take in the sight of Coral. She stretches over my head by several stories, shimmering in the soft light. Thousands upon thousands of tiny crevices make up her height. Her entire structure moves and shifts like she's alive.

"She's stunning," I say. Every Artefact has its own type of beauty, but I can see why Bain thinks his girl is just a little more.

"She is," he says proudly, laying a gentle hand against her. "How are you?" he asks Coral, pausing as though he expects an answer.

Then he gestures to me. "Whenever you're ready. We shouldn't linger here too long. I'm not supposed to let you in here, and..."

He doesn't finish the thought.

"Of course," I say, and then, wasting no more time, I also lay a hand on her.

"Hello? Can you hear me?"

I wait, knowing it always takes a few seconds.

"It's Lor. The Heart Queen."

They all seem to know who I am.

That's when I'm sucked into that same shapeless void. Only this time, I'm surrounded by rippling blue waves. There's no up or down, just an endless stretch of nothing.

Heart Queen. Welcome.

My chest loosens. None of this has been a fluke. This is my purpose. These Artefacts talk to *me*.

You have finally come.

"Were you expecting me?"

There's a long pause before Coral answers.

Yes.

"Why?"

You must fulfill your destiny, Heart Queen.

Those words send a shiver creeping over my scalp. *"What destiny?"*

To save the Queendom of Heart.

Pressure wells in the center of my chest. Part of me understood this would be asked of me, but to hear it confirmed feels like another stack of bricks cemented to my shoulders.

"I'm supposed to save it?"

Surely you understand that by now. Why else do you think we've been helping you?

" 'We'? As in the other Artefacts?"

Yes.

"Why?"

It could have all been so much worse.

I blink. *"What could have?"*

Coral pauses for several seconds, almost as if she's gathering herself.

It has always been a condition of Imperial magic that should a ruler attempt to seize power for themselves, they would lose it all.

I wait for her to continue, understanding she's about to open another door that can never be closed.

But that is our *condition. One we decided at the beginning to prevent endless years of bloodshed. That threat was enough to keep hundreds of rulers in line, save a few over the millennia, but we handled those with little trouble.*

I pause, sure I'm about to hear more about my grandmother.

When an unascended Primary attempts to seize power, the magic does react, becoming erratic and wild and difficult to control. As I said, we were able to smooth over previous incidents, but not on the day Serce tried to steal the crown. With her, there was too much power to contain.

It takes a moment for me to understand what she's saying. Out of precaution, they never shared the entire truth.

"Does this have to do with everyone losing their magic?" I ask.

Yes. That night, the Crown felt the magic spinning out of control. It began fraying apart, and it was only a matter of time before it devastated the continent in a permanent way. The Crown told Queen Daedra to slice out a piece of its jewel and pass it to the next Primary. In that way, the transfer would be incomplete and, therefore, the reaction less violent.

Still, your grandmother was strong beyond measure. The magic of Heart has always been very powerful. When the end came, the only way we could save everyone was to direct all the Imperial magic down into the earth as far as we could and then seal it off to prevent a chain reaction across every realm. It was the best we could do.

I press a hand to my chest, remembering when the Staff revealed what happened that day. My throat knots, recalling the way my grandfather wept over my mother when they sent her away to save her life.

We also hid the Heart Crown in a place where no one but its true owner would ever find it.

I nod at those words because that makes sense. Nadir had been sure only my magic would free it. Only I would have been able to feel that tug towards it.

Once we felt the worst danger had passed, we returned the magic to the other realms, but Heart was not yet stable enough. As your mother matured, it was still too volatile, and so we waited. When she gave birth to three children many years later, we had just enough control to bestow the first threads onto you and your siblings. And then we chose one to become the Primary.

I shake my head. Finally, all of these pieces are starting to fall into place. For the first time since I arrived in Aphelion, I feel like a fog is lifting.

"I'm still not sure I'm following. Can I bring the magic back?"

You've already started it, Heart Queen. Why do you think the roses bloomed for you? Why do you think you were the only one who could find the Crown?

"How do I do that?"

We cannot release all the magic into Heart until you ascend and take your throne. Only then can your queendom ever be whole.

I consider that statement. *That* has always been my goal. But the Empyrium want me to become Zerra.

"Can someone else do it?" I ask.

Not unless you give birth to a new Primary.

"I can't just give it to someone else?"

It's then I realize Coral said they bestowed the first threads of Heart magic onto my siblings. Willow, too?

"What about my sister? What if I died?"

Your brother's and sister's destinies lie elsewhere. There is no one else. It must be you or someone born of you.

"What happens if I don't?" My fist clenches against the rough surface of the Artefact, bracing for the answer.

Then we will have no choice but to disperse the magic of Heart throughout the continent, allowing it to meld with the power of the other realms. The Crown will crumble to dust, its magic lost forever, and Heart and its people will become only a memory. The longer we delay, the harder it becomes. We are running out of time. You must act soon.

I swallow hard.

There can be no other, Heart Queen. We are here at your disposal.

"Why are you helping me?"

Our job has always been to protect Ouranos's magic, and we do not hold you responsible for your grandmother's mistakes.

My throat knots up at those words. Why am I getting emotional over the sentiments of a giant enchanted object? Though, it's clear they're so much more than that.

While the continent can exist without the magic of Heart, Ouranos was created with seven realms, and it is our desire to see it restored.

My tongue feels numb, and a pinch shoots between my eyebrows as more pieces lock into place. Technically, my existence isn't necessary, and the Empyrium have other plans for me. If I don't take the Heart Crown, then they all die, and if I don't take the place of Zerra, then all of Ouranos is in danger.

The knowledge makes me feel both disposable and indispensable in the same breath.

Regardless, I came here to get my mate back. That is my first task. Then I'll figure out the rest. Or go down trying, I guess.

"I need the ark of Alluvion. I can't accomplish any of this without the ark. Do you know where it is?" I ask. When I schemed to talk to Coral, I only wanted to ask about the ark. I've already received so much more than I could have imagined, but I'm praying she knows where to find it.

I can show you.

"*You would do that?*" I breathe, almost ready to collapse in relief.

If that's what you require. My king does not need or use it.

"*Please, tell me where it is.*"

The scene around me melts away and then I'm looking at the throne from a different angle. The perspective shifts, zeroing in on one of the tide pools inset into the floor. I'm frantically studying the gently rippling surface when something glints in the light, and there I see it—the sparkle of virulence nestled between the rocks and coral.

Then I'm flung from the scene and find myself standing inside Coral's tank.

I spin around to find Bain watching me.

"What happened? You were in a trance," he says. "Did she speak to you?"

"Yes," I say, taking in his hopeful expression.

"What did she say?"

He's looking at me with such desperation that I need to tell him something. I didn't get a chance to ask for a message.

"She said . . . you take very good care of her and to tell you thank you."

"Oh," he says, his posture straightening. "Well, that's very nice."

"I have to go," I say. "Thanks for this."

Then I start running.

"Wait!" Bain calls after me. "Where are you going?"

I barrel down the tunnel and into the throne room. About two dozen pools circle the perimeter, but I can't tell which one Coral showed me—they all look kind of the same. I run between them, hoping a memory will spark.

Bain follows behind me as I spiral into panic, shoving everything I just learned into a pocket of my mind to deal with later. I need to find the ark and get out of here. "What are you doing?" he demands over and over as I continue to ignore him. "You cannot touch these!"

I drop into a pool, plunging my hands between the stones and coral. They scrape at my hands and knees, leaving hairline cuts. After I'm sure the ark isn't there, I stand up and run to the next.

"Stop this," Bain says, his voice taking on a desperate edge. "These are sacred!"

I plunge into the next one, splashing in the shallow water, hunting, searching in the sand and rocks. "Where is it?!"

"Where is what?" Bain asks. "If you don't stop this, I'll call the guards."

That gets my attention.

"No, you can't," I say, grabbing him by the shoulders with my dripping hands. "Just give me another minute. Coral wanted me to do this."

It's not a lie. She did tell me where the ark was hiding.

"Did she?"

"Yes," I say, running for the next pool, scattering crabs when my feet hit the sand. They nibble on my bare toes, and I hope they're not toxic or something. My fingers bleed, and I wince at the sting of salt water while red clouds billow under the surface. Thunder booms overhead, setting my already stretched nerves on edge. When I was speaking to Coral, the entire world melted away, and I completely forgot about the storm.

Where is it?

Still nothing. With only a few pools left to search, I'm growing desperate. What if Coral was wrong? What if Cyan moved it? What if she was lying to me?

When I reach the next pool, my memory clicks, sure I recognize that pile with a long oval-shaped rock balancing on top. With a cry, I drop down to shift the stones, and then there it is. The ark lies half-buried in the sand, sparkling in the dimness.

"I found it!" I cry.

"Found what?" Bain asks, bending over with his hands pressed to his knees.

"This is what Coral wanted."

Bain squints at it. "What is it?"

"It's . . ." I'm not sure how to answer, and a lie fails to materialize. "It's nothing."

I jump up, trying to wipe the wet sand off its surface.

"Thank you for your help. I have to go now."

I leap out of the pool, and without another word, I run for the door, hoping I won't be spotted on my way to an exit.

But then a body steps into the doorway and I slide to a stop, my wet feet squeaking against the smooth tiles. Cyan, the Alluvion King, stands before me, his arms folded and his head cocked, a sliver of moonlight illuminating his dark blue hair and a pale cheekbone.

"Going somewhere, Lor?"

CHAPTER 15

I stumble over my feet, catching myself before I face-plant into the floor.

Cyan watches me with a dispassionate expression, his feet spread wide like a wall, harboring no intention of allowing me through. The corner of his mouth curls up, and he looks like he's caught a cat with a canary in its jaws. And I'm the stupid cat. Or the stupid canary? Either way, I'm fucked.

"How long have you been waiting there?" I ask, gasping for breath. My heart gallops in my chest, my ribcage compressing into my lungs.

"Long enough to know you've stolen my ark and were planning to abscond with it. After all the hospitality I've shown you?"

"I . . . uh . . ."

I have absolutely no position of defense or explanation other than that's exactly what I intended to do. My gaze slides past him, and I wonder how far I can get before he stops me. He catches the direction of my stare and lunges, his hand circling my arm, squeezing tight.

"What are you doing with it?" he asks. All his previous feigned affability and cool demeanor are gone, his blue eyes flashing in the slice of moonlight that falls across his face. "How dare you come into my home and steal one of my most precious objects while desecrating my sacred tide pools?"

"I need it," I hiss. "More than you can possibly understand."

"You think that makes it right? To steal from me?" He squeezes my arm tighter, and I wince at the pressure against my bones.

"Let me go." I attempt to yank my arm from his grasp, but he holds on.

His jaw turns to stone. "You could have just asked," he says, and I scoff.

"You would never have given it to me."

"Now you'll never know," he says. "Instead of appealing to my good nature, you've now forced me to feed you to my pet sea dragon. Such a pity, Heart Queen. Just when you'd returned after all this time. I suppose your family truly *is* destined for nothing but ruin."

I yank again, but his grip is firm, and I'm starting to panic.

"I need it to save him!" I scream. "Please. I'm begging you."

"Save who?" Cyan demands. "Tell me what's going on."

"She has him. Zerra has my mate."

Cyan's grip on my arm loosens, his pale face turning ghostly white. "Zerra?"

"Yes," I whisper, knowing how insane I sound right now. "She...I saw her."

"What do you mean you *saw* her?" His voice is sharp, the syllables snipped.

"I was in the Evanescence. I saw the beginning of Ouranos and the rulers who received the Artefacts first."

I'm babbling and not making any sense, but Cyan slowly parses out my words.

"That's not possible," he says, peering at me as though he's trying to determine if I've lost my mind. I don't blame him. Everything I'm saying right now *does* sound impossible.

"I thought so, too, but I was there." I finally pull my arm from his hold and back up a few steps. "I wasn't lying when I said Nadir is dead. I killed him, but it was an accident."

"Your magic," Cyan says. "You lost control like you did in my bathroom."

"I meant to kill the Aurora's soldiers, not him. Then Zerra came to me, and she said she could save him. But she would do so only if I bring her the Alluvion ark. So you see, this is why I need it."

My chest heaves with shortened breaths as I clutch the ark to my chest.

"Please. I'm begging you. I can't live...I can't...I can't live without him. Even if he hates me for killing him, I can't let him die."

Cyan's hard expression softens, genuine remorse in his eyes, but I already know what he'll say as his head slowly shakes from side to side.

"Lor. I'm sorry, but I can't let you take it."

"Why not? What do you need it for?"

"I need it for my kingdom and my people. If you know of the arks, you understand that already."

"Can't I just borrow it? Coral said you don't use it anyway."

His eyes narrow. "Coral said *what*?"

He gazes past me, and I peer over my shoulder to find Bain in the doorway, watching us, his forehead furrowed and his hands clutched to his chest.

Cyan's gaze returns to me, his eyes darkening to navy pits. "*What* did you do?"

"Please," I say, brushing past the accusation.

"Do you think Zerra will give it *back*?" He arches a dark eyebrow and gives me a look that suggests I've got to be kidding him.

"Maybe?" I ask as I inch back another step. The ocean crashes outside, rain still falling, and I wonder if I can escape over the edge of Coral's aquarium.

"Give it back to me," he says, holding out his hand. "Give it to me now, and I'll try to grant you mercy. You can't escape this place. Guards are stationed everywhere."

I look behind me, watching as a line of said guards files into the throne room. Behind Cyan, another group gathers, all eyeing me with hardness. I'm surrounded.

"Bain," Cyan says, looking up at his father with tenderness. "Return to your room."

Bain nods and scurries off before the Alluvion king focuses his fierce attention on me.

"Lor. I'm sorry that Nadir is gone, but that is not my concern."

Cyan takes a slow step towards me, and I take another back, still clutching the ark.

"Give me the ark," he says again. "I can't let you walk out of here with it. She tried to take them once, and I've sworn never to let it fall into her hands."

"He's going to die," I say as tears fill my eyes. "I'll never see him again."

He takes another step, and I'm lost. This is over. It was an impossible task, and I never had a chance of succeeding, but a small part of me still hoped.

The sound of hurried footsteps draws Cyan's attention behind him.

Linden comes running towards us. "We have visitors," she says, her expression grim.

"Who?" Cyan asks.

"An army."

The king of Alluvion stares at her, waiting for the crushing blow she's about to deal.

"We believe it's the Aurora King."

CHAPTER 16

RION

"Would you like to feel him kicking, Your Majesty?" Rion turned away from the window to find the midwife wiping her forehead with the back of her hand. Meora had started bleeding earlier that morning and called for Lisette to ensure everything was right with the child.

"Good news, it was only a little scare," Lisette added. "Sometimes it happens as we near the due date, but the baby is fine. You have a strong one growing here." She wiped her hands on a cloth and beamed down at Meora, who lay on the bed, sweat coating her face, her hair a nest of dark tangles.

She looked at him expectantly, running a hand over her

bare, swollen belly as if hoping a sliver of affection would manifest for the child who would soon join their lives.

With his hands behind his back, he approached and stared down at her.

Nadir.

The Torch had confirmed it was a boy.

Meora had chosen the name to represent its connection to the celestial sphere.

But Rion saw it the other way.

This child was his downfall. The lowest point of his fortunes.

Perhaps it wasn't right to blame him. And Rion didn't blame *him* so much as he did the boy's mother.

He'd wondered, too, when all was said and done if he might summon up something close to affection for the child. Part of him had expected it after the bonding when there would be no turning back, but it had yet to manifest. When he closed his eyes and imagined him, this child born of his skin, all he saw was everything he'd lost.

Rachel had made good on her promise to depart from The Aurora, and he had no idea where she'd gone. It had been six months without her, and it was eating away at the edges of his heart.

Perhaps she'd return to see him in time, but something told him that would never come to pass. He'd lost the love of his life over a petty grudge and one night of random passion. He'd lost his heart for one mistake.

"No, thank you," Rion said, addressing Lisette's question before turning towards his bonded partner and giving her a curt bow. "I have matters to attend."

"We'll need to send out invites for the blessing," Meora said. "Since the birth will be soon."

Rion resisted the scowl that curved on his lips. They'd have to smile and pretend to be a happy family as the kingdom's citizens came to pay their respects to the next Primary and future king.

Outwardly, he wouldn't let his disdain show. He'd keep up appearances, at least until his father finally expired. Garnet was weaker than ever, the Withering ravaging what was left of his body. Still, the king clung on, and Rion was ready to tear his hair out.

"Excuse me," Rion said, and then he swept past the midwife and out of the room, heading for his wing in the Keep.

Recently, he'd made a discovery occupying much of his attention, and he could hardly wait to return to this object of his current obsession. One night he'd had a dream. He'd been exploring the vaults below the Keep and had come upon a chest. He couldn't tell what it was in the dream, but the moment he'd awoken, he'd descended into the bowels to explore.

It had been filled with journals. At first, he'd dismissed them as pointless history, but after another dream leading him to the same spot, he once again found himself down in the vault late one night, perusing the pages by the light of a glowing yellow orb suspended in the air.

They belonged to King Herric—the last Aurora King of the First Age. It was a miracle these relics had survived for so many years, but the airtight seal on the chest had preserved the pages, though they were extremely delicate.

He'd had the entire chest brought up to his study, where

he'd been poring over them every night. The first few journals contained little but mundane accountings of ruling and the same problems that plagued kings even millennia ago. But eventually, his interest snagged on a passage about when something changed in The Aurora.

> *The sky is dark again tonight. By my count, it's been nearly three weeks since the northern lights last appeared. Even worse, reports from the mines grow increasingly alarming. Tomorrow, I will journey with my advisors into the tunnels, though I fear what we will find. Without our jewels, The Aurora is lost.*

Rion felt the king's despair and understood it. He couldn't imagine what force would cause the jewels to disappear and hoped he'd never live to see it. Without its jewels, The Aurora would have nothing to trade, and he'd lose his position of power. While that passage had been interesting enough, it was everything that came later that truly held his attention.

Herric had been present at the beginning of the Second Age. And while the old stories held that an Artefact had been bestowed upon each ruler then, they left out some key details.

Like the existence of gods named the Empyrium and the fact that Herric had volunteered for Zerra's role and been turned down. But the history books credited King Elias as the first king of the Second Age, so what had happened to Herric during those early years?

Tonight, Rion entered his study and poured himself a drink before he settled on one of the soft velvet divans facing the window. The lights danced across the sky in ribbons of red and blue and green. The sight always moved him when so little else did.

Rion grabbed the next journal from the chest, flipping to the front. Herric was certainly verbose, and while normally Rion would roll his eyes at this level of self-indulgence, he found himself appreciating just how much this ancient king had revealed.

Recently, he'd finished a journal about Herric's trips to the Evanescence, where he'd whored himself out for information while searching for Zerra's weaknesses. He'd had every intention of finding a way to replace her.

Rion scanned the pages, searching for something interesting, skimming through Herric's self-loathing over using his body to achieve his ends. Rion shook his head at the dramatics. He would never hesitate to do the same if it meant he could become a god. What was sex anyway? Only one person in his existence had made it mean anything.

When the current volume produced nothing, he picked up another, landing on a passage about a dark substance Herric had discovered in the mines that could channel magic.

This was something new.

Rion sat up and leaned forward as he devoured every word.

> *It's taken years to dig deep enough, but we've finally found it—virulence. I don't know why I didn't remember it earlier, but the events with the Empyrium have weighed heavily on my mind. I felt the magic and power in that stone before I was taken to the Evanescence. It*

sparkled like it was alive. While I attempt to pick apart Zerra's weaknesses, perhaps there are other ways to take back the power I lost.

This magic I've been granted is a gift, but it is difficult to contain, and it does little to raise me above others. That little queen in Heart is said to be the strongest, and I cannot allow her the upper hand. Perhaps this material is the key. When infused with my magic, the stone alters its state, changing its properties and granting me abilities beyond my nature. Next time I visit Zerra, I intend to test for its other capabilities.

Rion continued reading, discovering that not only did virulence channel magic, but doing so would affect Zerra in adverse ways. He read about Herric's months of meticulous testing, weighing the pros, cons, and outcomes of channeling his magic through the stone in her presence. He'd read about witches who lived deep in the forests of The Woodlands who used stone or wooden carvings of someone's likeness to set curses upon them and had adopted the principle to create a set of objects intended to harm the goddess.

Rion then went on to read about the arks Herric had created in her image. He'd gifted one to each ruler in Ouranos, promising it would help control their magic. Through his testing, Herric had determined it would take vast quantities of magic used over time to bring Zerra down. While the rulers believed Herric had handed them a lifeline, they were slowly killing their goddess without realizing it.

Rion couldn't believe what he was reading. He'd never

heard of these arks. Did his father know about them? Was this information imparted only to the ascended?

But it then occurred to him that if Herric had gifted them to the other rulers, perhaps he had only made six. Rion looked around the room at the walls of his study and the glittering black stone walls of the Keep.

He stood up and placed his hand against the surface, attempting to feel something buried in the layers of stone. This Keep had been standing here throughout most of the Second Age. Again, King Elias was credited with its construction, but had *Herric* surrounded them with virulence, and no one had ever realized it? Rion sent out a tendril of magic, anticipation churning in his gut. It touched the stone, but nothing happened.

He frowned. Perhaps this wasn't virulence after all and he was wrong about how it appeared.

No matter the case, now he had to know more.

Was there more to be found under the mountain? Could he use it to conquer Ouranos? To finally take his crown?

Like the king who'd once ruled this kingdom thousands of years ago—it was time to start digging.

CHAPTER 17

LOR

ALLUVION—PRESENT DAY

The Aurora King.

Those words freeze us all in place for several tense heartbeats before Cyan's accusing gaze turns to me.

"What have you brought to my doorstep, Heart Queen?"

"This is not my doing," I hiss. "He must have tracked me here."

"How were they not detected earlier?" Cyan demands of Linden. "How did they sneak up on us?"

"One moment there was nothing, and suddenly they appeared. The storm must have obscured their approach." Her green eyes flash, and if I thought she hated me already, that's nothing compared to the bottomless loathing she feels for me now.

"Fuck!" Cyan says before he whirls on me.

He seizes me by the arm and drags me towards the door while he shouts out a series of commands to Linden. She tosses me the dirtiest look that has ever been tossed in the history of ever before she hisses, "It's exactly as I said. Your family brings nothing but ruin."

I swallow my nervousness, but it does feel like she's kind of right.

Cyan yanks on my arm and drags me down the hall.

"Stop!" I scream. "You're giving me up to him?"

"You come into my home, lie to me, deceive me, and then rob me? I'll be thrilled to see the back of you."

He's moving so fast that I stumble as we walk. Gods, he's pissed.

"How can you do this? You know what kind of man he is."

"I do, and that's why I don't want him threatening my home and *my* people. You are no one to me, Lor."

It's a fair point. I'd probably do the same thing. But I can't let Rion have me. If I don't return the ark to Zerra, Nadir will die. I'm almost out of time.

Magic hums under my skin, sparkling and crackling, and I flex my fingertips as Cyan continues to drag me through the palace, shouting orders at everyone we pass. The rain has eased up, the sounds of the wind and thunder no longer drowning everything out.

Activity flurries around us, and I consider my options. If I use my magic, I might kill a bunch of innocent people. Cyan included. I swore I would be more careful from now on, but he's forcing me into a corner.

As he tows me towards the entrance, I can practically feel the distance closing between me and the Aurora King, pressing in on me like an iron noose. It's like he's calling to me, reeling me in like the helpless worm I am. If he gets his hands on me again, I'm so very dead. Or worse. My entire life has been a lesson in things that are so much worse.

Cyan throws open a door and hauls me onto a high balcony that overlooks the city surrounding the castle. Rain falls in a steady drip, making everything glisten in the moonlight.

In the distance, Rion's army approaches, spreading across the horizon like a black stain. I thought I'd killed more of them, but he probably has endless resources to draw on. I'll never be a match for him, and I knew it wouldn't be that easy to kill him anyway.

"Cyan," I say, pleading. "Don't do this. I'm begging you."

He whirls on me. "How dare you?"

He snatches the ark from my clasped hands, scraping my already bloodied fingertips, and hands it to a guard.

"Keep that safe," he orders. "And don't let her near it."

The guard nods as he gives me a suspicious look. Great. This is just fucking great.

Rion's army marches closer, passing through the gates and down the wide boulevard bisecting the city. Screams echo from below as people cower in the safety of their homes. Alluvion's soldiers also move through the streets, trying to maintain order, but Rion's army ignores everyone, and I understand why. He didn't come here to level the ocean kingdom; he came only for me. But I also have no doubt he'll destroy everyone here if that's what it takes.

I jerk against Cyan's hold again and find myself surrounded by soldiers, including Linden. Anemone has also appeared, and she passes a quizzical look between me and her king.

"What's going on?" she asks.

"This thief tried to steal the ark," Cyan says. "Ate our food, slept in our beds, and then just walked into my throne room and *took* it."

Anemone's eyebrows draw together, and the look on her face makes guilt burn at the base of my neck. She looks so... disappointed in me.

"How did you know where to find it?" she asks.

Cyan pauses and looks over at me as if he's just remembered what I said earlier. "She *claims* Coral spoke to her," he says, squeezing my arm so tight I wince. "I'll throw you off this balcony if you don't explain yourself."

I grimace and then say, "Sometimes, the Artefacts talk to me."

"Liar!" he hisses. "The Artefacts speak only with the ascended."

"No, they talk to me," I say. "I swear to you."

"How did you get to Coral?" Anemone queries, and I glare at her. Does she have to ask so many damn questions?

"Bain was with her," Cyan says. "You tricked him."

"Uh... maybe?"

Cyan shakes his head. "You took advantage of a confused man to steal from me? How are you not ashamed of yourself?"

"I had no choice," I say, feeling as tall as a bug. "Zerra has my mate, and she won't give him back without the ark."

Something passes behind Anemone's expression as she exchanges a loaded look with Cyan.

"Why should we give a fuck about that?" Linden demands, still my best friend.

"Because Rion won't stop with me," I say. "He's up to something bigger. Something that will hurt you too. If he gets his hands on me, then he's one step closer to that goal."

Cyan glares at me. "*What* is he up to?"

"I don't *know*," I say, deciding now is the moment to add in a few more details I've kept to myself. I've got little else to lose at this point. I tell him about Nostraza and my magic, explaining the horrors Rion visited upon me and my siblings.

When I'm done stumbling through my hasty explanation, Cyan seems to consider my words as he looks at Anemone. They appear to be having some kind of silent conversation that I can't interpret. The hold on my arm loosens a fraction.

"She's lying," Linden says. "The Heart Queen would say anything to save her own neck."

Cyan's hand squeezes tighter again, and my shoulders sag. I want to kick her in the shins right now.

"I'm not lying," I say. "Look at my face. He did that. He left that scar on me with his magic."

"You could have gotten that anywhere," Linden says.

She's right. And what reason have I given any of them to believe me? All I've done is lie since they let me in here. My inability to trust anyone is becoming a self-fulfilling prophecy.

At the sound of a horn, we all turn to watch as Rion's army draws near.

When they reach the round plaza surrounding the palace, they spill into it like ink staining a clean white canvas. Rion sits on his horse at the front, all imperious arrogance in black armor with a sword strapped to his back. He looks like the Lord of the Underworld himself, come to drag me to the pits of hell. I remember with a jolt that this is Nadir's heritage. That the first king of The Aurora is his great-great-great-great-however-many-greats-this-goes-back grandfather. Goosebumps erupt over my skin.

"Cyan!" Rion shouts from below. "I've come only for the girl. Hand her over to me, and your people need not suffer."

Cyan isn't buying that, is he?

"You don't really think he's just going to turn around and leave once he has me, do you?" I ask, trying to pull my arm out of his hold.

"Well, I know he won't leave if I don't give you up."

Okay, good point.

"You won't be able to live with yourself if you do this," I say. "I can see that you're a good king and a good man. You really wouldn't hand over an innocent woman into the clutches of her abuser, would you?"

A conflicted waver flickers in his eyes—it's true that he's a good king. He's just protecting his people.

"Don't listen to her!" Linden hisses. "She fills your ears with poison. You think she didn't do the same to my brother?"

I grit my teeth and resist the urge to lash out. "I'm not," I hiss.

"Your Majesty!" Rion calls from below, and we all turn to face him.

I stare down at the Aurora King, hating everything. He looks too much like Nadir but nothing like him at all. He is the sum total of so much misery in my life. Exacting my revenge has always been a desire that sits in the center of my heart like a pellet of jagged iron, and gods, the vicious things I'd do to him if I ever got the chance. It would break both of us, but I'd consider every moment worth the price.

"Give her to me, and then we'll be out of your way. This girl is nothing to you. Or to anyone, really. Just an heir to a broken queendom that, soon enough, everyone will forget about for good."

Those words touch some deep, insecure part of me because he's right, isn't he? If we had never left Nostraza, none of this would be happening. The last drops of Heart magic would die with me, and that would be it.

But the people of Heart are counting on me. I can't let them die. It's been almost three hundred years and they waited, never losing faith. I refuse to let them down.

But Cyan won't care about any of that.

"I'm sorry," Cyan says, and my chest deflates. "But I have no choice."

He starts to drag me away from the railing, and I don't think. I forget all my earlier reservations. I don't consider what I'm doing. I just react.

My hand flies out, and I explode.

Lightning bursts out of me, bleeding across the sky in rough crimson streaks.

My ears fill with the unbearable sound of terrified screams and the crack of crumbling stone, and then . . . I'm falling.

CHAPTER 18

The balcony gives out, cracking and shattering as Cyan's grip falters, and we tumble to the earth in a shower of dust and wreckage. Pain digs into my body as time seems to slow before I strike the hard rock and even harder ground. My vision blurs as blood drips in my eyes and I'm pelted and crushed by debris. Covering my head, I try to stem the worst of the damage as chaos rains from above.

It takes a moment for my head to stop spinning. A haze of dust surrounds me, and I can't see more than a few feet through it. Slowly, I sit up, wincing at the ache in my limbs. I touch my head, my fingers coming away red. Screams and the sound of everything splitting and breaking fill the air. I seek out Cyan, Anemone, or Linden, but they're currently beyond my sight.

I almost killed myself, but it created the distraction I needed.

This is my chance.

I stumble to my feet, rocks sliding out from under me, and it's then I notice the rain has finally let up. Thank Zerra for small miracles. I shake my head. Not Zerra. Fuck that bitch.

I need to find the Alluvion ark and then I'll run as fast as my feet will take me.

Coughing up dust from my lungs, I stagger on a throbbing ankle. How long does it take for this Fae healing thing to kick in? It's been so long I hardly remember how it works. I pass the bodies of guards and palace servants. Some are still breathing, only knocked out, but some are clearly never waking up.

Guilt twists in my chest, because I did this. Am I any better than my grandmother, taking what I want and failing to acknowledge the consequences?

I swore I'd raze the palace to the ground if I had to. If Cyan had just listened to me, I wouldn't have had to resort to such drastic measures. But none of that quiets the nagging shame that burns at the back of my throat.

As a few begin to stir, I tear the cloak from a fallen guard and wrap it around my head, using a portion to cover my nose and keep the dust from clogging my lungs. I scan the ground, searching for the guard Cyan handed the ark to. He can't have gone far. I just hope he isn't buried under an immovable pile of rubble.

A body with pale skin and long indigo hair emerges in the fog. Cyan lies on his side, his limbs askew and his eyes closed. I stare at him and let out a breath of relief when I see his ribcage expand. Not dead. Just...momentarily impeded. I didn't want to kill him. I didn't want to kill anyone.

I stare in the direction of the city. I hear people shouting orders, along with more cracking and rumbling as they shift the debris. The haze continues to blind me, but it's starting to clear. I need to get out of here before anyone finds me. What happened to Rion and his army? I hope I took a few more of them out.

Finally, I spot the guard I'm seeking and cry out. As I fall to my knees, my hands land on the sharp rock, scraping my palms. They're still aching from my search in the tide pools, but I ignore it. I have more important things to do than worry about a bit of temporary discomfort. If I lose Nadir, I'll never be able to breathe again.

I pat his pockets, finding a telltale hard spot, but the opening is trapped under his body. He's enormous, and I try to shift him, but the angle is awkward and he's half-buried under the rubble. A knife hangs at his belt, and I slide it out before sawing through the fabric of his tunic. Voices in the distance move closer while the sky clears and dawn arrives with a wash of pink and orange.

Finally, I free the ark and yank it out of the guard's pocket, his eyes fluttering as he groans. I briefly consider knocking him out again, but I reason it'll be at least another minute before he's coherent enough to cause any problems. With the ark clutched to my chest, I stagger over the rubble and scoop up a fallen scarf to create a makeshift sling in which to carry it.

I've already decided to return to Aphelion. Once I get Nadir back, I need to find Tristan and Willow. Maybe they're already looking for me. If I were in their shoes, I'd do the same. That means south is my destination.

I continue picking through the debris then trip, landing on my knees. I wince at the scrape as it tears away my skin. The sky is almost clear now, but no one pays me any attention as they tend to their wounds and dig up those caught under the wreckage. I take a moment to scan the horizon for Rion, knowing that wherever he is, he's already looking for me.

Does he know Nadir is dead? Does he care?

Finally, I make my way to the edge of the palace and look up. My eyes widen at what I've done. I've torn off almost the entire front facade of the building, leaving the exposed guts underneath. Rubble is everywhere, nothing but chaos. I shake my head, tears filling my eyes. I wanted my magic back so badly, but I didn't stop to think about what it would mean. I'm not a queen or a High Fae—I'm nothing but fucking destruction. Linden is right.

I swore I'd do anything to save Heart and save Nadir, but at what point do I have to consider the cost of what I want versus those I might hurt along the way? I was a child when my life was taken from me for the sins of a woman I never met. That wasn't fair, but what I did here isn't either. I've been so afraid of people judging me against the things my grandmother did, and here I am, at the first opportunity, doing the same. Is this who I want to be?

I scan the distance, seeing black uniforms moving through the mess. Rion's guards are searching for me. I take another look at the destruction I've caused. It's done now. I can't undo this, but I need to think harder about how I use my magic again. Or at least find some way to fucking control it.

I also need to run, or all of this will have been for nothing.

I duck around a corner, keeping out of sight. No one lingers on this side of the building, and I continue around it until I come to the far side. Ahead of me is a stretch of endless beach, sand spreading in every direction, bordered by the ocean on one side and the rest of Ouranos on the other.

The Crystal Palace sits on an island with three bridges arching over the Sinen River. Either I head for one, which would mean entering the city, or I take my chances and swim across the channel.

I consider my options.

In the distance, I see the blue ribbon where the water splits the land. Heading into the city seems like a fool's errand. I'm covered in blood, and it will be glaringly obvious I was part of the collapse. I'll draw too much attention.

The beach is nothing but open sky and plain. Anyone looking this way will see me from miles away. Neither is a good choice, but I decide to take my chances with the sand.

Checking one last time that the coast is clear, I push away from the wall, and then I run.

CHAPTER 19

NADIR

THE EVANESCENCE

"**Y**our mate. She killed you," Zerra repeats after I don't answer for several long seconds. Her expression turns simpering, and she assesses me up and down. "She thought you betrayed her to your father and, in a fit of rage, unleashed her magic and killed you." She tips her head and purses her mouth into a faux pout. "Surely you remember something?"

She stares at me as I sort through my thoughts. Yes, I remember a bright flash of red and then nothing. I remember hands touching me and shoving me. It's finally clearing in the haze of my mind. Being rolled over grass and a sharp pain in

my feet and legs. Being dragged over the earth. Lor screaming my name over and over.

But I can't see any of it. It's like impressions on the backs of
my eyelids. Muted flashes that are more about feelings than
actual memories. Did any of it happen?

"And then what?" I ask, barely able to summon the words
over the clog in my throat.

Lor believes what my father said. She thinks I betrayed her.
Surely she would know he was lying. After everything we've
been through, how could she ever think I'd do anything to
hurt her?

"Then she got up and walked away," Zerra says.

"You're lying." I try to make it sound like a statement, but it
comes out far too much like a question for my liking.

"Oh, all right," Zerra says. "She cried a bit. Felt a *little* bad.
But then she dusted off her pants and ran. She said she was
planning to track down the Aurora King."

I narrow my gaze, sure Zerra has to be lying. Lor wouldn't
have just *left* after killing me. No matter how angry she might
have been, she would never have done that. And if she were
free, she wouldn't go after my father first. She would have
turned right around and run for her brother and sister. I'm
sure of it. I know her better than anyone, and the Lor I know
would have sought out her family above all else.

"That still doesn't explain how I ended up here," I say.

I'm attempting to piece through the shattered fragments
handed to me, and I need as much information as possible.

Zerra's expression turns to annoyance. "I invited you to
dine with me, not suffer through an interrogation." She plants

her elbows on the table and gestures with her chin towards the seat next to her. "Sit down."

I hesitate, and her eyes flash. The last thing I want is to dine with this woman, but I understand I'm backed into a corner right now. I survey my surroundings, searching for exits, but windows surround us on all sides. However, a window can be used as an exit just as much as a door. There is the issue of us hovering in the middle of nothing and the fact my magic seems to be blocked, but I just need to bide my time.

My gaze then snags on a surprising sight: three pedestals stand at the far end of the room, with three dark objects hovering above each one.

The arks.

Though I saw it for only a second, I remember the object the Mirror hurled at Lor.

"I see you're admiring my collection," Zerra says. "It's been quite a feat to get my hands on these. And soon, I'll have them all."

My attention moves back to her. "How so?"

"That's nothing to concern yourself with." She pats the end of the table in front of an empty seat on her right. "Come and sit."

After hesitating for a moment, I pad down the length of the table in my bare feet. My gaze pings to the arks again, and I consider how to trick her into telling me more. How does she plan to get the rest? This might be important for us to know.

The marble floor is cold, but the air is warm. As I approach, Zerra eyes me with naked hunger, and I repress a shudder. I pull out the chair next to her and sit. The position puts me closer to her than I would like.

"Hungry?" she asks.

"Not really."

I'm starving, but I don't want anything she's offering.

"Come now. I was mortal once, even if it was a very long time ago. You haven't eaten anything for days. You must be famished."

She ignores whatever I'm about to say and starts to pile food on my plate: strawberries and cheese, a slice of beef, and a chicken leg. She pours gravy over the top, picks up a fork, spears a potato, and holds it out to me. Reluctantly, I reach for it, but she pulls it back.

"Ah ah," she coos. "I want to feed my fiancé. It's so romantic, don't you think?"

I nearly choke on my tongue.

"Fiancé?" I croak.

I know this is a human concept—something to do with their type of bonding.

"Yes," she says, grinning.

"I . . . don't understand."

Zerra pouts again and holds up the fork. "You know, I thought you'd be much smarter than this. But that's okay. I've always preferred my lovers to be pretty and not much else."

Then she uses her other hand to stroke my bare chest. I shove away from the table, the screech echoing through the hollow room.

"Do not touch me," I snarl, and her bright blue eyes darken into swirling pits of anger. Her nostrils flare and she sets the fork down, folding her hands on the table.

"You're shy. I understand. But don't worry. Soon enough, you'll be craving my touch. Your ancestor was the same."

A thousand responses sit perched on my tongue, but I drag in a long breath, attempting to soothe my temper. I'll do myself no favors by antagonizing her.

"My ancestor?"

"Yes, the first Aurora King of the Second Age. We were lovers for many years."

"King Elias was your lover?"

"Not him," she scoffs. "The *true* first king."

I narrow my gaze, wondering what she's talking about. If she's being truthful, I do have to question my forbearer's judgment.

"Who?"

"Herric," she says, but that doesn't tell me anything.

"I don't know who that is."

"No, you wouldn't." She pushes my plate closer, seemingly done with this subject. "Feed yourself then. I can't have you passing out on me."

I eye her narrowly as she fusses with her napkin, avoiding my scrutiny.

"What happened with him?"

She stops and pins me with a look. "Eat your supper."

Leaving it for now, I pick up my fork, watching for any sudden movements. I slowly take a few bites and resist the urge to moan. I didn't realize until now just how hungry I am, and everything tastes incredible, but I do my best to temper my pace. I don't want her to get any ideas about starving me out.

She watches me intently as I eat and doesn't seem the least bit bothered by how weird this is. At least I don't have to make conversation.

"Better?" she asks when I've finished.

I make a noncommittal sound as she reaches out and picks up a decanter, pouring me a glass of wine. She places it in front of me and then leans forward as her hand slides up my thigh.

Red hazes my vision, and I leap up.

"I said don't touch me."

She rolls her eyes, which just really pisses me off.

Forget subtle exits. I pick up a chair and hold it over my head.

"What are you doing?" Zerra screeches as I storm towards a window and swing the chair with all my strength. It bounces against the surface, ricocheting and smacking me in the chest. I go flying, my back hitting the floor as I slide along the slick surface.

What the fuck.

With the wind knocked out of me, I lie still, trying to catch my breath.

Zerra appears above me, her eyebrows pinching together.

"What did you do that for?" she asks softly as if trying to lull me into complacency or speaking to an ill-behaved child. "I know this is all new, and it will take a little time to adjust. Besides, if you want to destroy my palace, you cannot do it with force. It requires a sacrifice. Worry not. You'll learn all the rules soon enough."

Before I can process what that means, her soft smile turns wicked as she wraps a hand around my arm and hauls me up. I try to wrest myself from her grip, but her hand is like iron. She drags me back to the table, and I'm compelled to follow. My bones creak, and I have no doubt she'd snap my arm in two if I continue to put up a fight.

"Sit," she says, tossing me back into a chair with enough force to nearly tip it over. "I was about to explain our wedding preparations, and I don't appreciate the interruption. It is my special day, after all, and the least you can do is listen to what I have planned."

I eye her warily as she settles back into her seat. "Now, I thought we'd have two kinds of fountains. Chocolate and sparkling wine. What do you think?" She looks at me expectantly and blinks her eyes. "Hmm?"

"You're asking me?"

"Yes. Of course I am."

It's clear she's starting to lose her patience.

"The dress. Once you see the dress, you'll be as excited as I am."

I really doubt that, but I keep my mouth shut.

She claps her hands, and two High Fae servants materialize. They're both stunning in the way of Fae, with long blonde hair that falls nearly to their ankles. They wear loose white dresses that I recognize as the ceremonial garb reserved for Zerra's disciples. They also wear the same vacant expression as all of Zerra's helpers.

Between them, they hold a dress made of folds of sheer white fabric, the train so long the end disappears out the doorway.

"Isn't it divine?" Zerra intones, and there's a beat of silence before I realize she's speaking to me. "Isn't it?" she asks again, her lips thinning to bloodless white.

I shrug because I have no idea how to answer the question—it means nothing to me—and I'm sure it'll annoy her if I fail to demonstrate sufficient enthusiasm.

"It's a dress," I say dryly, like the complete asshole I am.

Then I take a long sip of my wine, staring into the cup, before draining the entire thing and reaching for the decanter on the table. At this point, I'll have to drink this entire place dry.

"Yes but isn't it special?" she needles. "It's the dress of my dreams. I never got to have a wedding, you know. I was dragged up to this godforsaken place and forced to live here."

"Forced by whom?" I ask. I've never heard anything to suggest her words are true.

"The Empyrium," she says with a petulant sigh.

"Who?"

She turns her eyes back on me and obviously doesn't want to bother explaining anything else. She just wants me to shut up and do what she asks.

"They're the supreme beings who oversee Ouranos and all the worlds around us." She waves a hand as though they're there hanging above her. My eyes flick up as though I'm really expecting someone to be there. *Get a grip, Nadir.*

"I thought *you* oversaw Ouranos," I say, causing irritation to flash in her gaze. This is clearly a sore spot. Then I remember what Nerissa said back in Aphelion about some higher authority having created the Artefacts. The Empyrium. Who are they, and what is *their* role?

"Not exactly," she answers in a way that tells me she's done with my questions.

Fine, I don't care unless it might get me out of here. I tuck this into my pocket for now—I'll revisit the topic when the time is right.

"Where is Lor now?" I ask. "Can you see her? Do you know?"

It's the wrong thing to say because her fingernails dig into the wood of her chair arms, causing the entire frame to creak under her weight.

"Why are you asking me about that horrible woman?" she snaps. "She killed you!"

"Do not speak of my mate that way," I say, my voice as cold as an icicle hanging precariously over our heads.

"Why are you defending her?" Zerra asks, incredulous.

She cups her hands around her mouth to amplify her voice and then says in slow, deliberate speech, "She. Killed. You."

"That doesn't mean I'll allow you to speak ill of her. I'm sure she had her reasons."

"Are you kidding me?" Zerra says, and now I'm kind of enjoying myself.

"Forget her," she says. "You are marrying me now."

"I don't think I can do that. Surely you know what a mate bond is. You're the one who blessed us, after all."

She scoffs at that. "I didn't do anything."

That brings me up short again.

"You didn't? But mate bonds are blessed by Zerra."

"You think I give two shits about who fucks who on the surface?" she asks. "Mate bonds are the dominion of fate. I just made you all believe that so you'd worship me, hoping I'd bestow them on you."

"So you're not the divine, and you don't control the mate bond. What is it that you do up here?"

I see the moment she realizes she's revealed too much, her eyes widening before she clenches her teeth.

"This line of questioning is over."

She pushes up and saunters to where I'm sitting, plopping herself on my lap. It takes every ounce of restraint I possess not to dump her into a heap at my feet. I'll need to stay on her slightly less crazy side if I want to escape with my head still attached to my neck.

"Please get off me," I say, trying to keep my tone polite, but she ignores me, leaning in and pressing her breasts to my chest.

"We don't have to wait for the wedding night, you know," she says with a wink, dragging a finger along my jawbone and then pressing it to my lower lip. My head jerks as she slides the tip into my mouth, and then I *do* shove her off. Screw this.

She topples to the side, landing on her ass in a satisfying tumble of limbs.

"You bastard," she hisses, scrambling to her feet.

Well, it was satisfying for me.

Faster than lightning, her hand streaks out and circles my throat. She squeezes and then starts to lift me up. I can't resist. I claw at her arm, but I might as well be trying to fight a mountain.

"That's enough," she says, bringing her face close to mine. "This is your home now, princey-poo, and you are mine. Keep speaking to me this way, and I'll cut out your tongue," she warns. "Soon, we will right the wrong done to me so many years ago."

Then she hurls me to the ground and claps her hands. Two of her little minions appear again. They stare blankly at me before Zerra crooks a smile.

"Don't worry. Before long, you'll forget your mate. You'll forget everything. That's what this place does to everyone."

Her eyes flick towards her two helpers as her meaning becomes clear. These were High Fae who lived below once, but they've been here long enough to become these empty shells.

Icy dread trickles down my spine.

"Take him to his room," she says, waving her hand. "He can come out when he learns how to behave."

As I'm dragged away, one thing is absolutely clear: I have to get the fuck out of here.

CHAPTER 20

LOR

ON THE RUN

Sand churns under my feet, rubbing my soles raw. My ankle throbs, and my head pounds, but I press on, gritting through the pain. The sun starts to rise, transforming the sand into a burning canvas like walking over hot coals.

A large rock formation looms ahead, and I duck behind it to catch my breath, seeking a sliver of shade to cool off my overheating body. I'd give anything for a drink of water as sweat drips down my temples, mingling with the blood coating my face. I say a silent thank-you for my light garments at least.

Peering around the corner, I scan the horizon. In the distance, people tend to the fallen, scrambling over the wreckage.

Behind me, the river looms in the distance, and though it feels like I've been running for hours, it looks like I've barely covered any distance.

Once I can breathe again, I check behind me and run.

Eventually, I'm forced to slow my pace as my breath twists tight and my chest constricts. Every time I gauge my progress, I nearly weep. Why is the river still so far away? My stomach rumbles, and my mouth feels like it's coated with carpet. I run for the next large stand of boulders, seeking shade and another moment to rest.

Once I've recovered, I check behind me again, and my blood runs cold.

Two black shapes move in the distance. I recognize their armor declaring them as Rion's soldiers, and they're approaching much too fast.

Sucking in a panicked breath, I turn around and continue running as quickly as my tired legs will take me while I consider my next move. I could just blast them away, but I've hurt enough people for one day. These men serve Rion though, so why would I feel bad about that? But maybe they don't have a choice.

More importantly, I don't know if these two spotted me and started running or if they told the king first. If I use my magic, it'll be a bright flashing light revealing my exact location. I'm almost sure that if Rion knew I was running this way, he would come after me himself. I decide to take my chances and hope I can outrun them. Those uniforms look heavy, and the black fabric must absorb a thousand degrees of heat. Hopefully, it slows them down.

The sun beats overhead with an unrelenting force, and I'm

gagging at the lack of moisture in my mouth. I'd give literally anything for some water. Where is that rain when I need it?

Finally, the channel crossing looms in the distance, spurring me forward. When I peer over my shoulder, I see the Aurora soldiers gaining on me. A flash of metal reveals a canteen they pass between them—they have water, putting them at a distinct advantage.

I consider confronting them before I look ahead at the forest that grows beyond the beach. I need to be strategic. Think about the consequences of my actions. My best plan of escape right now is to let everyone think I'm buried in the rubble. It's the only chance I have.

Finally, I reach the channel. The river flows below a raised bank about six feet high, and I plunge into the water. It's the best thing I've ever felt in my life. The cool water mixes with the nearby ocean and is too salty to drink, but at least I don't feel like I'm about to melt into a puddle of fire.

I kick to the surface, exploding up, and immediately start swimming for the far shore. The distance is greater than I anticipated, and I'm already so tired. I haven't slept since the night before, and I'm running on nothing but adrenaline and a misguided sense of hope that I will somehow escape Rion one more time.

I look back to see the guards standing on the edge of the far bank. Will they jump in to swim after me? They're conferring with one another, and when I look back, I see that one of them has taken off running in the direction we just came. I have until that guard reaches the Crystal Palace before my presence is revealed.

The other guard is currently tugging off his boots and dropping his weapons. Clearly, he plans to come after me, but at least he must leave his essentials behind. I continue swimming, kicking like my life depends on it. I was always a decent swimmer as a child, and that long-buried muscle memory takes over.

Thankfully, the guard struggles as he slaps the water, his stroke gangly and inefficient. Finally, I catch a break.

I reach the far shore and scramble out of the river. I'd love to lie down and sleep for a hundred years, but I continue running as the beach gives way to the forest, turning south towards Aphelion and my brother and sister.

But first, I must get this stupid ark to Zerra and get Nadir back.

I stumble into the shelter of the trees and cling to a trunk for support.

The guard chasing me reaches the far shore, but I've gained a bit of a lead. Pushing off the tree, I disappear into the forest's cool canopy.

Instead of sand, my feet catch on rocks and stones, and I wince as they stab my soles. As I plunge deeper into the trees, the sound of rushing water draws me towards a stream. I weep in relief as I drop to my knees in the mud and scoop up handfuls of water. It tastes so sweet and cool and reminds me of that morning I woke up in Aphelion when Mags handed me the first glass of clean water I'd enjoyed in years.

It soothes my parched throat, and I dump more on my head, cleaning off the salt and blood crusting my hair and skin. I remember Tristan once telling me it's difficult to pick up anyone's scent in the water, so I splash along the edge, making my way downstream.

I listen for any sounds of pursuit, but I hear nothing, which bolsters my confidence. Hopefully, I have enough of a head start to escape. And if not, I might be forced to use my magic again. I just hope it's strong enough to stop Rion when I haven't caught him off guard. It's worked for me twice, but I can't rely on the element of surprise again.

After what feels like forever, and my feet have turned numb from the icy stream, I take a chance and climb onto the bank. Sinking against a tree, I slide to the ground to catch my breath. My entire body aches, my muscles quivering and loose. My stomach is hollowed out and in desperate need of something to fill it. I scan the forest, hoping to find something to take the edge off. We spent enough time in the woods as children for me to understand what I might turn into nourishment.

My eyelids are heavy, but I can't sleep. First, I have to get Nadir back.

"Zerra," I say, calling to the sky. I try to keep my voice tempered. I need her attention, but I also don't want to give away my location. "Zerra?"

She didn't say how I'd find her when I secured the ark, but I'm sure she's watching me from her perch. Or wherever the Evanescence resides.

My eyes flutter closed while I use my mind to call her.

Zerra. I have the ark. Come and find me.

I wait with bated breath before my eyes peel open. Nothing. I huff out a sigh and consider my next move. She'll find me soon enough. I have what she wants. For now, I have to keep moving and stay alive.

After giving myself another moment to rest, I struggle to my feet and listen. At first, I hear only silence, but then the sound of voices and someone giving out orders echoes in the distance.

I look up, and my blood turns to ice.

The sky is now blue, and the sun is out, but the sight is unmistakable. Ribbons of colorful light spear across the horizon, muted against the brightness of the day.

My chest aches at the sight, and I rub at it, wishing I could reach Nadir.

But the message is clear.

The Aurora King is here, and he's coming to find me.

CHAPTER 21

PRINCE RION

286 YEARS AGO

The whole of the Aurora court gathered in the throne room, every eye on their fledgling prince, who had entered the world in a fit of screaming and blood a mere three weeks ago.

It was a tradition in the court for the Torch to officially welcome the next Primary into the fold, and an entire gaggle of nobles had gathered to pay their respects.

Meora held the boy in her arms wrapped in a bundle of soft blankets. Rion stood at her side, looking down, peering into the scrunched face of the child—*his* child. Despite everything, Rion had hoped some latent rush of affection would manifest for his son, but it had yet to happen.

His gaze slid to his father, Garnet, seated on his throne. Barely a trace of breath remained in the king. Wisps of white hair fluttered meekly on a nonexistent breeze, his skin stretched over his frame so thinly it looked like it would rip at the slightest pressure. Still, he clung to life, refusing to move on.

Rion's fist clenched as he ground his teeth and rolled his neck. It was uncommonly warm in here with all these people crammed into the space. The flames from the Torch gave off an impressive amount of heat.

One by one, the citizens of The Aurora approached to greet the child. Meora beamed proudly, tipping the bundle to show him off, offering exclamations and giggling at everything the baby did, no matter how mundane.

Rion pinched the bridge of his nose and resisted the urge to snap at her to maintain her sense of decorum. Normally, the woman was a nervous wreck, and as much as that grated on his nerves, it was preferable to this bubbleheaded fool.

Once each noble had viewed the child, they moved to the king and queen, falling to their knees in respect. Rion peered again at his son, and inexplicably, the child seemed to notice him. Did he imagine the accusation in the baby's gaze? The knowing? The understanding that he'd already disappointed his father in more ways than he could possibly imagine?

Rion clasped his hands, spinning the wide ring he wore around his finger. He'd recently created it, chiseling out a piece of virulence to always carry with him.

He'd been testing the material for months, using his magic against it and keeping notes of his own. The process was difficult and complex, rarely producing the results he sought.

He'd wondered why the rulers hadn't used the arks in other ways, but he was starting to understand it wasn't as straightforward as it seemed. Herric had given them instructions on using the arks to control the strength of their own magic, but that was all he'd shared.

He also suspected *this* was what Zerra had come for all those years ago during the Burning. While she'd pretended it had been about loyalty, he wondered if she'd created the priestesses to root them out. If the arks were killing her, it stood to reason that she'd want to keep them close.

Rion hypothesized the rulers must have hidden them during the strife, which was why he'd never learned of their existence. It had all happened long enough ago that they'd fallen out of the collective memory. And The Aurora hadn't needed an ark.

Through Herric's journals, he'd also learned that virulence could be manipulated only with Imperial magic and that once used, it would work again only with the same vein of magic. Thus, no ruler could use another's ark.

Zerra's actions had lost her the trust of the Imperial courts all those years ago. She was a ruler in name only amongst the High Fae. Any support she had left was to be found in circles of humans or low fae, and that wasn't worth much.

Rion watched the Torch spark to life, the flames in its mouth burning with violet, crimson, and emerald. Now would come the time for the official anointing of the future Primary.

When Rion had come to the end of Herric's journals, he'd scoured the vaults for more but had turned up nothing else. What he couldn't understand was *why* King Elias was credited as The Aurora's first king of the Second Age and not Herric.

What had happened to him? And was it Elias who lived inside the Artefact now or Herric?

Ribbons of magic curled from the Torch and wrapped around Rion, Meora, and Nadir—one *happy* family—encasing them in a column of bright lights.

As the magic twisted around them, Rion heard that *voice*.

Rion.

It was low and rough, like something rusty dragged from under the earth—the same as he'd heard it on the day of his bonding. He'd returned many times since, hoping to hear the voice again, but eventually convinced himself he'd imagined it.

Rion, it whispered.

But here it was again.

Rion studied his surroundings, searching for the source of the sound. Everything appeared normal. Meora cooed at the baby, bouncing and swaying with the bundle in her arms. Suddenly, the ring on Rion's hand burned hot, and he did his best not to flinch as it seared his skin.

Rion, the voice said again.

The heated sensation faded as Rion held completely still, listening for the voice to return. His gaze wandered to Garnet, who watched Nadir with the love in his rheumy eyes that Rion should have felt. Maybe he'd just been waiting to meet his grandson before he finally moved on.

Rion, came the deep voice again as the virulence blistered his finger.

He narrowed his eyes, studying the glowing Artefact in the middle of the room. Last time, he'd thought it had come from the Torch, and now he was almost certain. But he wasn't ascended, so why would it be speaking to him?

Rion, it said again.

"Who is this?" he said under his breath.

Don't you know? You found my journals, did you not?

Rion blew out a sharp breath. Herric?

All you needed was a little guidance. A nudge towards them.

Rion thought of those vivid dreams. Was it possible a dead king had led him to that chest?

I've been waiting for someone like you for a very long time.

Rion looked around, studying the ceiling and walls, the faces in the crowd. Was someone playing a prank? Or was he losing his mind?

The virulence, the voice said. *Ussssse it.*

Rion blinked. Use it for what?

Alter the Torch's course, the voice said. *You have the power.*

Rion's eyebrows pulled together as his gaze flicked around the room.

At that moment, the Torch's magic surrounding Nadir and Meora swelled, filling the air with ribbons of light obscuring them from view of everyone in the room. He channeled a thread of his own magic into the virulence, and then, against every instinct—against everything he'd ever known—he filtered it into the Torch.

At first, it resisted the intrusion, trying to shove his magic out. But he gritted his teeth, propelling more power into it. He pushed against the barrier holding him back.

That's it, came the rough voice again. *You're doing very well.*

Emboldened by those words, Rion channeled more magic into the Artefact as the voice continued encouraging his efforts.

"Now what?" he heard himself saying. Meora gave him a curious look through the translucent bands of light surrounding them. He schooled his expression into coldness, and she quickly looked away.

Now, decide what you want it to do.

Rion hesitated. It? As in the Torch?

His gaze fell to Nadir, who stared up at him with that same accusing glare.

You want to punish the boy, don't you?

Without really understanding, Rion forced more magic into the Torch, and though he couldn't hear it, he could sense its surprise. Rion attempted to wrest control of its magic, and it fought him, trying to push him out.

He winced as his ring heated again, pain searing his skin. He reached into his pocket, where a polished stone of virulence sat, and wrapped his hand around it for strength. With another press of magic, he felt the Torch's resolve crumbling.

There was a shift, a moment, when Rion realized he'd taken control.

His gaze went to Nadir, and Rion forced out another ribbon of the Torch's magic, concentrating it on his son. He touched it to the baby's forehead, the power camouflaged by the ribbons already swirling around the room.

Immediately, Nadir began to scream, his little fists bunching and his face turning red. The child thrashed in his blankets with such force that Meora stumbled.

Gasps around the room accompanied a chorus of horrified whispers.

"What's happening?"

"What's wrong?"

"Nadir?" Meora sobbed. "What's wrong?"

Rion paused for one more breath before he pulled the magic away. Meora hugged the child, bouncing up and down and making soothing sounds.

"It's okay," she whispered as tears slid down her cheeks. "What's wrong, my baby?"

After another moment, Nadir's cries calmed, his little body jerking with hiccups. Rion studied the boy with cool detachment. Then he slid his magic away from the Torch. He felt its relief as he withdrew, and it continued bathing Nadir and his mother in a benevolent light.

The incident was soon forgotten as the ceremony came to a close—congratulations and refreshments were passed around the room. He noted the look on Meora's face, a mixture of relief and confusion, as she showered Nadir with kisses.

But Meora hadn't forgotten.

She stared across the room at Rion, fear darkening her expression as she pulled Nadir against her, some instinct telling her she'd need to protect him against his own father.

Rion wouldn't forget either.

He'd controlled the Torch. Forced it to do his bidding. The former king of The Aurora had helped him, and Rion was too eager about his discovery to wonder why.

His gaze wandered to his father, sitting on his throne with the dark crown of the Aurora King perched on his head.

Finally, Rion had found a way.

Finally, Rion would get his crown.

Chapter 22

Gabriel

Aphelion—Present Day

This place has gone to hell. Everything has spun out of control between riots in the streets and the palace falling to pieces. Smoke hangs in the air and the sounds of mild explosions have become a part of Aphelion's daily backdrop.

Through it all, my brothers continue to search for Atlas, sending reports to me regularly. Atlas is a royal who has never had to fear for his life. While he learned how to wield a sword with proficiency, my brothers were trained nearly to the point of death in every art of war imaginable, including tracking down an escaped prisoner. Since his magic is mostly ineffective against them, especially as a group, it's only a matter of time before they close in on our former king. I pray daily for news, but I haven't yet decided if his capture will come as a relief or simply another burden.

Without my brothers here, almost everyone around me is an incompetent fool.

"Gabe," Tyr says softly from where he sits in a chair under the window. We're in the king's study. I'm so used to referring to it as Atlas's, but is it really Tyr's? I've envisioned this day so many times, but nestled in that murky fantasy was the idea Tyr would rise up and take his place as king.

But so far, he remains an empty shell, intent on staring at the wall, and I'm not sure what to do. I don't blame him for this state. Atlas caused this, and I shouldn't expect anything from Tyr. He doesn't owe us anything.

The heads of all of the twenty-four districts sit around the table I had brought in because Tyr refuses to enter the council chamber. Though he hasn't explicitly said so, I think it's a place of too many painful memories and the last thing he remembers from when he was still a king. No one hears his soft plea because these peacocks are all too busy arguing with one another.

"Are you okay?" he asks me so softly that I barely hear the words, only see the shape he forms with his mouth. My heart feels like lead in my chest. I don't know if I'm strong enough to help put him back together. He needs a better man than I could ever be. He needs a different purpose.

"I'm fine," I say, gruffer than I intend. None of this is his fault, and I know that. I've always known that, and despite playing witness to my every shortcoming, he's never judged me for who I am.

I watch the High Fae surrounding the table. They include Commander Cornelius Heulfryn of the most affluent Twenty-Fourth District, whose daughter is currently making my life hell, down to the head of the First District, where the more modest citizens of Aphelion live, though their stations are far above those of the low fae. Currently, everyone is arguing about the leadership of the kingdom.

According to Tyr, the Mirror sat silent when he stood before it for two hours yesterday while they all watched. Something tells me he wasn't entirely forthright about that but isn't ready to discuss his future. I can't blame him for that either.

By rights, Tyr has always been the king, and there should be no question of who should lead. The district heads claim Tyr isn't fit to rule in this state, and it's hard to argue with them. They can't force him to descend, but they can question his leadership. The Artefacts' role is to decide who is the most fit to rule, but their choices are sometimes imperfect. I assume it's because their vision is limited and even they can't know the future.

My gaze wanders to the streets, where I hear the distant crash of the ongoing riots. Glass shattering and panicked screams. The sounds and the fighting swell and ebb with each passing day. Just when I think things might have finally calmed down, something happens to revive them anew. Ash hangs perpetually in the air, clouding the blue sky, and the ocean is a dark blot, littered with charred wood, clothing... and invariably, more bodies than I care to think about.

What none of these Fae in this room understand is that if Tyr isn't meant to rule, then that dubious honor belongs to someone else. And I'd stake my life on the fact that someone *is* right for the role.

Someone who the Mirror already chose years ago, dooming us all to this fate.

Someone who not a single person in this room would approve of.

The door to the study pops open, and Hylene slides through the gap. Every eye in the room draws her way, a few sentences cutting off mid-complaint. It's easy to understand why. There's something about her that garners attention wherever she goes. She might be the only person within spitting distance with more than two brain cells to rub together.

After the events of Tyr's reveal and Lor and Nadir's capture, Hylene remained in the palace. She explained that she'd been helping them by getting herself invited to the bonding and keeping an eye out while they snuck into the throne room. Thankfully, the Aurora King's soldiers only knocked her out and didn't inflict any permanent damage when they overpowered her.

"Don't mind me," she says as she saunters down the side of the room. She's wearing Aphelion gold, and the contrast with her fiery hair makes it look like the sun itself is walking through our midst. The bodice is cut scandalously low, showing off her rounded breasts, fitting snugly to her curvy hips. I shouldn't be thinking about my desires at a time like this, but they have a mind of their own. "Just came to see what all the screaming is about. I'm sure it's positively *riveting*."

Several eyes in the room narrow as they try to work out if they've all just been insulted.

She gives me a small wave before bending down to peck Tyr on the cheek. Inexplicably, the two have bonded. She has a quiet way of sitting beside him in a manner he seems to need and appreciate. I even heard him laugh the other day, a sound that made my heart almost crack in my chest. I can't remember the last time I heard Tyr laugh.

"Someone needs to be in charge," says a male High Fae who rules over one of the middling districts. I truly can't keep them all straight. This was something Atlas was a master at. He knew them all by name, who their bonded partners were, who their children were. I tuned it all out, thinking that none of this would ever be my problem. Joke's on me, I suppose.

"Well, it's not going to be *you*," a female across the table says.

"I didn't say that it was," he replies through gritted teeth, and then the conversation erupts again, voices clashing and flying as they vie for the upper hand.

I have no idea how to fix this, what answers to give them, or how to solve any of it. Someone *does* need to be in charge, and right now, it appears to be me, which isn't doing anyone any favors. I drop into my chair at the head of the table and rub my temples, a stabbing pain building behind my eyes. I can't seem to shake this headache.

My gaze slides to Tyr, who watches with his hands on the armrests, his face expressionless. Then I turn to Hylene, who sits on the sofa with her legs crossed and miles of bronzed flesh exposed by the slit in her dress. Gods, I need to get a grip.

I let everyone argue for another minute as I try to formulate a plan. What do I want? To get them to stop fighting. None of them seem concerned enough that Atlas has run. I haven't had any luck figuring out how he escaped or who might have helped him. Was it someone in this room, hoping to seize power in a void?

A sharp clap draws my attention, and now Hylene is standing. "Everyone!" she says, her voice threaded with command. "I think that's quite enough!"

She snaps her fingers, and finally, the arguing dies down. "I think that's enough . . . ruling for today. Hmm? I've arranged drinks and food for everyone in the salon."

There are several blinks around the table and several wary exchanged glances. No one seems to know what to do.

"Everyone," Hylene says. "Please. Let's take a break and remember you all want what's best for your kingdom. There's no need for all this fighting, is there?"

She sweeps towards the door, and like they've all been enchanted, everyone slowly begins to stand.

"I've arranged for some added surprises," she says with a smile, and her eyes glitter, making it clear what she means. "This is all very stressful, and you all deserve a little relief."

She greets everyone by name as they exit. I almost pass out when I hear several of them thanking her. When the last one departs, she slams the door and leans against it, wiping her hand across her brow.

"Whew, I thought they would never leave."

"How did you just do that?" I ask. "I've been trying to get them to leave for two hours."

She shrugs her shoulders and smooths down her hair. "They can keep arguing in circles until they all drop dead, but until the Mirror decides what it wants, there's nothing we can do. In the meantime, they'll just have to accept that you're in charge."

"Tyr is in charge," I say, not sure why I'm so determined to cling to this fallacy.

"Of course. You're in charge as Tyr's proxy."

I narrow my eyes, but she presses my hand to her heart.

"It's okay," she says, and something loosens in my chest. "I know you want only what's best for him."

We both turn to Tyr, who watches us, still with that dispassionate expression. I wish I could wake him up, but I don't even know where to begin. Hylene lets go of my hand and moves in front of Tyr.

"How are you?" she asks, placing her hands on the sides of his chair before she sinks down. "Do you want to go to bed?"

Tyr nods slowly, and I hold in my sigh. This is all he does. Sleeps and sits there staring into nothing. This is all he's done for decades, and I know he's dealing with his personal demons, but the cuffs are off, and I can't rein in my disappointment that removing them did absolutely nothing. I need to be patient. He wore them for a century. I can't expect him to return to who he was in an instant.

"Let's go," Hylene says, helping Tyr stand. She takes small steps as he slowly shuffles along next to her. He looks like a young man, but he might as well be dead for all it matters. Though his heart still beats, Atlas killed him nonetheless. I fear I'll never get him back.

Hylene and Tyr leave the room, and I draw a deep breath before deciding to follow. Hylene speaks quietly as I trail behind until we reach the king's suite. Guards flank the massive golden doors and a High Fae female moves to draw the left one open as we approach. Hylene thanks her, and I swear the soldier nearly passes out as she gives Hylene an adoring look. This woman has an effect on everyone.

We settle Tyr in his bed, and he's asleep before we can even finish closing the curtains.

I stare at where he lies, at the brittle ashen hair that spreads over his pillow, wondering if this is all he'll ever be. Hylene moves to stand next to me and leans against my side. She's warm and soft, and my hand fists before I look down at her.

"It's going to be okay," she says.

"I don't think it is."

"It will be. Whatever is on the other side of this might not look exactly as you envisioned, but everything will work out. One way or another."

I run a hand down my face. "You really believe that?"

"I know it seems hopeless right now, but we'll figure this out."

"We?" I ask.

She shrugs. "I'm in the middle of this now, and I like to see my way to the end of things."

She blinks up at me with those big green eyes, and for the first time in as long as I can remember, something stirs in the hollowed-out recesses of my heart.

Gods, this is truly the last fucking thing I need right now.

Chapter 23

Nadir

The Evanescence

I pace the length of my room, feeling like a wild animal tethered inside a cage. I can't tell how long I've been up here, but it feels like it's been months. I'm invited to dinner every night while Zerra makes lewd comments loaded with innuendos. She seems convinced that because this King Herric was her lover, I, too, will succumb to her advances. In fact, I get the unsettling sense she thinks I'll replace whatever role he once played in her life.

I've been doing my best to play nice during our dinners, attempting to lull her into a false sense of security. She's revealed a few things as a result. Like the fact she sent Lor on a mission to retrieve the ark of Alluvion.

But that information only adds to my confusion. Why would Lor agree to that? I'm not sure I even believe it. If Lor had the choice, she would have gone to find Willow and Tristan. Unless Zerra is holding something over her. I wonder if it might have something to do with me, but Zerra doesn't seem inclined to ever let me out of here.

I also get the sense she doesn't like Lor, thanks to a regular stream of underhanded comments that make me see red, but I can't begin to figure out why. What could Lor have possibly done to make Zerra dislike her so much?

Beyond that, I've learned a bit more about the Empyrium and my ancestor, King Herric, who was indeed the first king of the Second Age, but something happened to him that Zerra hasn't yet revealed. It does seem clear that he hurt her, but given the way she's treated me, I'm not all that inclined to feel much sympathy. Something tells me I would have sided with him.

The "wedding" is coming up, and it's imperative I get out of here before then. Not only does the idea make my skin crawl, but she's made it clear that once it takes place, she'll be coming for my . . . body. I shudder at the idea of becoming like one of her servants who move about this place like soulless ghosts, trapped here forever.

I rub my chest and the constant ache that blooms behind my ribs. I miss Lor like I miss air. I want to hold her in my arms and bury my nose in the scent of her hair. Inhale that combination of roses and lightning that always makes me feel like I've come home. I miss her skin and those eyes that see me in a way no one else ever has. I miss that mouth and her sarcasm, and I'd give anything to have her yell at me right now.

I touch the window, pressing against it with all my strength, already knowing it's useless. Zerra made a comment about requiring a sacrifice to destroy her palace, and I've yet to puzzle it out. After our first dinner, Zerra returned my magic, but I quickly understood it's to remind me that it has no power here. That *I* have no power here.

It seems to only work alone in my room, and I've tried using it to free myself in every form I can manage—with every ounce of strength I possess—but it makes no difference. I'm losing my mind, stuck in this place.

I need Lor.

A knock at my door stops me in my tracks. I've learned to dread that sound, knowing I'm about to be dragged to yet another uncomfortable dinner. They don't wait for my answer. The door swings open as two of Zerra's minions enter.

They both wear gowns of light, almost sheer material that floats around them and drapes to the floor. Their shiny hair is curled and pinned, and their faces are painted with artful lines of black around their eyes, their lids and cheeks dusted with shimmering powder. It's become obvious Zerra doesn't like anything to be less than shiny and perfect in her presence.

"Her Majesty requests you for dinner," says the one on the left, her voice distant and hollow. Her name is Tia. She dips into a curtsy, and I repress a long, exhausted sigh.

"She's asked you to wear this," says the other. Her name is Diana, and she holds out a silver jacket embroidered with glittering stones along the collar and cuffs. It's the height of tacky and ostentatious. Even if it weren't, I don't want anything from this goddess.

Still, I'm trying not to make too many waves that will either get me killed or prevent my escape. In fact, I'll keep playing the willing captive, hoping to glean more information from her. Zerra seems inclined to see what she *wants* to see, so I don't have to pretend too hard. I roll my neck, working out the tension that wrenches on my muscles, and grit out a stiff smile.

"Thank you," I say, and Diana holds it open for me.

I walk over and slip my arms into the sleeves before she shrugs it onto my shoulders, smoothing them down.

"That fits you very nicely. Her Majesty will be pleased," Tia says, and I grunt.

"Great."

"Come along," Diana says. "Dinner is ready."

They both turn and expect me to follow. Like a good little pet, I do.

Another thing I've learned is that Zerra can only clearly see and summon the living into the Evanescence when they call for her. Otherwise, they must agree to her invitation or be dead. I remember Lor screaming for help in my half-conscious state and this must be how Zerra ensnared both of us.

These poor women were simply praying to Zerra when they were dragged here against their will, so I'm trying not to take my frustrations out on them.

The door opens, and we proceed along the strange glass pathway. I've become a bit more accustomed to it, though it's still dizzying. The path bends to the left, where another round floating room appears.

Diana opens the door and gestures for me to enter, revealing a bedroom where everything is white, the floors covered in thick fur rugs. A massive bed of white wood, covered in white sheets and pillows, sits against a wall, but it's the view that makes my breath catch.

Huge arched windows extend from the high ceiling, revealing a range of snow-capped mountains receding into the distance. It's the first time since I arrived that I've seen anything other than a stretch of formless blue sky and clouds.

Zerra sits at a dressing table, staring at herself in a small hand mirror. She looks up at my entrance and sets it down before standing.

"What is this?" I ask, gesturing outside.

She shrugs. "Sometimes I like to change the view. The mist can get so boring."

"Where exactly are we?" I ask, moving towards the window and scanning the horizon. While the view might be different, it still doesn't appear real, like someone copied a mountain and redrew it a thousand times.

"We're somewhere above, below, beside Ouranos."

I turn around. "What does that mean?"

She twists a hand in the air. "The Evanescence is everywhere. I can't explain it."

I frown as she approaches, scanning me from head to toe.

"Shall we eat?" She gestures to the small table in the middle of the floor set with silver dishes and a giant candelabra topped with dripping candles. I follow and sit down as she spoons food onto my plate. It threatens my entire sense of calm when she feeds me like I'm a child, but I dig my hands into my thighs, reminding myself that I'm pretending to be nice.

When she's heaped my plate with food, I give her a smile that I hope appears genuine before I manage a few bites.

"What did you do today?" I ask.

Her eyebrows draw together, and she shrugs. "Why?"

"If I'm staying for a while, I'd like to know more about you."

That answer seems to please her, and she leans forward, resting her elbows on the table.

"Just sprucing the place up," she says and waves out a hand, suddenly in a good mood. "I can make anything happen in the Evanescence. Food. Parties. Wine. Fucking. Anything your lurid little heart desires."

I try to appear interested in her answer as I force down another bite of food.

"Can you control what happens on the surface?"

She typically refuses to humor this line of questioning, but she pauses for only a heartbeat before she replies. "My role on the surface is to keep watch over the Artefacts and ensure they're doing their job. I am also the conduit for their magic."

"What about what happened in Aphelion?" I ask, hoping to keep her talking. "Atlas has been pretending to be their king. Aren't the Artefacts supposed to stop that?"

She spins the stem of her wine glass and takes a sip. "Yes. That. Well, I was getting around to dealing with it."

"It's been nearly a century."

"Has it?" She blinks her big eyes. "Time moves in its own way up here."

"Isn't that your *job*?" I ask, trying to keep the judgment out of my voice. Probably not all that successfully.

"I knew that jacket would suit you." She reaches out and dusts my shoulder before she adjusts the lapel, clearly trying to change the subject. I guess that's the end of her chatty mood. I resist every urge to throw her hands off me.

"I think we'll have one just like it made for the wedding—perhaps with some gold here."

She presses her hand to my chest and then tips her head with a smile. "Won't that be nice?"

"Zerra," I say. "I have a mate. We can't get married."

"You just said you were staying."

"Yes, but I'm not marrying you. I can't."

She shoves me in a playful way, but it's a bit too forceful to be believable. My chair nearly tips due to her strength, and I grunt as I right myself.

"Don't be silly. Your mate won't be alive much longer."

Those words snap me to attention. "*What* does that mean?"

She hums to herself as she stands up and strides over to the window.

"Zerra," I growl, following her across the room. I grab her arm to turn her towards me.

"What the fuck does that mean? If you touch her—"

A sharp slap cuts off my words, my head snaps to the side, and I taste blood in my mouth.

"Do not grab me," Zerra says, calmly smoothing down the front of her dress. "Her presence is a threat. And soon, you won't even remember her. Soon, all you'll need is me."

If I thought I was angry before, it's nothing compared to the visceral anger now churning in my blood.

"I'll destroy you," I hiss, taking a step towards her and backing her against the window. "If you lay a hand on—"

A movement catches the corner of my eye. The mirror lying on Zerra's dresser flashes. Our eyes meet, and something in her expression tells me to go and look.

I'm moving across the room before I know what I'm doing, and then I see her.

Lor.

She's running through a forest. Her feet are bare, and her face is covered in blood and dirt. She's crying and stumbling, shouting something I can't hear.

"Lor!" I scream as she careens into a tree and presses her forehead to it as tears mingle with the blood on her cheeks. "Lor! Can you hear me?"

My entire body trembles as my fingers go numb. She's there. She's alive, but she needs me.

I whip around to look at Zerra, who's watching me with her hands folded in front of her and that same infuriating smile on her face. I stalk over, holding up the mirror.

"What's happening to her?" I ask.

"Oh, she's succeeded on her little errand," she replies with a gentle shrug of her shoulders.

"The ark?" I ask, my teeth grinding so hard that I'm worried they'll crack out of my head.

"Yes. She's done rather well. Better than I expected, really. The only problem is that your father showed up and is currently hunting her down." She tips her head and pushes out her lower lip. "Pity."

I lift the mirror and stare into it, watching Lor run through the trees. Her movements indicate that she's trying to hide. My father can't get his hands on her. She stops every once in a while to scan the sky, her mouth moving as though she's trying to keep quiet, but it's obvious she's calling for Zerra.

"Lor!" I shout again, but it's no use. It's clear she can't hear me. "Help her!" I say to Zerra. "Do something! Let me go!"

Zerra laughs, and the sound is like knives plunging into my ears.

"Come now. Surely you know better than that?"

I roar and run for her, not sure what I plan to do, but I need to *do* something. I slam into her, but it's like running into an iron pillar. She tosses me aside, and I fly across the room, hitting the far wall as my head snaps against it.

I drop to the floor, groaning and clutching the back of my head, trying to catch my breath. A smear of blood coats the wall where cracks spiderweb out. She's watching me, not a hair out of place, and I leap up, prepared to attack again, when I'm seized around each arm by two pairs of iron hands.

Tia and Diana have me in their grip, and apparently they possess the same unnatural strength as their goddess. I fight and struggle against their hold, but I'm like a small child fighting two grown warriors despite being physically larger than all of them.

"Let me go!" I scream. The mirror lies at Zerra's feet, and I see flashes of Lor, still running. "Lor!"

"Take him away," Zerra says. "I grow tired of your theatrics, Herric. You may come out when you can behave."

"Help her!" I roar. "Lor! Lor! I love you!"

But it's no use. I'm dragged out of the room and returned to my prison yet again.

Chapter 24

LOR

Paralyzed, I stand transfixed by the Aurora King's magic, watching his ribbons of light ripple across the sky.

It's a message and a warning. I will not escape him again.

I plunge into the trees, running blindly, my arms and face scraped raw by tangles of vines and branches. I feel nothing as blood trickles into my mouth and into my eyes. I wipe it away, and I continue running. My only mission is to get away. Every time I escape, I only make him angrier and angrier.

I understand because that's how I would feel, and the Aurora King and I have something in common: We'll stop at nothing to get what we want.

As I weave through the bushes, I keep one ear peeled for sounds of pursuit. I can't use my magic—at least not the useful and destructive kind—or it will immediately give away my position.

"Zerra," I whisper. "I have the ark. Find me. Come and get it and return my mate."

I repeat the words on a loop to give me something to focus on while hoping she finally hears me. Part of me suspects she's toying with me right now. Some deep premonition tells me she's enjoying watching me run for my life.

That's when an idea occurs to me. It's a risky move and probably the worst plan I've ever had, but when have I ever let that stop me?

If Zerra won't come to me, then I'll force her out.

I slow to a walk, surveying my surroundings. A distant rustle and crack signal that Rion's men are nearby. Sounds come from every direction, and it's clear that without my magic, I can't outrun them. I can stay hidden for a while, but sooner or later, they will find me. I could blast them away, but more will follow. So many more. I'm vastly outnumbered, and the Aurora King isn't the kind of man to make the same mistake for a third time.

But I can't make my plan look too obvious, or they'll suspect I'm up to something.

Slowly, I angle my trajectory, estimating that if I keep on this path, I'll bisect theirs at a distant point. It will look like I'm too scared to think straight and just don't know what I'm doing. I hope. I jog through the trees, and there's no faking the ragged breaths scraping from my throat. I'm exhausted and on the verge of collapse.

"Zerra, where the fuck are you?" I try again. "Please don't make me do this."

The sounds of Rion's guards grow louder as they crash through the bushes like a herd of hippos. They're so confident about my capture, they're not even attempting stealth.

Now it's time for the incredibly stupid part of my plan. I have to let them see me.

A branch lies across my path, and I wince as I bring my foot down on top. The crack echoes through the forest like a lightning strike a split second before a voice shouts, "There she is!"

I twist in the opposite direction, running as fast as I can, weaving through the trees as I hear them gaining on me, narrowing my window of safety.

Rocks and branches stab and sting my bare soles, but I feel none of it. Adrenaline floods my limbs, keeping me upright, but it won't last long. I've been running for hours, and my strength is long gone. Dozens of soldiers surround me, filtering out like mist until I spot their black uniforms in every direction. They're closing in on me like I'm an injured deer, and I hope I've played this correctly.

When I'm surrounded on every side, I grind to a halt in the center of a small clearing, spinning around and around, my hands clutched to the sling holding the ark as dozens of soldiers emerge through the trees, all swagger and confidence.

I have two options right now.

The first is to use my magic. I could take them all out at once, but that would only buy me a temporary respite. Rion will send more guards, putting me right back in my current position, running for my life as I grow weaker and weaker. Eventually, they will wear me down.

Or I allow them to move closer and hope against every hope that Zerra is watching. Everything is counting on it.

"What've you got there, sweetheart?" a guard with mean eyes asks me, gesturing to the sling.

I don't bother answering. His little pea brain wouldn't comprehend the magnitude of what I hold even if I drew him a picture with captions.

"Stay away from me," I say, holding out my hand. This bastard smiles. He isn't the least bit afraid of me. Surely he saw what I did back at the palace? Everyone always underestimates me.

"Our king would like a word," he says. "If you come quietly, he promises no harm will come to you."

"A word? And then what? He'll let me go?"

The stupid grin slips from his face, and it's clear he has no idea how to answer that.

"That's what I thought," I say as his expression morphs into an ugly scowl.

"You're surrounded," he says. "There's nowhere you can run."

I scoff. He's right, but I planned it this way. I just hope I haven't misjudged everything.

"You have no idea who I am, do you?"

"You're from Nostraza," he says. "An escaped lunatic."

"That's really what he told you? The magic that destroyed the Crystal Palace was mine. I could kill you all right now."

I see the falter in his eyes. He didn't connect that with me.

Rion is such a piece of scum—he doesn't even tell those loyal to him what they're walking into. I could fry them all where they stand, and he knows it. Anything to get what he wants. But we can both play this game.

"So come and get me," I taunt. The guard looks to his left and his right, and he must give some kind of secret signal because they all begin to advance. I stand my ground, willing my magic down, though it wants to break free. It senses danger and wants to protect me.

Another step. They're nearly on me, and I cast my gaze to the sky.

Then, several things happen at once.

A guard reaches out and snatches my wrist on one side while another grabs my arm and bends it so hard that I cry out as my knees buckle. *Zerra. Where are you?* Another hand grabs my hair and wrenches my head back. I'm met with the first guard's eyes—they're triumphant now, a sneer on his face.

"Here she is!" he yells.

Rion appears at the edge of the clearing, one hand fisted in the other like he can't wait to tenderize me to a pulp. Fear curdles my insides. He takes a slow step, cocking his head and savoring my distress. I'm such an idiot. What have I done?

Black smoky magic spills from his fingertips, surrounding him and then spreading to me like a cloud of toxic dust. My magic drains away, my fingertips dulled from sensation. He stops before me, and the guard pulls my head back further, forcing me to look at him. Rion's mouth turns down in a mock pout as his finger reaches out to stroke my chin. I try to jerk away from his touch, but I'm held firmly in place.

Then he grips my face in his large hand with such force I whimper.

"You can keep running," he says. "But I will always find you, Heart Queen. You fooled me once when you were a child. I'm not too proud to admit I underestimated the slip of a girl who lay on that table all those years ago. But I won't make that mistake again."

He lifts a hand and flicks his fingers as someone emerges from the trees. This one carries a collar made of the same glowing blue stone I recognize from Tyr. The same material I broke through last time Rion had me. I buck harder, trying to wrench myself free.

"You destroyed my cuffs. How did you do it?"

I shake my head as he squeezes my face, tears slipping from the corners of my eyes. I don't know how.

"These have been fortified with a special layer of protection," he says with a dark smile. "I will need your magic soon enough, but for now, you're only an annoyance."

"No," I say, trying to break from his grasp as his smile turns colder than an arctic wind.

The guard approaches with the collar as panic swirls in my gut. I notice it's a duller blue, the edges tainted with black. I'm about to be caged again. I try to call up my magic, but Rion's dark power blocks mine and I spiral into panic.

I attempt to scramble away as the guard approaches. He holds the collar open, reaching for me, ready to clamp it around my throat, and then . . . I dissolve into nothing.

CHAPTER 25

White smoke fills my eyes, mouth, and lungs. I hack at the intrusion, my body an amorphous collection of bone and muscle until it comes back together and I'm once again on solid ground. I lie on a cool marble floor with my cheek pressed to the tiles. It feels strangely good. I groan as I shift. My feet ache, my soles so shredded, they sting from the cool breeze. My skin burns from the beating sun, cooked to a crisp. My hair hurts where the guard grabbed me, and I feel the bruising on my arms and chin from Rion and his guards.

But I'm alive, and most importantly, I escaped him again.

A slow clap rouses me from the twisting coil of my thoughts, and I have to close my eyes to stop my head from spinning before I force it off the floor to find the source of my mocking. Of course, I already know who stands there. I recognize the weird, intangible emptiness of this place. I remember the smell. It's both sweet and fresh but also reminds me of nothing.

My plan worked. I was counting on Zerra's desire to keep the ark out of Rion's hands, and instead of just reacting, I forced myself to think and it *worked*. Tristan would be furious with me, but he couldn't argue with the results.

Of course, none of this answers the question of why she ignored me at first or why she waited until the last second to rescue me.

A set of perfectly manicured toes appears in my vision, and I will myself to look up before I finally push myself into a seated position.

"I have the ark," I say. "Where the hell were you?"

She purses her lips, and her nostrils flare as though she can't believe my rudeness.

"I was right here, waiting for you."

"Why did you wait to rescue me?"

She lets out a tinkling laugh, like calcified golden bells.

"I was enjoying the show so much. You are a resourceful one, aren't you? Not especially bright, though. What made you so sure I would rescue you?"

"Because you wanted the ark," I say.

She turns and walks away a few paces before she spins around again. "Hmm. Perhaps."

I sigh and shake my head. "Okay, whatever. I don't really care." I pull the sling off my head and hold it out to her.

"You have it now. Give me Nadir."

She approaches me again and reaches for the sling. I resist

every instinct to snatch it back, but I'm aware I am the one with no cards to play. For a split second, I cling to it, her eyes flashing before I release it. She lifts the sling and feels the object through the fabric as a smile tilts up the corner of her mouth.

"Well done," she says. "You just walked in there and stole it right from under him."

She doesn't utter the second statement in an admiring way, more like she's musing at my audacity.

"Well, you left me no choice."

"You must really love him," she says, almost like it's a question.

"Yes." There's no point in pretending. I already laid out my heart the last time.

"That's very...commendable." She holds out the sling and twists her hand before it dissolves into thin air and then reappears at the other end of the room, where four pedestals stand, each with an ark hovering above it.

I squint, making out the details of the arks of Tor, The Woodlands, and Celestria. I knew she had them, but seeing them sitting all together kindles the spark of an idea.

"This will look so nice in my collection."

"Yeah, great," I say, pushing a lock of sweaty hair off my forehead. "I'm so happy for you."

The corners of her mouth twitch as though she's amused. Or gassy. It's kind of hard to tell which.

"If you'll just give me Nadir back, we'll be on our way."

"He's very angry with you," she says. "I told him what you did."

"I don't care. I would have told him too."

Zerra's answering laugh is full of derision.

"Of course you would have. Noble Lor."

"What is your problem with me? Why are you so…" She tilts her head in expectation, waiting to hear what I'll say. But maybe I shouldn't insult her right to her face.

"Amazing," I finish lamely. The lie is so obvious she narrows her eyes.

"I'll pretend you didn't say that. I have another mission for you."

A growl builds in my throat. I kept trying to ignore the voice that told me this might happen. She will not keep him from me. I will *destroy* her.

"I did what you asked. Give me back my mate."

"But you're very motivated right now."

My shoulders hunch with aggression as I take a step towards her. "You promised me."

"I did," she says, touching her bottom lip. "But I've never been very good at promises, have I?"

White hot rage churns in my gut, burning a line of fire through my chest. She stares at me with that haughty look, and I imagine carving out each eye and her nose with excruciating slowness, leaving her mouth intact so she can listen to the sound of her own brutalized screams.

"You can't do this! Return him now!"

My voice echoes off the high corners, and I suck in a long breath, trying to temper my reaction, even as I boil with fury inside. "Whatever else you want, I'll do it if you give him back. I swear it."

She seems to consider that. "But how can I be sure? I have your loyalty right now, but if I let you go, you might turn against me."

"You're a god. Surely you're not scared of *me*."

Her eyes narrow with such coldness that I wonder if I've touched a nerve. What does she fear? What does the goddess Zerra worry about? Does she know what the Empyrium want from me? How does she feel about that? I'm desperate to ask, but I'm not sure if the question will set off another list of reasons for her to torture me. She doesn't seem very happy, but maybe she likes her role, and if she knows I'm to be her replacement, what might she try? I doubt she'll believe me when I say I want no part of it.

"Of course I'm not," she snaps. "But I don't trust you."

I hold out my hands and approach her slowly, like trying to appease a snarling beast. "Listen, I swear I will do what you ask, but Nadir knows more about Ouranos than I do. He knows all the rulers and can get us an audience anywhere. This will go faster if I have his help."

I give her a forced smile as she scans me from head to toe. She seems like maybe she's considering it.

"You must think I'm a fool," she replies, and my shoulders sag, my emotions cycling between anger and defeat as Zerra makes my head spin.

"No," I say, rubbing my face and the back of my neck, realizing how filthy and sweaty I am. What I wouldn't give for a cold shower and some soap right now.

"Besides, you won't need his help. You already know Aphelion extremely well."

"Aphelion?"

"You're friendly with the warder? The rebel leader?"

"I . . . sort of?"

"I want their ark."

Yeah. I knew she was planning to say that. Fuck me.

"They won't give it to me."

"You figured it out once. You can do it again."

I knew she would say that, too. She folds her hands together, all prim and elegant like a creepy porcelain doll that wakes up at night to murder the family it lives with.

"I can't steal from Gabriel."

"Why not?"

I shake my head. I don't know. It just doesn't feel right. I already harbor enough guilt for what I did in Alluvion. I can't leave a trail of destruction everywhere I go. A voice reminds me that I *am* my grandmother. Her brand of chaos resulted in one big strike, but I'm tearing through Ouranos, knocking things over one at a time. I'm no better.

Zerra gives me a tight smile.

"If your conscience is troubling you, then I guess you'll have to convince them to give it to you."

"How am I supposed to do that?"

"*That* is not my concern. Not if you want your mate."

My rage builds with each sentence, charring me from the inside.

"You promised you'd give Nadir back!" My voice rises with every syllable. "And what happens if I get it from Aphelion? You'll give him back to me then? Why should I believe you? Why would I believe a single fucking thing you say!"

My body trembles as I step towards her. "You lied to me once! Why should I believe you aren't still lying!"

Zerra takes a step back, matching each of my own.

"Calm down," she hisses, but I'm beyond that now. She'll want the ark of Heart next and retrieving that from Rion will be impossible without Nadir.

"Give me my mate! Where is he? Nadir!" I scream his name so loud that my voice cracks. "Nadir! Can you hear me? I know he's alive. I know that if he weren't, I'd be sick. Give him to me!" I stomp towards her, my bare feet slapping the marble with purpose. Zerra backs up. "You promised, you witch!"

"That's enough," Zerra says, swiping her hand through the air. An invisible force drives into my chest, throwing me backward as my stomach lifts into my throat right before I crash against the tile, my skin squealing along the slick surface. I gasp at the emptiness in my lungs, trying to suck in mouthfuls of air.

A shadow falls over me, and Zerra looks down. "I told you what you need to do," she says, her blue eyes flashing. "You'll get Herric back when I'm satisfied."

Herric? What's going on? Her expression is blank but for the pain pooling in her eyes. I study her for a moment. He *hurt* her. It's then I realize she never had any intention of returning Nadir.

"Well, I'm not doing it!" I shout. I lurch to my feet, look around the room, making a decision. She's taking him from me? Then I'll take something from her. What Herric did doesn't give her the right to do any of this.

I call on my magic, and for a moment, it struggles to surface. Zerra glares at me with her jaw hard and her eyes narrowed. I realize she's trying to prevent me from using it. Gritting into my reserves, I dig into my power, drilling down into pulsing crimson rivers until I feel it swell, smashing through her walls.

She gasps as she stumbles back, and magic builds in my fingertips, crackling along my limbs. Before she can recover, I unleash fire while keeping the arks in my side view. Crimson lightning bursts out of me, filling the room with my screams of rage. A force knocks me to the side, but my magic continues, unleashed and wild. I couldn't contain it even if I wanted to.

I hear a distant scream and someone cursing my name as I tumble through the air in a cloud of dust and stone and marble. End over end, I flip until the world snaps around me and the same white fog that delivered me here wraps around my chest and throat, constricting tightly before I find myself back on land.

More debris falls from above, pelting me with a hailstorm of sharp stings. Once again, I'm in a forest where everything around me is quiet. I scan my surroundings, looking for something that seems familiar. Where did she drop me this time? The only consolation is that I don't appear to be near Rion and his army, though I trust nothing.

I don't even notice I'm crying until a hot tear hits the back of my hand. I've lost Nadir. She's never giving him back. She's using him to replace Herric, who betrayed her in the worst possible way. I scrub at my wet cheeks, anger stirring inside of me like hot coals.

"You fucking bitch!" I scream at the sky until my voice gives out. When I can't scream anymore, I pound my fists against the earth. Finally, I fall quiet, breathing heavily as I push my hair back from my face. This isn't getting me anywhere.

I stand up and brush off my leggings, but there's little point. I'm filthy and ragged, and now I'm here without food or water or any idea of where I am.

I've lost Nadir.

That's when my gaze snags on a dark object nestled in the grass. My breath catches as I stagger over and drop to my knees, picking up the ark of The Woodlands, carved with Zerra's likeness holding the Staff.

I did it.

I intended to break out of that room but also to take some of it with me, including the arks. I can't believe it worked. Frantically, I search through the trees and bushes. The debris forms a wide circle of marble and stone, and I lose track of the time it takes to collect them all as the sun passes overhead.

Eventually, I gather all four arks. The same one I stole from Alluvion, along with those of Celestria and Tor. Clutching them to my chest, I peer up at the sky, unable to believe my dumb luck.

But Zerra will come for these. Whether she knows of the Empyrium's plans to replace her is now secondary. She spent centuries hunting these down, and now, with one fell swoop, they're in my hands.

A sob chokes from my chest. I wish so badly Nadir were here. He'd know what to do.

What do *I* do?

Aphelion.

It was always my destination. I've lost my mate, and an unhinged god wants my head on a pike. I need to go to my safe place. The one thing that has always been my home. I have to find Willow and Tristan.

Chapter 26

Nadir

I pick up a chair and hurl it at the window with all of my strength. It smashes apart, landing in a pile of splinters, but it has no effect. Still, I stare at the wreckage with a sense of grim satisfaction.

I've been at this for days. Ever since I saw Lor in Zerra's mirror. I've screamed myself hoarse, demanding to be let out. My magic is powerless against the walls and windows of this room, simply dissipating or ricocheting off the surface, so I've resorted to less elegant means.

My room is a scene of destruction, like a forest decimated by termites. No one has tried to stop me, and I suppose it's because nothing I'm doing has the slightest effect. And even if it did, where would I go? Zerra said we're in and around

Ouranos, which means nothing to me. Can I get back home on my own? What I know is that I'm not getting anywhere trapped in this room. I have to find Lor. If my father gets his hands on her . . . he will make sure she doesn't escape again.

With the last chair lying in pieces at my feet, I scan the room, searching for something else I can use. The door comes and goes, which is very disconcerting. It appears in different places whenever someone enters to bring me food, though it's been a few days since that happened. Thankfully, I've made it last, though I'm reaching the end of that, too. Zerra is punishing me for my disobedience. She called me Herric. Something tells me this is all so much worse than I originally thought.

A flash catches the corner of my eye through a window, and I spin around.

Red lightning fills the sky far in the distance. It sparks and cracks across the pristine blue, illuminating fluffy white clouds with blood-red streaks. I'm momentarily stunned until my brain catches up.

"Lor," I croak. There's no other possibility or explanation. I won't accept one. It *has* to be her.

But I've destroyed everything around me—the bed, the tables, the chairs, the wardrobes. Not that any of it has been of use. I consider how hard it would be to drag the bathtub out here.

Out of frustration, I run for the window, hurling my body at it, using my shoulder to pummel the glass. And then I lose my mind, punching the surface, left, right, left, right until my knuckles bleed. I scream for Lor, frustration and rage oozing from every cell.

Blood smears against the glass, and then . . . a hairline crack forms. I stare at it in disbelief, blinking a few times.

A sacrifice. That's what Zerra said. My blood? Or rather . . . my suffering.

I punch the window again, my hand screaming in agony as more blood paints the surface and more cracks spread. I think of how the wall crumbled when Zerra threw me against it. *Finally*, we're getting somewhere.

I continue punching the window until my hands are numb with pain, but I'm making progress.

I back up to the far side of the room and run at the window, wincing as I collide into it with my shoulder. But more cracks form, spiderwebbing out like a million tiny lifelines.

Fuck. Yes.

Again. I run for the window, using my other side to give my shoulder a break. Again. More and more cracks form. Eventually, it has to give. I pick up a sharp splinter of wood and carve a long gash into my arm before swiping it over the glass as the cracks continue spreading.

"Hey!" comes a voice. Tia stands in the doorway, staring at what I've done. "You mustn't do this," she says, like we're discussing the weather. I glare at her, and she must see the resolve in my eyes because something spasms in her expression.

"Come!" she yells behind her, finally displaying a sliver of emotion. "The prisoner is escaping!"

She keeps shouting for help, and I'm out of time.

So I back up and launch myself off the far wall, running in a blur towards the window, using all of my weight as I spin up my wings. The glass gives way in a shatter, and I'm almost too surprised to react. Especially as my wings blink out a moment later, my arms and legs windmilling as I start to plunge.

Shit. Shit. I try to spin up my magic again, but it's gone.

I plummet down, down, and then crash, leaves and branches scraping against my skin. I come to a juddering halt, landing on something both soft and hard, accompanied by the crack of branches. Stunned, I stare up at the sky for several long seconds, realizing a bush cushioned my fall.

Lor's magic is gone, the sky littered with white clouds and an endless carpet of blue. I tamp down the swell of fear that threatens to choke me. What happened to her?

It takes me a moment to extricate myself from the tangle, and I land on soft grass with one knee planted to the earth. I inhale several long breaths, trying to focus. My body aches, my wrist throbs, and my hands are a bloodied mess. I open my fist and close it again, grunting at a lash of sharp pain. I'm sure I broke something, but it was worth it because I couldn't stay trapped in that room a moment longer.

Finally, I look around me, taking in my surroundings.

It's peaceful, everything smooth and perfectly rendered. There's no other way to describe it. The grass is eerily perfect, with every blade the exact same height and shape. The bush I crashed into is made of thick green leaves that look almost real, but the color feels off. They're green, but not a green you'd ever find in nature. Every leaf is perfect like they've all been cut from the same idealistic pattern of what a leaf should look like.

Slowly, I stand up and listen. I hear the gurgle of a stream in the distance and the tweet of a bird here and there. A dragonfly, larger than my hand and in every color of the rainbow, flits past me with a soft buzz.

Off in the distance, I think I hear soft voices mingling in the cadence of numerous conversations. Slowly, I put one foot in front of the other until I reach a line of hedges, again all perfectly made like I'm inside a child's dollhouse. The voices grow louder, and it almost sounds like a party. The clink of glasses is backdropped against gentle music and floating laughter.

"Oh, hello," a voice says, and I turn to find a stunning High Fae female watching me. She's wearing a loose grey silk dress, has deep brown skin and long silver hair, and looks like she must hail from Tor. If I'm not mistaken, she's actually the spitting image of Queen Bronte.

"Are you new here?" she scans me from head to toe. "You seem a little young."

I open my mouth, unable to respond, as she steps closer and peers at me. "You must be Garnet's son," she says, her eyes growing wide.

Garnet. The name stills the blood in my veins.

My grandfather's name was Garnet, but . . . surely not. She thinks I'm my father.

"You really don't look old enough, though." She's still studying me. "Nevertheless, you'll probably want to see him. Come on. We didn't know you were coming, but sometimes that happens. One of you just drops in." She searches behind me, and I turn around to see what she's looking for. "Where is your bonded?"

"I . . . was just looking for her," I say. That causes a wrinkle to form between her eyes before it softens away.

"Oh, I suppose it's possible she ended up somewhere else, but that is unusual. No worries, she'll make her way here eventually."

I'm not sure why I lie about who I really am other than if someone discovers I'm not supposed to be here, they'll throw me out. And I suddenly have a strange, bone-deep urge to see the man I know only from stories and paintings.

"Will you take me to see my...father?" I ask, and I don't have to fake the ballooning emotion that swells in my chest.

"Sure. Come this way," she says brightly, leading me towards a gap in the hedges framed by a marble arch.

"What were you doing out there looking for me?" I ask.

"Oh, I heard you fall," she says. "I always like to be the first to greet our newcomers. It can be quite disorienting."

"Thank you," I say, because after that shitshow with Zerra, encountering someone kind feels like a cool breath on a hot day.

"What's your name?" I ask.

"I'm Greye," she says, her eyes crinkling at the corners with her smile. *Greye.* I remember the name. She was a queen of Tor many centuries ago.

We enter what looks like a party. The hedges border dozens of white iron tables surrounded by plush armchairs where other High Fae sit enjoying wine and food. I see Fae representing each of the realms, all marked by their distinctive coloring and features.

I'm in the Evanescence. That I knew, but now I'm where the descended go, surrounded by the kings and queens of Ouranos's past. My first instinct might be to panic that I've died, but this isn't how it works, right? I haven't ascended yet, so this can't be my resting place. All I can assume is that when I broke out of Zerra's palace, I landed in a different part of the Evanescence.

Greye weaves us between several tables as I feel the weight of many curious eyes. She says hello to a few onlookers, tapping their shoulders lightly as their gazes burn into my back. She doesn't introduce me to anyone, which is probably for the best.

In the distance, I see a table surrounded by several people with black hair and varying shades of brown skin. I feel a weird shift in my heart at the sight. I know those faces. I've seen them all rendered in oil paintings that I used to study when I was a boy, wondering if any of these ancestors could have shielded me from my father's hatred.

There's Verde, the third king of the Second Age, and Iris, the queen after that, my great-great-great-great—I'm not sure how many I have to add—grandmother. She's the first to spot me, her dark eyes finding me in the distance. They narrow imperceptibly before they open wider. She taps the arm of the man next to her, and that's when I see him. After studying his portrait for more hours than I can count, I know him. Wearing a black shirt and pants, he looks just like my father with his dark hair cropped short.

My grandfather looks over, and confusion crosses his face. He was expecting his son. And while I do look a lot like my father, it's clear he knows that I am not Rion. Garnet, the former Aurora King, presses himself up to stand as I slowly approach. I must look insane right now. I'm covered in blood, my feet are bare, and my clothing is in shreds.

"Nadir?" Garnet says, and I blink.

"Yes," I say. "You know me?"

"Of course I do."

He nods as he approaches, and now everyone around the table watches me. I run a hand over my head, suddenly feeling self-conscious under the scrutinizing gaze of my ancestors. I feel judged, weighed, and found lacking, though I'm not sure why.

"Why are you here? Where is your father?"

I look around the clearing, noticing several other people staring at us now.

"That's kind of a long story," I say.

"Then come with me," my grandfather says. "I know somewhere we can talk."

CHAPTER 27

I n a daze, I follow my grandfather through the garden until
we reach a quiet corner surrounded by hedges. He gestures
to a stone bench and invites me to join him. A small table sits
next to me, and a moment later, a silver tray topped with a
plate of pastel-colored desserts and a decanter of pale wine
appears out of thin air. My grandfather chuckles at my blink
of surprise.

"The Evanescence provides everything you need. Help
yourself."

I'm not really in the mood for sugar, but alcohol—that I can
do. I pour myself a generous glass and knock it back before I go
for another.

My grandfather watches me quietly, assessing. It doesn't
make me feel weird for some reason. It feels natural. After I

drain another half glass, he folds his hands together and rests them on the table.

"Now, do you want to tell me what you're doing here? Where is your father?"

I finish the rest of the glass and pour out another before I begin. I recount the last few months. Being sent to find Lor. Finding her. Finding out she's my mate. Being killed by Lor, apparently, if Zerra was telling me the truth. I rub my chest at the ache sitting behind my ribs. I can't tell if it's because of what she did or because I miss her so fucking much. Probably a little of both.

"And then Zerra locked me up and wanted to marry me," I say. "So I busted out of my room, and I fell . . . here." I sweep out a hand. "I saw Lor's magic across the sky. She might be here somewhere, and I have to find her." I pause. "Where am I exactly?"

My grandfather spreads his hands. "You are still in the Evanescence, but Zerra's domain surrounds us, and we are at its core."

"I'm not sure I get it."

"You don't have to. It's one of those things that simply is."

I shrug and take another long sip of my drink, trying to settle the constant shake of my limbs.

His smile drops off his face a moment later. "Your father," he says. "I always hoped he would change."

"He didn't," I say. "He's only become more twisted and cruel."

"I heard you," Garnet says. "When you spoke to me."

I blink. "You did?"

He nods and reaches out to squeeze my wrist. With no other parent figure to talk to, I'd often pretended my grandfather was still alive and would speak with him, but the last time was after the Second Sercen War. I'd returned from the front lines a broken shell of a man. Mael and I spent many years healing together, and when Amya was born, she became the only bright light in my life for a very long time.

I confided in him, talking to him for hours about what we'd seen and done. It felt like he was the only one who'd understand.

"I wish I could have answered you," he says sadly.

"Can you see what happens to us?"

"Only those who share Imperial magic and only when you call for us."

"I wish I'd known that," I say, and he gives me a sad smile.

"I won't lie and claim I was always a good king. I made mistakes. I did so many things wrong, but my greatest regret will always be how I failed my only son."

"How did you fail him?" I ask.

He shakes his head. "I wish I knew. As a small boy, there was always something dark about him. A deep remorselessness. I put it down to the immaturity of youth, but as he grew, it never really went away. When I realized it was a problem, it was too late to do anything about it. He was already his own person.

"But when you spoke to me, I understood you turned out . . . differently," he says, tipping his head as he studies me. "And when I realized that, it eased so many worries."

"I'm no saint," I say. "I've done many things I'm not proud of."

"Perhaps, but you've never carried that same darkness, Nadir. You don't delight in the suffering of others the way he always has."

I huff out a wry snort. "That might be the nicest thing anyone has ever said to me."

Garnet throws his head back and laughs. It's a warm sound, and my chest constricts, thinking about how different our lives might have been had he remained with us longer.

"Is what they say true?" I ask, needing to know. "Did my father force you to descend?"

The smile vanishes from Garnet's face again.

"It wasn't my choice," he says. "I didn't want to leave you or your mother. When you were born, I saw the way he looked at you. The way he—" My grandfather's eyes flick to me with pity.

"Hated me," I say. "It's okay. I know."

Garnet sighs and waves his hand as a goblet appears in his grip. He takes a long sip and sits back.

"He blamed your mother for entrapping him, but that is not the kind of woman she is. He built up this *fantasy* in his head where he was the only one who'd been wronged. She loved you from the moment she fell pregnant, but I know she wished she could go back and undo everything, too."

I nod because I know that's exactly what happened. My father played stupid games with his lover and lost. He used my mother and then blamed *her* for it when things veered off course.

Garnet sighs and runs a hand through his hair. "Though the Withering had ravaged me almost completely, I held on, terrified of what he might do without me around. I fought against the descension as hard as I could, though I knew he was doing everything to undermine me."

"So what happened?" I ask.

He shakes his head. "One night, he came to my room, lifted me into my wheelchair, and took me to the throne room. I don't know what became of my guards and nurses, but I have my suspicions. I was too weak to question what he was doing, but I had enough presence of mind to ask the Torch what was happening. If it knew anything, it didn't answer."

He closes his eyes as the memory haunts him. I want to reach out to him, but I'm not sure he'd welcome it. I think of the way my father always reacted to any kind of affection with disdain. Lor is the only one I've ever felt comfortable touching without limits or fear of judgment.

"And that's when I knew my end had come."

"How?"

"I've had many years to contemplate what happened that day," my grandfather says. "I believe he manipulated the Torch. Somehow, he found a loophole in the Artefacts' conditions."

"How is that possible?" But just as I say it, I suspect I already know the answer.

"He used magic I've never seen before," Garnet says. "There was another voice. Someone else inside the Torch?"

"Someone else?"

My grandfather nods, his expression pinched with confusion. "It was a voice I'd never heard before. It was instructing him on what to do. I don't really understand it all, but the voice explained how Rion needed to contain the magic from breaking free so he could claim the crown."

As I stare at his face, I think about how my father hurt us all so much. He didn't care about anyone but himself.

"Was the magic black and made of shadows?" I ask.

He looks at me and blinks. "How did you know that?"

"Because he's still using it," I say.

Garnet considers that. "I can't say I'm surprised."

"Do you have any idea what it might be?"

"Something older and murkier than Fae magic," he says. "Your father has always had a way of finding the world's darkest places."

I'm gripping the glass in my hand so tightly that I'm surprised it doesn't shatter under the pressure.

"You can't see him?" I ask. "Like you can me?"

He shakes his head. "No. He's been lost to my sight for a long time."

"Because of the dark magic?"

"That is my guess."

"Is there anything else you can tell me?" I ask. "Why would he have wanted the ark of Heart?"

"I don't know for sure, but with everything you've told me, I wonder if it's all related to that voice."

I consider that, biting the inside of my cheek.

"I wish I could be more help," he says. I see the regret in his eyes. Part of me wants to stay here for hours and ask him a thousand questions about my family and his life, but I have to find Lor.

"What are you thinking about?" he asks softly, and in his expression, I see years of loss and the man my father took from me. Add that to the list of everything he's taken. I haven't seen my mother in many weeks, and now I can't even get a message to her. I pray that she's okay.

"I need to get out of here," I say. "I have to find Lor. She might be here too."

"Your mate," he says, a small smile lighting his face. "You're very fortunate. Tell me about her?"

"She's . . ." I break off. Where do I even begin to describe her? Her bravery and her loyalty. Her stubbornness and her vulnerability. The way she rushes into anything without a care for herself and would do anything to protect the ones she loves. How do I even begin to describe how fucking alive she makes me feel? Knowing she's out there alone, being subjected to god knows what at my father's or Zerra's hands, is tearing me apart.

"She makes me want to be the best version of myself," I say, realizing how true it is. "She's like the sun, and everything else is just the stars lucky to be moving around her."

Grandfather smiles at that. "Well, she sounds very special."

"She is."

"Then you'll need to find her."

"What if she landed here too?"

"We'll ask Greye. She always keeps an eye on these things."

Garnet rises from his seat, and we enter the garden once again. A few curious stares find us as we weave through the tables. I see the same female High Fae that greeted me and Garnet waves to her.

"Can you tell us? Has a young woman found herself here?" he asks Greye.

"No," she says very confidently. "I've been watching for his bonded, but no one else has entered the garden. It's very peculiar. Are you sure he belongs here?"

"Thank you," Garnet says. "No, he doesn't belong here."

He turns to face me. "She must have ended up back in Ouranos. Let's get you back to her."

"Can you do that?" I ask.

He nods as he starts walking again, and I follow. "Lucky for you, I happen to know the way out of here."

We pass through the garden, where we're met with more curious stares. My grandfather smiles and says hello as we exit out the other side, leading us back into the strangely symmetrical forest.

"This way," he says, winding down a narrow pathway lined with bushes. A cave materializes out in the distance, and he points to it.

"Through there. It will take you back to the surface."

"How do you know that?" I ask, eyeing the dark opening warily.

"Oh, you're not the first living person to wander in here," he says. "Zerra does like to play."

I curl my lip at that.

"Can you go through there? Can you come back?"

"Oh no," he says. "I'm dead. Once, we'd had a bit too much wine, and I dared your Great-Great-Great Aunt Sophie to jump through it, and for about seven long seconds, we thought she was gone, but then poof. She appeared standing right here next to us. So we spent all night tossing ourselves into it, but alas, we returned every time." He laughs at the memory, and I find myself smiling as I look back in the direction we came.

"I wish I could talk to them all," I say, and he gives me a sad smile.

"It's not your time yet. You'll get your chance, and when you come to see us, we'll be waiting for you with open arms. Go and live, my boy. Do better than your father did."

"I'll try," I say. "Thank you."

"Go on. I hope it will be many, many years before you return."

He opens his arms, and I hesitate.

"What is it?" he asks with a curious tip of his head.

"You're not what I expected," I answer. "Given how my father is ..."

Garnet's arms flop to his sides as he nods. "I won't pretend I was always a good man or a good father, either. But sickness and death have a way of softening us all. I, too, regret so many things."

That I can understand. He spreads his arms again and with a sharp breath I fold against him. He hugs me tightly, and I allow myself to revel in the comfort of his embrace. What might my life have been if someone had been there to hug me as a child?

"Live a long and happy life with your mate. I look forward to meeting her when it's time."

After another second, we pull apart, emotion knotting my throat. There are so many things I want to say, and he must sense what's on my mind because he adds, "Someday, my boy, we'll have all the time in the world to talk about everything. But for now, you need to go home."

Slowly, I nod, turning towards the cave.

Standing at the threshold, I look back at him.

He gives me one last smile and then bows.

With a salute, I turn and step through the dark opening.

And then I plummet down.

CHAPTER 28

RION

Rion stalked through the forest, winding his way through the darkness of the trees. Night had fallen hours ago, and he'd waited patiently in his study, nursing a strong drink, as the Keep settled into the ignorance of sleep. His research missions were always kept secret. He couldn't risk anyone tracking his movements.

It had been decades since he'd forced his father to descend, finally taking his crown. Decades since he'd attempted to conquer Ouranos until that witch Serce had fucked up his plans. Without his magic, he'd lost so many potential years of experimentation, and only recently was he strong enough to start trying again. He'd find some way to accomplish his goals that had been thrown off course all those years ago.

When his parents, Zerra rest their souls, had departed this world, he'd wasted no time performing the ascension with Meora at his side. Herric had talked him through it, ensuring a smooth transition thanks to the power of the virulence.

As Nadir aged, he'd grown no closer to the boy, who was now a man, and there would be no bridging that divide.

Rachel still consumed his thoughts, though sometimes he'd look at his bonded partner across the room and wonder if he'd wasted his chance at happiness. Perhaps he'd been too short-sighted in clinging to this idea of a woman who'd left and never looked back.

It had also been decades since he'd seen or heard from her, though she was content to withdraw large sums from the account he'd set up for her. Try as he might, he couldn't uncover who she was sending to The Aurora to retrieve the gold. Even under pain of death, the moneylender had been unable to identify anyone, saying they always came late, just before closing, their face hooded in shadows.

Rion had stationed guards outside the building, hoping to catch them in action, but the culprit always escaped their surveillance. It made him wonder who Rachel was consorting with to have such resources at her disposal. And then realized it was the very money he was providing that probably had set her up with anything she'd need.

Maybe someday she'd forgive him. Maybe someday they would be together again. But the more years that passed, the more he understood it would never be.

Overhead, ribbons of light rippled in the sky—blue, red, violet. Rion wasn't a sentimental man by any measure, but something about the sight never failed to move him. In spite of everything, this magic and these lights were part of him, part of his soul, and what made him tick.

After stealing out of the Keep, he emerged from the tree line into a large clearing at the base of a mountain. A twitch tugged at the corner of his mouth. Despite the strength of his Aurora magic, it still wasn't enough. He recalled those helpless years when he'd been powerless, like a piece of himself had been carved away.

He had read the anguish in Herric's journals about his desire to create power beyond what the Empyrium had given him. Rion, too, wanted more, but he vowed not to make the same mistakes as the previous Aurora King.

He hadn't heard the voice in the Torch since he'd forced his father to descend, and there were moments when Rion wondered if he'd imagined the entire thing.

Checking behind him, Rion ducked out of the trees and crossed the clearing. Not that anyone would be following him—he'd found a way to conceal himself using the magic of virulence, making himself invisible to anyone until he was right upon them. It was an added layer of precaution he used on these late-night crusades. He'd discovered the ability before the First Sercen war and used it to conceal his army when he'd snuck up on Serce so many years ago.

Lately, he'd been experimenting with the idea of infusing magic into the rock so that he could impart the abilities of virulence onto others. Such as his soldiers if he needed them to complete tasks when not in his presence. This was proving difficult so far, and he hadn't yet figured it out. Tonight, he had other plans.

He approached the mountain and laid his hand on the cold surface, channeling out a thread of magic. The mountain shifted, revealing a door and then a staircase carved into the stone winding into the depths.

After they'd uncovered the virulence, Rion had commissioned a small group of low fae to work on a secret chamber where he could experiment without prying eyes. Now he came here regularly to discover what new wonders waited if he could just unlock them from the sparkling black stone.

He wound down the stairs, his footsteps echoing in the silent chamber. It was dark, but he felt his way down until he was deep enough to cast a light to illuminate his descent. The glowing yellow orb hovered overhead as he wound further down the stairs.

As he went deeper, the sound of voices and activity floated up signaling low fae busy carving out a new section of the cavern. He needed more space to test out his latest theory.

He emerged to find the roof soaring overhead. Along the walls, piles of virulence waited, the black stone glittering in the low torchlight like a hoard of treasure. Only it was so much more valuable than mere jewels.

Every eye in the room swung his way at his entrance, and he regarded them with a stony expression. He wanted them to fear him. He wanted them to know if they ever revealed his secret, he would hunt them down and make them pay in ways they couldn't even imagine.

"Your Majesty," said the foreman, Surius, as he shuffled over with hunched shoulders and wringing hands. He was low fae of some variety, with skin like tree bark and long pointed ears sprouting with tufts of white hair. Rion couldn't be bothered to learn all of their various types. "Everything is ready, as you asked."

Rion said nothing, just tipped his head and then walked slowly around the room as everyone waited in rigid stillness, hoping to avoid his wrath. What he saw pleased him, which was a welcome, if unexpected, surprise. It was so hard to find good help.

"Excellent," Rion said. "You've done well."

Rion wasn't above praise when deserved, but meeting his exacting standards was rare.

He walked over to one of the piles of virulence and picked up a nugget, tossing it in his hand and catching it again in his large palm. Pinching it between two fingers, he held it to the light, studying the sparkle. This had become his favorite sight.

While the virulence worked by channeling magic, Herric had also discovered that by focusing it in specific ways, one could elicit different and far more powerful outcomes. During his reign, he'd kept an eye on the other rulers and the arks and seemed almost amused at the audacity of the first king of Aphelion, Cyrus, who was the studious sort driven by the pursuit of knowledge. Cyrus hadn't been content to believe everything Herric had told him about the ark and had conducted his own research and experimentation.

In that way, he'd created the warders, imparting their wings, and creating the oath that bound them to their king.

Herric's notes didn't mention if Cyrus had discovered any-thing else about the stone, but Herric was confident the Aphelion king would never uncover the full extent of his secrets, residing all the way on the other side of the continent.

Rion had been particularly intrigued by the ability to reshape matter with the right mindset. Herric had suggested that, to a degree, virulence could almost read your mind, feel your emotions, sense your thoughts, and alter your magic in a way that could be very interesting and potentially useful.

"You there," Rion said, pointing to one of the low fae. She was small, coming only to his waist, with soft pink skin, blue hair, and those ridiculously elongated ears. He thought this one might be a sprite. "Come here."

The sprite trembled under his gaze, her entire body shak-ing. Rion gave her a moment to gather herself. She was right to be afraid, but in a few moments it wouldn't matter, if things went the way he hoped.

He stared at her until she found her courage and then tip-toed over, her hands clasped in front of her heart. With her big dark eyes, she looked up at him and said, "Your Majesty?" It came out as a breathless squeak.

"What is your name?" Rion asked. He didn't really care what her name was, but for some reason, asking seemed to ease their apprehension. Perhaps they believed he wouldn't hurt them if he knew it. Perhaps in a better man that might be true, but Rion had never had such compunctions.

"I am Lily," she said, sounding a bit more confident now.

"Lily, you're going to help me with something very impor-tant today," Rion said. "Would you be willing?"

He didn't actually intend to give her a choice, but this also seemed to make them feel better. Lily's eyes darted around the cavern, meeting those of her brethren. Most of them looked away, and then she turned back to Rion and nodded.

"Yes, Your Majesty."

"Very good," Rion said. "I will need you to hold still no matter what happens. Try not to move."

Lily was already shaking too hard to answer.

Rion channeled magic into the piece of virulence clutched in his hand. Black smoke wrapped around Lily, enveloping her in darkness, and she slowly began to transform.

Her limbs stretched out, thinning into bony appendages, and her body elongated, her ribcage expanding, followed by her neck and her head. Everything ballooned up to unnatural proportions, her bright pink skin melting away, leaving behind mottled grey flesh. Her entire body convulsed, collapsing to the ground into a heap of dark limbs.

The sound was unbearable. Screams, discordant sounds, bones snapping, flesh stretching, tearing, and being put back together again. Lily screamed and screamed, and the sound was music to Rion's ears. It was working. If the virulence could do this, then there would be no stopping him. He would be nearly a god.

He barely registered the others' presence in the cavern. They watched on in horror, and he couldn't imagine what they were thinking.

After several minutes, Lily had transformed into a demon of his own making. Nothing was left of her innocent gaze, just a dead emptiness and a vicious cruelty ending in sharp teeth dripping with saliva. Rion made a slow circle around the creature as it watched him, its breathing rattling in and out of its chest.

He didn't fear it. As of this moment, he feared nothing.

"I think you need a new name," he mused as it snarled and hissed, its too-large head loping from side to side. "Let's call you the . . . ozziller. Perhaps you'll find a new home in my forests until I can make use of you."

He looked around the room at the terrified faces of everyone pressed against the cavern walls. He sighed, knowing he would have to deal with them. He gestured to the foreman, who took a moment to shuffle towards him.

"Your Majesty?" Surius said, his voice dry and thin with terror.

"You have all done well tonight," Rion said.

Very well. This would give him the edge he needed in another war for the domination of Ouranos. Maybe he could finally claim the ruined territory of Heart in the process. It had resisted all of them, almost as if magic had prevented it, but could virulence make a difference? He could barely contain his smile, his heart lighter than it had been in years.

Then he turned on his heel and headed for the exit, hearing the same voice calling after him, "Your Majesty, what should we do with . . . it?"

Rion turned to look at him and gave him a feral smile.

"Whatever you like."

Then he snapped his fingers and exited the cavern, sealing it behind him with a wall of magic.

A moment later, the sounds of horrified screams and ripping flesh followed him as he made his way back to the surface.

CHAPTER 29

LOR

WHO THE FUCK KNOWS?—PRESENT DAY

I huddle against a log hidden in the trees, tucking into myself as the chill in the air seeps into my bones. Night fell hours ago, and I've been pushing in the direction that I'm pretty sure is south, though I must admit my inner compass could be skewed. My feet and body and soul are so sore and tired, and I need a moment to rest. I need a moment to feel sorry for myself.

Nadir. Is he gone? Can I use the arks to bargain for his life? Or was the moment I lost control the moment I lost him for good? My chest is so tight, I can hardly breathe, and I suck in mouthfuls of humid air, wishing all of this would end. I want to die too. I want to give up. I just want it all to stop hurting so much. My head bounces before it snaps up again as I try to fight off a wave of bone-deep exhaustion.

Adrenaline has kept me moving for the past two days, but even my rage can't keep me upright anymore. I found water and an apple tree yesterday, so I'm not entirely starving, but gods, what I wouldn't give for a thick slice of buttered bread and a platter of roasted meat drowning in gravy.

I nod off again, my temple smacking the log before I rest it against the surface with a groan. Thunder rolls in the distance, reminding me I need to find shelter. What's the worst that can find me out here? I've faced down the vilest monsters already. But I really don't want to be eaten by some wild animal. What an undignified way to go. I snort at my stupid joke and stupid self and resist the urge to start crying again.

My hand tingles with the sparks of my magic. It saved me again, but I have to find a way to control it. I didn't care if I hurt Zerra. I wanted to make her suffer, though I realize that plan might have been shortsighted. I can't kill her if I want to avoid becoming her. Surely as long as she's alive then I'm safe? Or do the Empyrium plan to do away with her first? Why did they leave me with so little information? I broke through whatever enchantment she attempted to use on me, which also means I'm at least as strong as her. A fact she won't have missed.

I squeeze my eyes shut and whimper.

Why is everything so complicated?

My mind blurs out, dragged down by exhaustion as I fight the pull of sleep, blinking as I shiver. More thunder rolls overhead as rain starts to fall. I curl tighter into myself, sniffling as the temperature drops. I should get up. I should keep moving.

Nadir. I miss you so much.

Lor.

I dream of someone saying my name in the distance, and I twitch, my eyes fluttering open like I'm falling. They slide shut as I continue shivering. The wind has picked up, knifing through my thin clothing as rain mists over my skin. Idly, I wonder if there's some way to start a fire, but I'm too cold to move.

Lor. Can you hear me?

There it is again. It sounds like Nadir, and my heart twists in my chest. In the darkness, I reach for him, but I feel nothing. I want to touch him. Hold him. I want him so much.

Lor! Tell me you can hear me!

Wait.

My eyes snap open, and I sit up.

Lor! Can you hear me?

I blink, looking around. I'm awake. Did I just imagine that?

Can you hear me? Please hear me.

"Nadir," I whisper, pinching the skin on my arm hard.

"Ow!" I hiss. Okay, I'm definitely awake.

Nadir! I shout back in my mind, and then a wave, like warmth and honey and sunlight, washes over me.

Lor!

I'm already up and running, weaving through the trees, every ounce of pain and fatigue forgotten.

"Where are you!" I scream. "Nadir!" I'm crying so hard I

can barely see where I'm going. The rain falls harder, making the ground slippery and blinding my vision.

"Nadir!" My voice cracks. "Nadir!"

"Lor!"

I alter my course at the sound of his voice, crashing over brush and rocks, my already battered feet tearing up against the rough forest floor.

And then I feel him. I sense him. I remember that night in the settlements when Rion's men captured me, when a wave of something sharp and warm filled the space behind my heart. Desire and rage and every longing course through my limbs, threatening to tow me under.

A distant rustle in the trees has me picking up my pace.

"Nadir!" I scream again, needing to feel his name on my tongue.

"Lor!" comes his voice, and I've never heard anything so beautiful in my life.

Then he materializes through the dim light, running towards me, and my heart nearly stops.

"Nadir," I choke out. "Nadir . . ."

We crash into one another at top speed. He picks me up, wrapping me in his arms as my legs circle his hips. We spin around and around, squeezing one another so tight that I fear we might shatter.

"Oh, my gods," I sob into the curve of his throat, inhaling the scent of his hair, reminding me of crisp winter nights and falling snow. "You're alive. I'm so sorry."

He buries his head against my throat and says, "I'm sorry, can you ever forgive me?"

I pull away, framing his face with my hands.

"Forgive you for what?"

"What my father said about helping him—"

"I know it wasn't true," I interrupt.

"You're sure?"

"I only doubted for a moment. He got under my skin, and I'm so sorry. Nadir, after everything, how could I doubt you? From the second we met, you've done nothing but share every truth and give up every secret in your heart. Of course I'm sure. I know you would never have done that."

"Oh, thank gods," he says. "I thought . . . I worried . . ."

"He was just trying to drive a wedge between us, but that will never work. Do you hear me? I don't care what happens—nothing could ever make me stop loving you. Do you understand?"

He nods, his eyes searching my face as though he's trying to confirm I'm really here.

"I'm sorry I killed you," I say, choking out a sob.

"That really happened? Zerra told me, but—"

"It was an accident. But I did it, and Nadir, it killed me, too. I died in that moment and have been dying through every moment since. I've been doing everything I can to get back to you."

"What happened with her?" we both ask at the same time.

"Fuck, she's insane," he says, and I nod. "I don't want to talk about it right now."

Then he kisses me, our mouths clashing together as we drink in the calming power of each other's presence. "Gods, I was so scared I'd never see you again," he murmurs against me, his hands gripping my thighs.

"Me too," I say. "When I thought you were dead—" I can barely get the words out, but he swallows them down, kissing me again like a man drowning in the abyss.

We kiss, and we kiss until we can barely breathe as the rain coats our skin and lightning flashes overhead, thunder shaking the earth. We don't need words to convey how much we need each other as he drops me to my feet and tugs on my leggings, pulling them off before he lifts me up again. I reach between us, fumbling with the laces of his pants, shoving them down, freeing his already erect cock. My hand wraps around it, and it's so warm and soft and hard, and he groans into my mouth.

"I've missed you so fucking much," he murmurs into the curve of my throat. "I thought you'd hate me forever."

He moves me against a tree, my back hitting the rough surface as the curve of his thick cock dips into me. It slides in slowly, spreading me apart as my head tips back, and I cling to his shoulders. He thrusts his hips, filling me with a long, deep sigh.

Thunder and lightning continue flashing overhead as rain drenches us in sheets. But I don't care. A few moments ago, I was cold and scared and lost. But Nadir is here, and I have been found.

"Fuck," he hisses. "Fuck, I was so scared, Lor." He pulls out slowly, each inch like an awakening before he thrusts back in so hard I feel it to the depths of my very spirit.

"Me too," I sob, unable to hold back my tears as we move together, our heartbeats, our souls, our minds once again whole. "When I thought you were dead, I died too, Nadir. I never, ever want to feel anything like that again."

His hand grips the back of my neck as he brings my head towards his. Our foreheads touch as his other hand digs into my thigh, and he churns his hips.

"Never," he says. "We will never be separated again. I don't care if I have to chain you to my wrist."

"Okay," I say, not caring how ridiculous that sounds.

As we continue fucking, our movements become more erratic. I cling to him like I'm falling, knowing I nearly lost him. My magic sparks under my skin, red lightning twisting up my arms and legs as his ribbons of light filter out, both forms of our power melding together. I remember this from the last few times we had sex, but my magic is no longer locked away.

"Nadir," I whisper as he thrusts into me. "My magic. I can't control it."

"I've got you," he whispers back. "Look at me."

Our gazes meet, and he buries himself into me as his magic wraps around mine—not to repress it but to soothe it. It responds to his power, my sparks lining up into some form of order. It sings against his magic, and for the first time since we left Aphelion, it doesn't feel like it's spinning out of control.

He tells me he loves me, and I do the same, and then we come together in a burst of heat and slick, wet desire, my soul reborn from the earth and molded back together. I've never wanted to be anywhere so much. Our magic flares bright, exploding around us in a halo of red and green and blue. There's no destruction, though—it's just...beautiful. The perfect marriage of our spirits. He helped control it. I knew he could.

Thunder claps overhead, and the rain falls harder as we cling to one another, already soaked to the bone.

"We should try to find shelter," he whispers.

I want to tell him that I don't care if we get wet. I want him to take me under the lightning and thunder over and over again as I scream his name. But a chill is setting in, and I'm momentarily reacquainted with the fact that I haven't eaten properly in days. I shove my legs into my now soaked leggings, which is a feat unto itself.

"Gods, we're a mess," I tell him as he takes my hand. Both barefoot, our clothing is torn, and scratches and blood cover our skin.

"You've never looked more beautiful, Lor," he says with every ounce of sincerity, and I feel the delicate seams of my equilibrium pulling apart. I can't get over the fact he's standing here, alive and whole. "But let's find you somewhere to dry off. Then I can finish everything I've been thinking about for months."

"Months?" I say. "It's only been days."

He blows out a breath and rubs his hand down his face. "Later. We'll talk about this later."

I nod and tug on his hand. "I left some things behind. We need to get them."

He follows me to the spot where I was sleeping. I scoop up the arks, cradling them in my arms, then turn around to find Nadir's shocked expression.

"Where . . . the hell did you get those?"

I cringe and hug them tighter. "I stole them from Zerra."

His mouth gapes. "You did *what*?"

"She refused to give you back and . . . Let's talk about this when we're dry?"

"Right." He takes them from me and stuffs them into the pockets of his loose pants. Then he tugs my hand, and we begin to run through the forest, searching for something to use as a shelter as the rain pounds us from above.

"I see a light," he says, pointing through the trees, and I squint through the darkness, picking up on the same yellow glow.

"You think it's safe?" The Aurora King is still no doubt looking for me, and somehow Nadir managed to escape Zerra, and she's probably after both of us.

"Only one way to find out," he says, guiding me down the path.

We emerge from the trees to find a small village surrounded by a stone wall, and I almost cry in relief. Of course we don't exactly look like well-to-do travelers at the moment, but maybe someone will take pity on us.

"Come on," Nadir says, tugging me towards the gate.

"But we have no money," I say as we enter. The streets are mostly empty except for a few hurrying people who pay us no mind as they attempt to keep themselves dry. The rain continues to drench us, turning the street into muck. Gods, my feet are disgusting.

"Let me worry about that," he says. We spy a sign that indicates an inn with rooms for rent.

We open the door and step inside the warm common room filled with travelers eating and drinking. Thankfully, the rain actually washed away a lot of the blood, improving our haggard appearances by the merest fraction.

A human woman stands at the bar, and she turns to face us, eyeing us up and down, her gaze pausing at our bare feet before she places her hands on her hips and raises an eyebrow.

Or maybe not.

"Can I help you?" she asks, her voice dripping with skepticism. I have a feeling she'll throw us out on our asses when she discovers we don't have a dime.

"A room for the night, please," Nadir says in his most formal, princely voice. It almost makes me burst into laughter because it sounds nothing like him at all.

"You have money?" she asks.

"Not at the moment," Nadir replies, and she opens her mouth, about to order us out. He raises a hand and then lets out a tendril of his magic in a swirl of green and purple. Her gaze follows the trail.

"You're a royal," she says, not in an impressed way, but in a resigned one.

"I can assure you that you will be compensated more than fairly if you allow me and my companion to spend the night."

She eyes us warily, but I can see she's already lost this battle.

"Fine," she says, holding up a finger. "But don't cause any trouble."

"We would never," he says with a wink that almost elicits a smile. How could anyone resist the Aurora Prince when he turns on the charm?

She hands him a key from behind the bar. "Second floor. Last door on the left."

"Thank you," he says, keeping his head high, and like water isn't literally puddling under his feet.

"Also, could we get some hot food, clean clothes, and about twelve bottles of wine?"

Chapter 30

After the innkeeper graces us with another scathing look, she nods a quick, gruff yes, and then we scramble upstairs. A fire is already crackling in the hearth, and I make my way over, holding my freezing hands to the heat, my fingers aching from the thaw. I start to peel apart my clothes, struggling to extricate myself. They're heavy and crusted with blood and sand and dirt, sticking to every crevice of my body.

The sound of running water comes from the bathroom, and I grab a blanket and wrap it around myself. I enter to find Nadir already stripped down to nothing, facing the tub with his hands on his hips. I lean against the door, taking a moment to admire every inch. The carved ripples in his back and his hair swooping over the curve of his shoulder. Those two divots in his lower back that bracket the entry to the round firmness of his ass. My gaze travels lower, sloping over his thighs, noting the way the candlelight glints off the arch of his calf. Even his ankle bone manages to stun me.

"I feel you ogling me, Lightning Bug," he says, peering over his shoulder and flashing me a smile that both breaks and stitches up the pieces of my heart.

"Can you blame me?" I ask, moving closer, wrapping an arm around his waist, and pressing myself against his back. My nose buries into his skin, and I inhale deeply, drinking in the scent of cold winter nights and the wind cutting off snowy peaks. The scent that has become my safety and my home. The soothing call in the dark when I'm stumbling blindly through shadows.

My hand spreads over his stomach as my fingers forage along the ridges slicing over his torso. The lines of muscle and the hard angles of bone and sinew. I slide my hand higher, caressing the lines of his sculpted chest, circling a finger over a nipple, making his breath hitch.

I open my mouth and gently sink my teeth into the curve of his shoulder, wishing I could consume him. Keep him. Never let him go.

"You're killing me," he says, his voice soft.

"Not this time," I reply. "This time I'm here to save you."

A low growl rumbles in his chest, causing a spike of heat to flare between my thighs.

"Can I offer you a seat in the tub?"

I nuzzle my cheek against his back, savoring the heat of his skin. "I don't know, I rather like this."

His laughter is low and soft. "I do, too, but we have a problem."

"Hmm, what's that?" I stick out my tongue and stretch onto my tiptoes before I lick his earlobe and then suck it between my teeth, deriving the most exquisite satisfaction from his answering shiver.

"That you're touching me, but I'm not currently touching you."

I laugh softly. "Doesn't seem like a problem to me."

I drag my fingernails over his stomach, loving the flex and shift of his muscles as he attempts to hold himself still. "Does this bother you?" I ask, dragging my fingers lower, the trail of hair under his navel feathering against my fingertips.

" 'Bother' . . . is not the right word," he says with a low moan as my hand drifts lower. His skin radiates heat, and I drop the blanket still clutched around me before I press my body against his. Skin to skin, we stand in the swirling warmth as the tub fills with steaming water.

"Don't move," I whisper as my hand circles around his erect cock, wrapping it firmly before I slide my hand down then pump him with several strong strokes. His hips move with each decline, and I blow over the back of his neck, watching an eruption of gooseflesh spread over his skin.

"Lor," he practically whimpers.

"Shhh," I say. "I just want to touch you."

"As long as I get my turn," he growls as liquid heat pools below my navel and drips between my thighs.

"In a minute." My hand continues with long, languid strokes, eliciting a reaction from each vein and pulse.

"Fuck," he hisses. "Please."

"What do you want to do?" I say in a teasing voice.

"I want to do everything," he says. "Touch every part of you. Taste every part of you. Be everything for you, Lor."

"You *are* everything for me," I say, and he peers over his shoulder, his eyes hooded and brimming with lust.

"I will never be enough for you, but I will keep trying until the day I die."

"Don't say that," I whisper, reaching up to kiss him softly. "You are more than enough."

His eyes flutter as I stroke him harder and faster, and our faces hover an inch apart as we breathe in each other's space.

I want everything too.

Our eyes pin together, and he sucks his lower lip between his teeth as I grip him firmly. He covers my hand with his and guides me as we stroke him together.

The steam from the bath curls up, slicking our already flushed skin. Nadir grunts as he grows harder and thicker before he comes, his warm release coating my hand. He turns around so I'm facing him and then guides my hand towards me, dragging his cum over my stomach and my breasts, circling my nipples. He paints over me, drifting lower and lower before his hand slides between my legs, and he uses his release to circle my clit before dipping his finger inside to mix with my own wetness.

"Fuck, you're so beautiful," he whispers. "So fucking perfect."

He kisses me hard and then pulls away.

"Get in the tub. It's your turn."

I smile and then do as he asks, stepping into the hot water before he joins me and sinks in. He pulls me down so I'm nestled between his legs. The water is stingingly hot, and my toes finally start to thaw for the first time in days. I lean against him, resting my head on his chest and feeling the beat of his heart. For several minutes, we sit in silence, listening to one another's breaths as Nadir softly runs his hands over my shoulders and down my arms and back up again.

"Are you okay?" I ask after a minute.

"I am now." He twirls a lock of my hair between his fingers. "Do you want to tell me what happened?"

"I do, but not right now. How about you?" I look up at him, and he gives me a rueful smile.

"Same, I guess."

"I want to go back to Aphelion. I need to make sure Tristan and Willow are okay. I'm worried about the others, too."

He blows out a sigh.

"Yeah, me too." Something crosses his expression.

"What is it?"

"I'm just wondering if that's where my father will search for you." He gives me a pointed look. "I know you don't want to talk about it, but I assume he is still after you?"

"Yes," I say. "You should assume that."

He shakes his head and rubs his face. "We'll talk about this. After."

"After?"

"After I enjoy you a bit more," he says with that smirk that always manages to rip out my heart.

He captures my chin between his fingers, and I wince. Nadir's eyes darken as he gently tips up my face, noting what I assume is a mottling of bruises courtesy of his father.

"Who did that?"

"Who do you think?"

"I'll fucking kill him."

"I know." I place a hand on his chest. "But let's return to 'enjoying' for a minute, please?"

He growls low in his throat and kisses me as his hands smooth over my thighs and stomach, slipping over the water and soap in a way that feels decadent. His hand moves between my thighs, and my legs fall open as his gentle fingers slide along my core.

"Mmm," he murmurs into my throat. "I've missed this. Feeling how wet you get for me."

He circles my clit, and I gasp, my arm reaching around to grab behind his neck.

"It was less than a week," I say, and he laughs low and dark.

"It felt longer for me, and even a moment without you is too long. Don't you know that by now?"

His fingers continue to tease, dipping into me and then back out as circling around.

"I missed you too," I say. "Every single moment, I only wanted to get back to you."

"When I couldn't feel or hear you anymore—" He breaks off with a shudder. "I was sure she was preventing it."

"Maybe it was the Evanescence," I say. "What if it cuts people off from the surface?"

A moan slips from my lips as he touches me, his fingers plunging into me with a thrust.

"Maybe," he says. "All I know is I never want to go back

there. At least not until we decide we're done with this life. Together."

I exhale a breathy whimper as he drives his fingers in again.

"Fuck," he says. "That sound. It makes me so fucking hard. I need to be inside you, Lor."

"Yes," I gasp as he fingers my clit again. "Please."

I flip around and straddle his hips, kissing him. Bending his head back and just *devouring* him. I want to taste him and feast on him. Soak up his essence and every piece of him until he becomes a part of me. We kiss, and we kiss like the world is ending, and maybe it is, but if we don't survive, then maybe it will have all been worth it because at least we had this. And that's all I ever really needed.

"Lor," he moans into my mouth. "I don't know how I lived before you or how I'll ever live without you."

My hips rock into his, the hard length of his cock rubbing against me with the most delicious friction.

"You never will. From now until the sun burns out and the mountains crumble into the sea, I will be yours, Nadir. This is my promise."

I'm not ready to tell him yet what fate might await me, but I will tell him after this. He deserves to know. None of it changes how I feel, and if anyone can help me sort this out, I know it's him.

He stares into my eyes, and I see the promise written in them. We were nearly lost. The Aurora King almost broke us one more time, but never again. Zerra tried to keep us apart, but nothing and no one will ever find their way between us.

"I don't know how I got so lucky," he says.

"I might say the same thing."

Then I reach between us and guide the head of his cock into my entrance, slowly, so slowly sinking down as he clings to my hips like he's being shredded apart bit by bit.

I take my time, savoring the stretch and the way he fills every inch of me. When I'm fully seated, I wait, remembering the first time we did this. Remembering when I'd fought so hard against it but then I finally fell, and the plummet was the greatest feeling of my life.

"Are you okay?" he asks, tucking a lock of hair behind my ear and trailing a finger along my cheek. There's so much concern and love in his expression that my heart expands in my chest. This cruel prince who kidnapped me and tied me to the foot of his bed while he threatened to feed me to his pets. This cruel prince who isn't so cruel as long as he loves you. The prince who took my heart and held it in his hand and forced me to see him. But who would have handed it back to me if I'd asked.

"I'm okay," I say, and then I lift up and drop down as we slowly churn together, our breaths mingling and hearts aligning in this divine bliss.

"I love you," I say. "I need you to understand just how much I love you."

He quirks a smile, and the sight makes my heart seize in my chest. "I know, Lor. I know you didn't want to—"

I cover his lips with my finger.

"No. That isn't true. I wanted to. From the very beginning. I never didn't want to."

He smiles, and it's bright and beautiful, and I ride his hips, clinging to his shoulders as he guides me up and down. Our magic weaves together, his ribbons taming my lightning. We move as one, exploding together before I fall against him, and we sit in the tub, wrapped in one another, until the water grows cold.

Then we exit the bath and cocoon ourselves in warm towels before he sweeps me up into his arms and carries me to the bed. We snuggle under the covers, and he folds himself around me so I'm nestled into the curve of his body.

This is where I belong.

He is where I've always belonged.

CHAPTER 31

We sleep late the following day, desperately needing rest. My eyes peel open to the smell of coffee and bacon wafting up from downstairs. We had only a few bites of food before we passed out, and my stomach growls. The sound is enough to wake Nadir, whose lashes flutter as he gives me a lazy smile.

"Morning, Lightning Bug."

"Morning," I say, snuggling up to him.

"How are you feeling?"

"I'm tired and sore, but I'm so happy you're here," I say as my stomach protests again. "And hungry."

"Well, we can't have that, can we?" he asks before he lifts the covers and scoots out of bed.

"Where are you going?"

"I'll be right back." He digs into the pile of clothing provided by the innkeeper, finding a pair of pants and a tunic that are a bit tight for his large frame.

Then he leaves the room, and I take my turn digging through the clothing, finding a pair of soft brown leggings and a smaller tunic that fit well enough. There's something about fresh, clean clothes and fresh, clean skin that feels like the most incredible luxury after the dirt and heat of the sand and the forest and that sweat-slicked escape I barely survived.

A moment later, Nadir appears carrying a tray laden with breakfast. He sets it on a small table in the corner and we sit down across from one another. I almost weep at the taste of coffee and how my teeth sink into the greasy ecstasy of buttered toast. I used to be so acquainted with hunger, but I've grown softer since then. I can't grit my way through it like I used to, but I refuse to feel bad about that. No one should ever have to feel that way.

"So, tell me what happened," Nadir says, and I sigh. I need to tell him so many things, but so much of it scares me. "Go back to the beginning. How about when you killed me?"

My expression drops, and he reaches over to grab my wrist. "Lor. It's okay."

I rub my face with my other hand. "It's not. I thought I—"

"But you didn't. I'm here."

"Yes, but I fear it made things even more complicated."

"What do you mean?"

"I have a lot of things to tell you."

"Okay, I'm listening."

With my hands wrapped around my mug, I take a long sip

of coffee, preparing myself. I tell Nadir about waking up in his father's cart and everything that came after it.

"I broke through a pair of those cuffs—the glowing blue ones? Tyr was wearing them, too."

"You mean arcturite?" Nadir asks, his eyebrows climbing.

"You had them on, too, but I suppose Zerra must have removed them."

"You broke through arcturite." He sits back in his chair, his voice full of disbelief.

"Your father commented on that too. He had more when he tried to recapture me. Is that a big deal?"

Nadir laughs and shakes his head. "It's a really fucking big deal. Arcturite is one of few things that can cut Fae off from their magic. It's technically illegal, but obviously, anyone can get their hands on it with enough money and resources. You shouldn't have been able to do that."

"Oh," I say. Okay then. That's an interesting development.

"So you have no control over your magic?" Nadir asks me next.

"I can control my healing but not the lightning. It's just a raging torrent. All or nothing. What did you do when you helped it?"

"I'm not entirely sure," he says, "It just felt right. I could sense it spinning out, and I used mine to soothe it."

"You might need to do that again."

"Of course. But we'll want to figure out how to control it without my help."

I nod.

"And then what?" he asks. "What did you mean that killing me might have made things more complicated?"

"It's all a blur, but meeting Zerra wasn't the first time I ended up in the Evanescence," I say. I go on to explain what I saw in that strange room with the seven original rulers of Ouranos. The creation of the Artefacts and the arks. And how the first Aurora King fell from grace.

Nadir is silent for a moment. "So you're telling me my great-great many-times-over grandfather is the Lord of the Underworld." He snorts and shakes his head. "Why . . . doesn't that surprise me?"

"Don't do that. You know that has nothing to do with who you are, Nadir."

"Do I, though?" He blows out a breath. "She called me Herric. I think . . ."

"He hurt her," I say. "Yeah. She said his name to me, too."

I squeeze his hand and then let go as I twist my fingers together, because I'm not sure how to tell him the next part. He's silent after I explain that I think the Empyrium want me to replace Zerra, his expression stunned.

"Why?"

"I don't know. They said something about me being a queen without a queendom."

"That's . . ." He trails off. "I'm not sure what to say. If that's what you want—"

"I don't," I say, interrupting him. "I *don't* want that. We'll find another way, and I will fight this with everything I have."

"Oh, thank fuck," he says, clutching his chest. "Because I

was about to lose my mind." His eyes darken. "No one is taking you from me."

I give him a soft smile.

"Does Zerra know about their plan?" he asks.

"I'm not sure," I reply. "Did she say anything?"

His expression darkens. "I think she knows, Lor."

"Tell me what happened."

He blows out a breath. "Your story is pretty crazy, but mine is up there too."

Nadir then recounts his time in Zerra's Palace as my hatred of her spirals deeper and deeper.

"She seems to have a vendetta against you and I couldn't figure out what you might have possibly done to her. She said something about you being dead soon, and I lost my shit, but I got nothing else out of her."

I bite the inside of my cheek. "So she definitely knows. But how?"

"This Empyrium must have told her?"

"But why would they do that?"

"I'm not sure," he says.

"What else happened?"

He continues speaking, recounting how he woke up and how he broke out of Zerra's palace. The sadness in his voice when he recounts his time with his grandfather breaks my heart.

"Whose voice was in the Torch?" I ask when he tells me about how Garnet was forced to descend.

"I can't even begin to guess," Nadir says. "If we knew, it might answer some questions about what my father wants from you."

I shake my head. "We never really discussed what Cloris said. She claimed she went to your father and revealed me and Tristan and Willow, but what did he want? What did she promise him?"

Nadir presses a thumb to his lip. "When you first disappeared from Nostraza, he didn't seem to care other than making sure you were dead," he says, and I watch as he continues. "But then he changed his tune and suddenly seemed intent on me finding you."

"So maybe Cloris promised him something—whether the ark or something else—but when he couldn't get to my magic, he gave up." He looks up at me. "And something happened during those weeks you were looking for me."

"Maybe," he says as we both fall into silence.

"Zerra tried to force you into having sex with her?" I ask after a minute, my voice low and deadly.

He sighs. "Yeah. The extra fucked-up part is it's obvious that anyone she brings up from the surface eventually succumbs to this weird kind of numbness. All her servants and helpers were like ghosts—present but not really there. After a living person spends enough time up there, that's who they become."

"I'll kill her," I growl, and Nadir's face cracks.

"I love it when you're possessive, Heart Queen."

"I mean it," I say. "She was already on my list, but now—"

"Lor, if she dies, then does the Empyrium get what they want from you?"

I sigh and take a sip of coffee.

"I had considered that," I say, my heart feeling heavy. If

this fate is inescapable, then I've been contenting myself that maybe Nadir could live with me. But even if he was willing to abandon his life on the surface, I couldn't let him suffer the fate he just described. I also tell him what D'Arcy said about the death of one's mate because now I'm wondering if the same thing might affect him if I'm sent to the Evanescence for good.

"You weren't kidding when you said it was complicated," Nadir says with a weary sigh as I offer him a weak smile.

We both fall into silence as we pick at our plates. I was starving when I woke up, but I've lost my appetite in the face of the ever-mounting odds piling up against us.

Then he gives me a serious look. "How did you destroy her palace? What did you sacrifice?"

My brow furrows, and I let out a deep breath.

"What is it?" he asks.

"You," I say. "When she refused to give you back, I thought I'd never see you again, and I wanted to hurt her. When she said Herric's name, I realized she never intended to release you. So I lost control—I truly thought you were gone forever."

He slides from his seat and drops to a knee, his hands folding with mine. We press our foreheads together, needing only to hear our breath and feel our hearts beat.

"So now what?" Nadir says after a moment.

"We stick to the plan and head back to Aphelion."

I look at him and nod, neither of us saying what's next. We have to find the Crown so I can ascend. We need to get the arks of Aphelion and then Heart. That means confronting Rion once and for all. I started in The Aurora as a child and ended up in the Sun Palace, but everything keeps pointing me back to where I spent so many miserable years.

My gaze drifts north. Both Rion *and* Zerra want the ark of Heart for what I can only surmise are very different reasons.

Either way, we must get it back.

"Back to Aphelion again," I say.

Hopefully, not for the last time.

CHAPTER 32

NADIR

Once Lor and I dress in our borrowed clothing, we head back downstairs. I still don't have any way to pay the innkeeper, but I'm hoping I can convince her money is coming her way. I'll make up for our imposition later.

We brush past the bar and head for the door.

"Where are you—" the innkeeper asks, but I raise a hand.

"As I said, you will be compensated for our presence."

She plants her hands on her hips and gives me a dubious look.

"Just not today," I say with a smile. "But you will."

She looks towards a man in the corner who watches us both, his eyes shadowed by a hood. Some goon she hires to pummel anyone skipping out on their bill.

"Your friend there doesn't stand a chance against me," I say, and the innkeeper raises an eyebrow. "This would be much less messy if you'd just believe me."

"Please," Lor says. "We will send you something. I swear it. We've run into some trouble and lost our things, but I promise we're good for it."

Whatever she sees in Lor's face causes the woman's expression to soften.

"Fine, then," the innkeeper says. "May you be cursed if you're lying."

Lor gives her a smile. "Absolutely. Get in line."

The woman's eyebrows scrunch together, and Lor's face stretches into a grin. The woman waves us off, and if we had more time, I'm pretty sure Lor would convince her to pay us instead.

We stumble into the street and look around to find our bearings. The innkeeper revealed we aren't far from Aphelion, but it will take us a few days to get there on foot.

We'll need some provisions for our trip back. I don't think I should fly us. I'm worried . . . I say to her through our bond.

My eyes cast upwards towards the heavens. As long as we don't call for her, she shouldn't be able to summon or see us, but hovering in the sky feels a little too close to her dominion. I don't really know if that's how it works, but caution is probably wise. However, I was relieved to find I *could* use my magic again and that she doesn't have that kind of sway over me on the surface.

I have a feeling she'll try to get me back up there somehow, I add with a shudder.

Lor comes up and places a hand on my chest. *You under-stand that no one is taking you from me either. I'll destroy her if she so much as touches another hair on your head.*

I clasp my hand over hers and then wrap my arm around her waist.

You make my knees weak when you talk like that.

She snorts a laugh. *I mean it.*

I know you do, Lightning Bug. I mean it too.

She has no idea just how much I mean it. I thought I lost her when I was stuck up in that prison in the sky. I thought she hated me. I thought it was the end, and I never want to know that feeling again. I love her with every piece of my heart and will do anything to protect her.

"Lor!" comes a voice that has us both spinning around, instantly on edge. A familiar figure runs towards us, and the sight is so incongruent that it takes a moment for my brain to catch up.

"Willow!" Lor screams, and then she starts running too. They clash in the middle of the street, wrapping their arms around one another.

"Where have you been?" Willow cries as she hugs her sister.

"What are you doing here?" Lor asks at the same time.

Out of the crowd emerge three more figures—Mael, Amya, and Tristan—that make my heart squeeze. "Thank Zerra," Amya says, throwing her arms around me. "I thought he was finally going to finish you."

"I'm not that easy to kill, little sister," I say, and she gives me a watery smile.

"I know that."

Mael claps me on the back, and then we embrace. "I'm so fucking glad you aren't dead," he says.

"Don't get mushy on me."

He laughs, and then we join Lor and her siblings. Lor hugs both of them, too.

"What are you doing here?" she asks again, and then they fill us in on what's been happening in Aphelion.

"What a disaster," Lor says.

"You could say that again," Mael agrees. "Gabriel looks like he wants to hurl himself off a cliff."

"We need to go and see him," Lor says. "Do you think they've tracked down Atlas?"

She looks around like he might suddenly appear in the middle of the street.

"The warders will find him," Amya says, sensing her apprehension.

"Where have you two been?" Tristan asks. "What happened?"

Lor sighs. "That is a very long story."

"Do you have any money?" I ask Mael. "We had to impose on the innkeeper's good graces."

"Of course," Mael says, digging into his pocket and pulling out a sack of coins.

"Excuse me a moment," I say before I return to the inn. The innkeeper stands at the bar, pursing her lips together.

"As promised," I say with a shit-eating grin before I deposit the sack on the countertop.

She lifts an eyebrow as she sidles over and lifts it, weighing it in her hand. It's more than enough to cover our room and food for the night, and she knows it.

"And there will be more," I say. "For your kindness. I don't know what we would have done otherwise."

She eyes me up and down and must decide I'm sincere because she finally cracks a reluctant smile.

"Who are you, anyway? A royal, I know, but who?"

"I'm...the Aurora Prince," I say, and her eyes widen. "If you ever need a favor, you know where to find me."

"Safe travels," she says, and then I'm about to turn away when an explosion bursts in my ears, shaking the entire building. Screams echo from outside before a ball of fire shatters through a window, crashing into the middle of the long communal table bisecting the room.

Everyone jumps up, screaming while they scramble to escape. Outside, I see more balls of fire raining down on the village.

"Lor." I dash outside, scanning the street. She's running towards me, and I see Mael and the others trying to help everyone else find safety.

"We need to take cover," she says, grabbing my hand as the six of us weave through the chaos.

"What's happening?" Mael asks. "What is this?"

I look up at the sky to watch the falling balls of fire, and I know what's causing this. *Who* is causing this.

We find a barn on the outskirts of the village. It's not the best place to hide, but it's made of stone and less likely to catch fire. Inside, we find a dozen people already huddled against the far wall.

"Lor, I don't think we should hide with the others," I say, pulling her back.

This is Zerra, I add through our bond.

Lor nods as she stares at the roof. *Why can she see us? We didn't call for her.*

"What's going on?" Tristan asks.

"You four stay here," I say. "Take cover and wait this out."

"Where are you two going?" Willow asks.

"We're going to draw this away," Lor replies.

"I don't understand," Amya says.

"We'll explain everything after," I say. "Meet us at the town gate after this dies down."

If any of us survive, of course.

The building shudders at the impact of another fireball, and everyone jumps.

"Nadir," Mael says with a warning in his voice. "What are you doing?"

"Just . . . trust us," I say. "We'll see you soon."

Then I look at Lor, and we turn and start running, heading for the forest. Maybe we can find somewhere to hide. We weave through the trees, attempting to escape as Zerra's fire rains from the sky.

CHAPTER 33

GABRIEL

APHELION—THE SUN PALACE

My glass tumbler sloshes with the strongest orc wine this side of the Beltza Mountains. The viscous green liquid could burn a hole right through the crystal, not to mention what it's probably doing to my organs. All I care about is making my head swim and my limbs soft while allowing me a moment to escape. It's the first time in weeks that I've felt like I can breathe.

Not a single one of my problems has been solved, but this shit is good.

Hylene sits beside me on a plush settee as we stare across the sea. The secluded balcony offers a stunning view while keeping us from prying eyes.

"How are you feeling?" she asks softly.

I tip my head against the sofa, my lids fluttering closed. The alcohol swirls in my blood as I listen to the pounding of the waves. The constant thrum calms the beat of my racing heart.

"Like shit," I answer after a moment, and she laughs. This is what I like about her. No matter what I say, no matter my mood, nothing seems to offend or faze her. She takes everything I do in stride like she sees something in me and is just patiently waiting for me to stop being a pain in the ass and become a better person. I can just be myself when she's around. There's no judgment or criticism. There's just her with those beguiling green eyes, that infectious laugh, and, if I'm being frank . . . those luscious fucking curves that make my dick stir.

Speaking of which, I open one eye and twist my head towards her. She's leaning over, and I get a view of her creamy skin, her breasts swelling into the deep vee of her robe. She's definitely not modest in her attire, so this getup isn't for me, but nothing is sexier than a woman who's this confident in her own skin.

Maybe a small, feeble part of me wishes this getup *were* for me, and I try to tell myself no. I shouldn't be getting a hard-on for her, but I'm also sure I'm not imagining her interest.

Or maybe I am.

Maybe I'm hoping because I'm so starved for . . . everything. My brain is just fucked-up and sending the wrong signals. It wouldn't be the first time.

"Is there anything I can do?" she asks. "Besides the obvious, of course."

The obvious is solving this mess. Figuring out who should be leading Aphelion. Finding Atlas and bringing him the justice he deserves. Deciding what brand of justice is suitable for his crimes.

"Probably not," I say. "Unless you can wave your hand and take me away from all of this forever."

She gives me a sad smile. "You know you really wouldn't want that. You are loyal to your kingdom and your king. You could never abandon them."

I snort wryly and take another swig of my drink.

"You want to bet?"

The worst part is that as much as I don't want her words to be true, they probably are. And that makes me an idiot. I want to be able to pick up and walk away. Go down to the docks, board a boat to some other, distant land, and never look back. Rewrite my history and erase my existence.

But she's right. I'm a sucker, and I don't have the guts.

"Maybe there's something else," I say as my eyes dip again to her impressive cleavage. I pull them back up, not wanting to stare like a lech. Her smile suggests she knows what I was just doing and doesn't mind. Noted.

"What?" she asks, giving me a mock innocent smile. "What could possibly take your mind off all of this?" She sweeps out a hand, and she has a point. But I'm desperate for a distraction. I don't want to think about anything important. Nothing that matters too much. The pain of this constant responsibility is caving my shoulders inwards. Once upon a time, I was forced into a life of subservience, but maybe that's what suited me.

It turns out I'm much happier when someone else makes

the decisions and faces the harsh consequences of those actions. I can't help but feel like I'm doing everything wrong.

I lick my lips as I scan her body. She's wearing a light robe over what I hope is nothing. Would that be too much to ask? Is that something I should even be wishing for?

"I want to feel . . ." Gods, what is wrong with me? Why can't I just tell her what I want? I never have trouble just coming out and saying it.

"I want to see what's under there," I finally say, and her eyes light up.

She looks down at herself, touching the collar and sliding her fingers along the incredibly soft silk. But I doubt it's as soft as her skin.

"Oh, you mean this?" she asks as she plucks at the tie that circles her waist, giving me a coy smile.

"That's probably inappropriate," I say.

"Is it? Why?"

"Fuck. I don't know," I say. "I'm trying to be responsible or something."

She grins. "Even the most responsible kings are allowed a little indulgence."

"I'm not a king," I remind her.

"No, but you're carrying the burdens of one."

Good point. She pulls on the ribbon holding her robe together, and for a brief, sparkly moment, I'm the happiest Fae in all of Ouranos.

It turns out she *is* wearing something underneath, but the pinch of my disappointment isn't too sharp because the nearly translucent scraps of underwear are the next-best thing. As I imagine what they're concealing, I decide this might be even better.

She stands up from the divan, and I drink her in, noting the way the sheer fabric reveals her tight pink nipples and the smoky darkness between her thighs.

She allows me a moment to enjoy the sight—she knows exactly what she's doing—before she places a hand on each side of my head and brackets my knees. The position gives me an eyeful of every soft curve and line, the lushness of her hips and her breasts, and I want to sink my teeth into her soft, creamy flesh.

"How's this?" she asks. "Does this help?"

"A little," I say with a sly smile.

I feel a fuckton better, but I want more.

"Oh?" she asks, then plants one knee on the cushion next to my hip and then her other before she hovers just above me, maintaining a sliver of space between us. The heat of her pussy immediately filters through the fabric of my pants, where my cock is already hard.

"How about this?"

"This is . . . good," I say.

"What else do you want? What else would ease this stress, Gabriel?"

"I want to touch you."

She looks at my hands sitting obediently on the cushions, and laughs. This woman is pure sin and seduction. Even her laugh shoots straight to my stomach, stirring up wells of emotion I thought were long dead and buried.

"Then touch me," she coos. "Wherever you like."

I don't wait to be told twice, my hands clamping on to her thighs as I slide them down. She's just as soft and warm as she looks.

"Sit down," I tell her because her pussy is just barely touching my now throbbing cock, and it's making me crazy. "I need to feel you."

She laughs again, but she obliges, heat spreading through my groin and over my hips as we both sigh. Her eyes twinkle. "I've wanted to do this for a while."

Those words surprise and thrill me in equal measure.

"Me too," I say, and she leans in close, pressing her breasts to my chest.

"Where else do you want to touch me?" she asks. "Surely my knees aren't the subject of your fantasies?"

With a grunt, my hands slide back up, settling into the creases of her hips.

"Do you need me to draw you a map?" she teases.

I growl low in my throat. "I assure you I don't need a map."

"Then what are you waiting for, Captain?"

My inhale is ragged as I slide my hands inwards, my thumbs sweeping over the damp fabric of her underwear. She lets out a breathy sigh that nearly makes me come in my pants. Fuck. I'm like a horny teenager.

I tease the edge of the lace as she starts to squirm, creating excruciating friction. My chest loosens, and I let out a sigh weighted with relief. This was what I needed. A bit of skin and someone who doesn't expect me to be anything other than who I am.

My fingers slide under the fabric, where I find her molten

heat, and I let out a shudder that makes gooseflesh erupt over my entire body. She peers down at me, licking her lips as I circle her clit, drawing out a breathy moan.

"Sir!" An urgent voice blasts through my thoughts.

We both look over at the interruption. A guard stands in the doorway, and his eyes widen before he looks down with his hands behind his back.

"Captain, I was sent to find you," he says to his feet.

"What is it?" I snap. I can't get a fucking break around here.

"Captain, the low fae have breached the palace walls and demand an audience with the king."

"Great," I mutter.

Hylene slides off me and retrieves her robe before we rush through the hallways as thunder claps overhead. Clouds roll in, the weather changing swiftly. I try not to take that as an ominous sign.

We emerge into the front courtyard, where torches illuminate the darkened evening, casting the world into razor-sharp shadows.

The kind where demons lurk and the ruin of a kingdom waits.

Hundreds of people gather outside the palace walls, chanting into the night. Dozens more have flooded through gates ripped off their hinges, pressing against the line of Aphelion soldiers attempting to hold them back. They're calling for the king, their voices high and fever pitched, their arms stretched towards the palace as if trying to brush it with their fingertips.

The sight is chaos, bodies churning and writhing, and for a moment, I can't move. I can't breathe. My training never prepared me for anything like this.

I catch sight of two guards parting to let someone through before Erevan stumbles past the line. My jaw clenches. I should have known he was responsible for this.

A guard strides next to Erevan as he approaches, a hand on his sword, ready to take Erevan down should he make any suspicious movements.

"Captain," he says. "The rebel leader asked to speak with you."

"Erevan," I say. He's rumpled, his clothes askew, and his blond hair hanging in his eyes. "What is this? What are you doing?"

"They want justice. They want what they deserve."

I shake my head, my hands spreading wide.

"I don't know what you want me to do," I say. "They want justice from Atlas, but he isn't here to offer it."

"Then let us meet with Tyr," he says. "Have him repeal the laws and answer for his brother's crimes."

My jaw clenches, and our gazes meet. "You know I can't do that."

"Why not?"

"Because Tyr cannot repeal the laws on his own, and he can't have this conversation." I stop myself from explaining further. Erevan has seen Tyr. He has to understand that he can't deal with this.

"He is still the king, Gabriel. No matter what happened, these people are still his duty."

"I know that," I snap. "But it's not possible right now."

"Then when? They won't be placated any longer. They demand and deserve justice."

He flings a finger behind him, where the crowd pulses, arms raised, their chants swelling into the air. The line of soldiers continues to struggle against the crowd when a frantic scream rises above the cacophony, drawing our attention.

A group of low fae and soldiers have converged in the middle of the mess, clashing as they fight. Screams and shouts and someone yelling, "Stop! You're trampling her!"

I brush past Erevan and storm over. "Stop this!" I shout. "Stop it now! I order you!"

Everyone continues to shove and push while I thrust myself into the center of the tangle. "By command of the king, stand down!" I shout louder this time, and finally, they take notice. Someone is screaming and sobbing, and the crowd parts to reveal a small body on the ground covered in blood with someone crying over them. It's hard to tell, but I think it's an elf. Everyone stares, paused in the stillness of shock.

I whirl around to face Erevan, pointing at the dead elf. "Is this what you wanted?"

Erevan has gone pale, his jaw slack.

"Tell them to move out," I snarl. "We will deal with this. I swear to you they will be heard, but I need time. Tyr needs time, and we need to find Atlas." I drag Erevan towards me and force him to look at the dead elf. "Don't make this worse."

Finally, Erevan stirs out of his daze and nods, lifting a hand. It takes a moment for others to notice the signal filtering through the crowd. He looks at me, dark circles under his eyes, his expression more lost than I can ever remember.

"Erevan," I say into his ear, using a low voice. "If Tyr chooses to descend, then you understand what must happen. I know you don't want this but—"

He lifts his hand, cutting me off.

"I'll deal with this," he says, refusing yet again to talk about his destiny. The one the Mirror chose for him that fateful day a century ago. "But this is a warning, Gabe. You can't keep ignoring them much longer."

Then he tugs on his jacket and strides away, passing through the line of guards. He shouts a few words to the watching low fae, and it's a measure of just how much they respect him that they slowly follow, carrying the body of the elf with them, filing out as they cast wary glances in my direction.

"Repair and then fortify the gate," I say once they're all gone. "And double the wall guard."

"Yes, sir," answers a soldier as they move into action. I watch for a moment, conscious of so many eyes on me. Hylene stands beside me with her patient presence, but I'm far too aware these soldiers under my command must be questioning everything I'm doing.

Then I spin around and am once again caught off guard by the sight of two figures I thought I'd never see again.

"Lor? Nadir?" I ask. Behind them are Mael, Amya, and Lor's siblings, along with more guards, who've obviously brought them in through another entrance.

"Hey," Lor says with a wave. "Looks like you've got your hands full here."

They all look like shit. Like they've been chewed up and spit back out, their clothes torn and all in need of a bath or five.

"What the hell happened to you?" I ask.

Nadir and Lor exchange a wary look.

"That's a bit of a long story," she says. "Maybe we should go inside and talk once you've dealt with things out here."

I run a hand down my face as raindrops begin to patter against the ground. I look past the wall where the crowd still mills, but they seem settled enough. We've averted disaster for one more day. But just barely.

"I guess you better come inside," I say to Lor.

We enter the palace and make our way towards the king's study.

"How did you find each other?" I ask, gesturing to the entire group.

"We ran into one other in a village a few days' travel from here," Lor says. "It was kind of a miracle."

"Where were you coming from?" I ask.

"Alluvion," Lor says, and then adds, "Kind of. Also, the Evanescence."

My eyes almost bulge out of my head at that. "What do you mean the Evanescence? Like *the* Evanescence?"

"We'll try to explain everything," she replies, exchanging another look with Nadir. It's clear these two have been through something incomprehensible.

Finally, we arrive at the study, and everyone gathers in the room. Lor and Nadir stand at the front with their hands clasped as they address me, Hylene, and Tyr. It's obvious the others know this story, but they wait patiently as Lor and Nadir take turns explaining everything.

She chokes on her words, and it's clear how much strain she's been under. After she reaches the end of her tale, she falls silent before Nadir fills in his half. It's a wild story that gets weirder by the moment, and if it were anyone else, I might question the truth of their words.

But it was obvious from the first time I met Lor that she was no ordinary prisoner.

"How did you get Zerra to stop attacking?" I ask.

Lor shakes her head. "I'm not sure. Once Nadir and I moved into the forest, it stopped." She exchanges a worried glance with Nadir that I can't parse out.

"I'm not sure what else to say other than what the fuck?"

"I know," Lor says. "There's something else."

"What else could there possibly be?" Hylene chimes in.

"I kind of stole the arks from Zerra," she says, and Nadir digs into his pockets, tossing the lot on the table. The dark rocks imbued with silver sparkles clink together, and I stare at them in disbelief.

"I stole Alluvion's, but I can't do that to you. I should never have done it to him either, but I was desperate," Lor continues.

"I don't know where the ark is," I say.

Lor's shoulders drop. "I was afraid you'd say that. Everything we've learned suggests that only the ascended have knowledge of the arks."

Every eye in the room falls on Tyr, and as if sensing our scrutiny, he looks up.

Hylene maneuvers herself across the room, then drops to a crouch and takes his hand. She whispers something in his ear, and though his face remains expressionless, he dips his head.

"The ark," he says in that soft, thin voice that breaks my heart every fucking time. "Of course. I know where it is."

CHAPTER 34

LOR

The relief that expands in my chest at Tyr's words almost makes my legs collapse out from under me.

Hylene smiles and strokes his hand. "Can you show us?" she asks softly, and Tyr nods.

Then, with obvious difficulty, he heaves himself up from his seat. It's clear it's a struggle, his movements dragging in slow motion like he's been submerged in cold tree sap. My eyes burn with tears at the sight of him. I don't know him, but I can't imagine what kinds of horrors he must have suffered under Atlas.

Tyr hobbles to the edge of the room and stops in front of the bookcase near the window. That's when I spot it. Sitting right out there in the open like just another random object on a shelf.

Though maybe I'm being a little unfair because it *is* encased in glass, clearly meant to protect it. Tyr looks at it and then walks over to the desk, where he picks up a dagger lying on the surface. He lifts his hand and slashes his palm. A line of blood swells to the surface.

"Tyr!" Gabriel shouts, already moving towards him. "What are you—"

Tyr holds up the bloodied hand and shakes his head.

"It's okay," he says softly. Tension vibrates in Gabriel's frame. He wants to do something. He's worried about Tyr, and I wonder about their relationship. How long have they known one another? He is *Tyr's* warder. He never really belonged to Atlas.

Then Tyr shuffles back to the shelf and presses his hand to the glass case. The front pops open, allowing access to the ark.

"Only I can open it," he says before reaching in and taking it out.

"But that's . . ." Gabriel says, staring at the ark. "Isn't that the object used to create the warders?"

"It is," Tyr says. "The Mirror explained the process when I ascended..." He shakes his head as his voice trails off. He makes his way back to me holding the ark to his chest. I look at Nadir, who's watching the Sun King.

"I want you to take it," Tyr says. "Please."

"Just like that?" I ask. I'd kind of expected I'd have to plead my case a bit more or, if worse came to worst, stuff away my conscience and steal this one, too.

Tyr draws a ragged breath. "The Warders were a mistake. This was a mistake," he says, gesturing to the ark. His voice is filled with apology as he looks at Gabriel.

"If there's anything the last one hundred years have taught me," Tyr says, "it's that no one should ever be forced to carry out the bidding of another."

Gabriel swallows heavily, though his posture remains erect.

"However, before I hand it over, I must do one last thing. Will you allow me that?"

I nod because I think I already sense what he's about to say.

"It is time to free them, once and for all."

"Other than a warder's own death, the only escape from the warder bond is his king's death, but that kills the warder too," Gabriel says, his voice dead like he's recited the words a thousand times.

Tyr dips his head, acknowledging his words.

"That is true," he says. "*Or* I can choose to free you with this."

He holds up the ark.

"I'm sorry," he says, tears filling his blue eyes. "I should have done this so long ago."

So many emotions cross Gabriel's face—sadness, anger, confusion. And a profound sense of loss. Atlas could have chosen to free them at any point.

"Thank you," he says, dropping his head either out of respect or in an attempt to hide the tears that I'm pretty sure he doesn't want anyone to see.

"Do not thank me," Tyr says. "If I had never allowed this tradition to continue, then nothing Atlas did would have been possible. I am as much to blame for all of it."

"No," Gabriel says. "Don't do that. Just because someone has power doesn't mean they have to use it."

Those words strike something deep in my chest. I think about the destructive power of my magic and realize how true they are.

"Do you know how to do it?" Nadir asks.

Tyr shakes his head. "I know some of it, but I will speak with the Mirror while we wait for the others to return. It's time I make some decisions anyway."

Everyone in the room is silent, their eyes on Gabriel, who seems to be two seconds away from falling apart.

"I'm going to . . ." He shakes his head. "I'm just going."

Then he abruptly spins on his heel and stalks out of the room.

I don't know why I do it. Gabriel and I have always had a complicated relationship, and maybe I'm the last person he wants to see right now, but I bolt for the door.

"Excuse me," I say before I follow Gabriel, running to catch up. His steps are sure and quick, and he ignores me as I fall in next to him. I have to jog-walk to keep pace with his long legs.

I open my mouth, but he cuts me off.

"Don't," he says. "I don't want to talk about it."

"About what?" I ask as he gives me a side-eyed glare. "Oh, you mean the whole prisoner to your king thing?" I raise a hand and mime buttoning my lips shut.

"Totally not what I was going to ask you about," I say, and he gives me another skeptical look. "I mean, I don't really care, you know?"

Of course, I don't mean that, but my answer seems to shake something loose, his shoulders and his wings dropping and the tightness around his mouth easing.

"Then what do you want, Final Tribute?"

"You know, you could stop calling me that," I say. "I am literally a queen."

Gabriel snorts. "I don't see a crown on your head."

I can't help the smile that creeps onto my face, and I swear I catch the faintest hint of amusement in his eyes. There's something so normal and nostalgic about this moment that my chest tightens with acute longing for our surroundings to settle into a simple and normal place.

"Don't you dare fucking cry," he says. "Or I'm sending you back."

"How dare you? I don't cry."

That finally earns me a quirk of his mouth.

"You still haven't answered why you're following me like a stray kitten."

"I just wanted to know that you're okay," I say, bringing him up short.

"Why? I've been a dick to you since the day we met."

I shrug. "You really have, but . . ."

"Lor . . ."

I reach out and grab his arm. "I understand now how much pressure you were under. How little control you had over everything and that your personality isn't all your fault."

It takes him a moment to realize I've just insulted him, but that elicits a dry laugh before he keeps walking. I scurry along. The hallways are all dimmed with low light, devoid of the parties and music I remember during my first stay inside the Sun Palace. I wonder where everyone is. From what the others told us, there have been constant riots and fighting in the weeks since we've been gone.

Where have all the rich nobles run to? Their homes in the city? Or further away, where none of this can touch them?

"Where are we going?"

"*I'm* going to send a message to my brothers," he answers. "I don't know where *you're* going."

I ignore that comment, keeping pace with him as we wind through the palace until we reach an aviary filled with carrier doves. He opens a wooden box attached to the wall and retrieves a slip of paper and a pen.

With a gesture for me to follow, we open a gate and step out onto a balcony. White doves sit in cages behind us, cooing softly. The vantage offers a view of Aphelion and the miles of farmland and forest beyond.

"Where are your brothers right now?" I ask.

He shakes his head as he writes on the paper. "They're closing in on him."

"What will you do if they find him?" Our gazes meet. I know the punishment for treason in Aphelion is execution. Is that what Gabriel has planned? I suppose he's not technically in charge, but he does seem to be the one everyone is going to with their questions.

The look on his face tells me that he knows what I was about to say and that the same thing has been weighing on his mind.

"What are you planning to do with him, Gabriel?"

He shakes his head. "I don't know."

He runs a hand through his hair and peers into the distance. "It was all going to come down eventually."

"You did the right thing," I say. "In case you were wondering."

He squeezes his eyes shut. "I don't know if I did. The city is in chaos."

"Because of what Atlas did, not you."

"Thanks," he says, though I can tell he doesn't really believe me.

"You deserve answers from him," he says, and I blink. "If anyone does, you're at the top of that long list." He inhales and runs a hand down his face. "I know some of the reasons, Lor. Before everything went down, he shared some of them."

"Does it have anything to do with everything we just told you?" The more I learn, the more I'm sure Cloris's promises to Atlas are the source of Aphelion's current strife.

"Possibly, but I'm beginning to suspect he was led astray."

"I think I'd like to hear it from him," I say, and Gabriel dips his chin.

"That's fair. I hope you get that chance."

"I wish I'd known about all this during the Trials."

"Would it have made a difference?"

I grip the stone railing and lean back. "Maybe? For us?" I say, and that wins me a rare smile.

"I'm sorry I was such an ass," he says. "I didn't understand what you were doing there, and I was worried about Tyr."

I sense something in the way he says his king's name. I noticed it in the study, too. The way Gabriel looked at him.

"Were you two ever in love . . ." I venture, and he nods.

"A very long time ago. But that's over. How can we ever go

back after everything? He's seen me at my worst, and though I don't blame him for Atlas's actions, I'm not sure I'll ever be able to see anything else. How do we ever get past that?"

I think I understand what he means.

"Nadir's father killed my parents," I say, and Gabriel turns to me, his brow furrowing. "I spent so much time hating Nadir for that. I pushed him so hard, and even though I knew I felt something for him, I didn't want to."

I lean against the wall, placing my elbows on the ledge.

"But we found a way through it."

"You're mates. That's different."

I shake my head. "Even if we weren't, I'm sure we would have ended up here."

"Yeah. I don't think that's what fate has in store for us. That's not what I want anyway."

I nod and look across the horizon.

Gabriel scribbles a few more words onto the paper and then rolls it up. He opens a cage and retrieves a bird in one of his large hands.

"Would you mind?" he asks, holding out the roll. I tie it to the bird's ankle, and then Gabriel faces the wall, pausing with the pigeon clutched in his hands.

"What did you write to them?"

"To hurry home. That soon they will finally be free."

Then he lifts his arms and thrusts the bird into the sky, his wings ruffling softly. We both stand side by side, the breeze tossing our hair, watching until it disappears from view.

CHAPTER 35

RION

232 YEARS AGO

The letter dangled from Rion's fingertips, a missive on parchment sent to tear out his heart.

Rachel was dead.

After so many years of wondering where she was, he'd finally found her. Only it was too late to do anything with the knowledge.

She'd thrown in her lot with the wrong sorts of people. Gangsters who prowled the underground lairs of Tor, dealing in illegal trades of arcturite while also indulging in gambling and the skin trade, all of it conducted outside the confines of the law.

Rachel had been used as bait against a gang leader and taken as a hostage. When her side failed to deliver on their rivals' demands, they slit her throat. And that was it. She was gone.

Rion covered his eyes, his head hanging between his knees. His chest rattled with the uncomfortable weightiness of a heart that could never be put back together. His fingers were numb, and his stomach heaved like it was trying to turn itself out.

Rachel was dead.

He looked up, staring out the window, watching the lights ripple across the sky. Tonight, they brought him no comfort. Tonight, they left him feeling as empty as his soul.

He stood up and approached the window, pressing his forehead to the cool glass.

A tear, one long buried, slipped down his cheek. He couldn't remember the last time he'd wept. Probably when he'd been a child.

He turned away and walked to the bar cart, not bothering with a glass, as he picked up a full decanter and tipped the entire contents down his throat. He drank it too quickly to notice what it was. He didn't care. All he wanted was to numb this knifing pain searing through his limbs.

When he was done, he tossed the decanter aside, barely registering the shatter of glass as it hit the floor. He blinked, waiting several long seconds for the warmth of the drink to filter through his blood. His head swam, and he closed his eyes, trying to focus on remaining upright rather than the dull pain throbbing in his chest.

Rachel was dead.

What had he hoped for? Why had he clung to the idea that someday they'd find their way back to one another? He'd chosen his crown over her, but it had never filled the space she'd left. He wanted to hide away inside a deep cavern in the darkest recesses of the mountains. He expelled a long breath as his body curved inwards, trying to disappear into itself.

A joyful screech outside drew his attention, blasting through the headache already forming behind his eyes. Rubbing his temples, he sucked in a sharp breath when another squeal bounced against the inside of his skull.

He stormed across the room, whipping the door open.

Amya ran around in circles on her chubby little legs while Nadir chased her, pretending to trip as though he was having trouble keeping up. She squealed when Nadir finally scooped her up and peppered her with kisses.

Meora stood watching the scene with her hands clasped and a warm smile on her face.

Over the past few years, Rion had found it in himself to let her in, attempting to carve out a sliver of happiness with this family that he'd been given no choice but to accept. Though he'd never feel the way he had about Rachel, he'd found a corner of his heart where he'd allowed himself to release the hold on his rage.

He'd tried to make the best of it. Tried to forget what his heart truly wanted, but watching Meora now, that old anger bubbled to the surface, reminding him that this was not the life he wanted. Rachel should have been the one standing there looking over his family, healthy, safe, and whole.

All three stilled when they caught sight of Rion standing in the doorway, his frame hunched as he gripped the frame, the news of Rachel's death crumpled in his hand. Amya stared at him with big black eyes as he stalked towards Nadir.

"Give her to me. I'll play with her," he slurred.

"You're drunk," Nadir said, his voice cold.

"I'm fine." He reached for Amya, but she screamed, throwing herself against Nadir and wrapping her little arms around his neck.

"Amya," Rion said. "Come to your father."

He grabbed her by the waist, but she screamed louder, the sound echoing off the walls, making his head throb like a knife wedging into his brain.

"Amya!" he said, gritting his teeth. "That is enough."

He heaved her out of Nadir's hold, but she screamed and clawed and scratched him, her tiny hand gripping Nadir's shirt so hard her knuckles turned white.

"Na-eer!" she screamed. "Na-eer! I want Na-eer!"

Rion struggled with the girl as she squirmed like a slippery eel in his arms.

"That's enough!" Nadir said, his voice filled with venom. He pulled Amya away, and the girl folded herself around her brother, wrapping her legs and arms tight. "Leave her alone. Can't you see you're frightening her?"

Rion's nostrils flared as he stared at his children. They hated him. Both of them. He couldn't blame Nadir for his feelings—he'd been a terrible father—but Amya . . . Rion had thought Amya was a chance to try again. To fix the mistakes he'd made with his son. But she was only a toddler and already hated him too.

He looked over to where Meora stood, her mouth parted with surprise and her eyes wide. Gods, he hated *her*. Despite convincing himself otherwise, he still hated her as much as ever. When he saw her standing there staring at him with that *judgment* in her expression, he snapped.

He stormed over to Meora as the expression on her face morphed into terror. He seized her by the arm and started dragging her out of the room.

"Father!" Nadir shouted. "Stop this! Go back to your study."

Rion rounded on his son. "Don't fucking tell me what to do," he snarled, his words slurring into one long garbled string. Amya still clung to Nadir, where she peeked out from the safety of his arms before quickly looking away, burying her face into her brother's shoulder, her little body shaking with tears.

"Don't let him follow," Rion ordered a nearby group of guards, pointing at Nadir. "And if you *try* to follow, you can say goodbye to your mother once and for all."

He let the threat hang in the air as Nadir glared, his jaw hard.

"Come on," Rion said to Meora, spinning around and dragging her away, her feet tripping over each other.

"Father! Stop this!" Nadir's voice followed him, dogging his steps. Rion breathed out a sigh of relief as they turned a corner, putting his son out of reach.

They reached Meora's apartments, and he flung open the door to her bedroom.

"Rion! I'm sorry!" she cried. "I'm sorry."

What was she apologizing for? Did she understand anything?

He shoved her hard enough that she tripped, landing on the bed. She flipped over to face him as he stood above her.

"You will remain here from now on, out of my sight, unless royal duty requires otherwise."

Then he spun around and stormed out of the room, followed by her sobs.

As he stalked down the hall, Nadir appeared at the end, still holding Amya.

They passed one another, their exchange filled with loathing, neither one saying a word.

The look in his children's eyes would have been enough to shame any decent man into some kind of remorse, but Rion had never been a decent man.

CHAPTER 36

LOR

The next morning, I'm having breakfast with Nadir, Willow, Mael, and Amya in a Sun Palace suite. Gabriel said we are welcome to stay as long as we need. Hearing that we were back in the city, Nerissa also arrived last night. I sit on the edge of the bed with Nadir while the others find chairs around the room.

I feel a certain way about sitting here in this gilded castle, surrounded by guards, while the citizens of Aphelion battle in the streets, but right now, this can't be our fight. I can't lose sight of the fact that the Aurora King is up to something nefarious and that the world around us is crumbling.

My magic is back, which means that I must once again confront the Heart Crown.

Tristan knocks on the door and enters with his pack in his hand. He places it on a table in front of the large fireplace, and we all watch him pull out a bundle of fabric and unwrap it, revealing the Crown.

When we made the trek back to Aphelion, Tristan shared that he had it with him. I nearly broke down in relief at discovering it hadn't landed in Rion's hands after all.

"I can't believe you carried it with you," I say. "What if something had happened to it?"

"We thought you might need it," Willow answers.

"It was safer with us than here," Mael adds.

I nod because they're probably both right.

"Besides," Tristan adds as he holds it up. "I think it actually led us to you."

"What do you mean?"

"I can't explain it exactly, other than I kept having a sixth sense of what direction to go. And then . . . we found you. I think it was trying to get back to you."

The Crown sparkles in the sunlight filtering through the windows. The red jewel is so deep and vibrant that it's almost hard to look at.

I feel its presence immediately.

It looks different because it *is* different. *I* am different.

"It's awake," I whisper.

Nadir lays his hand on my knee. "Lor?"

"I can feel it."

I press my hand to my chest, thinking of the way it called

to me in the Heart Castle with that thrumming vibration in my bones. I felt it the whole way back to Aphelion while it sat in Tristan's pack traveling next to me, but I asked him not to show it to me yet because I wasn't ready to face the disappointment if it still refused to acknowledge me.

The feeling has shifted, too. It's brighter and clearer. Much like my magic, it was muted, but now it glows with the full force of its brilliance.

"It's definitely awake," I say again, and Tristan gives me a look that tells me he understands what I'm going through. I think he might be the only person in the world who truly does.

"Then you need to talk to it," he says, holding it out to me.

I place my cup of tea on the side table and wipe my palms on my thighs before I reach out and accept it with both hands. The moment my fingers touch the cool metal, a surge of lightning twitches under my skin.

This is nothing like my connection with the other Artefacts.

This Crown is a part of who I am.

Nadir wraps an arm around my shoulders.

"Take your time," he says, but I shake my head.

"I . . . don't want to. I've been waiting for this for so long."

He gives me a crooked smile. "Then go for it, Heart Queen."

I inhale a sharp breath, watching the faces around the room.

"We'll be here to protect you," Willow says.

"This is probably going to change everything," I say.

"Probably," she agrees.

"But you should be used to that by now," Mael says, and I snort out a laugh.

Then I place the crown on my head and close my eyes.

This time, there is no pause. There is no delay.

Immediately, I'm sucked into a whirling void, my heart leaping into my throat, and then I land, collapsing into a heap on a surface of pure white stone.

This, too, is different. This is no shapeless void spreading into nothing. I'm in a garden bursting with thousands of red roses, and my chest twists.

I am home.

I take in my surroundings for another few seconds before I push up to stand. The sky is a wash of pure blue dotted with fluffy clouds, the sun a perfect yellow sphere. Roses. Roses bloom in every direction as far as I can see. A white stone path interspersed with benches along the sides stretches before me, and my breath catches when I notice a figure standing in the distance.

"Hello?" I ask as the figure approaches. I see it's a woman with long black hair wearing a sweeping red gown. Her dark eyes burn with emotion, and my heart wedges in my throat as she draws nearer, tears misting my eyes.

It's been so many years, and I was a child the last time I saw her, but her face lives in my memories and . . .

It's my mother.

"Lor," she says, stopping a few feet away with her hands clasped at her waist. "I've been waiting for you."

I open my mouth, but no sound comes out. My fingers and toes have gone numb, and my cheeks are warm. I don't know how to react.

She takes a step closer and then spreads her arms as tears

slip down my cheeks. Before I know what I'm doing, I trip towards her, collapsing against her as her arms wrap firmly around me.

"Mother," I whisper, my heart tying into knots. "Mother."

"Lor," she answers as she rubs the back of my head, and I sob into her shoulder. Inhaling deeply, I'm transported to a small cottage in the woods and the scent of her sweet buns that I loved to help make. And the unmistakable smell of roses. I always wondered why she smelled like that, but now I understand what it meant.

A thousand memories flood back with such clarity that it makes my head hurt. My mother tucking us in at night. Singing us lullabies even though she couldn't carry a tune. I remember the sunlight reflecting off her dark hair as she hung the sheets to dry in the backyard. The way she'd laugh when my father would chase us around her, nearly upsetting the basket of clean laundry. I remember her soft touch and her soft voice. I remember how she made me feel safe. And loved. Most importantly, she made me feel loved.

But I also remember her face as our father shoved us into that underground cellar when Rion's army arrived. I remember the necklace she always wore, the red jewel reflecting in the light as she unhooked it from her neck and pressed it into Willow's hands, making us promise we'd keep it safe. I remember the sounds of her screams as she was taken from our lives.

"Mother," I gasp as I sob and sob. "I miss you so much."

"I miss you too, my baby," she says, stroking the back of my head. "You have no idea how much."

"How are you here?" I ask, finally pulling away to study

her face. I'm taller than her now, and she looks so much like me and my siblings. I remember the freckles that dusted her cheeks and the light brown slivers in her eyes. That tiny mole on her earlobe.

Suddenly, I remember everything.

"I have much to share with you," she replies. "When you're ready."

I scrub my eyes with the back of my hand.

"I don't know if I'm ready for anything else," I say.

She gives me a sad smile. "I can understand that."

She directs me to a bench, and we settle on it. I have so many questions and don't know where to start.

"I'm sorry I didn't tell you more about who you are," she starts. "I thought I'd have more time, and you were so young. I didn't want to frighten you. I thought . . ."

She shakes her head. "I thought I'd have more time."

"How much do you know?" I ask. "About us now?"

"Only some things," she answers. "Tell me, what happened after we died?"

I take a deep breath. "Are you sure you want to hear? It's not . . . pretty."

She clutches a hand to her heart. "My children's pain will always be mine, too, Lor. I knew that from the moment I laid eyes on your brother. It is the lot of a mother to wear her heart outside of herself from the moment her children are born."

"Okay," I say, again laying out my truth.

And this time, it *is* the truth. I give her everything. Every ugly moment and every secret I know. She accepts it all with stoicism, but I see the pain that passes behind her eyes.

She doesn't ask me to stop. She doesn't ask for anything but the cold, unvarnished truth.

When I'm done speaking, I feel like I've been talking for hours, my throat hoarse and sweat beading on my forehead. She started crying a while ago, quiet tears running down her face.

"I'm so sorry, Lor. I wish..."

I take her hand and squeeze it. "No. Let's not do that. Let's not make this anyone's fault but those who caused all of this. I admit I've spent time being angry with you for leaving us all in the dark, but I understand it, too. I love you, and I miss you, and I don't want to spend whatever time we have here debating who was right or wrong. I know that you did your best."

The words come out in a rush, and the look she gives me nearly breaks my heart. She touches my cheek in the way only a mother can and smiles.

"I knew you would grow up to be someone remarkable, Lor. I knew your heart was always as big as the sea. Even when you seemed intent on making foolish decisions, you'd always find a way to come back from them."

I can't help the tears that continue to fall. They come in coursing, endless waves, channeling every moment that I've missed this woman with every piece of my heart. She wraps me in her arms as I cry and cry, giving everything to my mother, who couldn't be there to comfort me through the years. They wash away a darkened slice of my soul that I thought was broken forever, her love and her touch healing over scabbed wounds scratched deep under the surface.

It is a cleansing. A rebirth. But I already know I won't be allowed to keep her forever.

As I cry, she cries too, and after a while, we finally pull away again.

"What are you doing here?" I ask, and my mother shakes her head.

"I come on behalf of the first Heart Queen of the Second Age, Amara."

"You do? Why? Where have you been?"

"She thought it might be better to hear it all from me," she says. "And I've been with your father."

"Is he here too?" I ask, hope flaring in my chest, but she shakes her head.

"Alas, it could only be us. A former Primary and her future."

"Oh," I say, trying not to let that disappoint me too much. My mother is here, and that's more than I ever dreamed possible.

"Where is he? Where have you been?"

"We were granted passage into the Evanescence upon our deaths," my mother says. "The Artefacts agreed that while I never ascended, they would still afford us that honor."

I remember what Cedar and Elswyth said when we were in The Woodlands, realizing this explains why they never found our parents' bodies. Though Tristan and I fantasized for a brief second that they might be alive, the truth is actually comforting, because they deserved this as their resting place.

"Why?" I ask.

"Because of you, my girl," she says. "While my destiny as the Heart Queen was never meant to be, it lives on in you."

"That's kind of what Coral told me."

She nods. "The magic lives inside you."

"But if I don't ascend or have a child of my own, then it will be lost forever," I say, repeating what Coral told me. "Then Heart will die."

My mother nods. "That is the message Amara sends as well."

"I can't bring a child into this. Besides, I don't think we have that much time."

"I think you may be right," my mother says.

"What did you mean that it might be better hearing it from you?"

Her lips press together.

"I've been sent not only to offer some clarity about past events but also to warn you."

"Warn me?"

"Zerra knows the Empyrium seek a replacement."

My mother's gaze slides to me, the expression on her face clear.

"And she knows it's me," I say, finally confirming what Nadir and I already suspected.

"She has sought to kill you," my mother says. "And she will stop at nothing to do so."

I rub my face. "Yeah, I was kind of getting that from the fireballs falling from the sky."

My mother smiles. "I've missed that dry sarcasm."

I laugh. "I don't think you enjoyed it much when I was twelve."

She laughs too. "Being your mother wasn't always easy, but I knew that ferocious spirit would do you well in the end."

"So what do I do about her?"

"You will need to . . ."

"Kill her before she kills me?" I ask, and my mother nods.

"Can't the Empyrium just take care of her?"

"It may be some time before they return," she says. "They do not experience the days and weeks the same way you do on the surface. And by then . . ."

I mimic slicing a knife across my throat.

"So how do I kill her? Please don't say the arks."

"The arks," my mother replies immediately, and I groan.

"Well, the good news is that I kind of stole most of them."

My mother exhales a surprised laugh and shakes her head. "For some reason, I'm not surprised to hear that."

My answering smile is rueful.

My mother inhales. "Most?"

"I don't have the ark of Heart. It's with the Aurora King."

My mother winces. "You'll need it, Lor. And you'll need each respective ruler to destroy their ark. Only the king or queen, or possibly their Primary, will have the strength to destroy it. If they are unbonded, they may still require the help of their Primary."

I drop my head into my hands.

"Oh, sure. No big deal. We'll just invite them all to a tea party and ask really nicely."

My mother rubs my back, her touch soothing. "I'm sorry that you must be the one to shoulder this burden. None of this was your fault."

"It's kind of what I expect at this point." I push out a breath from my mouth. "What if I just ascended before the Empyrium took me? Could I save Heart?"

My mother shakes her head, apology in her eyes. "You would still require an heir to pass the magic on to before they took you. You'd simply be delaying the inevitable. Plus, Zerra is an integral part of the ascension process, and it would make you vulnerable to her, giving her a chance to strike."

I scrub my hands over my face. There are roadblocks in every direction I turn.

"There is one more thing," my mother says, hesitating.

"Oh gods, what else?"

"It's not a bad thing. At least, I don't think it is."

I arch an eyebrow.

"Queen Amara is rather certain that for you to have the strength to destroy the ark of Heart, *you* must be bonded, as you do not have a Primary yet."

"Right," I nod. "I suppose that makes sense."

"The magic of Heart has always been the strongest, and as magic is channeled into virulence, it grows stronger to the point that the ark of Heart is nearly indestructible." She spreads her hands in a helpless gesture. "What I can offer you is the knowledge that you will be vulnerable to Zerra's sight when you're near an Artefact unless you're shielded by a large quantity of virulence to counteract it."

That explains how Zerra saw us in the village and why she stopped attacking when Nadir and I moved away from Tristan and the Crown. And also why she could see me when I carried only the ark of Alluvion—it wasn't enough to hide me. I think about the Aurora Keep, made entirely of virulence. Was Herric trying to hide from her?

"Interacting with the surface also weakens her," my mother

adds. "In fact, it's extremely difficult for her to do so, especially now. So it may be some time before she can act again, which is why you must move swiftly."

I groan and lean back, staring at the sky, wondering how everything got so royally fucked-up. Then I look at my mother, who watches me carefully.

"What if she succeeds?" I ask.

"Then the land will continue to react, growing worse and worse unless the Empyrium return to choose another. She is becoming too weak."

"And we have no idea when they'll be back," I say, and my mother takes my hand and squeezes it. "Is there any way to avoid becoming Zerra when they do return? I don't want this. If I manage to destroy the arks, then I want to go home."

My mother shakes her head, her lips pressing together. "Amara confirms it must be a king, a queen, or a Primary. Only they will have the strength to act as the conduit for the Artefacts. But only *you* can save Heart, which is why she sent me."

I chew on the inside of my cheek as I consider that. If it must be a ruler or a Primary, that leaves only a handful of people in Ouranos for the job. And I can't ask anyone else to shoulder this burden for me. I can't even tell anyone this. If Tristan or Nadir knew, they might try to take it on themselves to save me, and I could never live with that.

"So the Artefacts want me to somehow do both?" I ask. "Satisfy the Empyrium *and* save Heart?"

My mother grimaces. "Or find another way."

"But you can't tell me what that might be?"

She shakes her head slowly. "I'm sorry."

I bark out a wry laugh and then drop my head in my hands before I look up.

"Can't I just stay here with you forever?"

She gives me a soft smile. "While I would like that very much, I don't think it's possible." She takes my hand. "Besides, your brother and sister need you."

"I wish they could see you too."

"So do I," she says with such sadness that my heart twists.

"Tristan is a Primary," I say. "Of The Woodlands."

"So perhaps I'll see him someday."

I open my mouth to tell her that I don't want to leave.

"And your mate," my mother says. "He needs you too."

"I need him," I say. "But I might lose him."

My mother takes my hand and squeezes it. "I'm so happy you found someone who loves you so much, Lor. You deserve happiness in your life, and you will find a way through this. I believe in you, and I love you. I wish I could do more to help, but no matter how dark it gets before the end, never forget how much you were loved."

She lays her other hand against my cheek, and I press mine over it, savoring the warmth of her touch. My eyes close as I cry, clinging to her. A moment later, her hand disappears, and when I open them, she's gone.

I'm back in the Sun Palace with everyone staring at me. I blink, wiping away tears with the back of my hand.

"What happened?" Tristan asks. "Are you okay?"

I exhale a long, shuddering breath.

"I don't know . . . I saw our mother."

CHAPTER 37

NADIR

"What do you mean you saw our mother?" Tristan asks, his face pale with shock.

Lor twists her hands in her lap as she looks up at her brother. I wrap an arm around her shoulders, where she sits next to me on the bed.

"I'm sorry," she whispers as tears build in her eyes. "I—"

Willow stands up from her chair and strides over to sit on Lor's other side, taking her hand.

"What happened?" Her expression is so kind and understanding that my chest tightens.

Lor then recounts what she saw with the Crown.

I listen with swelling alarm. This is getting more and more complicated by the moment.

I found my mate through the most unlikely set of circumstances, and all I want is to disappear with her somewhere we can be alone to explore one another, where I can protect her. Everyone is trying to kill her or cage her, but they'll have to go through me first.

"So we have to go after Father," Amya says, and I can see what she's thinking. We always knew that it would come to this one way or another. Us against him. I remember every moment Amya and I confided in one another. One parent was absent, and the other was a monster. Even though I was a grown Fae by the time she was born, there are so many bleak moments we shared. It's taken me many years to admit it to myself, but there were so many times when he willfully made me feel like nothing more than a scared child.

"There's something else we need to do first," Lor answers, and I register the worried look on her face.

"Such as?" my sister asks.

She looks at me. "My mother said I'd have to bond to have enough power to destroy the ark."

I nod and blow out a sigh.

Do you think what Cloris told us is true? I ask.

You know it is.

"So you and Nadir will bond," Mael declares. "Why do both of you look like you're going to your funerals? Don't tell me we're still playing this 'Ooh, we don't want each other' game. You're fucking mates."

"Give us a little credit," Lor snaps, and the irritation in her voice makes me smile. "Of course we're not doing that anymore."

Lor turns to look at me. *Are you ready for this?* she asks in my thoughts.

I give her a half smile. *I've never been more ready for anything, Lor.*

We have to tell them.

We both turn to look at the others, and I guess it's time for us to come clean about this other hitch in our plans. Lor explains the complications with a mate bond between two Primaries and what happened with her grandparents.

"So if you two bond, you'll blow up half of Ouranos?" Willow asks, crestfallen at the prospect. "But you love each other."

"It's not all bad news," Lor says. "Apparently, it can be done with the right precautions."

"What precautions?" Amya asks.

"That *is* the bad news," I say. "We'll need to ask Cloris Payne."

"Well, fuck all of us," Mael says, echoing what we're all thinking.

"That crazy witch is still there," Amya says. When I raise an eyebrow, she adds, "I thought it would be a good idea to keep an eye on her, so I've had someone watching her."

"Good," I say. "That was good thinking. Thank you."

"You're planning to see her again?" Willow asks. "What if she's dangerous?"

"I don't think so," Lor says, chewing on her bottom lip. "I almost killed her once, and something tells me that if she were capable of overpowering us, she would have done so last time."

"I don't know," Tristan says. "That seems risky."

She holds up her hands. "What other choice do we have?"

Tristan's jaw hardens. We don't see eye to eye on much, but his sister's safety is one area we agree on.

"So we'll go see her," Lor says to me, "and then figure out what we need to do before we go after your father." She waits for my confirmation, and I reluctantly nod.

"And we also need to reach out to the other realms and convince them to destroy their arks," I say, amplifying the tension in the room. I'm not sure if they'll listen to us, but we have to make them see this is important for all of them. Maybe the only positive working for us is that there isn't an Aurora ark to destroy and we won't have to rely on Father for that.

Lor blows out a breath and runs a hand down her face.

"Alluvion will *not* help me after what I did."

I tip my head and consider. "Cyan isn't a fool. It's possible he can be reasoned with. And we aren't asking any of this for us. Not really."

Lor snorts out a dry laugh. "Not if you saw what I did to his palace." She drops her face into her hands and groans.

"I think we have to try," I say. "And while we're at it, perhaps one or two can be swayed into helping us beyond destroying the arks. We don't know what my father is planning, but I'm worried that it will be more than we can handle if we try to go in alone."

"Cedar promised us his allegiance," Tristan says, and I dip my chin because he's right about that. Tristan. Another Primary. I can see the longing in his expression. The desire to get to know the king he's intended to replace someday. I hope we can give him that chance.

"What about the queens of Tor and Celestria?" Amya asks.

Lor shakes her head. "I don't know. They knew I was lying too…"

"What about Aphelion?" Amya adds. "Do you think Tyr can…"

She trails off, and I fill in the words she doesn't voice.

"But we don't know if he can even use his magic anymore?" I ask, and she nods. "All good points. We'll discuss it with Tyr and then ask the others to meet with us. The heir of Heart has risen from the ashes despite every odd, and we can convince them to at least hear us out."

Lor gives me a worried look, and I squeeze her shoulder.

"Where do we meet them?" Tristan asks.

"Somewhere kind of neutral?" Amya asks.

"No," Lor says. "They need to see it for themselves."

"See what?"

"That the magic of Heart has returned. Whatever happens with both Rion and Zerra affects them, too. No matter their personal feelings for me or our grandmother, they must help us or risk losing so much more."

The corner of my mouth lifts up in a small smile. She's breathtaking when she's like this. All fierce determination and bravado. My queen who acted like a queen even when she was a far cry from one.

She looks at me. "Can you get a message to Etienne? Is there anywhere in Heart suitable for receiving the kings and queens of Ouranos?"

"I will right away," I say. "I'm sure there's something we can work with."

"Okay," Lor says with a firm tip of her jaw. "We ask them to meet us in one week. I don't think we can afford much more time than that."

"Agreed," I say.

"We'll see Cloris and find out what precautions are needed to complete the bond."

"And hope that whatever she says is the truth?" Mael adds.

"Right," I answer. "And isn't impossible to execute."

I see the uneasiness that flashes across Lor's expression, and I lean over to press a kiss against her temple. *We're going to figure this out one way or another.*

Don't worry, Lor, I say through our bond. *We'll fix all of this.*

She gives me a tight smile.

"So we have a plan," she says, clearly trying to put on a brave face.

I just hope any of it works.

CHAPTER 38

LOR

A low rumble rouses me from sleep as the room shakes. My eyes peel open, and the rumbling stops. Was I dreaming? I look at Nadir, who lies next to me, his face relaxed with slumber.

I sigh and roll back, staring up at the ceiling. After relaying everything I'd seen and learned, thanks to my mother, I didn't miss the expressions on Tristan's and Willow's faces when they realized what had happened and how much they wished they could have seen her too.

They both looked like she'd died all over again, and I knew there was nothing I could say to make it hurt less. I can't imagine what it would have been like to be in their shoes. I'm not sure I would have recovered. I wish so much I could have given them that moment.

Another rumble shakes the room, harder this time, vibrating through the bed, and now I'm sure I'm not dreaming. I reach over and shake Nadir's arm.

"Nadir, wake up," I say. It takes a moment for his eyes to slide open, and he stares at me with a small smile on his face.

"What's up, Lightning Bug?" he asks before he takes note of my expression. "What's wrong?"

Another rumble shakes the room, and he sits up.

"What do you think that is?" I ask.

Nadir runs his hand down his face. "I don't know, but I'm guessing we're in for another problem."

I slide out of bed and pad over to the window to stare out across the city of Aphelion. The early morning sun is rising, casting the world in golden light. Our room offers a view of the gilded buildings and streets and the ocean beyond.

Another rumble shakes the room, stronger than any before, enough to knock me nearly off-balance. I clutch at the brocade curtains to steady myself, and a moment later, I feel Nadir standing behind me.

"We should go find Gabriel," I say.

Just as I'm about to turn away from the window, something catches my eye. Another strong rumble shakes the entire room, and now, in the distance, I see it. The city is collapsing before our eyes.

I watch in horror as the edges along the shoreline start to crumble, the buildings falling against each other as they shatter. The glass muffles the roar that vibrates through the floor.

"Nadir," I whisper. "Is this Zerra?"

He stares out the window, witnessing the destruction, our foundations shaking so hard we cling to the glass before us. The room tips as the chandelier overhead tinkles with crystals knocking together. I jump when a pitcher falls off the nightstand and smashes against the floor, along with a tray full of glasses sitting on the table.

Nadir looks around us. "We should run for cover," he says.

"Where do we go?" I ask.

Nadir grabs my hand. "Under the bed."

We huddle underneath, and Nadir wraps his arms around my waist, pressing me against his strong chest as we wait for the rumbling to subside.

After what feels like forever, it finally stops. My ears ring with the weight of the silence.

What caused this? My first thought was Zerra, but does she have this kind of power? My mother said that interacting with the surface drains her for a while, so has she recovered from her earlier attack?

But this feels bigger than only her, and I'm sure this is another manifestation of the world crumbling beneath us. It *is* Zerra, not because she's causing it but because she continues to grow weaker and weaker. Whatever it is, we're running out of time on every side.

We ease out from under the bed and walk back to the window. I cover my mouth and gasp at the sight in the distance. A large chunk of the city has fallen prey to the earthquake, and dozens of buildings have toppled and been crushed beneath the weight of stone.

I shudder to think how many bodies are buried and how many lives were just lost.

"Let's get dressed," Nadir says. "We have to look for survivors."

Just as we are about to turn away, a loud crack draws our attention back to the window because this isn't over yet. The land splits apart like it's been shattered through its heart, a large crevice spreading wide. In a sluggish puff of smoke and shadows, dozens of buildings disappear with a roar.

I step back, my hand pressed to my chest, unable to believe what I'm watching. It takes only a few seconds, but it feels like hours before the dust settles again.

"No," I say, my voice a whisper. The chances of anyone surviving that are nothing.

"Let's go," Nadir says, crossing the room and finding a shirt and pants before tugging them on. I blink away the threat of tears and follow him, donning a pair of leggings and a tunic.

We fling open the door to find the palace has become a sight of chaos. The panicking servants must have friends and family living below. They're running back and forth, shouting orders and crying, many apparently at a loss for what to do.

We push past, knowing there isn't much we can do for them now, and emerge outside in the courtyard, where we find Gabriel, Mael, and Hylene already doling out orders.

"Look for survivors!" Mael shouts to a line of soldiers.

A row of palace healers wearing long robes with crosses on their chests stand at the ready.

"I can help," I say, holding up my hand. "With the injured."

Gabriel turns to scan me from head to toe as if doubting my claim.

"Don't look at me like that," I say. "I can help heal the survivors."

He rolls his eyes. "Well, I guess you can't inflict any more damage."

"Oh, well, thank you for that ringing endorsement," I snap. Our eyes meet momentarily before we both break into grins despite everything.

"I kind of missed you, Final Tribute," he says. "But don't let that go to your head. I'm under a lot of stress, and I'd miss a diseased ferret right now."

I press a hand to my forehead and pretend to swoon. "You always know just the right thing to say to me, Gabriel."

"Can you really help?" he asks, his expression turning serious now.

I nod. I think I can. I'm pretty sure. I was able to use my healing magic on Nadir without blowing anything up, and I think I can do it again. I hope. These people need me, and I have to try.

"I can help too," Tristan says, coming up next to me. "A little."

I look at him and then take his hand, squeezing it.

Gabriel turns to us both, his mouth opening and then closing.

"I literally don't understand anything anymore," he says, and then, with that cryptic statement, he turns on his heel and starts shouting orders. When he's several feet away, he turns to look at me and my brother. "Well? Are you two coming? We need to set up a temporary infirmary."

As Gabriel walks away, I turn to Nadir and take his hand. "What are you planning to do?" I ask.

"I'll help search for survivors," he says. "I can help shift some of the heavier rubble with my magic."

Then he pulls me in and wraps his arms around me tight. I know what he's thinking—we almost lost each other not that long ago, and everything around us is falling apart. We just need to hold on to each other a little bit tighter while the storm rages around us.

I kiss him, and then I turn around to follow Gabriel. He's walking away, Tristan falling in line beside me.

Behind us walk the other healers, everyone's posture straight with purpose. We all file into a room near the palace gates that's clearly used for medical purposes. A few small white beds line up against the far wall, and an array of silver metal cabinets stand against another.

The healers start opening them and pulling out supplies: bandages, ointment, needles, and thread—everything we might need. Without the magic of Heart, Aphelion's healers are dependent on these implements. The weight of this mission and its purpose flutters heavily in my stomach. I *have* to save the magic of Heart.

Someone thrusts a loaded box into my hands, and then, once everyone is armed, we start marching back out of the room and out through the palace. Gabriel says nothing, his shoulders hunched, his head low, and I can't imagine the stress he's under right now. I run up to walk next to him. "Hey, are you okay?" I ask.

He looks over at me and shrugs. "I don't have time to think much about that. I just have to keep going. You know?"

"Yeah, I know that so well, Gabriel."

He gives me a soft smile, and it's weird seeing him look at me like that. Like he's actually, maybe, a bit happy to have me around, even if I still annoy him.

We enter the city, marching through the streets surrounded by a contingent of soldiers. Up ahead, more healers and soldiers scurry about, setting up a big white tent in the middle of an open square. A line of people is already forming, everyone covered in cuts and bruises, some of them holding their arms, others limping on injured knees and ankles.

We don't have any beds, so we use sheets and blankets to create makeshift pallets on the ground as we begin the task of healing the survivors.

Over the next few hours, I use the second half of my magic. That soft, velvety ribbon feels dense and solid as I mend limbs, seal up cuts, and, in one case, repair an entire chest of broken ribs. I don't understand why I can control this side of my magic when the other is so difficult to contain.

It's hard work, and my brow beads with sweat. As I'm healing, I catch a few curious glances directed at me and Tristan. He's across the tent at another bedside, using his thinner vein of healing magic to smooth over cuts and bruises.

It's been a long time since anyone has experienced the healing magic of Heart. Many of them must have seen the red lightning when I destroyed the throne room, and I worry they'll reject us because of our grandmother, but they mostly seem grateful for our help.

I lose track of the hours until I notice the sun is starting to set. My stomach rumbles with hunger. They've been feeding us small bites of food, but I've been too busy to bother with much. I've been trying to keep myself hydrated, but that's about the extent of it.

Nerissa sits by a pallet next to Tristan, tending to a cut on a survivor's head, and he leans over and says something that makes her laugh. Tears burn my eyes at the sight, and I admonish myself. Now is not the time to lose myself in daydreams. *So he made a girl laugh. Get a grip, Lor. They aren't pledging undying love to one another yet.*

She finishes with her current patient and then leans down to plant a kiss on Tristan's cheek before she walks away to replenish her supplies. My brother's attention remains glued on her as she disappears through the crowd. When he looks back, our gazes meet. I smirk, and he glares until his expression turns into a sheepish smile before he shakes his head.

Turning away, I survey the helpers, noting how none of the nobles have made their way down here, content to remain in the palace and do nothing.

But then I spy Halo and Marici entering, wearing simple pants and tunics with their sleeves rolled up and their hair tied back. Halo spots me first.

"Lor!" she cries and runs over. We throw our arms around one another and hug tightly. "I heard you were in the palace. What are you doing here? How did everything go with the Mirror? We saw your magic. Was that really you?"

She's talking a mile a minute as Marici comes up beside her, and I hug her next.

"I'm back," I say. "And I took a little detour after I spoke with the Mirror." That's a mild understatement.

"Spoke with the Mirror?" Halo asks. "What does that mean?"

I blow out a breath. "I said I couldn't tell you everything before, but it's probably safe enough now." I scan our cluttered surroundings. "But maybe not here? We'll be leaving again soon, but I'd like the chance to talk."

"Of course," Marici says. "In the meantime, we came to see what help we could offer."

I look at them as tears burn the backs of my eyes.

They were my first two friends outside of Willow and Tristan. I reach out to grip their hands as a wave of melancholy washes over me. Why does it feel like this might be the first of many goodbyes?

"Did I ever thank you for being so nice to me during the Trials?"

They both exchange an uncertain look.

"We weren't, though," Halo says. "We were awful to you."

"You came around," I say.

"We don't deserve your thank-you. We should have been nicer to you from the beginning and never listened to that horrid . . ." she trails off, biting her tongue.

Like it or not, Apricia is still set to become her queen. Or is she?

"What happens to you now?" I ask. "With Tyr back?"

"I'm not sure," Halo says. "We're all kind of in limbo. I doubt he wants . . ."

"Yeah," I say. Tyr doesn't really seem to be in a mindset to bond to Apricia *or* run a kingdom.

"Anyway," Marici says. "What can we do?"

I set them to work and then return to my patient's bedside.

A while later, a heavy hand lands on my shoulder, and I look up to see Gabriel standing over me. His skin is pale, and the circles under his eyes are dark with worry.

"How is it out there?" I ask.

He shakes his head, disbelief written into every line of his face.

"Is this the thing you told us about? The magic?"

"Yeah," I reply. "I think so."

He sighs, rubs a hand along the back of his neck, and rolls his shoulders. "So there's no controlling this."

"Not yet," I say. "But I'm trying to figure this out."

"By replacing Zerra?"

"No," I say. "I am not doing that. I'll find another way."

He gives me a skeptical look, and guilt twists in my chest. I should want to do this for the good of Ouranos, shouldn't I? Am I being selfish? If it can only be another ruler or Primary, then why is my fight to remain free any more important than theirs?

Part of me doesn't care. Ouranos has never done anything for me or my family. Everyone sat by and let Rion torment us for over a decade, and then when I was finally released, I was thrust into a contest that nearly killed me. Everyone in Ouranos is trying to use me for their own ends. But that also isn't fair to the innocent people who've had nothing to do with any of this. It also isn't fair to the people of Heart—the only ones I truly need to be loyal to—if they lose everything.

"I'll find another way," I repeat, hoping that's true.

"Sir," a soldier says, coming up to Gabriel. "The tally is currently sitting at five hundred twenty-six dead and one thousand forty-two injured."

Those numbers make my blood run cold. So many people. Even one is too much. And that doesn't even account for those we lost in the chasm forever.

"Thank you," Gabriel says, his voice twisted with emotion.

The soldier bows and then walks away before Gabriel looks down at me. His eyes go to the man I'm trying to heal—a large gash sliced across his forehead. "Thank you for helping, Lor. After everything we did to you, you didn't owe Aphelion any more of yourself."

Then he spins on his heel and walks away, leaving me staring after him in shock.

Now I know the world *must* be ending because did he just say something nice?

CHAPTER 39

We spend the day and night helping clean up the wreckage. The city feels like it's dangling on the edge of a knifepoint. Rumors are spreading, and some of them are closer to the truth than anyone would like. Not that Gabriel is trying to keep this knowledge from anyone, but it might also cause a mass panic, and that's the last thing anyone needs.

The sun is rising on the following day when we all meet in the palace, occupying one of the large dining rooms where the cooks have been bringing in food on a regular rotation so the soldiers, healers, and anyone else on duty can stop in and grab something whenever they need.

Last night, I found a spare moment to catch up with Halo and Marici and revealed everything to them. They were as shocked as everyone else and only wished the best for me. I wish the best for them too and pray that if we come out the end of this, I will see them again.

Nadir and I now find ourselves in a quiet moment, sitting with Gabriel, Erevan, Tristan, and Mael. After the quake, the rebel leader appeared at the palace, and I watched from a distance as he sat in a serious conversation with Gabriel for a long time. When they were finished, Erevan remained here, helping deal with the aftermath.

Everyone is exhausted, and no one says much as we pick at our food and occasionally sip our drinks.

"We need to meet the other rulers in two days," Nadir finally says, looking at Gabriel. "We sent the missives just before the quake."

"We understand. Thank you for all of your help."

I exchange a look with Nadir. I feel terrible about abandoning them right now.

"I'm sorry," I say, but Gabriel waves me off. "If you really think this is a part of some bigger change in Ouranos, then you need to deal with it. This is only a minor thing compared to what might happen if it continues."

I nod and take a sip of my water. It's boiling hot in the room despite every window flung open to the breeze. The air is filled with smoke and ash, which does nothing but coat everything in a depressing layer of grey dust.

"The heat," I say. "According to the Empyrium, that's what happened to Aphelion last time."

I look around the room, half expecting Zerra to be standing there, smirking at me. If she didn't cause the quake, I'm still all too aware that she might strike again at any moment, which seems like a good reason to clear out of Aphelion as soon as possible. They've got enough on their hands.

"Can we talk about the ark?" I ask.

Gabriel shrugs his shoulders. "Tyr said you should have it. Who am I to argue with my . . . king?"

He keeps stumbling on that word.

I nod. "We actually don't want to take it anymore, but we do need him to destroy it with his magic," I say. "And since he's unbonded, he might need his Primary's help. In Tyr's case, it seems almost certain he would."

Gabriel stares at me before he sighs and rubs a hand down his face.

"Do you think he can?" Nadir asks. "When was the last time he used his magic?"

Gabriel shakes his head. "I couldn't tell you. Certainly not since before Atlas cuffed him."

"Do you think the arcturite affected his abilities?" Nadir asks.

As he and Gabriel discuss the implications of extended exposure to arcturite, my gaze slides to Erevan, who watches everyone with a guarded expression like he wants to escape through a window. Atlas isn't the Primary, so it must be someone else related to their family.

"Is it you?" I blurt out.

Erevan sits up straighter. "Me what?"

"Are you the Primary of Aphelion?"

Gabriel's gaze darts to Erevan and then back to me. "Lor—"

"Sorry. I don't mean to pry, but if Tyr can't use his magic anymore, then we might need your help."

Erevan's shoulders drop, and I sense he's been carrying a lot of weight on them for a very long time.

"I . . ." He sighs. "Yes. I am the Primary."

"You?" Nadir asks. "And Atlas knew?"

Gabriel nods. "The day the Mirror told Tyr, he ran straight to me and Atlas." He pauses. "That was the beginning of the end."

"How long have you known?" Nadir asks Erevan, leaning forward.

"Maybe all along," Erevan admits. "But Tyr told me right before Atlas . . . Well, before he did everything."

"What do you plan to do?" Nadir asks, and Gabriel and Erevan exchange a loaded look. I place my hand on Nadir's arm, indicating that maybe this is none of our business, even if I am the one who started it.

"I don't know," Erevan says, his words clipped. "I don't want to be a king."

A shuffle at the door draws our attention to Tyr, who stands beside Hylene, her hand gripped around his elbow. We all pass looks around the circle, wondering how much he heard.

Gabriel stands up. "Tyr . . . I'm sorry. I . . ."

Tyr raises a hand, and Gabriel snaps his mouth shut as Hylene escorts the king into the room with slow steps. It's nearly painful to watch him.

Hylene pulls out a chair and Tyr settles into it as we all watch in silence.

"Tyr," Gabriel says, his voice pained. "You should stay in bed."

"I'm fine," he says, his voice a little more forceful than his appearance suggests.

He turns to look at me. "You need me to destroy the ark. Please tell me everything, Heart Queen."

I nod and then fill him in on the rest of the details. I watch his hand open and close like he's reaching for his magic.

"I can still feel it," he says after I stop speaking, and my chest heaves with relief before he adds, "But it's not the same as it was."

"But it's still Imperial magic," Nadir says. "You're still the ascended king."

Tyr dips his chin. "All I can do is try." Then, his gaze moves to Erevan. "Or ask for help from the Primary and the soon-to-be king of Aphelion."

Erevan looks like he's just been kicked. Gabriel sits up in his seat, alarm spreading over his expression. Erevan can only ascend if Tyr descends into the Evanescence, and then he will be gone forever.

"No," Erevan says, a firm set to his jaw. "You're not going anywhere."

"Then we need your magic," Nadir says.

Erevan shakes his head. "I swore an oath never to use it until the low fae have been granted use of theirs again."

"But—" I open my mouth and then snap it shut at the dark look Erevan tosses me. It's clear from his expression that he has no intentions of wavering.

Tyr tips his head slowly and gives Erevan a look up and down that suggests his cousin doesn't really have a choice in the matter.

"Then I will try. After the warders return and are released," he says, and then more firmly, "*We* will destroy it."

Erevan gives no sign of acknowledging that statement.

"Any sign of Atlas?" I ask, and Gabriel gestures to a piece of paper on the table.

"They're getting closer. I'm hoping they'll return any day now."

Nadir nods. "We appreciate all of your help."

We're due to arrive in Heart in two days. But I'm not quite done with everything I need to do here. There's one more person we need to see.

I turn to Tyr and ask, "Before we leave, do you mind if I borrow the ark for one last errand?"

CHAPTER 40

Nadir and I make our way through the city, heading for the Sixteenth District, one area that mostly avoided disaster in the quake.

Cloris Payne claimed she knows how to manage the bond between Primaries, and while I have no expectations that she'll be willing to help us, I'm arriving with a bargaining chip.

We stop in front of the Priestess of Payne as thunder rolls overhead, pausing outside the building to remember the last time we were here.

"I can go in alone," Nadir says, his hand gripped around mine. The last time I saw Cloris, she told me Rion had caused the scar I wear on my face so proudly. I touch my cheek as though I can still feel the pain of those long nights in the Keep where he tortured me until it felt like my skeleton had been ripped out of my body.

I shake my head. "I'm not afraid of her."

Nadir gives me a tipped smile. "I know you aren't."

"Then let's bargain with this bitch," I say, and we make our way up the white marble stairs.

"We're here to see Madame Payne," I say, and the stunning High Fae female at the front desk blinks at us with her big eyes.

"She's very busy—"

"Tell her Lor is here," I say, cutting her off. "And tell her we don't have time for her bullshit. We want to see her now."

The Fae's eyes widen, and I know none of this is her fault, but I refuse to stand around waiting for her high and mightiness to grant us an audience. We have what she wants, and she *will* give me what *I* want, so help me.

"Of course," the Fae hostess says when it's clear I mean business. She dips into a curtsy and then scurries off, whispering something to another High Fae, this one male. He looks at us, then turns down the hall, off to deliver our message.

The woman returns. "Would you like to wait inside?"

She gestures down the long hallway that leads to the large room made to look like a temple of Zerra with its pool and greenery.

"No," I say. "We won't be here long."

She nods, and we wait only a few seconds before the male reappears.

"She'll see you," he says, and Nadir takes my hand as we follow him up the winding golden staircase. We enter a dark paneled hallway and are then ushered into Cloris's study, covered in thick woven rugs and filled with bookcases and ornate furniture. This time, she doesn't make us wait. She's standing in the middle of the room wearing a silk burgundy dress, her silver hair pulled into an intricate braid, and her cane clutched in her fist. She's all sneering smugness, and my fist clenches as I resist the urge to clock her across the mouth.

"Heart Queen. Aurora Prince," she says as the door closes. "Have you come to keep up your end of our bargain? I assumed I'd see you again soon enough." The corner of her lips curl up. "Because you're in . . . love."

She says the last word like it's carrion, spitting it out like sinew on dry, caked sand.

"Have you ever loved anyone?" I ask, and she laughs.

"Do you think I care?" she scoffs. "You think you'll trick me into revealing my bleeding heart? Not all of us are so weak."

"Fine," I say. "No, I will not be helping you find the ark of Heart."

Her eyebrow arches up in disdain. "Then what are you doing here? You will not beat or torture the answer out of me, girl. I'll die rather than reveal anything to you."

"That's what I thought you'd say," I reply, looking at Nadir.

He's not in love with my plan but conceded it was kind of the only option we had.

"So we've brought you something I think will convince you."

"What could you possibly—"

Her words cut off as I dig into the pocket of my tunic and pull out the ark of Aphelion. I'm banking on the notion that Cloris doesn't know I stole the others from Zerra, worried she'll demand the rest from me too. How often does she converse with her goddess, and *why* hasn't that goddess found me again?

Last time, Cloris told us Zerra was dying because everyone was using their magic with impunity and draining her. Cloris had part of the story but not all of it, which leads me to believe she isn't as *in* with her goddess as she thinks. It also makes me think Zerra is feeding different truths to different people, hoping to prevent anyone from having leverage to use against her. Perhaps she's more clever than she seems.

Cloris stares at the ark in my outstretched hand and then at me. "You're giving this to me?"

"In exchange for the knowledge of how Nadir and I can bond," I say.

She's trying to keep her cool, but the manic light in her eyes gives her away. She wants this so badly she can taste it.

Cloris inhales a sharp breath and straightens her shoulders. "Our bargain was for the ark of Heart."

"Which is currently somewhere in The Aurora in the hands of the king," I say. "You said you've been searching for all of them, so I'm offering you this one."

I study her face. There's nothing to suggest she knows I have the others, only that intense longing for the object cradled in my hand.

She shakes her head and peers up at me. "I want this *and* the ark of Heart for the knowledge you seek."

I suspected this would be her ask. Give an inch, and they always ask for a mile.

"Fine," I say, tucking the ark back into my pocket. I take Nadir's hand. "Then we'll be on our way."

We turn to leave, but she calls out as I predicted she would. "Wait."

"What?" I ask.

"Listen," Nadir says, dropping my hand and stepping towards her. He's taller than her by a good foot, plus he's fucking scary when he's pissed. She takes the smallest step back at his approach, though she tries to cover it up. "We can find this information out from someone else. If you know, then someone else knows too. But there is only one ark of Aphelion to be had. So you'll take Lor's offer, or you can fuck right off. We have things to do, and you're wasting our time."

Cloris's eyes flash with fury, but she must hear the sense in Nadir's words. Her jaw clenches, and she holds out her bony, trembling hand.

"Fine. Give it to me, and I'll tell you."

Nadir snorts but defers to me, glancing over his shoulder in question.

I move to stand next to him. "No. You're going first because, as he just pointed out, you're getting the better end of the bargain," I say.

Technically, it's true. We might be able to find this information on our own, but we're also running out of time.

"How do I know you won't run as soon as I tell you?" she asks.

"Of the two of us, you are the one who's been trying to screw me over. You're the one who's been lying to everyone. So I'm the more trustworthy one in this relationship." I hold up a hand. "You have my word that we will not run."

Cloris lets out a long, slow breath.

"Very well," she says and then smiles in a way that suggests neither of us will like this answer. "It's very simple. You will need both Artefacts, and there are a series of lines to recite in addition to those required of a normal bonding."

"What lines?"

"I don't have them memorized, but you'll find them in a book known as the Book of Night."

"Where will we find that?" Nadir asks, and Cloris shrugs.

"At one of the priestess temples, I suspect."

I look around the study. "You don't have one?"

"No. Your grandmother destroyed my copy."

I study her, scanning her up and down. I think she's telling the truth.

"That's it?" Nadir asks.

Cloris tips her head.

"No. There are two more things you need to be aware of."

"What?" I ask. She's enjoying the process of stretching this out as long as possible, feeding us drips of information to maximize their sting.

"First, you'll need a High Priestess, of course. I told you Serce made the mistake of trying to do it herself."

I narrow my eyes, trying to parse a lie in her words. I think she's being honest, as much as it guts me to admit it.

"So you'll still need me, and I will trade this knowledge for the ark of Aphelion, but if you'd like my help, I'll still require the ark of Heart as payment."

I sigh and pinch the bridge of my nose. My mother said I had to bond to destroy the ark, but will I be strong enough to get it from Rion without it?

"Why did my father want the ark?" Nadir asks. "You never explained that. Is that what you promised him?"

Cloris considers the question. "It was not the ark I dangled before him."

"What then?" I ask.

"It was you," she says. "The territory of Heart had resisted conquering over two long, bloody wars, and I simply suggested that with the Primary and her magic in his possession, he might finally be able to take it."

"Would that have worked?" Nadir asks.

Cloris shrugs. "Maybe."

Nadir looks at me and I shake my head. She lied to Atlas and Rion to get at me. She could be lying to us right now. She's obviously a master.

"That's why he was so angry when I refused to show him my magic," I ask as my stomach knots with this knowledge that I've craved for so long.

She nods. "He was convinced I'd lied, and the Primary was gone."

I think about what Nadir said and how Rion's interest in me shifted after Gabriel stole me from the Hollow. So why did he start searching for the ark of Heart?

"What's the second thing we need to do?" Nadir asks a moment later.

"Oh, that," she replies, and that's when her face stretches into a wicked grin.

"For the bonding to work, one of you will have to give up your role as the Primary."

Nadir and I both grind into stillness at those words, and Cloris laughs in delight.

"Oh? Did you think it would be so easy?" she sneers. "If you want that kind of power, it requires a *sacrifice*. Can your *love* stand the test?"

I narrow my eyes. "You're telling us the truth?"

She laughs again, tipping her head back with glee.

"It's the truth, Heart Queen." She studies me. "Or perhaps not a queen anymore." Her gaze slides to Nadir. "I haven't met many men who'd give up their power for a woman."

I cannot pass the role of Primary on to anyone else. Coral said it *had* to be me. If I don't ascend, then Heart loses everything.

But his answer is a derisive scoff. "Then you underestimate what I'd do for her, *High Priestess*."

I exchange a look with him, reading the sincerity in his eyes, my heart twisting in my chest. There's a flicker of something in Cloris's expression before it morphs into a scowl.

Nadir takes another step towards her, and this time, she visibly backs up. "How does one give up one's role as Primary?"

Cloris blinks several times before she recovers. Nadir has completely thrown her off with his reaction. She expected him to balk at giving up his crown, but I also can't help but wonder if he understands what he's doing.

She clears her throat. "You will have to ask the Torch when the bonding is performed."

Nadir looks back at me, seeking confirmation that I'm done with my questions.

I swallow a ball of tension in my throat. "And that's everything?" I ask again. "The full extent of it?"

"That is everything," Cloris says, holding out her hand. "Now, I will take the ark. And I will *consider* performing the ceremony for you once you find me the ark of Heart."

I glare at her, and then I hold out the ark of Aphelion. The black stone glitters in the light, and I can *feel* its power even if it isn't mine. She studies me, her calculating gaze sweeping me from head to toe. She will do everything to ruin me. I can see it written on her face. No matter what she says, she harbors centuries of anger towards my grandmother, and I will be the culmination of her revenge. This witch already tried to steal me, and when that didn't work, she used every resource she could to get at me.

She reaches for the ark, and I allow her hand to close over it as a light of triumph sparks in her eyes. But I hang on to it, and she looks up at me, her face twisting into a frown.

With Nadir standing at my back, ready to offer his control, I unleash my magic, a lightning bolt slamming into her chest as the room explodes. Books fly from shelves as they collapse into splinters. Cloris screams and bends at the waist, clutching herself.

Fury curdles in my limbs as I filter more magic into her body while Nadir's magic curls around mine, keeping it in check. Just barely. I *want* Cloris Payne to understand everything I'm capable of.

She groans and wails, rolling on the ground, just like when I attacked her as a child. This time, I feel no remorse or guilt about my actions. She is responsible for everything that happened to me and my siblings. To my parents. I ended up in the Trials because of her. Rion killed my parents because of her.

She could have let us live in peace, but she dragged us out into the world and played with our lives for her own benefit. We will find another way to complete the bond. I'll be damned if I let this monster take another thing from me.

Magic funnels into her body, charring her from the inside out and frying her to a crisp. I don't kill her—I'm not sure I even can after what happened last time, so I pull my magic back because I don't *want* to kill her. I want her to live knowing that I am stronger. That I could have destroyed her, but I'm choosing to allow her to live. Let her goddess punish her for failing her yet again. Those two deserve each other.

As I stare about the ruined study, my breath drags in on a ragged gasp. Surveying the spoils of my destruction, I feel only grim satisfaction.

When my magic cuts off, I stalk towards her and stand over her broken body, ash falling over her like snow. A crash signals the collapse of the far wall, exposing us to the outside air. As tendrils of hair whip across my cheeks, I don't even blink as I glare at her.

She looks up at me and groans, her blackened fingers reaching for me, her chest rattling with a dry breath.

"That's for everything. For telling Rion and Atlas about me. For trying to use me. For every moment of misery that me and my siblings lived in Nostraza."

I crouch down and get in her face, dropping my voice to a deadly whisper.

"Don't ever think you have power over me, Cloris Payne. I will fucking ruin you if you hurt anyone I love ever again."

Then I stand up slowly as she blinks—the stark contrast of her eyes against her blackened skin is positively ghoulish. She moans, the sound withered and cracked, and I try to summon up an ounce of remorse.

"Do you understand me?"

She whimpers, but I see the defeat enter her eyes. The understanding that she's been bested, once and for all.

"Stay away from me," I say. "From my mate and my family."

Then I spin around, take Nadir's hand, and we exit the room, closing the door on Cloris Payne for the very last time.

CHAPTER 41

GABRIEL

With my hands behind my back, I stand outside the aviary, staring across Ouranos. Clouds roll in overhead, thunder churning in the distance. Why is it always raining lately? Combined with the heat, it's so humid that even my bones feel like they're sweating. A scuffle at the door draws my attention to Hylene, who stands with one hand propped on the frame.

"You need some company?" she asks, and I scan her from head to toe. She's in a soft yellow dress that worships her curves, her red hair piled on her head with a few curls falling around her shoulders. We haven't had another moment to revisit our interrupted encounter on the balcony, but I'd be lying if I said I hadn't thought about it many times since.

"Of course," I say, and she moves next to me, resting her

elbows on the edge of the wall. We both face the distance, comfortable in our silence. It's nice to be around someone who doesn't feel the need to fill every pause.

More clouds tumble in, the sky turning grey. The temperature continues to climb, resulting in a sticky, cloying mess that makes me even more anxious.

"How's Tyr?" I ask after a few minutes.

"Asleep," she says, and I sigh. A gentle hand rests on my arm. "He needs to build up his strength."

"I know. I just wish—"

"I know."

She moves closer to me, the heat of her body pressing against mine as the wind tugs at our hair and clothing. The first small patters of rain hit my skin as my arm wraps around her hips almost involuntarily, drawing her nearer. She leans a head on my shoulder and peers up. As I look down at her, our mouths are so close that I can feel her warm breath on my lips.

She smells like orchids and vanilla. Like leather and silk. She licks her lips, and I zero in on the movement, imagining what it would be like to bite down on the lower one. My head moves, and our mouths brush with the barest flutter as my heart flips in my chest.

"Captain!"

"Fucking hell," I grumble as I look up to find a soldier standing in the doorway. Can we not get a fucking break around here? Hylene looks over and then at me, a small smile playing on her face.

"What is it?" I ask, my teeth gritted.

"Captain. The warders have returned...and they have the

king." He shakes his head as if trying to clear it from the lies weighing down every corner of this palace. "I mean . . . the prince."

My breath hitches like a roundhouse kick to the stomach. It takes me a moment to process those words as I cling to Hylene for support. I've been bracing for this moment, but now that it's here, I'm not ready at all.

I nod slowly. "Take me to him."

The soldier spins on his heel, and we rush through the palace, emerging into the courtyard. Dozens squeeze together in front of the gate, reaching through the bars, their arms outstretched as they scream for Atlas and his head.

Word of his capture has spread quickly, and they've come in droves bearing their metaphorical pitchforks. I scan the parapets, hoping no one gets any ideas of climbing over. Though we repaired and fortified the gate after the last incident, I don't have enough soldiers to adequately control this.

Atlas kneels in the center of the courtyard with his head down and his hands cuffed behind his back. The sight chills my blood, making my stomach clench. My emotions straddle the line between wanting to tear him apart with my bare hands and vomiting in a corner until I have nothing left.

The eerie blue glow of arcturite highlights his shoulders and jaw and the ragged strands of coppery brown hair that fall in his face. I hate the sight of those cuffs. My tongue catches in my throat as I force one foot in front of the other, approaching slowly.

I nod to my brothers where they surround him, their wings spread and their hands hanging loosely at their sides, on the alert for sudden movements.

"Atlas," I say, and he slowly looks up with cold and tired,

bloodshot eyes. The spidering veins tell a story where I read so many things. The years we've shared. The childhood we spent together. Everything we've been through. The pain he caused. And the laughter, too. Perhaps he was my friend once.

"Gabe," he says as I come to a stop before him. He doesn't attempt to rise. He just looks up at me as though he still wears that stolen crown on his head.

He blinks at me, saying nothing with his chin lifted at an arrogant angle. I see no contrition in his eyes. Only the certainty that he had every right to do this.

Is he truly such a lost cause?

"You stole the throne, Atlas. You locked your brother away for decades. You nearly killed him. And then you murdered two of your warders. The greatest crime of all for a king of Aphelion," I say as if he needs a reminder.

I hope I don't imagine the flicker of uncertainty that crosses his expression then. Atlas might be many things, but even he's not this big a fool.

The crowd outside the gate grows increasingly agitated, the noise swelling to a pulsing crescendo on the verge of bursting.

"Secure the wall," I say. "If this mob enters the palace, I can't protect the . . . Sun Prince."

Atlas's eyes flash at those words. I will never refer to him as my king again.

A moment later, Erevan appears at my side, his gaze on the crowd.

"They want him," he says, gesturing to the wall. "They want justice."

I blink, knowing this was inevitable.

"What would you have me do?" I ask. *Please. Someone tell me what to do.*

"I would have you release him to me. Let those who suffered the greatest under his rule have him."

I open my mouth and then close it. It would be a neat and tidy solution. Atlas would get what he deserves, the people would get a scapegoat, and I wouldn't have to figure out what the fuck to do with one of my oldest friends. Erevan is practically handing me an out on a silver platter. But even if it might be the easy escape, I can't let them just tear him apart. I could never live with myself.

"You fucking traitor!" Atlas roars, finally stumbling to his feet as he lunges for Erevan. "You always wanted this, didn't you?"

He crashes into Erevan, his large frame knocking into one of the guards. With his hands bound, his weight lurches, and they all go down in a heap. Atlas thrashes on top of Erevan like a wild beast.

"You wanted my crown!" Atlas roars.

"I never wanted it!" Erevan shouts. "You know that!"

"Why did the Mirror choose you?" Atlas screams, a broken, anguished sound in it.

Several members of the council have arrived to witness the false king's capture, and at that, everyone in the courtyard stills. Atlas just blurted out the final secret we've all been dragging around like a sack of hammers for a hundred years. But he's oblivious, still bucking and thrashing against his restraints.

"Someone get him off!" I yell, seizing Atlas by one arm as Rhyle grabs him from the other side.

Erevan raises his hands as he struggles to his feet. Atlas snarls and lunges uselessly for him.

"Atlas. Stop this!" I say, and he turns to me, his eyes practically rolling in his head.

"You're planning to give him the crown," Atlas accuses. "He's spent years fighting against the peace of Aphelion, and you're just going to give it to him!"

"I wouldn't have needed to fight anything if you weren't a tyrant—" Erevan shouts, but I get between them, pushing out my hands.

"Stop it!" I yell, my voice rising over the shocked drone of everyone witnessing this pitiful spectacle. "Both of you fucking stop it!"

Finally, they both go quiet.

"I'm not doing anything," I say to Atlas. "I have no power over who will rule Aphelion. Besides, its rightful king still lives."

Atlas glares at me.

"Take him back to the dungeon," I say to Rhyle. "Don't remove the cuffs under any circumstances. And put a round-the-clock double watch on him. No one sees him without my permission."

I see Lor and Nadir appear at the edge of the crowd. They took the ark to Cloris Payne, hoping to fool her into a bargain. Her gaze catches mine, and she tips her chin imperceptibly, indicating they were successful. At least something is going right.

Atlas catches the direction of my stare, his gaze falling on Lor. He blinks like he can't quite believe it. Slowly, she approaches, looking down at him, her expression giving nothing away, but something passes between them. No matter what Atlas did, I know Lor believed in him for a short time.

She takes in the measure of him, the arcturite cuffs around his wrists, the defeated look on his face, and I don't think that I imagine the glimmer of satisfaction that shines in her eyes.

Atlas's gaze narrows as he studies her before turning back to me.

"What do you plan to do with me?" he asks as he dismisses Lor. Clearly, his fate is his main concern.

I shake my head. "I don't know, Atlas."

"Gabriel—"

"Take him away *now*," I say to Rhyle, cutting off whatever Atlas wants to say.

I can't stand to look at him a moment longer.

My brothers haul him up from under his arms.

"Gabe, please," Atlas pleads. "Please don't do this. I know you. You'll regret this."

The tether on my temper is so close to snapping. I approach him, hissing in his face.

"Do *not* tell me what I will regret. I regret so many fucking things, Atlas, but this will never be one of them."

It takes four warders to restrain him as he thrashes and screams and fights against his bonds.

You'd think he could go out with some dignity, but I guess that's asking too much. This excuse for a man will always be who he was. The sight of the once glowing Sun King is pathetic to behold.

To the sounds of the chanting crowd, my brothers haul him into the palace, bearing the weight of his lies that have finally caught up with and will soon become the end of him.

CHAPTER 42

LOR

Seeing Atlas again is a shock to my system. I wasn't pre-pared for this onslaught of emotion. Nadir wraps an arm around my neck and drags me close, speaking against my temple.

"You okay?"

"Yeah," I say. "I think so."

Atlas used me and abused me, but I am at the bottom of the very long list of his victims. While I could hold on to my anger, I also want to step aside and make room for those he lied to for a century. For those whose lives he's affected in unalterable ways.

Whatever my personal grievances, they're nothing com-pared to what Gabriel, Tyr, and the other warders had to endure. The pain is written into their faces, etched into the haunted look in their eyes.

Atlas spared only a glance for me. I never mattered to him anyway, and knowing that doesn't hurt as much as it might have once.

He's yelling at Gabriel now. Pleading for mercy and for himself, but I don't know how he can stand there and look anyone in the eye.

He's dragged away into the palace as thunder booms overhead and the rain starts to fall in thick sheets. Now that the show is over, everyone scatters. We make a break for the palace, where we find Gabriel standing with some of his brothers, all of them murmuring soft words to each other.

Gabriel leans against the wall, pressing his arm to the surface and then dropping his forehead. We all watch him as he drags in several long breaths. Hylene walks over and runs a hand down his back, stretching onto her tiptoes to whisper something in his ear.

I exchange a curious glance with Nadir. Seems these two have gotten close.

Suddenly, he looks up, and his gaze finds me.

"You want answers from Atlas?" he asks, and I nod. "Then come."

He doesn't wait for my response before he pushes off the wall and stalks down the hallway, his footsteps ringing in the silence. I look at Nadir, who nods, and then I take off after Gabriel, running to catch up.

His gaze remains forward as we march through the halls. I

resist the urge to fill the silence for once, sensing he needs me to shut up.

We finally approach a wide archway and then enter through a set of fortified doors flanked by six guards wearing the livery of Aphelion. They both acknowledge Gabriel as he yanks on one of the handles before we head down the spiraling stone staircase.

Fire-lit torches guide us down through the gloom and into the dungeon, where I enjoyed a brief stay myself. Many of the cell doors stand open, and Gabriel catches my stare.

"Low fae broke into the palace and released their friends and family from the cells during the riots," he tells me.

"Good," I say. "That's good."

"Yeah," Gabriel agrees as we proceed past more guards and to the end, where four warders flank the locked door of a cell. They greet Gabriel and then bow to me, their eyebrows climbing.

"Aren't you the Final Tribute?" one of them asks, eyeing me up and down. I remember his name was Rhyle.

"She's the Heart Queen," Gabriel says. "Show her the proper respect."

I glare at Gabriel. Some might argue the Heart Queen deserves little from Ouranos, but he's giving me a look that suggests maybe he's a little proud.

Rhyle stutters and then bends at the waist. "I'm sorry, Your Majesty," he says, standing back up. "If it's not impertinent to ask, then what were you doing in the Trials?"

"That's what I'm hoping to find out," I answer, gesturing to the bars. He and the other warders step out of the way, revealing Atlas kneeling in his cell.

I approach and wrap my hands around the cool iron, pressing my face close.

"Atlas," I say softly as he ignores me. "Why?"

The word hangs in the air, waiting.

Slowly, Atlas lifts his head. He scans me from head to toe, his eyes narrowed with suspicion. There was a moment when I thought he felt something for me, and when I thought I felt something for him.

"Because I was destined for more," he says. There is no arrogance in his tone—only a statement of fact that proves just how deluded he is.

"How did you trick the Mirror?" Gabriel asks. "How were you getting away with this?"

Atlas cocks his head and stares at Gabriel. "I am the most gifted illusionist to ever grace this kingdom, Gabe. It wasn't hard."

Gabriel lets out a long breath, and I can't believe what I'm hearing.

Did the Mirror not know?

"Did you know?" I ask Gabriel.

"I suspected," he answers. "It was the only thing that made sense."

"That's why you kept it covered," I say. "Just in case."

"And never stepped in front of it when anyone else was in the room," Gabriel adds. "It took me a long time to notice it, but once I did, it became so obvious."

I think back to the times I was in the throne room with Atlas. The day I arrived here when I found out about the Trials, Atlas had sat at the front of the room, out of sight of the

Mirror. And at the end when I'd lost my shit, he'd told *Gabriel* to bring me to the Mirror. He didn't do it himself.

"Wow," I say because while it's awful, I'm almost impressed. "That's one hell of a cover-up."

Atlas glares at us both.

"Proud of yourselves?" he asks. "Now that you've figured it out, can you leave me alone?"

"No," I say. "I want answers. What did you want from me?"

I think I understand though. After discovering he was never the true king, it all became much clearer, but I need to hear him say it.

He narrows his gaze. "I was going to be powerful beyond measure," he says. "She was going to help me."

It takes me a moment to put it together but of course.

Cloris. I'm so glad I fried her.

"How?" I ask.

He rolls his neck and shoulders, jostling the glowing blue ring surrounding his throat. "There was a magical object that would help reverse the Mirror's decision and allow me to bond with you."

"But you weren't the king, and you could have bonded to her at any point," Gabriel says, and the heat of Atlas's glare is enough to melt the bars around him.

"And what good would that have done? Everyone had to see the *Mirror* choose her."

I shake my head.

"Cloris lied to you," I say. "The magical object is an ark, and I doubt it can do what she told you. She was using you from the very beginning. She never had any intention of helping you."

"Why would I believe that?" Atlas asks.

"Why would you believe *her*? She wanted to use my magic to find the ark for Zerra."

That causes his eyebrows to pinch together.

"Zerra?"

"Yeah," I say.

"I don't understand."

"No. I wouldn't expect so," I reply.

"So explain it to me."

I look over at Gabriel and then back at Atlas. "I don't think there's much point in that anymore."

"Why not?" Atlas asks, and then he looks at Gabriel, and whatever he sees in his face makes something crumple out of him. I realize then that Atlas really thought he'd talk his way out of all this, but Gabriel must follow through for his kingdom and its people.

Gabriel stares at Atlas, and I watch as a silent message passes between them. I can't imagine the oceans of hurt and unspoken words conveyed in that look.

"How did you break out of here?" Gabriel asks. "How did you kill Drex and Syran?"

A gleeful light sparks in Atlas's eyes. "You think you know me so well, don't you?"

"What the fuck does that mean?" Gabriel growls as he wraps his hand around a bar, his knuckles turning white.

"It means you've never understood everything I'm capable of. No one has." Gabriel just stares at him, clearly at a loss for words. "Besides, I still have some friends left in Aphelion. Not everyone thinks the way you do."

Gabriel rotates his shoulders. "I suppose you won't give me names?"

Atlas doesn't respond. He glares at all of us, his jaw hard.

Gabriel leans in closer. "Why the low fae, Atlas? Why did you do any of it?"

Atlas's eyes turn flat, the corners of his mouth turning down. He waits on his knees, his hands pinned behind his back, the shine of the once golden sun king tarnished to rust.

"You won't answer that either?" Gabriel says.

Atlas watches Gabriel, his face unreadable. And all I see before me is a prince who tried to take what didn't belong to him. He used everyone around him, including me, but in the end, he will not be the victor.

It's in that moment that I choose to forgive him. Not for his sake, but for mine. I will no longer live with this in my heart.

After we leave for the settlements tomorrow, I will never think of him again.

I look up at Gabriel, who's still watching Atlas, then he drags in a very long breath and says, "Very well. Then for committing treason, for impersonating the king, for killing two of the king's warders, you are found guilty. As per the laws of Aphelion, you will be executed for your crimes against the true Sun King and everyone in this kingdom."

He pauses as Atlas's face drains of color.

"And though no one can technically punish you for it, for crimes against the low fae as well."

Atlas's entire body jerks like Gabriel slapped him across the face.

"Gabe," he hisses, finding his tongue again.

"Don't bother, Atlas. After your execution, my brothers and I will be released from our duties as warders. We will no longer be slaves to Aphelion or to you."

"What?!" Atlas says. "You can't do that!"

Though I can see the slight tremble in Gabriel's limbs, he lifts his head high and holds his shoulders straight, his game face on.

"This is the last time we'll ever speak," he says. "Goodbye, Atlas."

He then looks at his brothers and bows to each of them. Spinning on his heel, Gabriel stalks away to the sounds of Atlas shouting after him.

I run, catching up with Gabriel. Turning around one last time, I see the warders embracing one another, their faces pressed to each other's shoulders.

Soon, Aphelion can begin to heal.

CHAPTER 43

NADIR

The morning after Atlas's capture, we gather our things, preparing for our journey to Heart. Neither Lor nor I arrived with much, but we've stocked up with some new clothing and necessities. After we learned about Zerra's sight when we're in proximity to the Artefacts, I summoned Etienne to get the Crown away from us and to a safe location until we need it.

Two days ago, while out walking, I came across a blacksmith selling some of the most beautiful weapons I've ever seen. They sparkled in the sunlight, and when my gaze fell upon a dagger anchored with a red, heart-shaped stone in the hilt, I couldn't help myself.

I retrieve it from where I've hidden it as I watch Lor stuff her pack. I catch her solemn expression. She hasn't said anything about what happened with Cloris, but I know it's on her mind.

She looks up, catching me watching her, and gives me an uncertain smile.

"Are you okay?" I ask, and she shrugs.

"I'm...nervous." She tips her chin towards my hands. "What's that?"

"Something for you," I say as I approach with the dagger and hold it out to her. She looks at it, her gaze pausing on the heart stone, and then looks up at me. "I saw it and thought it would be perfect for you. As long as you don't mind having something from Aphelion."

She presses her lips together and shakes her head. "I don't mind." She reaches out and accepts it, pulling the blade from the sheath. "I think my feelings about this place have changed. Atlas will receive justice, and yesterday, I chose to forgive him for what he did to me. I won't live with this in my heart or my mind anymore."

She blows out a breath and looks up at me, and I'm so proud of how much she's grown, my heart feels on the verge of bursting.

"And now they can all try to start over."

The blade shines in the sunlight, and she tips it left and right, the reflection bouncing off its surface. "It's beautiful," she says. "Thank you."

She approaches and loops her arms around my neck, stretching up on her tiptoes.

"I love you," she says.

"I love you too." My hands find her waist as I pull her in closer.

"You don't think I'm a monster for what I did to Cloris yesterday?"

I arch an eyebrow. "Why would I think that? You know how hard I get when you're violent, Lightning Bug."

She huffs out a laugh and slaps me playfully on the shoulder. "I forgot who I was talking to."

My smile tips up. "You know I love you no matter what. And that witch deserved it. If you hadn't done it, I would have destroyed her on the spot."

I take her chin between my fingers and kiss her deeply, reminding her just how much I love her. How this thing I feel for her extends straight through the earth to a place with no end. If fate is intent on separating us, I'd be happy to spend countless years—lifetimes if I had to—waiting for her because what we have is inescapable. Inevitable. As constant as the moon and stars.

"We should get going," I say as I pull away, and she nods before sliding the dagger back into its hold.

We meet the others in the palace entry and say our goodbyes to Gabriel, Tyr, and Erevan. I notice Tristan and Nerissa in the corner, wrapped in each other's embrace, as she looks up at him, speaking quietly. My gaze slides to Lor, who also watches her brother. It's none of my business, but I can see how much she wants this for him.

I look away and then embrace Hylene, who will remain in Aphelion too. Apparently, she's comfortable here, though she refused to give me details on what exactly she's been up to with the captain of the king's warders. I'll get it out of her eventually.

My gaze snags on the golden tattoo on Gabriel's neck, and I watch as he absentmindedly touches the spot. He notices my attention and his hand drifts away. Gabriel and I have never had the freedom to be friends, but had we been born into different circumstances, I think we could have been great ones.

Soon, Tyr will release the warders, attempt to destroy the ark, and send us a message when it's done. He asked for some time to work up to it, and I'm praying he can summon enough power. But we still have a long road to travel before we've destroyed all the arks, so we can allow him time.

I reach out my hand, and Gabriel takes it before we wrap each other in a hug.

"Thanks for everything," he says gruffly.

"I didn't do anything," I reply. "But I'm glad you will finally be free."

Gabriel looks around and gives me a rueful smile. "Not yet, exactly," he says. "How do you do it? Make decisions you know will affect everyone?"

I blow out a slow breath. "All you can do is let your conscience guide you. Nothing you do will ever make everyone happy, but I've always found that following my beliefs usually serves me well."

Gabriel squeezes his eyes and pinches the bridge of his nose.

"You'll figure this out," I add.

"Probably not, but at least I'll go down trying."

I clap him on the shoulder. "That's the spirit."

Then his gaze falls to Lor, and they study one another for a moment. She rushes towards him and throws her arms around his neck. I can tell he's not quite sure what to do with that because his arms hang limply at his sides before he finally wraps them around her waist.

They hug for several long seconds before they pull away.

"I'm sorry we can't stay," she says. "Will you be okay?"

"Eventually. I hope. Maybe." He rubs his hand down his face. "Thank you for all your help after the quake. You and your brother."

"It was no problem," she says. "But we better go."

We say our goodbyes, and then we depart.

Etienne has returned and will use his magic to transport us to Heart in groups of two. Lor and I are the last to arrive. As we appear outside the walls of the first settlement, I notice the way Lor's shoulders lift, as though being here fills her soul.

I squeeze her hand, and she looks over at me with a smile.

"This way," Etienne says, and we fall into step next to him, passing through the gates. "The others went on ahead."

We make our way through the streets, and several people notice our presence. There's no need to hide Lor any longer, but now is not the time to reveal everything either. Their curious glances follow us, but no one stops us. "Rhiannon convinced one of the wealthier merchants to give up his home for a few days," Etienne explains.

Quite frankly, I'm a bit surprised there *are* wealthier merchants in the settlements, but I suppose power will always grow in a vacuum. We pass through the village and head into the outskirts on the far side, delving into the trees.

"Where are we going?" Lor asks.

"Lord Maida built this house many years ago," Etienne says. "Apparently, he finds the village depressing."

Lor lets out a derisive snort. "How charming."

We wind through the trees for a few minutes before coming upon a black wrought iron fence with a tall gate spanning the pathway.

"He also wants to keep everyone out," Etienne says wryly.

"Who is he?" Lor asks.

"He claims he's a very distant descendent of the Heart family," Etienne says, and I hear Lor's sharp intake of breath. "But as far as anyone can discern, he's likely full of shit."

"Why do you say that?"

"No one can remember him from before the breaking," Etienne says. "But he did show up with money and helped fix up some areas of the settlements while also establishing many of the buildings you see. And then he built himself this."

Etienne pulls out a key and unlocks the gate, swinging it open for us.

The short walk leads us to a modest home two stories high. Though it's not extravagant, it's clearly well tended and loved, as evidenced by the verdant garden, blooming with red roses, and the sculptures that dot the pristine green lawn.

"Why have I never heard of this place?" I ask, and Etienne shrugs.

"He mostly keeps to himself. Doesn't like to mingle too much."

"And where is he now?" Lor asks.

"Rhiannon has a seaside villa in Alluvion," he says. "Some

rich suitor gifted it to her years ago. She offered it to him for a few weeks, and he jumped at the chance to enjoy a little beach holiday."

I cast my gaze about. Though the home is nice, this forest is gloomy. A sense of foreboding hangs in the air, and I understand why he took Rhiannon up on the offer.

Etienne swings open the door to find Rhiannon already on her way down the hall.

"Lor! Nadir!" she exclaims. "It's so good to see you again."

She wraps Lor in a warm embrace and then folds me into a hug. It has a motherly sort of affection to it, and the act makes a knot swell in my throat. I need to see my own mother soon. It's been too long, and I fear for her safety given my father's recent behavior. But I can't leave Lor's side either.

Rhiannon talks a mile a minute as she leads us up the stairs, chattering with excitement about meeting Willow and Tristan. She then takes Lor and me down a hall, showing us which rooms she's designated for the other rulers of Ouranos.

Nothing is very fancy—they're all used to more luxurious surroundings—but I don't think anyone will be insulted by what we're offering. They all know there's very little left of Heart, and quite frankly, this is nicer than I was anticipating.

"I saved this room for you," she says, swinging open the door. "Etienne might have mentioned that you two would be sharing?"

She cocks her head and studies us.

"Yeah," Lor says, looking at me. "You remember when you told me my grandparents were mates?"

Rhiannon's eyes widen a fraction. "Of course?"

"When you told me about their magic reacting...well, I realized that Nadir might be mine."

"I remember you started acting strangely," she says before a wide smile spreads over her face. "Oh well, isn't this wonderful? After you're settled, I have so many questions for you. If you don't mind? I've always been fascinated by mate bonds."

"Sure," Lor and I both say. After everything she's done for us, it feels like the least we can do.

Rhiannon opens the door and gestures us inside, and that's when Lor gasps. This room offers a view of the Heart Castle in the distance, the white spires peeking over the tops of the trees.

She presses a hand to her chest and swallows as my hand settles on her lower back.

"You okay?" I ask, and she nods.

"I want to see it again," she says. "Last time—"

"Let me send Mael and Etienne to do a quick sweep and make sure it's safe."

I don't bother trying to talk her out of it. I already know what will happen if I do.

"Willow and Tristan can come too."

"Of course," I say.

She looks up at me and gives me a watery, if grateful, smile. "Thank you."

"I thought you'd like this one," Rhiannon says from the doorway, her voice soft. "There is food downstairs whenever you're ready."

She closes the door, and we drop our bags and clean up from travel before we head to the main floor to find the others.

Mael and Etienne leave immediately to check out the castle while Lor explains her plan to Willow and Tristan.

"If you want," Lor says. "If you're not ready, you can stay here."

She clasps her hands, and I can tell she's trying not to appear too hopeful. She desperately wants them to see it.

"Of course I'm coming," Tristan says, and Lor smiles before turning to her sister.

"Willow?"

I watch the older sister of Heart look out the window. From the first floor, we catch glimpses of the walls surrounding the city visible through the trees.

"I don't know," she says.

Lor drops to her knee and rests her arms on Willow's thighs.

"What's making you hesitate?"

"I'm scared of how it will feel."

Amya reaches over and clasps Willow's shoulder, and Willow folds her hand over hers.

"It's overwhelming," Lor says. "I won't lie. But I had Nadir with me, and he made it feel a little less scary. A lot less scary, actually, and you'll have me and Tris."

My heart seizes at those words, and I resist the urge to clutch my chest. Did she really feel that way? We were so at odds then. It felt like a bridge we'd never be able to cross.

"We won't let anything happen to you," Tristan says. "And if it's too much, we can always leave."

"Nadir and I will wait outside," Amya says, laying a gentle hand on the back of Willow's neck. She looks up at her, and I sense the trust that passes between them. There hasn't been much time to discuss what's been going on with them, but it's easy to see they've grown closer. "You say the word, and I'll fly you out of there."

That elicits a nod from Willow. "Okay. I can do that."

Lor breaks into a grin and wraps her arms around her sister. "I can't wait to show it to you," she whispers.

Willow presses her cheek to the top of Lor's head, and they hold on to one another for a long time before they finally break apart.

After that, we fill up our stomachs and wait for Mael and Etienne to return. When they give us the all clear, we prepare to leave.

It doesn't take long to push through the forest before we arrive at the border of the desolate plain that Lor and I crossed many weeks ago.

"This is where it happened," Lor says.

"It's . . ." Willow says, her voice trailing off as she stares at the wreckage.

"I know. But we're going to fix this," Lor says, and I hope she believes it. I believe it. Somehow, we will fix this.

"Come on."

We continue over the rough terrain until we reach the crumbling wall surrounding the city. The roses continue to bloom, each flower so bright and precise that it's hard to believe they're real.

"Nadir said they started growing when Atlas took me from Nostraza. Coral told me they are blooming for me," she says, her voice thick with emotion.

She picks a rose and buries her nose in its center. I see her in a flash, somewhere in a distant future. Standing with a crown on her head, wearing a long red dress, the sun gilding her dark hair with a golden halo. She looks over her people, happy and content. And I'm there with her because I will always be with her.

Cloris said one of us had to give up our role as Primary, but the choice was easy for me. This is where she belongs.

She looks over at me, catching my stare, and nods. I see the thank-you she shares in her eyes.

"Amya and I will wait here," I say, placing my hand on her nape and pulling her closer to kiss her temple. "Just call if you need us."

She nods and then reaches out, taking the hands of Willow and Tristan on either side.

They stand together at the threshold, looking over their family's ruined queendom.

"Ready?" Lor asks, and Willow and Tristan nod.

She looks over her shoulder and blows me a kiss before the three siblings of Heart enter their homeland together, hand in hand, for the very first time.

CHAPTER 44

LOR

QUEENDOM OF HEART

W illow squeezes my hand so tight that my fingers are going numb. I knew this would be hard, but I'm here to guide them every step of the way.

Tristan and I share a careful look.

Things didn't go according to plan the last time we were here. If Rion is anywhere near Heart, then we'll probably know soon enough. Etienne and Mael scouted the area, and I don't want to be a jerk, but the last time Etienne assured me everything was safe, it wasn't.

Still, I have my magic and Nadir and Amya are watching over us. Plus, Tristan grows stronger with every passing day.

"It's . . ." Willow whispers. "It must have been beautiful."

"I said the same thing," I reply.

We continue walking, picking over the ruined sidewalks and past the crumbling walls. When I was here with Nadir, we were so focused on finding the Crown, and I was so overwhelmed that I didn't have the chance to really study this place.

I see the outlines of a building that might have been a shop once and another structure with a partially collapsed curved dome on top, as well as narrow buildings that might have been houses at one time. We walk through a plaza with a statue planted in the center, the top half long gone, leaving only the bottom of a woman's dress.

"Who do you think it was?" Tristan asks, catching the direction of my gaze.

"Amara," I say. I don't know why, and maybe it isn't, but I like the idea of the first Queen of Heart standing watch. The Empyrium said the first rulers of Ouranos were good kings and queens, and I need a role model more inspiring than my grandmother.

We continue walking, taking in the relics of our grandparents' ruin. Interspersed between everything are vines and roses. The contrast between life and death, between the past and a possible future, makes my chest tight.

Finally we reach the castle wall and pass into the crumbling courtyard. I note the spot where Nadir and I stood when he said the roses started to grow for me. The same spot where I looked at him and knew I was already falling.

Hand in hand, we stand at the base of the castle, peering up at its jagged spires and the once white stone now grey and mottled by history.

"You okay?" I ask Willow, and she nods, though I can tell she's putting on a brave face.

"This is . . . harder than I thought it would be. You know?"

"I know," I say and squeeze her hand.

We enter the castle and walk down the hall in single file. This was where Rion's soldiers entered, finding us in the throne room after that night when I screamed at Nadir that I would never be his. I can smile at the memory now as I peer over my shoulder. Even if I can't see him, I know he's there, just beyond the walls, watching after me.

The reminder of our somewhat rocky relationship makes me think of Tristan.

"How did you leave things with Nerissa?" I ask my brother, whose eyebrows climb up his forehead. He bends down to pick up a stone before tossing it, then catching it in his hand.

"It wasn't serious. We agreed to leave it open-ended for now. I don't know if I'm ever going back." He pins me and Willow with a serious look. "Right?"

"Maybe," I say.

"It was just nice to feel something." He pauses and then adds, "It's been a long time."

Willow and I exchange a look. While fewer female prisoners lived inside Nostraza, Tristan also had his fair share of flings.

"Remember Seraphina?" I ask, and Tristan snorts.

"How could I forget?" He shakes his head at the memory of the mortal woman who swept into Nostraza when Tristan was nineteen. She was almost twice his age, and she had been stunning before Nostraza did what it does to everyone.

She oozed charisma, and Tristan spent the better part of

six months following her around like a lovesick puppy. Eventually, like all prisoners in Nostraza, she succumbed to the cumulative weight of its environment, and Tristan moped around the prison for another good six months.

"She practically made me a man," he sighs wistfully. "The things she taught me . . ."

"Gross," Willow and I both chorus, and he grins as we continue walking.

What Tristan had with Seraphina or anyone who came before or after was never love. It was lust and release. Something to cling to in the bleakness of our days. I remember that feeling all too well.

"You will feel that again," I say to Tristan. "If it's not Nerissa, then it will be someone else. Gods help me, I will make sure you do."

He presses his mouth together. "I'm not sure I'm ready anyway. I need time to sort out everything up here." He points to his forehead, and I nod, understanding exactly what he means.

"This way," I say, turning left, preparing to save the throne room as our last stop. I lead them through the charred hallways as crumbled brick and mortar crunch beneath our boots.

"I'll be honest, there isn't much to see," I say. "Most of it looks like this. Nadir and I explored nearly every inch when we were looking for the Crown, but there is something I think you'll both like."

Willow is rubbing her chest, making a strange face.

"What's wrong?" I ask.

She shakes her head. "I feel weird."

"Weird how?" I ask.

"I don't know. I'm sure it's nothing. I shouldn't have skipped lunch—I'm a bit lightheaded."

"Are you okay?" Tristan asks. "We can always come back later."

"Absolutely not. I'm fine." She gestures to me. "Lead the way."

I give her one more skeptical look.

"Come on. Seriously, it's nothing," she says.

"Okay." I take them to the library, where the portraits of our grandparents hang.

"Here," I say, leading them into the room. "Turn around."

We all do at the same time, and once again, the sight takes my breath away.

Our grandparents stand on either side of the door, larger than life, rendered in paint by a carefully skilled hand.

Neither of my siblings says anything as they stare at the portraits.

"They're incredible," Willow eventually breathes. "She was so beautiful."

"She looks just like you," I say, and Willow smiles.

"And our grandfather," she says. "He looks . . . kind."

"He does," I agree, remembering I thought the same thing.

Tristan's jaw is hard as he stares at the portraits, still saying nothing.

Willow and I give him a moment as we both move closer. Willow stands under Serce, the Heart Queen who broke the world, looking up. Last time, I'd been too full of emotion to remain here long—but now I study my grandmother's face, looking for signs of who she might have been.

She loved her family and her home. She loved her mate so

much that she had been willing to do anything. I consider my own actions and wonder if I'm in any position to judge her. I've been tearing through Ouranos, leaving my own path of destruction. And now I'm also planning to bond with my mate whatever the consequences.

After another minute, I look back at Tristan, but he still hasn't moved. He just stares at the portraits silently, something passing behind his expression that I think I recognize.

"Tris, you okay?" I ask finally. "Tris?"

He looks at me as though he'd forgotten we were here.

"Are you okay?"

"Yeah. I'm fine." He tears his gaze away from the portraits. "What else should we see?"

He's clearly not fine, but I won't push him. We can discuss this later, when he's had time to digest everything.

"The throne room," I say. "This way."

We wind our way through the castle. We were here for only two days last time, but I remember every corner like they're tattooed into my memories. How can anyone say that I don't belong here?

We step inside and come to a stop. It's even more overwhelming than I remember.

I look around, noting the evidence of the battle with Rion— shattered stone littering the floor where he fired his magic. In the middle of the room lie the traces of the night Nadir and I spent talking and staring up at the sky. Even the small circle of stones where we lit a fire remains.

"What happened here?" Tristan asks, pointing at the pile of rubble behind the thrones.

"That's where we found the Crown," I say. "It was behind that wall."

I glance over at Willow, who's staring around the room with her lips parted. She looks a little pale and keeps rubbing her chest. We really should get her something to eat. We'll stay here another few minutes and then head back to the manor. It's getting late, and we could all use some sleep.

Tristan stares at the twin thrones, and I'm not sure which of my siblings needs me the most right now. They're both having very different reactions—ones I might have predicted. Willow all wide-eyed wonder in her endless optimism, and Tristan with his more practical and cynical outlook. As much as I love Willow, Tristan and I have always been two peas in a pod.

Willow's gaze traces the roses that spiral up the pillars and clamor across the ceiling. Are there more than the last time? It's hard to tell, but I think so.

"The roses," Willow says. "I know you told me about them, but Lor—" She cuts off and stops. "This is all so much bigger than we ever imagined, isn't it?"

Tristan and I watch as she scans her surroundings, a tear slipping down her cheek. She scrubs it away with the back of her hand.

"I wish they could have told us," Willow says. She looks over at me and Tristan as my brother runs a hand over his head.

"I'm angry with them," he says, and the words sound like a confession he's been clinging to for a long time. "I didn't want to say anything, but I'm so fucking angry with them."

"Tris—" Willow says.

He shakes his head and then rubs his chest. "I miss them so goddamn much. I wish more than anything I could have seen Mother too, but fuck, I'm so furious they left us to deal with all of this on our own."

"They had no choice," Willow says.

"I don't mean *that*. I know they didn't. They could have *told* us. They had to know someone might find out their secrets one day. They just... didn't *tell* us."

Tristan paces back and forth, inhaling deep, ragged breaths. While I've been bewildered and confused by their choices, I also didn't know our parents like Tristan did. I don't remember them the way he does.

"And those people!" he shouts, gesturing towards the library. "Our grandparents! How could they have been so stupid and selfish? How could they have done this to us!"

"Tris..." I say.

"No! I'm so fucking mad! Okay? I know Willow can see the bright side in anything, and Lor, you're dealing with all of this with a lot more maturity than I am because I am so fucking pissed, and I can't keep quiet about it anymore!"

He spreads his arms, looking left and right.

"This could have all been ours. This life. This place. And not just us. All of those people out there. They left us with nothing! They left everyone with *nothing*! They just took what they fucking wanted and didn't care!"

His voice bounces off the stone, echoing in the space with the pain in his words. I agree with every single thing he's said.

"We could have grown up with our parents! With our family! We could have had a life that wasn't just existing with secrets. We wouldn't have spent twelve fucking years in that prison, barely clinging to that pathetic excuse for a life.

"And Lor! Lor—you wouldn't have been forced into those Trials. You wouldn't have been forced to do all of this! You found your mate, and now you're going to lose him, and I might not like him all that much, but you seem to really love him, and *fuck*, all I've ever wanted is you both to be happy!"

With his hands on his hips, he spins away, and I watch his shoulders heave, feeling the heat of his frustration burning the backs of my eyes.

Willow and I allow him a moment to stew in his anger as we trade worried glances. Our brother has always been our rock. Our safe place to land when life in Nostraza became too much.

He looks up and keeps pacing as a tear drips from the end of his nose. He sniffles and wipes it away. It's been a very long time since I've seen my brother come undone.

Willow and I exchange another look that becomes a silent signal, and we both move, planting ourselves on either side of him. He stops short when he realizes I'm in his way.

"What—"

I throw my arms around his waist, and Willow does the same from behind. It takes him a moment to realize what we're doing, but when he does, he curls into us and just . . . *lets go*.

I feel the drain of his heart. The strain in his sobs. The release of a thousand emotions and worries and hurts he's been burying for a very long time.

We clutch one another, holding on in this ruined place that should have been our home. Willow and I start crying too, the sound of our sorrow echoing in the dusty, forgotten corners of Heart.

But then the strangest thing happens.

It takes me a moment to notice it. It's an odd sound—something stretching and squeezing, snapping and crackling like twigs underfoot. And then I see it. Vines covered in rosebuds creep across the ground like snakes, stretching towards us. The sight *should* be alarming, but something tells me we have nothing to worry about.

They crawl closer, then stop a few feet away and peel off the ground. Tristan and Willow have noticed now, and we all pull apart. More vines climb up the pillars around the room and up every wall, coating them in curtains of green. They continue climbing, stretching over the ceiling, filling every corner and every recess.

The vines around us form an arch over our heads, and then everything starts to bloom. Buds expand over every inch of the vine, unfurling in scarlet bursts, petals spreading out like they're greeting the morning sun.

They open in a wave until we're surrounded—until every surface is a blooming tapestry of brilliant red roses. Tristan, Willow, and I stare at each other wide-eyed, unable to comprehend the sight.

It's then I notice another vine creeping across the floor, inching towards Willow. She inhales a sharp breath, but I'm still sure that no one needs to be afraid.

Slowly, it crawls closer and then gently winds its way around her ankle.

"Lor," she whispers.

"It's okay," I assure her. "I think it's okay."

The vine climbs higher, circling around her knee and then her thigh. Willow holds completely still, her eyes never leaving it.

"Willow—" Tristan says, about to reach for her, but I stop him.

"Don't," I say. "It's . . . fine."

He knows I would never let anything happen to her, so he nods and stands back as the vine crawls up Willow's legs and hips then circles her torso and travels down the length of her arm. She watches it, her gaze steady as the rose-covered tendril winds around her fingers. Willow lifts her hand, pointing it towards the sky.

We all wait, suspended in this moment, wondering what new revelation is about to change our reality yet again.

Willow rubs her chest as a spear of red lightning drops from the sky, exploding against her hand. She screams, and I scream, and Tristan yells in surprise.

When it's over, she stands unharmed.

She lowers her hand, her fingers spread wide as she stares at her palm. The vine then unwinds back in the other direction before it melds with the others.

"What just happened?" I ask, but I think I already know.

We bestowed the first threads of magic on you and your siblings.

"Was that . . . ?" Tristan adds.

"Magic," I say as footsteps pound down the corridor and Nadir and Amya appear at the door.

"We saw Lor's lightning," Nadir says. "Is everything okay?"

"It wasn't me," I say. "It was Willow."

Chapter 45

"What?" Amya asks. "Willow?"

My sister shakes her head and rubs her chest again. "I feel something. I think..."

The Aurora Prince and Princess then take note of our surroundings. It's impossible to miss the thick carpets of flowers and vines climbing over every surface.

"What happened?" Nadir asks.

"We were standing here, hugging," I say, "and they started growing."

"And then one of the vines showed me I have magic."

"You felt it," I say. "When we came in here."

The corner of her mouth ticks up in an uncertain smile. "I didn't know that's what I was feeling."

"Willow! You have magic?" Amya says, running over and throwing her arms around my sister. They kiss and then hug for several long seconds.

"I think so," Willow says, looking to me and Tristan.

"Try it," Amya says. "Just concentrate on that feeling in your chest."

Willow holds out a hand. "Back up," she says, and we all give her some space.

A moment later, magic springs from her fingertips in crimson whorls, but it isn't lightning like mine. It's light and airy and twirls around the space, forming into . . . roses. They float across the room, tumbling down like rain. She pulls her hand back and clutches it to her chest before she looks at me.

"Lor," she whispers, and I stumble towards her, throwing my arms around her.

"I'm so proud of you," I say, and we hug before we pull apart. "I confess the Alluvion Coral said something to me that made me wonder, but I didn't want to say anything, just in case."

We stare at the roses lying at our feet.

"I'm not sure how useful that is," Willow says, her nose scrunching.

"It's beautiful," I say, "Absolutely perfect." I step back to let Amya hug her again.

"How do you feel?" Amya asks, framing my sister's face in her hands.

"I'm . . . I never really cared that much that I was the only one without it, but . . ." Her face splits into a smile. "I have to say it does feel really good."

"What do you think this means in terms of Heart magic?" Amya asks. "Is it possible Lor isn't the only one who can bring it back?"

She winces, realizing what she's just said. If Willow could become the next Primary, then I could take my place in the sky, lost to all of them.

"Sorry," she says, shaking her head. "I didn't mean..."

"Coral and Amara told Lor it wasn't possible," Nadir says.

"Lor is the Primary," Willow says firmly, her tone brooking no argument. "This has always been her place. Even if I could, we are not losing her."

My gaze meets Nadir's.

Even if Willow *could* take my place in Heart, I still have to kill Zerra before she gets to me.

"You'll need to learn how to use it," Amya tells Willow. "I'm sure there's more you'll be able to do."

"That makes two of us," I reply. "Though you're probably a natural like Tristan."

I look at my brother. I see the happiness in his eyes for Willow, but I also remember the angry words he shouted only minutes ago. As Amya and Willow chatter away, I take his hand and hold it.

"Me too," I say. "Everything you said."

I catch Nadir watching the two of us, his expression contemplative.

"You're so much better at rising above it, Lor."

I snort. "Are you serious? I'm a raging ball of chaos."

Tristan laughs. "You are, but... you persevere."

"Tristan, don't sell yourself short. You practically raised

me. I am the way I am because of you. It wasn't fair that you had to, but I owe so much to you."

Everyone has fallen silent during my little speech. When we see everyone staring at us, the tips of my ears go pink.

"What?" I ask, "What are you all looking at? Can't a sister get a little sentimental?"

"Come on," Nadir says, approaching us and wrapping an arm around me. "If you're ready to go, we should get some sleep before tomorrow."

We all nod and then file back into the ruined city that surrounds the Heart Castle. I wonder if I'll ever see this place again—as its queen, not as a reluctant god forced to give up everything.

It's not happening. Nothing is keeping us apart.

I squeeze Nadir's hand.

I hope that's true.

We continue walking, and the sun has set by the time we make it back to the manor house. The windows are dark, save for a few glowing in the distance. Etienne and Mael meet us at the tree line.

"How did it go?" Etienne asks.

"Willow has magic!" Amya exclaims.

"Well, hot damn," Mael says with a grin. "The three of you are unstoppable now."

"Now?" I say, pressing my hand to my chest in mock offense.

"Right, sorry, no one ever stood a chance against you, Heart Queen."

"And her brother and sister," I add, and everyone laughs.

Rhiannon greets us as we enter the house, curiosity written

on her face. I promised I'd answer some questions about the mate bond, and I'll fill her in when we chat.

"I've received word the other rulers are on their way," she says. "Everyone will be here by morning."

"Okay," I say. "Then let's hope they're willing to listen and that Cyan or my aunt don't kill me on sight."

"They'll have to go through me first," Nadir growls.

I cock my head and wince.

"Maybe that's what I'm afraid of."

CHAPTER 46

RION

R ion shuffled through the papers on his desk with a grim sense of frustration. He'd been working on a new set of amendments to the laws governing The Aurora's mines. He needed unrestricted access to the labor of the low fae. They were moving too slowly for his liking, and he wanted to extend the length of their shifts while also conscripting more workers.

One of Herric's journals lay open next to him. In it, the former Aurora King claimed that virulence was an inconstant material. The deposits found closer to the surface were less potent, almost to the point of being devoid of magic. He'd used them to build the Keep, wanting to be surrounded by the material without inadvertently alerting anyone else to its power. It had the added bonus of shielding him from Zerra's sight as he'd worked on methods to destroy her.

It had been his ode to himself. A monument to all the things he'd accomplished so far and the dreams he had yet to fulfill.

Rion had read those words seized with a sick sense of desire.

How far could he go? How much power could he amass? Would it be enough to fill this aching hole in his chest?

From Herric's notes, it became clear that the virulence used to create the arks was from a deposit so deep that Herric couldn't seem to map out its location. In his cynicism, Rion wondered if Herric had purposely created this mystery lest anyone happen upon these notes. The former king also hadn't deigned to speak to Rion in centuries, further adding to his frustrations. Almost as if he was purposely keeping this information from him.

But it was the strongest virulence the former king had ever encountered, and Rion wanted it.

He returned to his papers, reading them over again.

Once he managed to force these amendments through, Rion could conscript as many low fae as he wanted, no longer concerning himself with their base needs, like food and sleep and water. If one died, he could just replace them, and maybe then he'd find what he was looking for.

He opened the top of his collar and stared out the window before he pushed himself up and strode through the Keep to find himself alone in the throne room. He'd been spending a lot of time here lately. The Torch's presence had a calming effect, and those warm flames flickering in its mouth allowed him to forget for a short while.

He marched up the dais and dropped onto his throne, leaning back while crossing an ankle over his knee. He pondered in the massive room's stillness, watching the lights ripple across the sky through the ceiling's glass dome.

It had been a difficult week. Another riot inside Nostraza, and this time, that girl—Serce's granddaughter if Cloris Payne was to be believed—had disappeared. He'd already confirmed her two siblings remained behind the prison's walls, and as far as he could tell, it seemed she'd died in the Hollow. Still, Rion wanted to be sure.

He'd sent his disappointment of a son looking for her. He knew Nadir would keep his secrets. Even if he hated him, Nadir had no choice but to be loyal. Rion had too much insurance to use against him.

Rion had pretended the girl was no one. She might have been the heir of Heart, but her magic was gone, and she *was* useless.

He should have killed her all those years ago, except that wretched priestess had convinced him otherwise. Why had he let her talk him into anything? She'd convinced him he could use the heir of Heart to claim the land that refused to be claimed, but it was all lies. She had a silver tongue and just enough feigned authority to make Rion fear Zerra's wrath. Despite his opinions about their god, she was still a god.

When he got his hands on the girl, he'd do what he should have done twelve years ago—end her and do away with the brother and sister, too. This chapter in the history of Heart would finally be over.

You're on the right track.

A voice popped into Rion's head, and he shot up in his seat.

Herric.

After all these years.

"What?" Rion asked into the empty space, hardly daring to believe he'd returned.

Heart cannot be claimed as long as its heir lives.

Rion narrowed his eyes. "Where have you been?"

Below. I am the Lord of the Underworld.

His breath hitched at those words. Was this what had happened to Herric?

"How? I don't understand."

I pushed too far. I continued to dig and dig until, one day, it became too much. I was trapped, forced to remain here at the bottom of the world amongst the souls of the dead, where I rule without challenge.

"How did you become the lord?" Rion asked, and Herric chuckled.

What a very predictable question.

Rion pressed his lips together in annoyance at the condescension in Herric's tone.

I am the only living being on this plane. I claimed this crown when I lost my own. My nephew Elias had already been named Primary and took over in my stead, burying the truth about me.

"He's the one inside the Torch?"

He is.

"How are you speaking to me then?"

There are many things I can do, Rion. Things your mind cannot even begin to comprehend. But I grow tired of this place. It is dead.

I want to feel sunlight on my face. The wind in my hair. I want to see the aurora lights in the sky. It's been so long.

"And what do you want from me?" Rion asked as a warning pricked up the back of his neck. Why was Herric contacting him *now*?

Find me the ark of Heart. You've read my journals—do you understand what they are?

"How am I supposed to do that? The arks are all hidden. Or gone."

Use the Primary.

"There is no Primary," Rion said, though at that moment, he realized that probably wasn't true.

There is. The magic of Heart still lives deep in the earth.

"Where do I look?" Rion asked as thoughts cycled through his head. The prisoner was dead, or so he presumed, which meant the Primary might be someone else. The brother was of Woodlands magic, and the sister had no power of which to speak. Perhaps he'd have to hunt through the settlements searching for the Primary. The old magic of Heart had always followed through the female line.

That is what you must discover.

"What if I could find the ark without the heir?"

It's possible. However, I still require the Primary to use it.

"Use it how?"

There is great magic inside the ark of Heart. Amara was the strongest of us. And after I'm done with the heir, you can kill her, and the people of Heart will die. Only then will the land stop fighting you.

Rion chewed on those words. "And what do I get in exchange for all of this? Freeing the Lord of the Underworld?"

Herric chuckled again, the sound like chains dragging over stone.

Why stop at Heart? You seek a source of the most powerful virulence in existence, and I am surrounded by it. You want to use it and learn to control it. You want to know everything it is capable of.

I can teach you, King Rion of The Aurora. I can show you where I failed.

I can give you everything.

CHAPTER 47

LOR

PRESENT DAY

Morning comes all too soon. I wake up wrapped in Nadir's arms, his warm breath dusting the back of my neck. We stayed up late talking with Rhiannon and fell asleep instantly after returning to our room.

We slept later than I'd intended, but we aren't scheduled to meet with the other rulers for another hour. Still, we should get up, have something to eat, and dress.

When I shift, Nadir groans and tightens his arms around me, dragging me closer.

"Where are you going, Lightning Bug?"

"The meeting is soon," I say.

He groans again. "Great."

I roll over to face him, studying his eyes. They swirl with specks of blue and green. He gives me a small smile.

"What are you thinking about?"

I shake my head. "I don't know. Everything."

"It's going to be fine."

I give him a tight smile. We still haven't discussed the bombshell that Cloris dropped about one of us giving up our crown. Nadir said it would be him, but I still want to confirm that he's sure about this or at least talk about how he's feeling. But it's like we're moving a million miles a minute, and there hasn't been time.

Finally, we drag ourselves out of bed when breakfast arrives. I eat lightly because my stomach is twisted into knots. I don a simple red dress with long sleeves and a sweetheart neckline that Rhiannon supplied. It's time to remind everyone of who I am.

"Ready?" Nadir asks.

"Not really," I say.

He cups my cheek with his hand and drops his forehead to mine. "Let's go, Heart Queen."

At the top of the stairs, we see Rhiannon and Etienne talking in low voices, their heads bent close. She touches his arm and then looks up at the sound of our approach. If I fail to save Heart, Rhiannon and Etienne will lose everything, too.

"Good morning," she says brightly as Etienne dips his chin. "Everyone's here."

Nadir and I clasp hands and make our way down the hall.

At our entrance, everyone in the salon turns towards us. The large room is covered with floral wallpaper and a thick fur rug. It boasts a bank of windows along the far side draped with heavy velvet curtains. In the middle is a low table surrounded by an array of armchairs and sofas where some of the most powerful people on the continent sit.

Bronte, the queen of Tor; Cedar and Elswyth, king and queen of The Woodlands; D'Arcy, the queen of Celestria; and Cyan, Linden, and Anemone from Alluvion. My brother and sister, and Mael and Amya, are also in the room. Etienne follows in a moment later.

"Hi," I say, addressing Cyan, already knowing I can't avoid this conversation. His eyes narrow, and he stands up from his seat. Today, he's wearing long grey pants and a thin green tunic. Apparently, he does own shoes, because his feet are stuffed into a pair of leather sandals.

"Hi?" comes a bitter voice. Linden is already standing, her teeth bared, and her posture curved with aggression. "Hi? You left our kingdom in shambles, and you presume to stand there acting like nothing happened!"

She leaps, and I step back as Cyan and Anemone seize her by each of her arms while Nadir steps in front, shielding me with his body.

"Back off," he says with a snarl, and I shudder to think what these two would do if they were alone in a room with me as the subject of their quarrel.

"She stole from us!" Linden screams. "She's no different from her grandmother! Vile, selfish witch!"

I straighten my shoulders, trying not to let her words affect me. She's right. I stole from them, and maybe I am just like Serce, but I'm *trying* to do better than she did.

"I had no choice," I say, pushing past Nadir. He stands at my shoulder, ready if I should need him.

"You had a choice. You always have a choice," Cyan says. "Don't give me that bullshit."

"Fine. I had a choice. And I chose myself and my mate over a piece of rock. Happy now?"

Cyan's lips press together. "You destroyed half my castle. Killed people."

"I regret that," I say. "I am truly sorry for everything, but you were planning to give me up to the Aurora King."

"Cyan's answer is a skeptical look.

"Will you hear us out?" I ask. "Nadir and I have some things to tell you. Things that seem incomprehensible, but I assure you are all real. And for whatever it's worth, I have your ark and intend to return it to you today."

"But?" he asks, arching an eyebrow as he senses my hesitation.

"If you'll listen, I'll explain everything."

"Fine," Cyan says. "But this better be good."

I snort a derisive laugh. "It's something all right."

Over the next hour, we start explaining, and when we finish speaking, we're met with surprised silence.

"This is impossible," D'Arcy says, but there is no conviction in it. Our tale is too out there, too wild, not to be true. Why would we make all of this up?

"I know it sounds that way," Nadir says. "But I was in the Evanescence. I saw my grandfather, and he said that my father used some kind of alternate magic to coerce the Torch into forcing him to descend."

Bronte shakes her head. "If the Artefacts can be manipulated in such a way, then this throws everything we've ever believed into question."

A grim silence circles around the room. She's right. It shakes the foundations of everything Ouranos has been built on for thousands of years. Zerra is a lie. The Artefacts aren't what we thought they were. And all this time, we've actually been the puppets of some distant entity that doesn't appear to care all that much whether any of us live or die.

"Beyond that," Cedar says. "What about Zerra? You mean to tell us we've spent our lives worshipping a spoiled, selfish brat?"

"That appears to be the measure of it," I reply. "The Empyrium may have had noble intentions . . . I think? But it's clear they have no idea how life moves for those with mortality, even when you have the long life of the Fae."

"This is all . . ." Bronte says.

"Monstrous," Elswyth finishes.

"So you see why I did what I did?" I ask, addressing Cyan and my aunt. "I know it was wrong, but I had to."

A pause hangs around the room.

"There's also something more you need to know about my grandmother."

Nadir reaches over and takes my hand. I don't want to share this, but they all deserve to know why they lost their magic for fifty years. They should never have been punished for what Serce did.

I look at Linden, who's staring at me like she wants to wrap a rope around my neck and tighten it. What I'm about to share won't help matters.

"Someone needs to restrain her before I do," I say, pointing to my aunt, who narrows her eyes. Cyan looks at her.

"Linden will control herself," he says with authority, and I can tell she wants to argue. Then he adds in a softer voice, "Killing the girl won't bring your brother back, my love. Let her speak."

I watch some of the air deflate from her rigid posture. "Fine," she says sharply. "I'll kill her later."

"Thank you," I say, rolling my eyes. I guess that's the best I'm getting.

I explain what happened with the bonding that went wrong.

"Primaries cannot bond," D'Arcy says.

"It's not that they can't," Bronte interrupts. "It's just that it's always been considered a bit taboo."

D'Arcy wrinkles her nose.

"Anyway," I say. "It *is* possible, according to Cloris Payne."

"Cloris died that day," Cyan says, rather forcefully. "What do you mean?"

"I'll get to that part," I say, wondering what his problem is.

I then go on to explain what happened when my grand-mother tried to steal the magic of Heart.

"I knew it was her fault!" Linden hisses. "She killed him."

Physically, she holds herself back, but her expression seethes with anger. I see the hurt and loss in her eyes. She misses her brother. I can't blame her for that. I'd want to do the same if anything ever happened to Tristan.

"Linden," Cedar says softly. "It is not Lor's fault. Surely you see that. Wolf agreed to the bonding as well. She is our family."

"She is not—" Linden starts, but I interrupt her.

"I'm sorry," I say. "I'm sorry. I wish I could take all of this back. I wish I could have stopped all of this. I wish my grandmother hadn't done it and they were all alive. I wish that I could take your pain away. Our grandmother's actions killed our parents, too. It was because of her that we were tossed into the worst prison on the continent when we were children."

A tear slips down Linden's cheek, and she scrubs it angrily away.

"You are our family. *Please.*"

Linden shakes her head, and I know I haven't won her over, but there's something slightly softer in her ire.

"Go on," she finally says, and I nod, understanding that's the best I'm getting right now.

"What does all of this have to do with Zerra?" Cyan asks, picking up our conversation.

I blow out a breath.

"I was taken to the Evanescence, where the Empyrium told me they wanted to replace Zerra."

"Sounds like she needs it," Cedar scoffs.

"And when I wore the Heart Crown, I saw my mother," I say.

Bronte whistles. "How many surprises do you have for us, girl?"

I go on to explain everything my mother told me, and when I'm done, I've shocked them all yet again.

"This is one hell of a twist you're in," Cyan says, and I see the softening in his expression. He might finally understand why my hands were tied.

"Lor," Elswyth says, drawing everyone's attention to her. "How can we help?"

"There are two things we need," I say. "The first is that the arks must all be destroyed, and you are the only ones who can do it."

Amya appears with the arks in her arms and deposits them on the table in the center of the room, where they glitter faintly in the light. It's hard not to feel the intangible power they give off. Bronte reaches out and picks up the ark of Tor, studying it.

"When I ascended, the Stone told me this existed, but Zerra has had it in her possession for a long time. I never expected to see it," she says.

I notice D'Arcy peering at the pile like she doesn't want to look but can't help herself.

"And we need a High Priestess," I say. "One who won't kill me or drag me back to Zerra."

Anemone shifts in her seat and clears her throat. I think she's about to say something, but she remains silent.

"Where will you find a priestess?" Bronte asks. "It's not like they're walking around everywhere you look. It's miles to their closest temple, and that's assuming anyone will even help you."

"She's right," Cedar adds. "If what you say about Cloris is

accurate, then they probably will either kill you on sight or capture you for Zerra themselves. The legends say they can communicate with her."

"Why should we do any of this?" D'Arcy interrupts. "This sounds like your fight. And that's assuming I believe a word you've said."

My shoulders sag.

"You don't believe us?"

"It's . . . impossible," she says, repeating her earlier sentiment.

"Is it? Or do you just not want to believe it?"

She purses her lips together and folds her arms, not deigning to respond.

"Wow, you sure attract a lot of drama," Anemone says, scanning me from head to toe.

"That's me," I say wryly. "I don't want it. I don't want to be a god. I want to reclaim my queendom and bond with my mate."

"After everything you've told us, you cannot risk a bond!" D'Arcy says, slamming her hand on the armrest. "This is madness."

"We weren't asking for your permission," I say.

"No, but you want our help," she spits back.

"We will do whatever we can to help," Elswyth says. "Cedar and I swore we'd assist with whatever you need, and that hasn't changed."

Relief untwists in my chest at those words.

"Really?"

"Really."

She gives me a kind smile as Linden huffs.

"Enough," Cedar says to his sister. "I do not hold the heirs of Heart responsible for Wolf's choices. He stood by and let it happen, too. And these three certainly aren't to blame for any of that."

Linden's eyes darken to the deepest shade of pine trees at midnight as she presses her mouth together so hard her lips turn bloodless.

"If you can't join in a productive conversation, then perhaps it's best you leave the room." Cedar pins her with a challenging look, and if I didn't already like him, I'd hug him right now.

Linden doesn't respond; she just stands up, and I think she might actually leave, but instead, she walks over to the window, spins around, and folds her arms before she leans against it, one foot planted against the wall. She glares at me, and I rub my face.

"And finally, I guess what we also need is protection. Only I can destroy the ark of Heart, just like only you can destroy those lying in front of you, but we have no idea what we're going into beyond that."

"Our armies are yours," Cedar says without hesitation.

"Thank you," Nadir says. "But I don't think that's what we need."

Everyone watches him as he sits forward in his seat with his hands clasped between his legs.

"My father's army outmatches yours by the thousands. Even if we combined everyone's in this room, it wouldn't be enough. Maybe if we had Aphelion, but that isn't an option right now."

D'Arcy huffs, reminding us of her displeasure.

"And it's clear not everyone is amenable to that anyway," he adds, looking at her.

"So then what?" Cedar asks.

"I think we should go quietly," Nadir says. "We'll need to reach the Torch to complete the bonding, but first, we have to figure out what exactly my father is up to."

"So I'll go in," Amya says from where she perches on the arm of my sister's chair.

Nadir shakes his head. "I don't know if he trusts you anymore."

"Maybe not, but if anyone can get close to him in this room, it's me."

"If he suspects anything, there's no telling what he'll do," Nadir says.

"I know that," she answers, picking at the lace of her skirt. "But what other choice do we have?" She gives Nadir a look that dares him to argue with her.

"I'll go with her," Mael says. "Your father has never considered me a threat or worthy of his notice."

"What will you say if he asks where I am?"

"That we don't know. That we tried to convince you to come home and give up the girl, but we can no longer support your reckless choices."

Mael winks at Nadir, and he gives his friend a rueful smile.

"He'd probably buy that," Nadir says. "Anything that makes me look like a fool."

"I won't support this," D'Arcy says again. "You cannot repeat the history of your grandparents. You must find another way. Why should I destroy my ark? This was stolen from my queendom and belongs to me. I do not care if *you're* forced to live in the Evanescence."

"There is no other way," I snap. "Zerra is trying to kill me, and I don't know how long we have before she catches up with us. If I die, then the magic of Heart will be gone and then you're all at risk too."

"What happens to it?" D'Arcy asks. "Magic cannot just disappear."

"It goes to all of you."

I say the words matter-of-factly, knowing I have to tell them the truth.

"So you want us to save magic for *you* when we could all become more powerful? Do you think we're fools?" D'Arcy challenges.

"Is that really what you want?" I ask, standing up. "Is that really the queen you want to be? Do you want to be like Rion? Or Zerra? Like my *grandmother*? Aren't you listening to what I'm saying? This isn't about just me or Heart!" D'Arcy blinks her big black eyes. It's the slightest reaction, but I sense my words reach something inside her.

"What will you do when she is dead? How do you plan to avoid becoming Zerra? What will happen to Ouranos if you do not take her place?"

Any of the people in this room *could* take her place, but I still can't tell them. I can't let anyone else shoulder this load on my behalf. I will find another way. I hope. I open my mouth and close it. "I don't know . . . I haven't figured that part out yet."

She sniffs sharply and folds her pale arms.

"I want to save my people. I want to fix what my grand-mother did, and I want...I want to bond with my mate." A knot swells in my throat. "You lost your mate. You understand why I cannot give him up."

Her expression turns icy, and maybe that was the wrong thing to say.

"I want no part of this," she says and stands up.

She stops in front of me and Nadir, looking down her slim nose.

"A mate bond is a wonderful thing, but your happiness doesn't come before everyone else."

"That's not only what this is about!" I shout.

"Isn't it?" she asks with a tip of her head.

"I *know* you don't want to be responsible for the death of these settlements. What if this were *your* home?"

D'Arcy's jaw hardens as she quickly shakes her head. With-out another word, she storms out of the room. I watch her leave, my heart deflating in my chest. If we don't have every-one, then we have nothing.

"I will destroy the ark of The Woodlands, and I'll come with you to The Aurora," Cedar says a moment later. "Elswyth should return home to watch over the kingdom, but I won't let you face Rion alone. I owe this to my brother and to all of you for failing you twelve years ago."

"Thank you," I say, clasping my hands at my chest. "Thank you."

I look at the others. Bronte seems to be considering every-thing, while Anemone is giving me a curious look.

"What if you just ascended?" Bronte asks. "Wouldn't that give you enough strength?"

I explain what my mother said about needing an heir and how I'd be vulnerable to Zerra during an ascension.

"It wouldn't be that much use anyway," Anemone says.

"Why not?" I ask.

Anemone looks at me, smoothing her long blue skirt over her knees.

"While an Ascension does grant a ruler more power, it is but a shadow when compared to a bond, *especially* one between mates. Given that mate bonds are chosen by fate, it seems that you have found your purpose and your destiny."

"How do you know that?"

She inhales a long breath and then reaches up to the collar of her dress and pulls it aside. Everyone leans in as they note the marking tattooed into her skin. Each of the seven Artefacts rendered in miniature in precise detail form a circle. "I am . . . was . . . one of Zerra's High Priestesses."

I sink down onto the sofa and look at Nadir, my limbs trembling with a wash of hope.

"I don't understand."

She sighs and shifts as though what she's about to say makes her uncomfortable.

"A long time ago, I was chosen along with two of my sisters to seek out the remaining arks. You already know one of them—Cloris, of course.

"My name was Rosa then, and Zerra bid me to work my way into the good graces of Alluvion's king and steal the ark."

I snort. History repeating itself, indeed.

"Only things didn't go to plan." She looks at Cyan with warmth in her eyes. "We fell in love, and I knew I couldn't betray him.

"I spent years trying to placate Zerra, assuring her I was working on it and that it was just taking a little more time than I expected. But she is . . ."

"A bitch?" I offer, and Anemone nods.

"She grew more and more impatient, threatening all manner of consequences.

"So I faked my disappearance, changed my name, dyed my hair, and went underground for a long time. When I resurfaced, I was Anemone, a citizen of Alluvion's court and consort to the king."

"Whoa," I say.

"I would very much like to stop hiding," she says. "Should she ever discover my deception, she will no doubt kill me too." Her gaze slides to Cyan. "And possibly those I love."

She turns to me. "So if there is a way to end her, I will perform the bonding, Heart Queen, no matter the transgressions on my home. I understand what it's like to be at the mercy of Zerra's will, and while I wish you'd simply been honest with us, I understand your motivations."

Her gaze moves to Nadir. "I do understand what it means to do anything to be with the ones you love."

"I'm speechless," I say.

"Well, that's a first," Mael quips, and I toss him a glare.

"I also happen to have a copy of the Book of Night back in the Crystal Palace," Anemone adds.

My mouth opens in surprise. Finally, something works in our favor.

"And the bonding won't open us up to Zerra?" Nadir asks as Anemone shakes her head.

"She holds no dominion over bonds. Only the Artefacts are necessary to combine your magic."

I blow out a breath. That seems like good news, at least.

"Do you know why the arks affect her?" I ask.

"The priestesses know of dark magic, and the kings of The Aurora are not the first to meddle with its power, nor will they be the last," Anemone says.

"Zerra is the vessel that connects Imperial magic to the Artefacts and thus to the High Fae. I've always suspected the reason these items affect her so strongly is because the arks act in opposition to that, trying to sever that link, which, in turn, would kill her."

I nod. I'm not sure if that makes sense, but it doesn't really matter. All that matters is destroying them.

"Do you have any idea why Lor is immune to the effects of arcturite?" Nadir asks, and yet again, I sense everyone's shock.

Anemone's gaze traces over me as she nods. "It's not that the magic of arcturite can't be overcome, it's that it requires a great amount of power to do so. I've never heard of it happening before, but I suppose these are unprecedented times."

I return her nod, feeling like another brick has been stacked onto my shoulders.

"Thank you for all of this. We are so grateful," I say to Anemone after we're all silent for a moment.

Nadir dips his head. "We appreciate this very much. Will your kingdom destroy the ark?"

My gaze falls on Cyan. "If it will rid the world of Zerra and free Anemone from her shadow, then I do not hesitate," he answers. "I remain unbonded and do not have a Primary to call upon, so

I will do the best I can. From what Coral shared with me in the past, it was used only a little by Alluvion's former rulers and thus isn't likely to be as strong as some of the other arks."

"Thank you," I whisper, tears filling my eyes.

"And I assume that means we're all going to The Aurora," Cyan says, his tone wry.

"We will need the Torch and the Crown to complete the bonding," Anemone agrees.

A hard knot loosens in my chest. We're a long way from the end, but at least this is one step in the right direction.

My gaze slides to Bronte, who's watching everything with a deep furrow between her brows. She considers me with a sweep of her eyes.

"You're alliance with my father? Does this create problems for you?" Nadir asks, and Bronte's mouth presses together.

"I'm allied with your father in the way a mouse might befriend a lion, hoping to avoid its jaws."

"You're no mouse," I answer, and she laughs, her grey eyes sparkling.

"Perhaps, but our realms border one another, and it's always been prudent not to ruffle Rion's feathers." She pauses. "But I have no true loyalty to him."

"So will you help us?" Nadir asks before Bronte turns her attention to me.

"Little queen, I'm not sure what to make of any of this or of you, for that matter, but I will destroy the ark. I want no part of anything created by the Lord of the Underworld. Beyond that, I promise you nothing, but if you're all heading north— well, I just happen to be going that way too."

CHAPTER 48

NADIR

After our discussion with the rulers, Cedar, Bronte, and Cyan agree to destroy their arks in the morning once they've had some rest and have the full force of their power. We'll do it inside the ruined walls of Heart, hoping to contain any catastrophic blowback. I'm not sure what we'll do about D'Arcy yet. This endeavor is an all-or-nothing proposition. Maybe we can convince her yet.

Amya and Mael will also head out once we're done, returning to the Keep to discover anything useful, including where Father is keeping the ark.

The kings and queens who have agreed to join us will travel north in our company. I'm not surprised that D'Arcy declined to help us—she's never been one to get in the middle of anyone's affairs, even to her own detriment, but I'm grateful for the help we have.

I don't know how anyone could hear Lor's story or see the plea in her eyes and turn away.

It's late by the time we're finished talking, and Lor and I retreat to our room overlooking the Heart Castle. When I exit the bathroom, she's staring out the window, and I can practically see a million thoughts swirling around her head in the tense set of her shoulders.

I walk over and circle my arms around her waist, pressing my chin into the curve of her throat. Her hands slide over mine as she leans back and looks up at me.

"Nadir. We have to talk about the bonding and the final condition Cloris shared with us."

I sigh and let her go, rubbing a hand down my face and heading for the fire, bracing my hands on the mantel and dropping my head.

I'd already told her my decision, but I knew she wouldn't accept this without an argument.

"If you don't want to go through with the bonding, I'll understand," she says. "I can't ask you to give up your crown for me."

I whip around to face her. "Of course we're going through with it," I say. "How could you ever say that? Lor. I'm giving up my position as Primary of The Aurora." I stride over to her and wrap a hand around the side of her neck. "It was never a question."

"I can't ask you to do that," she says.

"You're not asking. I'm offering."

"Nadir...but what about everything you've wanted? All the years you've spent trying to bring down your father?"

I shake my head. "You still don't get it, do you, Lightning Bug?"

"What don't I get?"

"I never wanted a crown, Lor. That was never my motivation."

She watches me, those big dark eyes filled with conflict and emotion. Those eyes drown me every time I look into them.

"I want to end my father, not because I want a crown but because I want The Aurora to have a better ruler."

"And?" she asks.

I tip my head and smile. "While I can't be sure of who the Torch will choose, I have an idea."

Lor pauses, and then her eyes widen. "Amya."

"Amya," I say.

"Are you sure about this?" she asks.

Of course I'm sure. I've never been more sure of anything in my life. I could never ask Lor to give up everything she's fought for. Everything she dreamed of every night she rotted away in Nostraza. I can't give her those years back, but I *can* give her this.

"Lor, I want to end my father and release my mother from his hold. But what I want more than anything is to stand by your side. To be with you every day we have left on this earth. To stand with you and be your rock. To be your mate and your partner."

The flicker in her eyes is uncertain. "But I'll be stronger. I'll have more magic than you."

My answering smile is wry. "You're already stronger than me, Lor, in every way possible. It's what I love so much about you."

"Nad—"

I press my thumb to her mouth, silencing every protest she can summon. "Stop it. It's my fucking *honor* to do this for you. I promised I would burn down the entire world for you, and I meant it every single time."

"This isn't burning the world down," she says. "This is changing who you are."

I shake my head. "It's not who I am. I meant I'd do anything, and if it means changing a piece of myself, then I would do that too."

I sweep my thumb over her cheek, tucking a lock of hair behind her ear.

"What's bothering you about this?"

"I don't want you to regret it. I don't want you to resent me or the choice you made. I don't want you to do this just for me."

"I'm not," I say. "I mean, I am, but not in the way you're implying. I'm doing it for us. I'm doing it for Heart, The Aurora, and all of Ouranos. We can't beat my father without the bond. And you can't destroy the ark without it. This makes sense."

"Just because it makes sense doesn't mean you might not regret this one day. And didn't you tell me once you couldn't risk the magic of The Aurora going somewhere else?"

"If I'm no longer the Primary, there is nothing stopping me from killing him. If I step down willingly first, then the Torch will not punish us. And if we don't stop Zerra and my father, there will be nothing left to protect."

She blows out a breath and presses her forehead against my chest before looking back up. "How did we end up with villains on every side of us?"

I smirk. "I never thought I'd end up fighting for everyone. But that day we escaped my father in Heart, I knew then I was protecting you not for myself, but for every single being on the continent."

I touch her cheek, and she lays a hand over mine.

"I wish it didn't have to be this way."

"I don't care. I wish I could open my brain and let you see that I don't care about a crown. I have never cared about a crown. I care only for you."

Then I lean down and kiss her, hoping that I'm conveying everything my words are saying. I *don't* care. Maybe when I was younger I liked the idea. Even a few months ago, if you'd asked me the question, I might have told you I wanted it, but Lor has changed me in ways that I can never return from. The crown isn't important. What matters is family and friendship and this burning flame I carry for her in my heart. One that I won't let be snuffed out. The Empyrium aren't taking her from me, and Zerra certainly isn't, and we'll find some way through all of this.

My mouth finds hers, our lips fusing together in a slide of warmth. Her tongue grazes the seam of my lips, and I part them. We kiss, luxuriating in the decadence of its slow perusal, discovering one another over and over.

I've never been so grateful to live a nearly immortal life. I have never been so relieved to know that should we survive any of this, I will have so many years to explore every layer and facet of this incredible woman who, despite everything, has chosen me.

"I love you so much," I murmur as I pull her in closer, my hand sliding down her back and over the delicious curve of her ass.

"I love you too," she whispers.

And once we've bonded and Lor ascends to her throne, then we'll have another eternity to enjoy each other in the Evanescence. Even then, none of it will ever be enough.

I maneuver her to the edge of the bed, but at the last moment, she spins us around and pushes me down.

"Sit," she says, a smirk curling on her face. Then she falls to her knees and places a kiss on my chest. Her hands slide under the fabric of my tunic, exploring the map of my body, her fingers curving over the contours and planes as I respond with a shiver.

"Remember when I wouldn't let you touch me in the Keep?" she asks, and I chuckle.

"How could I ever forget?" My hands slide into her hair before I tip her face up to mine. "I remember everything, Lor. Every moment. Every smile. Every seemingly insignificant look. Every second has become a part of me, and I will do anything to hang on to this." I give her a smirk of my own. "And that was still the hottest fucking blow job of my life. Even the particles of dust I become someday will remember it."

She laughs. "Hottest? Surely I can top that."

My face splits into a smile. "Care for a challenge?"

"Always."

She leans down to kiss me before tugging up the hem of my tunic.

"Take this off," she says. "I still like looking at you."

I do as she asks, pulling it over my head and tossing it to the side.

"Last time, you refused to do the same."

"I did," she muses, and I'm almost positive she's about to defy me just to make me suffer, but she stands up and then slowly peels off her clothes. I can't take my eyes off her as she reveals every inch of her warm brown skin.

I love every curve and line. Every tiny mark. I study the scars left on her body, deciding at that moment to let go of the anger I feel every time I see them. When I look at her, I will see only the evidence of her strength and resilience. The proud way she holds herself and the loving passion she brings to everything. If she chooses to wear them as badges of honor, I can view them like that too.

I lick my lips as I think of the sweetness of her pussy as she allows me to drink in the flare of her hips and the softness of her thighs. Her round breasts that are the perfect size for my hands, and then her lips and her eyes and the nose that I love to kiss. The birthmark on her hip that I've just realized looks like a heart. How have I never noticed that before?

When our gazes meet, she smiles before approaching and falling before me again. Her hands slide up my stomach and chest, sweeping over my shoulders.

Then she reaches for the ties on my pants and slowly pulls them open. She hasn't touched me anywhere below my navel yet, but I'm already so hard I have to grit my teeth. She takes her time, humming as she drags out each lace with agonizing slowness.

She shifts close enough that I feel the barest brush of her breasts against my cock, and I choke on a moan.

"Lor," I growl.

"Yes?" She blinks up at me innocently.

"Hurry the fuck up, would you?"

She laughs, the sound churning from the bottom of her chest. It's warm and feels like sunshine, and gods, it's the most beautiful fucking thing.

"Surely you know better than to order me around, Aurora Prince?"

I grin. "I was hoping you'd go easy on me today."

She laughs again and then grips the waist of my pants and tugs. I lift my hips so she can slide them off. When she's done, she stares at my cock, and that makes me even harder.

"Is this what's bothering you?" she asks with mock pity, and I let out a sound that is half laugh, half sob.

Then she puts me out of my misery and wraps a hand around the base before she closes her warm, wet mouth over the tip and sucks.

"Fuck," I gasp. She takes me deeper, swallowing more of me. I'm not going to last. Her cheeks hollow out, and she slides up, her hand pumping me at the same time.

"Better?" she asks after she releases me with a pop.

"Better," I grit out as my hand slides into her hair. This time, I *will* be touching her. "You always look so fucking pretty with my cock in your mouth."

She grins and resumes her movements, drawing me deep as I shiver with each sweep of her tongue and the heat of her lips. My hips move, thrusting upwards into her mouth, sliding down her throat as my vision blurs and my fist tightens into her hair.

Her hands find my waist, and she grips it as she lets me take over, guiding her where I want. "Fuck, you feel so good," I growl, thrusting over and over. "That's my girl. Take all of me." And then I feel myself thicken before I come, spilling into her mouth.

She swallows me down and then slides off before wiping her lips with the back of her hand. "Hotter?" she asks, and I laugh.

"Fuck yes, Lor. Every single time is hotter."

She smiles, and then I pull her up so she straddles my lap. My hand slips between us, and she's so warm and wet that I nearly come again. My middle finger slips into her as she whimpers, my thumb teasing her clit while her hips writhe against me, making my cock hard all over again.

I flip her over onto the bed, and she lets out a delighted scream. Starting with her ankles, I kiss my way up her body, inhaling that smoky scent of roses and lightning.

When I finally reach her mouth, I consume her. My kiss is every promise I've offered and the heart that I've given to her body and soul. As we kiss, I nudge my hips between her thighs. Using my knee, I push her leg up, and then I position myself at her entrance, sliding into her hot, tight pussy as we both moan.

She feels like an endless cycle of want and need. Desire and friction coming together with the most exquisite bliss in our little corner of heaven. My hips thrust into her as my thumb circles her clit, my movements slow but forceful.

"Nadir," she gasps as she clings to my shoulders. Our eyes meet as I pump into her, the walls of her wet heat fluttering around me. I lean down to suck on her neck as I slowly bring her to the edge. Our magic rises, filtering out and twinning together. Gods, will it be like this every time? Every moment with her *is* magic.

I can feel her melting, and I want to make her fall apart. I want nothing more than to be the one who makes her cheeks flush and be responsible for those heady sounds every single day.

She cries out, her back arching as she comes around my cock, tightening with the most mind-numbing pressure. I continue moving, chasing another release, and then I spill into her again as our bodies roll together like the tides under a waning moon.

I kiss her again, and I could do this until the sun rises. I could kiss her forever. Until the stars burn out and the world turns to ash.

I just hope that day doesn't come anytime soon.

And if it does, that we're still around to see it because as long as I have her, it will all be worth it.

CHAPTER 49

GABRIEL

Atlas's capture does nothing to quell the chaos churning through Aphelion. I'd hoped it would simmer some of the boiling tempers, but all it's done is stoke the fires.

I suppose I was being too optimistic. Or rather, naive.

They know he's alive, sitting in a cell, and they want his head. But the low fae won't be satisfied with Atlas's death alone, and I understand. Undoing the century of damage he caused will take a long time. Laws need to be repealed. Reparations need to be made. I have no actual idea of what the finances of this kingdom look like—that has never been my responsibility—but I hope we can do something to compensate them, even though gold can never make up for the stripping away of one's dignity and rights.

The problem is I'm already acting on a thin edge of authority, and I don't have the power to do any of this.

A fact I'm reminded of as I sit in the council chamber to Tyr's left as the heads of the districts continue to argue. He didn't want to join us, but I convinced him that he needed to be here. He's been spending most of his time working with his magic, trying to regain enough power to destroy the ark. For now, it sits safely in the study in its case. I'm not sure what he's waiting for—how will he even know if he has enough magic unless he tries?

But Lor and Nadir said we have a bit of time, and I'm not pushing him yet.

Erevan sits across from me, and no one in this room trusts him. They know he's the Primary now, but these nobles all hate him.

"He blew up half of my district!" the head of the Twelfth District, Virgil, shouts. "What is he even doing in this room?"

Every eye swings to Erevan, who glares at Virgil.

"You all deserved it and worse," he says, his voice cold with fury. He's not even trying to win them over. I sigh and rub my forehead with two fingers, trying to massage away the ache building behind my left eye.

Though Atlas initially encountered some opposition to his new rules when he took over, the nobles quickly realized that it was beneficial to have the low fae corralled and "managed." They could pay them next to nothing to work in their homes and businesses, and any complaints were swept under the rug. They became far too comfortable with this new normal. There have been grumblings from a few corners of late, but not enough to compel anyone into upsetting the status quo.

So Erevan is right about all of it, and I understand the source of his anger, but this baiting isn't getting him anywhere.

"You hear that?" Virgil exclaims. "How can we support a king who believes this of his most valuable citizens?"

Oh shit, that is precisely the worst thing he could say.

Erevan presses his hands to the table and stands up, leaning towards him.

"Most valuable citizens?" he hisses. "No one in this room is more valuable than anyone who lives out there." He scans Virgil from head to toe. "In fact, I might argue the opposite is true."

"How dare—"

"How dare I? How dare *you* sit here in your fancy clothes and with your fancy houses and cast aspersions on people you've all taken advantage of and who are just trying to survive?"

Erevan slaps the table.

"The only right thing to do is repeal every law against the low fae," he says to a chorus of shocked whispers and gasps. "I had hoped that you sycophants would finally see reason and agree because it is the right thing to do, but the longer I sit here listening to you windbags, the more I realize you are all lost causes. You care for no one and nothing but yourselves."

Erevan hunches forward.

"You are not the king here yet!" accuses a female High Fae—the head of District Thirteen. Or is it Fourteen?

"No," Erevan says, "but Tyr agrees, and he *is* the king. In case any of you have forgotten?"

Every eye flicks to Tyr, who sits quietly with his forehead crumpled in worry. It's actually more emotion than I've seen from him in a while. Tyr does agree with Erevan. I've been there to witness many talks the two of them have had over the past few days. Well, Erevan talks, and Tyr nods and listens, but I understand that in Tyr's heart, he knows Erevan is right. He will free my brothers and me from our chains, and I know he wants to do the same for the people of his kingdom.

Something in me suspects he's waiting for Erevan to come around to the idea of ruling. He'll descend when he knows Aphelion is finally in good hands. The thought sends a cold dread spreading through my chest, but I know it's selfish to wish he'd remain here with me. And I also want him to find peace.

"Is this true?" Virgil demands of Tyr, who opens his mouth and closes it. Though Tyr is the king, he cannot repeal laws with impunity. The council was created many years ago, and any significant decisions like this must be voted on. While technically no one could stop him, it would be of little use to repeal the laws if there is no one actually to act on his wishes.

Though he can allow the low fae to move from The Umbra, these windbags, as Erevan so eloquently put it, can't be forced to welcome them.

"It's true," Tyr says in a soft voice, but if he was planning to say anything else, it's drowned out by a chorus of shouts and condemnations.

My eye catches on the door, and I recognize Halo, one of the Tributes. Seeing her frightened face and her hands clasped, my shoulders tighten. I was afraid of this.

Earlier this morning, Tyr asked that a message be sent to Apricia requesting she return to her home in the Twenty-Fourth

District. He'd spoken with the Mirror, which confirmed it had chosen her through Atlas's deception, and it wouldn't be right to proceed with a bonding.

In fact, every remaining Tribute was granted a pardon and told they could return to their former lives. Some might be happier about that news than others.

The Mirror told Tyr that he could hold his own Trial to determine his bonded partner at a later time. I doubt that will ever happen, but I was all too happy to have the news delivered to Apricia. I wanted to handle it myself, but then I was called to this stupid meeting.

I was hoping she'd go quietly with her tail between her legs, but from the look on Halo's face, I know that was also naive and wishful thinking. She spots me and then scurries to where I'm sitting. No one seems to notice; everyone is too busy arguing amongst themselves.

She bends down and whispers, "We need help. Apricia hasn't taken the news of her dismissal well."

I notice Cornelius Heulfryn eyeing the two of us from across the table. I try to decide whether soliciting his help would be better or worse. Can he calm his daughter down? In hindsight, maybe I should have discussed all of this with him to begin with. He's always struck me as a reasonable man, but I rushed through the process in my excitement to get Apricia out of here.

"I'm coming," I whisper to Halo. Then I look over at Cornelius and jerk my chin towards the door. He nods and pushes himself up, proving that he's also a smart man.

I stand too as Erevan gives me a quizzical look.

"Sorry, I need to go," I say. I feel bad leaving him and Tyr, but I have no authority here, and they'll have to sort this out on their own.

Cornelius and I follow Halo out of the room and through the palace into the queen's wing. Even from a distance, I hear the screech that's so adept at shredding every eardrum located within a square mile.

Halo walks in front of us with her hands clasped and tosses a worried look over her shoulder.

"What is the meaning of this?" Cornelius asks, peering down the hallway.

"I regret not telling you this earlier," I say, "but this morning, Tyr released the Sun Queen Tributes from their obligations and they were told they could return home."

"Could?" Cornelius asks, looking at me.

"Were asked to return home . . . in the case of your daughter."

The truth is the other Tributes were invited to remain at the Sun Court, but Apricia's letter made no such offer. I think Tyr couldn't stand the reminder. I think if he were a crueler man, he might have sent Apricia out of Aphelion altogether.

"I see," Cornelius says, his lips pressing together.

"It seems she's not taking the news well."

That's an understatement, I realize as we draw closer. The very walls seem to be vibrating with the sounds of Apricia's tantrum. Glass shatters, and furniture breaks. We pick up our paces, entering the large bedroom suite that has been the former residence of a line of Sun Queens to witness a most pitiful sight.

Apricia is a frenzied nightmare of screeching, wild hair,

and tears. She's trashing the entire room—ripping the sheets, smashing the mirrors and trinkets, and kicking furniture into the walls.

"I was supposed to be the queen!" she screeches. "That bitch stole it from me! I will kill her!"

I can only assume she means Lor, who is obviously responsible for none of this, but there was never any love lost between those two.

"The Mirror chose me! I was going to be a queen!"

She repeats the same mantra over and over, and she picks up another chair and hurls it at the fireplace. It smashes apart and pieces land in the hearth, a few splinters catching flame.

I'm worried she'll burn the entire place down at this rate. Cornelius watches his daughter with a mixture of sadness and resigned exhaustion. I don't know what kind of relationship he has with her, but then he says, "She's always been... difficult."

There's a threadbare weariness in his words that makes me take pity on the man. Perhaps he thought he'd gotten her out of his hair too. What a perfect match she could have made with Atlas. They could have driven each other insane until the end of time.

"Shall I call for more guards?" I ask over the backdrop of more glass breaking and furniture shattering.

"No," he says. "I'll deal with it. Grant her this dignity, at least. Everyone will already know within the hour anyway."

I nod and step back, allowing him the opportunity to calm her down. He approaches her with his hands in front of him like he's trying to trick a wild animal into trusting him.

When Apricia sees her father, she stops, a jewelry box poised over her head.

"Apricia," he says softly. "Put it down."

She shakes her head. Tears coat her face, and her shoulders tremble. She clutches the box to her chest.

"I was going to be a queen," she says with such broken agony that a tiny, withered part of my heart almost feels sorry for her. She too was brought here under a series of false pretenses and made to believe she was risking her life for a crown.

Whatever her faults, she was also a victim of Atlas's betrayal.

Of course, she could have been a little more gracious about everything from the beginning, and nothing Atlas did excuses how she treated anyone. Including Lor. Maybe especially Lor.

"I understand that," Cornelius says, his voice low and soothing. "But the situation has changed, and His Majesty has shared his wishes."

"But why not me?" she asks. "Is he planning to find someone else?"

He shakes his head. "I do not know the king's mind. But he *is* our king, and we must honor this request."

Apricia clutches the box tighter, and then she truly breaks down, sobbing so hard she can barely catch her breath. Fat tears roll down her cheeks as she hiccups over her loss. Cornelius approaches her and wraps his arms around her.

She folds into him, sobbing into his shoulder as he runs a hand down the back of her head. He lets her cry for a moment, then directs her towards where I stand. Apricia continues to sob, still holding the jewelry box. While he might have difficulty with her, it's clear that Cornelius Heulfryn loves his daughter.

A pungent bitterness coats my tongue at that realization.

My own father was a mean drunk who killed the only family I had. While I'm certainly far from perfect, I didn't deserve that. No one does. I hope Apricia uses this moment to take a hard look at herself and the person she wants to be.

As they pass me, Cornelius stops and nods.

"I apologize for this. Please send the bill for repairs to me. I'll take care of it."

I tip my chin. That's probably not necessary, but again, this isn't my call. I'm just glad she's getting out of here.

Apricia looks at me with bloodshot eyes. For once, there's no anger or calculation in her gaze. It's just flat and emotionless. I try to feel something other than relief. Maybe she'll find someone that can handle her and make her happy. Or maybe she'll live out her days as a miserable shrew. I don't really care either way if I'm honest.

Then Cornelius shuffles Apricia out, and I hear him say softly, "Come, my girl. Your time is done here. Let's go home."

CHAPTER 50

LOR

QUEENDOM OF HEART

The next morning, someone knocks on our door, and I slide out of bed to find Tristan on the other side, his hand running across the back of his neck. He's wearing a dark green tunic and black leggings with knee-high suede boots. His midnight hair has grown longer over the last months, curling in waves around his pointed ears and the base of his neck.

"Tris, what's wrong?"

"Cedar asked to speak with me."

"Oh," I say, immediately understanding why my brother is nervous. "Does he—?"

"I don't know," he says, cutting me off. "I don't know."

"Tris, it will be okay. It's not like this is a bad thing."

"Isn't it? What if he thinks it's a terrible thing? You saw how much Linden hates us."

He paces back and forth, and I've rarely seen my brother this nervous or unsure of himself.

"What's worrying you, specifically?" I ask.

He sighs and plants his hands on his hips, dropping his head.

"When you told me about it, I kind of just pushed it away. I didn't want to think about or deal with it. I was never prepared for this. I feel . . . overwhelmed, Lor."

By now, Nadir has appeared at the door, half-dressed and mussed from sleep.

"Everything okay?" he asks.

Nadir and Tristan exchange a look.

"Sorry. I heard what you were just saying," Nadir says. "Come in."

He jerks his head for Tristan to follow, and my brother hesitates for a moment before he enters. They're still warming up to one another.

"Sit down," Nadir says, and when Tristan hesitates again, he adds, "Look, I'm giving up my crown, and you're getting one. Things that neither one of us ever expected. I think we can talk about this."

Tristan's eyes move between us. "You mean—"

"Yes," Nadir says. "I will be giving up my place as The Aurora's Primary."

"You would do that for her?" Tristan asks.

"I would do anything for her. I hope that's obvious by now."

Tristan blinks before his gaze narrows, his eyes dragging over Nadir as if he's testing the truth of his words. Something softens in his expression.

"Thank you," Tristan says, bowing his head. "For taking care of her. For . . . being there for her. I know I've been hard on you."

Nadir raises his hand. "With good reason. You don't owe me anything."

Tristan's gaze slides to me. "Maybe not, but my sister seems pretty fond of you, and I—" He sighs and rubs a hand down his face. "And we're going to be family soon."

Tears burn the backs of my eyes as Nadir's face cracks into a grin.

"Then have a seat," he says. "Let's talk about this."

Tristan settles onto one of the divans arranged around a low table while Nadir and I sit across from him. Nadir scoots forward, his elbows braced on his knees and his hands clasped.

"Feeling overwhelmed about this is perfectly normal. But Cedar is High Fae and will go on to live for many years. You don't have to figure out how to rule a kingdom overnight."

"Right," Tristan says. "I hadn't thought of it that way."

"And Cedar is a good king. His people revere him. I don't know him extremely well, but he's been kind to you and your sisters, and I've only heard good things. Even if he can be an arrogant bastard sometimes . . . well, that kind of goes with king territory."

He smirks, and Tristan's shoulders drop. I watch as something passes between Nadir and my brother. They're more alike than they realize. Both fearless and loyal. Both full of passion for the things and the people they love. Both willing to do whatever it takes to protect them.

"So I should just go and talk to him."

"I think you should," Nadir says. "And forget about Linden. She lives in Alluvion and has no say in this."

"Do you want me to come?" I ask, and Tristan shakes his head.

"No. I think I can do this alone."

"Okay. You know where to find me if you change your mind."

"Thanks." He stands up, and Nadir holds out a hand. Tristan takes it, and they shake. "Thanks to you, too."

After Tristan leaves, I turn to Nadir.

"I think you might be finally winning him over," I say, and he shrugs as if it's of no importance, but I catch the bright, hopeful look in his eyes.

An hour later, we head down to meet everyone in the foyer.

Our plan is to use the walls of Heart as a buffer against whatever might happen when we destroy the arks. It's already in shambles, so how much more damage could we do? We're all going—Nadir and I, most of the rulers, Tristan, Amya, and Mael—basically, almost everyone with protective magic. Willow is staying with Rhiannon and Etienne to reduce any potential casualties. I don't know what will happen when we destroy them, but I imagine something big, loud, and explosive. And messy.

D'Arcy left late last night, returning to Celestria. I don't know how we'll change her mind, and I have no idea how we'll proceed if she continues to refuse.

At the end of the hallway, Tristan and Cedar emerge from a room, both of them smiling, and my heart lightens.

I catch my brother's eye, and he walks over.

"How was it?" I ask.

"Good," he says with a smile. "Good. He's thrilled and wants me to come and stay with them in The Woodlands after all of this is over."

"I'm so glad," I say. "How are you feeling?"

"Much better," he says. "I'm ... really looking forward to getting to know them all. You know?"

"I know," I say.

"Okay, everyone," Nadir says, and we all turn to him. "That's all of us. Let's go."

We file out of the house and head towards Heart to gather inside the city walls.

"How do we do this?" Nadir asks Anemone.

"Each of you will need to direct as much power as possible into your ark. It will be a matter of concentrating it into one point for long enough to essentially fill it to the point of bursting."

Nadir looks around. "Everyone move to higher ground. Use the walls or the rubble. Whoever goes first will stand here." He points to a spot in the middle of the large plaza where we stand.

"Any volunteers?" Nadir asks.

"I'll go first," Bronte says, her hand on the hilt of the sword at her hip and her chin lifted. Her pewter armor glints in the sun as a breeze tosses her shiny iron hair, and there's not an ounce of fear in her expression.

"Great," Nadir says, and then we all jog away from the center, each finding a place to observe from above.

Bronte pulls the ark from her belt and contemplates it before she places it on the ground and takes a few steps back. Her gaze sweeps over us, and she dips her chin to indicate she's ready.

I swallow a thick knot, really hoping this doesn't kill her. Or us.

From each of our perches, we spin out our magic. I have no idea what Mael is capable of, but when dark violet ribbons emerge from his fingertips, circling him like a cage, I'm somehow not surprised. He might play the role of the irreverent, but it's obvious he's also lethal.

My fingers curl into fists as I consider what to do with mine. It sparks under my skin, begging to break free, but I don't want to hurt anyone. A moment later, ribbons of Nadir's light magic circle around my limbs, and instantly, my magic calms.

"Better?" he asks, and I nod.

"Better."

He uses his other hand to join his magic with Amya's as the two of them create a protective barrier over our heads. Tristan and Cedar add ribbons of their dark green magic, while Cyan and Mael add their power, a net of water and streams of those dark ribbons enclosing the barrier to fortify the shield.

I hope it's enough.

Bronte focuses on the ark and then holds out her hand as her own brand of magic seeps from her fingertips. It's dense and solid mist, grey, silver, and white coalescing together.

Her magic hits the ark and absorbs her power. With everyone else concentrating on keeping the shield in place, I stare at the ark, watching as it pulls in more of Bronte's magic . . . It takes about half a minute before it starts to glow with silver light.

"Keep going!" I shout. "Something is happening."

I exchange a look with Nadir, who watches me, and then I look back at Bronte.

The ark is vibrating now, jumping around where it lies.

Don't stop, I say to myself, my lips moving with soundless words.

"Is it working?" Bronte shouts.

"I think so!" I shout back.

She continues filtering in her power as the ark glows brighter and brighter. A flicker appears above it, like an apparition emerging from its depths. Though the image is faint, it becomes obvious that it's Zerra. Fear floods the back of my throat as she stands with her arms out, glaring at Bronte. She bares her teeth, her mouth twisting into a snarl.

"Don't stop!" I scream. Something tells me that if Bronte lets go, we're all fucked.

Zerra's back arches, her mouth opening like she's screaming. Her head tips up, and then, in a flash of light, the ark explodes. I duck instinctively, but the barrier holds. After a few seconds, everyone releases their magic just as the sky fills with clouds and flashes of silver lightning streak across the horizon.

I listen closely and wonder if I hear a scream.

"Did you all see that?" I breathe. "She was there. Do you think she can get to us?"

Everyone shares a wary look across the plaza. No one was expecting that.

"Next one," Nadir barks. "Let's get this over with quickly. Cyan! You're up."

We repeat the process, and once again, the ark absorbs his magic until it must reach some kind of threshold and starts to glow blue. I hold my breath, hoping Cyan has enough power to see this task through. Again, Zerra appears in that barely there form, snarling and screaming without sound.

She spins around as if trying to see us. Can she tell who's killing her? Her fingers curl into claws as she sneers and then begins clutching herself, curving in on the pain. I swallow against the dryness in my throat. While I know this is necessary, watching her suffer makes my chest hurt. She was once a young queen forced into this role, and then someone she trusted turned on her.

Again, the ark explodes before the sky turns dark, more flashes of silver-white lightning forking across in jagged streaks. When she's gone again, I expel a short breath of relief. Cyan did it. And it seems like she can't reach us in this form.

"Cedar!" Nadir barks as he rolls his neck. We've all been shaken by the sight of Zerra. Before long, the broken pieces of the three arks sit in the center of the rubble. We clamor down from our places and stare at them as silver lightning continues to crackle across the sky.

"What do you think it did to her?" Tristan asks as he peers up.

I also cast my gaze skyward.

"I don't know," I say.

"What do we do about the last one?" Amya asks.

"I don't know that either," I say. "I don't think this works if we can't destroy them all."

"Does D'Arcy have a Primary?" Tristan asks.

"She does," Bronte says. "But the Celestrian Primary is still a child, far from the full force of their magic."

"So we're fucked," Mael says, and we all nod when I notice something falling from the sky.

Everyone's attention slowly turns towards it. A star streaks through the air, glowing brighter and brighter before it drops into the courtyard and hovers a few feet off the ground. I look around at everyone, but most of them seem just as confused as I am.

I notice the ghost of a smile plays on Bronte's face before the light dissolves, revealing the queen of Celestria standing at the end of the square, watching us.

"D'Arcy," I say as she approaches us on smooth steps while I try not to get my hopes up.

"I saw everything," she says, indicating the broken arks. "I still don't agree with your bonding"—she pins us with a dark look—"but I do understand what it is to lose your mate.

"Last night someone convinced me that this isn't about what I want. Celestria has always claimed neutrality in matters of Ouranos." She exhales a sigh. "But perhaps that is not the most prudent course of action in this case. I have no desire to witness the final death of Heart either."

Her gaze finds Bronte, and we all watch as they exchange a look. The queen of Tor dips her chin.

"I returned home to speak with the Diadem," she continues.

"It confirmed your story and the truth of your words." She studies me with her hands folded in front of her stomach.

"Does that mean you'll do it?" I ask.

She presses her lips together and stares me up and down. "I will do it."

Relief collapses in my chest. I exhale a sigh. "Thank you," I say, walking up and throwing my arms around her. "Thank you."

I feel her stiffen.

"Please," she says. "If you ever hug me again, I will rescind my offer."

I hear everyone trying to stifle their laughter, and then I drop my arms, wiping a tear that's slipped down my cheek with the back of my hand.

"Sorry," I say. "Sorry."

"Hmm," she replies, withdrawing the ark from her cloak. We all return to our places, prepared to repeat the process again. This still doesn't solve the issue of my impending fate as a god, but at least we're one step closer to giving me a chance to survive.

D'Arcy spins up her magic, focusing a concentrated beam of pure starlight into the ark. It's as beautiful as I imagined it would be.

The ark absorbs her light before it starts to glow. Again Zerra appears, wavering in and out. She spins around to face me, and it's then that I'm sure she can see me. Her form flickers again, and then suddenly, she becomes solid, like she's standing right there. I take a step back, stumbling over the rubble under my feet, feeling the stones give way.

"You!" she screams as her arms fling out. Silver lightning

spears from her fingertips as everyone blocks her with their magic, but Zerra is strong. I can see everyone struggling to hold her back as more and more magic filters from her hands.

Red lightning twists up my arms, my power swelling in answer.

Zerra flings out a silver whip of light. It circles around Nadir's ankle and yanks him towards her, dragging him over the rough ground. He roars as he fights and kicks, trying to break free of her tether.

"Nadir!" I call. I don't think. All I can focus on is the fact I'm about to lose him again. I leap off the wall, my feet slamming into the stones as I land in a crouch.

"Lor!" Someone shouts my name. "Don't!"

I ignore the call as I run for Zerra. I watch in horror as more of her silvery magic wraps around Nadir, like a caterpillar building a cocoon.

"Lor! Don't go near her!" he shouts as magic closes over his throat and chin, but she *will* not take him.

Zerra flings out a burst of magic and I react, blocking it. Red lightning surrounds me in a burst of jagged streaks. I pray everyone has taken cover. My pace never slows, and then I knock into her with my full weight. She stumbles, though she doesn't move from the circle of the ark.

Snarling, she blasts out more magic and I duck before I slam my hand into her chest, filtering out more of my magic, trying to inject it into her blood. We scream together as she bows, her back arching. She bends slowly like a tree fighting a gust of wind. With my teeth gritted, I cling to my power, shoving more of it in.

A moment later she snaps up, and I go flying, landing on the stones with a thud, scraping my palms and tearing the leather at my knees and elbows.

I noticed more of Zerra's magic surrounding Nadir, swallowing him up. All I can see now is the top of his head as the entire horrible creation writhes with his movements, still fighting to break free.

And then I'm up and running, once again slamming into her. She grabs my wrist and squeezes so hard my knees buckle. "You little brat!" she hisses. "You took my arks and my Herric. You won't get away with this."

Then she grabs me by the throat and lifts me up, squeezing hard enough to make stars burst in my vision. My feet dangle in the air, my toes just barely scraping the ground.

"Herric betrayed you," I choke out, yanking on her hand and trying to loosen her grip.

"I trusted him," she says. "The others refused to visit me. He was the only thing I had left from the surface."

I hear the anguish in her voice, and it makes a small piece of my heart twist with pity. She squeezes harder as she lifts me higher, and spots swim in my vision. Dimly, I register magic flashing around us as the others try to help, but they also don't want to hit me or Nadir.

"That's not Herric. You can't have him," I gasp as my legs flail uselessly against the air.

I grab onto her wrist and call up a blast of lightning. It spirals around her arm, over her shoulders, and down her torso, before her heart starts to glow right through her skin. She screams and then drops me. I roll over, coughing, trying to catch my breath, but I'm fueled by something primal and the need to save Nadir.

I leap up, grabbing her wrist before I douse her with another surge of magic.

Her eyes spread wide before she clamps a hand over my face. I jerk when I feel an opposing surge of her magic flow into my blood. My skin glows with that same silvery color, and we both cling to one another, battling for dominance.

I moan as it feels like I'm being cooked from the inside out. We are nearly equal in strength, fighting for our lives. But hers is coming to an end, and mine has barely begun.

Another blast of power sends me flying with a scream. I crash into the wall and collapse in a tumble of limbs. I try to get up, falling to my hands and knees as I stare at Zerra. She stands straight, flinging her arms wide as she bursts into silver light so bright I use my arms to shield my eyes.

The noise around the square mutes to nothing as rocks and debris fly towards her, the force tugging at our hair and clothing. She sucks everything in, and we all cling to the rubble as she pulls and pulls like a giant gaping mouth, preparing to swallow us whole. D'Arcy remains where she started, her stance hunched as she continues filtering starlight into the ark, but Zerra only has eyes for me.

I'm on my feet again, ignoring everything around me. I'm running as debris pelts me left and right, ignoring the jabs of pain. I hear my name. People screaming as I throw myself on top of Nadir.

My ears hurt from the absence of sound as she sucks every last drop of air towards her, and then ... everything pauses for a long unbearable heartbeat before she drops her head, staring right at me before it all reverses, everything flying out with a sonic boom that shakes the foundations of the earth.

Nadir and I go flying, tumbling end over end against the rubble. My body hits something hard and sharp, pain spearing through me as I roll down, crashing, bumping, and then eventually come to a stop.

Breathing heavily, I lie on the ground, willing my head to stop spinning. Blood leaks into my eyes, and I move to wipe it away, every limb seizing with pain. In a moment, the aftermath silences as everything again reduces to stillness.

Nadir. I roll over and let out a sob of relief when I see him lying a few feet away.

I drag myself over and throw my arms around him. "Are you okay?" I whisper, and he nods.

"I think so. She almost killed you."

"She almost took you."

He squeezes me against him before I lift my head, trying to see where everyone else landed. D'Arcy kneels in the middle of the chaos, the pieces of the broken ark scattered around her. I have no idea how she held on through all of that.

I scan the plaza. Where is Tristan? Amya? The action sends a stab of pain across my scalp.

Slowly, I roll over onto my hands and knees, ignoring the painful scrapes and bruises, when a sound draws my attention. The earth shakes with more snapping and cracking.

I look up towards the Heart Castle and then slowly rise to my feet, my injuries temporarily forgotten. The tallest towers shudder and then start to collapse, toppling against one another. They crumble together, crashing down, roaring against the silence as the entire castle slowly sinks into a heap.

I feel the force of the breeze it generates against my cheeks as dust coats the air, my skin, and my clothes. Time seems to stop as the castle finally implodes in a mountain of wreckage. It takes another minute before everything goes silent again.

With my mouth open, I look around. It seems like everyone is accounted for, though we're all bleeding from various scrapes and cuts. I take two steps, nearly tripping over the rubble, but Nadir is already behind me. I cling to him, my head spinning.

The Heart Castle is gone. I blink and blink, staring at the spot where it stood a few seconds ago. I can't look away.

"Do you think . . . that's a bad omen?" I ask.

Mael strides up next to me, his thumbs tucked into his belt loops. He's limping, and blood coats the side of his face.

"Well, Heart Queen. It definitely isn't a *good* one."

I glance up at him.

"But look on the bright side. You were going to have to rebuild it all anyway."

I choke out a sound that is half laugh, half sob.

Great. Just great.

But that's it.

We've held Zerra off for now.

We destroyed the arks.

Four down.

Two to go.

Chapter 51

Rion

Rion paced the length of his study, running his hands into his hair. They snagged on the greasy, limp strands. He hadn't been eating or bathing.

He was consumed with thoughts of his failure.

Of that *girl* who had fucking evaded him again.

How did she keep doing that? He *knew* who and what she was. Cloris had never been lying, and Rion had been too full of his own arrogance to see what had been in front of him the entire time.

But right now, she was still just a Fae girl with a tenuous grasp on her magic.

And somehow, she kept escaping him.

He'd had her under his nose for twelve fucking years. She'd been *right* there.

Through his hubris, Rion had assumed that she was expendable. When she'd failed to demonstrate any source of magic, she had become useless to him, or so he'd believed.

He recalled the moment he'd tracked Nadir to Aphelion, before securing a reluctant invite to the bonding. She'd saved him from Rion in Heart after Nadir had hidden her right under his nose. He'd been clinging to her, holding on as he'd encouraged her to find her power. He was the traitorous weasel he'd always known him to be. A disappointment before he'd ever drawn a single breath.

Something in their expressions—the way they looked at one another—told Rion she was special to her son. And that had made Rion's chest burn with a sour twist of envy. So he'd gotten into her head. Or at least he'd tried to by thanking Nadir for his help, hoping to drive a wedge between them. He didn't know if it worked. They escaped him together, but he also hadn't been with her in Alluvion.

Rion marched over to his desk and pulled out the oval picture frame in the top drawer. He traced the edge, his fingers touching the glass. Rachel beamed out at him, her luscious red lips stretched into a smile, part softness and part seduction.

That smile had managed to rip his heart out every time.

He'd been thinking about her more and more often lately. It felt like pressure was squeezing him from every side. He kept trying to make up for the void she'd left. But as his rule had stretched on for centuries, the hollow feeling in his chest had never closed up. He'd traded her for this life, and nothing—not his crown, not his magic, not his power—had come anywhere close to making him feel the way *she* had made him feel.

After her death, he'd broken. Whatever sliver of hope and light that lived inside him was gone. He'd given her up, and then he'd lost her forever. If she'd stayed with him, she would never have found herself wrapped up with the wrong sorts of people. She would be here, standing at his side.

The years had become a blur, and now he stood here facing the endlessness of immortality with this jagged chip lodged in his heart. Rion shook his head, crushing the picture to his chest, as his pulse threatened to burst through his ribs.

He'd already lost count of how many drinks he'd had today, so what was another?

He placed the frame on the desk and strode to the other side of the room, picking up a decanter of clear liquid. He sniffed it, but it hardly mattered what it was. The servants filled these almost daily, but their contents were irrelevant, provided they bordered on toxic. As long as it allowed him to numb himself for a few hours, he would have drunk the Lord of the Underworld's piss.

Speaking of which, the source of Rion's stress also had much to do with what lurked in that throne room. He was terrified to speak with Herric and tell him he'd failed yet again. How could it be this hard to capture one girl?

Without bothering with a glass, Rion lifted the decanter and drained half of it in several large swallows. Then he wiped the back of his mouth with his sleeve and closed his eyes, waiting for it to filter into his blood and just . . . take him away.

But it wasn't enough. These days, it was never enough. He drained the rest of the decanter and then hurled it at the wall, eliciting a small hit of adrenaline at the smash. But the relief was fleeting, and again, he started pacing.

He picked up another bottle and paused when it reached his lips. He'd just made a decision. He was done with this. He thought he wanted power, but what he really wanted was ... silence.

His feet were already carrying him through the Keep before he gave too much thought to what he was doing. His footsteps rang through the hallways as people leaped out of his way. Finally, he reached the throne room and threw open the door.

Though his nerves twisted with fear, he wasted no time.

"I'm done," he said to the empty room, then waited. He wasn't sure if Herric could reach him in the Keep, but the Lord of the Underworld's very presence was enough to bring even the bravest of men to his knees.

Done? came that dark voice, chilling his blood to ice. *You failed. Again.*

Rion ran a hand through his hair and tugged it.

And you're drunk again.

"Don't judge me," Rion hissed. "I give up. It's impossible. She can't be stopped."

Rion waited for the lashing he expected. The anger and vitriol. He braced himself for it, but he would accept it and find another way to exist. Maybe he'd descend and let his son deal with this shit. He was finished. Everything he'd tried to build was nothing but ash sifting between his fingers. Why bother?

I thought you wanted to understand the depths of the virulence. I thought you wanted to learn. I thought you wanted Ouranos?

"I don't care anymore," Rion hissed. "This isn't worth it. I'm done."

I knew you were weak.

Rion chuckled darkly and took a swig from the bottle.

"No, that shit won't work on me anymore. I'm done being manipulated."

He tipped the bottle back and drank deeply. Finally, he could feel the effects leaking into his blood. Another bottle, and maybe he'd finally be able to stop thinking and stop this churn of thoughts in his head threatening to destroy him bit by bit.

You loved a woman once, came the voice, which had Rion grinding to a stop, choking on his drink. *Rachel, was it?*

His body tensed, muscles seizing with confusion. "What does that have to do with anything?"

She died?

"How do you know that?"

I know many things. Have you not gleaned this by now?

"Do you know where she is?"

A long pause nearly had Rion climbing out of his skin. Herric was the Lord of the Underworld. He could speak with the dead. Rion reached for the Torch as though he could strangle the words out of it.

I know, Herric finally said.

"Where?" Rion asked, hardly daring to believe it.

She is here. With me.

The air in Rion's lungs turned to mud.

I wanted it to be a surprise when you found your way to me. But she lives in the Underworld, and when you open the door, you will be able to see her and perhaps ... Well, let's not get ahead of ourselves.

Rion's gaze narrowed in suspicion. It couldn't be true, but he wanted to believe it so much. What was Herric implying? Could he bring her back? He'd give up his crown this time. He'd give up anything to be with her. He wouldn't make the same mistake again. He'd have to find some way to deal with Meora, but she probably wouldn't even notice anyway.

If there was anything he'd learned in his discoveries of virulence, it was that anything was possible if you knew what questions to ask and, more importantly, where to look.

She said to tell you she still loves the taste of butterscotch.

Those words almost had Rion swallowing his tongue. Butterscotch. A quiet cabin in the Cinta Wilds at the height of summer, surrounded by fields of wildflowers. Rachel naked in his bed, her gleaming brown skin kissed by the sun. They'd been sharing ice cream, and one thing led to another before he found himself licking it off every inch of her body before she'd returned the favor. The hairs on his arms stirred at the memory.

He'd never been able to stand the smell of butterscotch after she'd left.

"What do you need?" Rion asked, running his hands through his hair and tugging on it so hard the roots ached.

The girl. The ark. You know what I want.

Open the Underworld and let me out.

CHAPTER 52

GABRIEL

The sky flashes with silver lightning against dark grey clouds. This has been happening for the past hour, but this storm brings us no rain, only a thick sense of foreboding.

A note arrived yesterday from Nadir confirming they had all the rulers together and that they'd be destroying the arks today.

I sense we're witnessing the outcome of that act.

"They're killing her," Tyr says from where he stands at the edge of the water.

He's shirtless, wearing only his breeches. Now I see how pale he is, how much the lack of sunlight has stolen from him. Once strong and muscled, he's now lean and rangy, like a rag doll that's had all its stuffing removed.

I keep an eye on him from a short distance, not entirely trusting him to stay safe. I wake up in a cold sweat every night, sure he's escaped his room and done the unthinkable. I've had everything he could use to hurt himself removed from his room, but I worry constantly.

He looks over at me. "They're destroying the arks." The sound carries over the crashing waves and the wind. He knows I'm there, always watching.

I dip my chin as Tyr opens his fist and stares at it.

He's struggling with his magic. The arcturite stole it from him. Or rather, Atlas did. Atlas, who still languishes in his cell, raging at stone walls as his actions continue to haunt us all. I made the call regarding his execution days ago but can't seem to bring myself to follow through on it. Soon, I will have no choice. I can't continue delaying forever.

Nadir's note also said they'd confirmed the best way to destroy the arks is with a strong blast of Aphelion Imperial magic, and that worries me too.

How will it affect Lor and Nadir's plans if Tyr can't summon enough power? What happens to Ouranos and to all of us? The rumblings in the earth are becoming more and more frequent. Another earthquake hit part of the coast yesterday and things are getting worse. At the same time, the temperature keeps climbing, and though we should be in the middle of winter, it feels like the height of summer.

"How long has he been standing there?" Erevan asks as he comes up beside me.

"An hour or so," I say as lightning flashes again. "They're destroying the arks."

Erevan studies the sky with an unreadable expression on his face.

"How was Atlas?" I ask. Though I refused to visit him again, Erevan had some questions he wanted answered.

"The same," he says, and I look over.

"Did you find anything out?"

He nods. "He gave me the names of those who helped him escape."

"And?" I ask when he pauses.

Erevan folds his arms and rubs his face. "He confessed that his power doesn't always work on the low fae."

My breath exhales sharply in a puff of disbelief. Suddenly, so many things make sense. Atlas, who has always been so fucking insecure about his magic, has proven yet again he was always beyond hope.

"*That's* why he did all this?"

"He was terrified of being discovered."

I don't know what to say. Atlas used the existing prejudice against the low fae and ensured their words and opinions would carry no weight, all to protect his fortress of lies and his ego.

I've been delaying the execution, but this revelation sweeps away the last shred of doubt I was holding on to just in case. There will be no redemption. There is no room to escape this anymore.

"Are you planning to keep watching him like this?" Erevan asks me a moment later, gesturing to Tyr.

I let out a sigh.

"What else should I do?"

He shakes his head.

"Erevan..." I look at him. "I know you don't want to discuss this, but we must."

He runs a hand over his head, his golden curls tossing in the wind.

"He wants to go. But he wants to destroy the ark first. He's gotten it into his head that he has to see this done. He feels like he's been useless for so long. This gives him the chance to do something. And he won't descend until you're ready."

Erevan says nothing as he squints into the sun, his gaze sweeping over the churning blue ocean. More silver flashes over the sky, and if I listen carefully, I swear I can hear a scream.

"We might need your magic to help destroy it."

I say the words tentatively.

"I'm not using my magic until the low fae are permitted to do so as well," he says, and I sigh because I knew he would say that.

"Erevan—"

He cuts me off. "You know, the day he told me the Mirror had chosen me, I saw my entire life go up in flames. It was the death of every freedom I'd ever had. It meant I could no longer fight for what I believed in."

"But why does it have to be that way?" I ask. "If you were king, you could make all the changes you've been fighting to win for so long. Why are you hesitating?"

"I won't, though," Erevan says. "If I'm king, then I'll always have to find a middle ground. I'll have to make decisions that appease the council enough to keep them from attempting to undermine me while I do what I can to ensure the populace stays happy."

He takes a long breath.

"Being the ruler of Aphelion means compromising on my

principles just enough that it will seem like I'm doing something when, in truth, I'm doing nothing at all. The council won't support all of my ideas. So I'll make some lukewarm promises they'll pat themselves on the back for, and nothing important will actually change."

"So what's the answer?" I ask. "Tyr can't keep doing this much longer, Erevan. I thought he might come back to us someday, but I don't think he even wants that anymore. I think he's ready to go, and I don't know how much longer he can keep hanging on. If you don't ascend and take your place, then what happens? Aphelion is left without a ruler, and . . ."

I trail off. I don't know what will happen. Anarchy. Chaos.

My gaze wanders in the other direction to the dark haze of smoke hanging in the sky. We're already wallowing in the pits of chaos. The low fae and their supporters continue looting and rioting, and the longer this continues, the further we slide into a place from which we can never return.

"Erevan," I say. "They're tearing the city apart. How much longer until we can no longer recover?"

He shakes his head, his gaze following the same direction as mine.

"I don't know, Gabe," he says. "We made this bed. We allowed all of this to happen. We lived in luxury while we forced living, breathing beings to suffer for one man's sins. All of us are responsible for that."

He looks at me, and I see the conviction in his eyes.

"Maybe the answer is to let it all fucking burn."

Then he glances at Tyr before he pins me with a dark look, turns around, and walks away.

CHAPTER 53

LOR

We arrive in The Aurora under the cover of night. Snow blankets the forest, and the wind whips through our clothing. Compared to just a few short weeks ago, the temperature has changed drastically as we've moved into winter. It contrasts vividly with the heat and humidity in Aphelion.

The lights ripple overhead, blue and green and scarlet, and I stare up at them, grateful they're here. I remember how the Empyrium told me The Aurora lost them at the end of the First Age. As many terrible memories as this place holds, the sight will always be beautiful to me.

Nadir wraps his arms around me, and I lean into him, realizing that I'm making new memories in their place. I look up at him and smile. We have everything working against us, and the odds of surviving are almost nothing, but I have him. No matter what happens, we'll have had this and each other, and I'm fighting for him and everyone I love, and that has to be enough. If I die, then at least I'll know I did that.

"Come on," he says, "you must be cold."

He uses his magic to envelop me, taking away the worst bite of the chill as we weave through the trees. The lights of the manor peek through the dense brush, and while my first visit to this place was anything but ideal, it, too, creates the sum of these moments. Those days in the manor when Nadir and I reached a tentative agreement to search for the Crown led us all to this spot.

Willow, Tristan, Bronte, Cedar, Cyan, and Linden follow behind us. After Etienne dropped us off, he returned to Heart to ferry Anemone back to Alluvion so she could retrieve the Book of Night.

Once D'Arcy destroyed her ark, she returned to her home in Celestria. I'm trying not to hold it against her—she did help us, and we were all nearly killed for it—but it'll be tough not to harbor a grudge.

As I note everyone's scant clothing, I realize they must be freezing.

Nadir uses some of his magic, which seems to help, but we better get them all inside.

When we enter the manor on a gust of wind, Brea is there to greet us.

"Welcome home," she says warmly, and I smile, remembering when she had to serve breakfast with me chained to the foot of Nadir's bed.

"Brea," he says. "We have some special guests with us."

She nods. "The princess sent word. We have rooms ready for everyone."

"Make sure you get them some warmer clothing, too," he adds, and Brea gestures for everyone to follow.

"Come," Nadir says, and he drags me up the stairs to his room, where we fall on the bed, wrapped in one another's arms. For several long moments, we hold each other. I can't get the image of the Heart Castle collapsing out of my head. Logically, I know a building doesn't matter. I understand it was just mortar and stones and not truly the legacy we left behind. I think of my grandparents' portraits, which already survived one tragedy, worried they're gone forever. Despite their actions, they're still a part of who I am.

I also can't stop seeing Nadir wrapped up in Zerra's magic. She almost took him again.

A soft shuffle from the corner of the room draws our attention, and we look over to see Morana and Khione in front of the fire. They're staring at Nadir with such longing in their dark eyes that I burst out laughing.

Nadir smiles and slides off me, kneeling on the floor. That's their cue because both giant ice hounds bound over, practically knocking him over as they paw at his clothing and lick his face, their tales wagging hard enough to snap right off. He laughs, and the sound twists in my chest.

Was this cold prince always capable of thawing? Or did I help him along?

Morana turns to me, placing her paws on my thigh, and I rub her head as she yips.

"You're not planning to eat me anymore?" I ask, and then she licks my hand with her rough tongue.

"I would never have let them eat you," Nadir says. "Perhaps just a nibble."

"Will you let me sleep in the bed tonight? No tying me up?"

He eyes me up and down. "Oh, I'd be happy to tie you up again," he replies, the suggestion in his voice clear.

"Or maybe we'll do it the other way around."

His eyes light up. "I like the sound of that, Heart Queen."

Khione whines, shoving her head under his hand for another dose of affection, when a knock comes at the door.

"Come in," Nadir calls, and it swings open.

Brea stands there again. "The princess and the captain have arrived and asked that you come downstairs to speak with them."

"We're on our way," he answers, and she nods, closing the door behind her.

Nadir reaches out and takes my hand. "Are you ready for the next part?"

"No," I say, shaking my head. "Not at all."

He kisses my knuckles and the red stone of my ring as my eyes burn with tears. I collapse against him, wrapping my arms around his waist as he presses his nose to the top of my head.

"I don't want to lose you," I say.

"You won't," he replies into my hair.

"You can't promise that."

"But I do."

I look up, seeing the conviction in his eyes.

My breath sticks in my lungs with the heavy certainty that

someone will soon take him from me forever. I can't let that happen. I will fight until I'm nothing but a pile of dust.

I let out a strangled breath. "Then let's go," I say.

The dogs trot in front as we head downstairs. Everyone is gathered in the library, perched on the various velvet upholstered chairs and sofas scattered throughout the room. Bookshelves line the walls and a fire roars in the hearth. The tall windows leak with plumes of colorful light, gilding everyone in rainbow edges.

Anemone, dressed in a tunic and leggings, has arrived with Etienne and the Book of Night. Cyan has also acquired some warmer clothing, and the dark colors seem to make his bright hair glow with even more brilliance.

"Have a seat," Amya says as Nadir and I enter. She stands with her hands clasped, the lines around her mouth tight. Her dark hair is slicked into a high bun, and she wears black leather leggings with a corset, all of it embellished with bright streaks of violet, emerald, and fuchsia. Though I wasn't expecting good news, she looks more worried than I'd like.

"What's happening?" Nadir asks, clearly picking up on the same feeling.

"So, we returned to the Keep prepared to convince Father that Mael and I had abandoned you to your own devices..."

"And?" Nadir asks.

"And he's not there."

A pause of silence echoes around the room.

"He never returned after I escaped them in Alluvion?" I ask.

"No," Amya says. "They returned, but everyone I've spoken to—his guards and attendants—all confirm that Father disappeared two days ago. His study is a mess—empty glasses and bottles lie all over the place with papers and books strewn everywhere."

Nadir shakes his head. "That . . . doesn't make sense."

"I know," she replies. "Mael and I searched through his things, but either he left, or someone took him."

"Did you find anything useful?" Nadir asks.

"I'm not sure. There was a chest full of journals. From what I could tell, they were written by Herric."

"What?" I ask sharply. Herric left journals?

"How could anything survive that long?" Cyan asks.

"I don't know that either," Amya says. "They must have been enchanted. There are dozens, and Father was definitely reading them. We found crumpled notes everywhere, too."

"King *Herric*," Cedar says, as if he's tasting the bitter syllables while we all share a wary look.

Herric, the Lord of the Underworld.

Is this connected? Have the strings been pulled from such a distance?

"So we can enter the Keep," Tristan asks, "without worrying about your father?"

Mael shakes his head. "I've questioned all his guards, and they could be lying, but it seems they aren't currently in contact with him. It's impossible to say. It could also be a trap, and we'd be playing right into his hands."

"But we need to get the Torch," I say.

"So we sneak in," Nadir says. "We would have had to do that anyway."

"What do we do about Zerra?" I ask, my gaze flicking

upwards. Along with the destroyed castle, I can't get the image of her screaming out of my head. The way she bent with pain and the look on her face when she sent that final blast my way. "If we go near the Torch, she might see us again."

"You said the Keep is made of virulence?" Anemone asks, and Nadir nods.

"It should shield you long enough to get the Torch. That amount would block out her sight."

"I wondered if that's why Herric built it."

She nods. "That would make sense."

"What about the ceremony?" Willow asks. "Can we all go in?"

"I don't think that's a good idea," Mael says. "It's one thing for us to sneak in, but all of you will draw too much attention."

"So, you will go under the mountain for the bonding," Bronte adds a moment later, and every eye turns to her.

Anemone nods. "That would work if we can find a large enough deposit."

"I think we also need to take a closer look at those journals," Nadir says. "Maybe that will give us a clue about where he went."

Amya nods. "We spent hours in there. If it's a trap, then he's either not worried about his study, or he's specifically waiting for both of you."

"He's likely to have the ark with him," Nadir says. "We might need to spring any trap he's set."

I wrap my hand around his forearm, and he covers his hand with mine.

"There's something else you all need to know," he says,

looking at me before he turns to his sister. "After we get the Torch, I also will ask it to release me from my role as Primary."

Collective surprise moves around the room. Everyone stares at the two of us.

"You're . . ." Mael says, trailing off. I wonder if he's ever been at a loss for a clever remark.

"We've discussed it and agreed that I would be the one," Nadir says.

"I've been wondering," Amya says. "I didn't want to pry. But—"

"But nothing. I want to do this. I'm choosing to do this—for Lor and me and for everyone in this room and on this continent. It has to be one of us, and it can't be her."

"But that means . . ." Mael says.

"That means it might be you, Amya," Nadir says, and the princess of The Aurora sighs out a long breath.

"I'm sorry if this isn't what you want and that it might alter the path of your destiny, too."

Amya squeezes her hands and nods as silver tears build in her eyes.

"I've never thought much about it," she says.

"You would make an amazing queen."

"The best," Mael adds warmly, making Amya smile.

She swallows, and I see it all so clearly.

Amya, with a crown and in a long black dress with those colorful strands of her hair spilling over her shoulders, stands before her people, maybe with my sister at her side.

"What if it doesn't choose me?" she asks, her voice a paper-thin whisper.

Nadir stands up and draws his sister into a hug. "I can't be sure, but something tells me you'd be perfect. It should have been you from the very beginning."

They hug tightly, and I wipe a tear from my eye. Even Linden looks somewhat moved, her stony expression softening just a little.

The prince and princess pull apart.

"This is going to feel so strange," she says, looking up at him.

"I think it's going to feel just right."

"You're sure, Nadir?"

"Amya, I've never been more sure about anything."

She nods as he turns to address the room.

"So I'll sneak into the Keep, find out what I can in my father's room, and get the Torch."

"I'm coming with you," I say. He gives me a dark look. "Don't even bother arguing. I'm coming."

He opens his mouth and then closes it before he says, "Fine."

"We'll come too," Amya says, gesturing between Mael and herself.

"Once we have both Artefacts, we can proceed," Anemone adds. "I'll study the book and ensure I have the process right."

"I will find somewhere to perform the bonding," Bronte says.

I give her an expectant look, and she shakes her head as though she can't believe she's agreeing to any of this. She convinced D'Arcy to destroy the ark, and despite what she claimed about just coming along when we headed north, she's offering more of her help.

"I know I said I was undecided . . . but I like you, little queen. You remind me of me."

"That's . . . I was in awe of you from the moment I saw you," I say a little breathlessly, and that earns me a warm smile.

"Etienne, you'll need to retrieve the Crown," Nadir says and Etienne nods. "Bring it directly to Bronte once she secures a location."

"Absolutely." He presses a hand to his chest and bends at the waist.

"We'll also come with you," Tristan says to Bronte, and Willow nods.

"We should make it nice," Willow says. "Find some decorations."

"Willow, that's not necessary," I say.

She turns to me, eyebrow raised. "My little sister isn't bonding to her mate in some dusty mountain cave without a little something to liven it up."

She glares, daring me to argue. This emerging form of Willow is so different from the sister I knew.

I offer her a grateful smile as everyone goes silent, lost in their churning thoughts.

It feels like the end. Like we've been running towards this place for almost three hundred years when our grandparents made a mistake that has rippled across centuries.

"Then we have a plan," Nadir says after another minute, returning to the business at hand.

"Not a very good one," Mael drawls.

"No," I say. "But when have we ever let that stop us?"

Chapter 54

The next day, Nadir flies me to the Keep, landing us on the balcony outside his father's library. Mael and Amya have returned the more conventional way and are busy blocking off the King's apartments from visitors under the guise of investigating his disappearance.

It's not a complete lie. We *are* looking for him, but we have ulterior motives.

The door has already been unlocked before we enter the room and survey the disaster of our surroundings. It looks even worse than Mael and Amya described. Broken glass and furniture lie everywhere, and it smells like we're in a distillery.

"What do you think happened?" I ask.

Nadir stands with his hands on his hips and shakes his head.

"I don't know. My father has always been in control of his emotions." He pauses and I see some long-buried memory pass over his expression. "Mostly, I guess. The only time I've ever seen him lose it was when he was drunk."

He runs a hand down his face.

"If you're feeling conflicted about going to hunt down your father to kill him, that would be understandable," I say, and he looks at me as his shoulders slump.

Then he takes a few steps into the room, slowly surveying our surroundings. "It's not that I feel conflicted, it's just that . . . I've never really known a single thing about him."

He spins around to face me, his arms spread out.

"What if there was a reason for all of it? I don't want to make excuses—nothing can justify so many of the things he's done—but what if, in his mind, he thought he was doing it for a reason? I've always assumed he just enjoys causing pain, but . . . all of this seems like a man who's *in* pain."

I say nothing, giving him a moment to gather his thoughts. He looks around the room as if weighing and cataloging every piece. I witness the storm clouds that pass behind his eyes.

"It doesn't matter," he says firmly. "I'll probably never know, and it *doesn't* matter. Nothing makes up for the things he's done."

With his jaw set, he stalks to the end of the room and starts sorting through the papers on his father's desk. I let him work through whatever he needs to as I start on the papers strewn about the divan in front of the darkened fireplace, lying everywhere like giant snowflakes.

I understand Nadir's conflict. No matter his faults, Rion is still his father, and I imagine that he always hoped that someday he'd turn out not to be the demon he thought. I watch him as he focuses intently on a journal, his eyes scanning the page.

A knock comes at the door, and Amya lets herself in.

"We've managed to move everyone out of this wing for now," she says. "Father's guards weren't happy about it, but Mael suggested that maybe they should be out looking for him instead of waiting around with their thumbs up their bums."

"I said 'assholes!'" he calls from the hallway, where he's standing watch.

She sits down next to me as she rolls her eyes.

"So he sent them into the Void to search."

"What if they find him?" I ask.

"Then they'd kind of be doing us a favor."

"Do you still think this might be a trap?" I ask.

"The more I learn, the less I think so. His attendants have reported that he's been drinking heavily, and they've been replacing several empty bottles a day. He won't let anyone touch this mess and has been holing himself in this room whenever he's in the Keep."

I exchange a glance with Nadir, who's listening as Amya's explanation confirms what he just said.

"But he seemed fine when we were here for Frostfire," I say.

She nods. "Apparently, he's been hiding it well."

She swivels around to look at Nadir, who stands at the desk with a fistful of paper.

"Do you have any idea what could have him acting like this? It doesn't seem like him, does it?"

"It doesn't," he agrees. "And none at all."

Amya nods and then stands up.

"Here are the journals I mentioned," she says. "We gathered all the ones we could find."

She opens a trunk at the end of the table. Inside are dozens of leather-bound notebooks. Nadir crosses the room and picks up the top one, flipping it open.

He scans the page for a few seconds.

"Herric," he says. "If these are real . . ."

"Whether they're real or not, it seems Father believes they are."

"So I guess we have some reading to do," I say.

I dig into the trunk and pass the books between us as we settle into our respective corners. Herric was thorough about his life, starting from an early age, but it's not until the jewels start to fade and the northern lights disappear that things start to get interesting.

Herric recounts his discovery of virulence and the detailed ways in which he manipulated Zerra. How he offered himself to her for years, trying to figure out how to take her down.

A sliver of sympathy swells in my chest for the queen forced to become a god. She could have lived out her days in Aphelion as a High Fae queen, perhaps not a very good one, but at least she would have been home. And then Herric betrayed her. Based on his accounts, their relationship was only about sex, but clearly, she felt differently about all of it.

Circumstance twisted her into the thing she is now too.

I continue reading and then find a passage that makes my blood run cold.

"He figured out how to manipulate the Torch," I say. "Look at this."

Amya and Nadir crowd around me, reading about how Herric made the Torch bend to his will.

"This is . . ." Amya shakes her head.

"Grandfather was right. If people knew this is possible, it would upset the entire order of things," Nadir says.

"I mean, would that be so bad?" I ask. "Isn't it a bit weird that we let some random objects tell us who is supposed to be in charge? They made a terrible choice with your father, and I'm sure that's not the only time. They have sentience, but it's obvious their sight is also very limited. Look what happened with Atlas."

"That was supposed to be Zerra's job," Nadir says as he takes the book from me and flips to the next page. "He forced our grandfather to descend, and when that still wasn't enough, he sought more power. That's what he wants from the mines and why he's gone so deep. It was never about jewels or protecting our trade exports."

"He wanted the power of the stone," Amya says.

"So your grandfather descended, and Rion got his crown," I say. "What does he need the ark of Heart for?"

Nadir stands up and starts pacing as he continues reading.

"The ark of Heart is incredibly powerful, as your mother said," he answers. "Only someone with the magic of Heart can use it, which is why he needs you."

He stops and looks at me.

"So the ark must be the key to something else," Amya says. "Something Father wants."

"Cloris mentioned that he wanted to conquer Heart the first time," I say. "But that doesn't feel like what this is."

Nadir nods. "I agree. Something changed."

We all fall silent, stewing in our thoughts.

"Keep searching," he says. "There has to be something else here."

We abandon the journals and start digging through Rion's things, all of us silent as we scan through papers, opening drawers and cabinets. Rion seems to have kept everything he's ever signed. Probably some kind of paranoid evil villain thing.

I see a crumpled ball of paper on the floor and reach for it. I pull it open and am smoothing it out when Nadir cries out, "Here!"

He's holding another piece of paper. It looks like an official document, but scrawled in the corner is a block of handwriting. "Look at this." He shows us the scribbled ramblings. The writing is shaky, like he'd been drinking when he wrote it, further evidenced by the dried wet marks on one corner.

Herric. Herric... Has her. Has her. Has...

The lines are written over and over, tipping at an angle like a descent into madness, becoming more and more illegible.

And then something clicks.

"What if Herric still wants to become a god?" I ask.

The words send a shiver over my skin as our gazes meet.

"Can we be sure he's still alive?" Amya asks.

Nadir rubs his chin. "What if Father was communicating with the Lord through the Torch?"

"Do you think he went... to the Underworld?" Amya asks. "Is that even possible?"

"Maybe if you know where to look," I say, holding out the crumpled piece of paper in my hand.

Nadir reaches for it. "Is that a *map*?"

"It appears so."

He studies the page before looking up and pointing to a spot. "He went under the mountains. Is this a door of some kind?"

"A *door* to the Underworld?" Amya asks, her eyes wide.

I retrieve the map from Nadir. "What if Herric asked him to get the ark?"

"But what good would the ark do him?" Nadir asks.

"I don't know," I say. "If he's still planning to kill Zerra, he'll need all of them, right?"

Neither Nadir nor Amya answers as I continue, "Or rather, he'd need to destroy them, just like we've been doing. What if we've been . . . helping him all this time?"

Cold dread spreads through my chest, trickling down my limbs.

"That . . . can't be," Nadir says, but the words sound uncertain.

"Herric must have promised him something," I say. "Who is the 'her' in those notes?"

Nadir and Amya share a look.

"I don't know," he says. "But something tells me we need to get the ark back immediately."

"At least we finally know where we might be looking," I say. "And we can assume he can't do anything with it until he has me."

"So we get the Torch, we perform the bonding, and then use the map to . . . travel to the Underworld," Nadir says, swallowing hard, like he can't believe he's just uttered those words.

"I don't like any of this," Amya says.

My gaze wanders to the window where the northern lights ripple across the sky.

I think about all the lonely nights I looked upon them, wishing for another life, wishing for freedom. I remember shivering in my bed, cold and hungry. I remember the hopelessness and the certainty that I would never get out of Nostraza alive. I remember my icy rage and my vows of revenge that became the only things that kept me warm.

I remember everything.

"I don't think we have a choice anymore," I say.

I hold up the map and look back at Nadir and Amya.

At my mate. At my second sister.

This family I never expected to find.

This family I'll do everything in my power to keep.

"We have to find him, and we have to get the ark. One of us will die, and I'm going to make damn sure it isn't me, but I won't live under his shadow anymore. This ends now. Once and for all."

CHAPTER 55

GABRIEL

W e stand in the courtyard of the Sun Palace under yet another grey sky. Thousands have gathered outside the walls to bear witness to Atlas's execution. The inevitable could no longer be avoided.

Though officially the order came from Tyr, I uttered the fatal words, and they sit heavy in my chest like my heart has turned to iron. There were a few feeble protests and arguments on Atlas's behalf, but they were quickly buried. It seems no one is in a forgiving mood. The few still loyal to him have been dealt with, too, though their punishments were more private and more easily delivered.

As the news filtered through the districts, I stood on the palace's highest towers, watching Aphelion's reaction. The celebrations of the low fae went well into the night, and while it seems callous to celebrate a man's death, I also understand their position.

I run a hand through my hair, expelling a heavy sigh. They all want to come closer, but I know this would turn into a blood bath if we allowed it. Almost every soldier in Aphelion is already marching through the crowd, struggling to maintain order.

In the center of the courtyard stands a platform. Off to my left, Atlas waits flanked by Jareth and Rhyle, the arcturite cuffs still binding his wrists and throat. His gaze slides to me, and he stares with fury and loathing. I don't know if he's trying to intimidate me, but I stare back, unflinching.

He made this bed. I'm only doing what I must.

Clouds gather in the sky as if they, too, understand what's about to happen. I feel the first gentle drops against my cheeks and hope this isn't an ominous sign.

"It's time," I say, my voice rough. Emotion wedges in my throat. Anger. Frustration. Resignation. I try to tease out its edges, searching for the guilt I expected.

The crowds beyond the wall surge and shout, chanting for Atlas's head. Everyone is here. The nobles. The council. I even see some of the fallen Tributes. Atlas owes them all something too.

"We're ready," says the executioner, who stands on my other side, and I breathe out one more time, trying to expel the last of Atlas's poison from my veins.

It is time.

I look behind me at Tyr, who stands between Hylene and Erevan. I watch them both. The past and the future, if only Erevan would stop being so damn stubborn.

Erevan nods and then drops Tyr's arm, intending to join me. Tyr asked to stay back, and of course, I couldn't deny his request.

I gesture for Rhyle and Jareth to come and follow the executioner to the platform. My brothers drag Atlas up the stairs. He stumbles along, his body limp, as he stares at me.

"Prince Atlas of Aphelion!" I shout, my voice rising over the increasing patter of rain. "For locking up the king. For impersonating the true ruler of Aphelion. And for crimes against all of us, you are sentenced to death."

A chorus of boos and cheers greet my words as Atlas's face turns white. Maybe part of him really thought he'd still get out of this. But after everything he did, I cannot allow him to live.

My brothers force Atlas to his knees as the executioner retrieves his axe, the sharp edge glinting despite the absence of sunlight. I blink. And I blink again, forcing myself to look as my stomach twists, threatening to climb up my throat before slumping at my feet.

"Gabe! Erevan!" Atlas calls as Jareth places a hand on his head and pushes him down. "Don't do this! I'm your brother!"

Erevan shakes his head and walks forward, bending down to murmur softly to Atlas.

"You are lost, cousin. You had so many chances to undo all of this. Do not beg for clemency, for you have never deserved it."

They are cold words uttered without mercy. Erevan is true to his convictions, and I admire the fuck out of him for it.

And that's when Atlas starts to cry. I haven't seen him shed a single tear since we were boys, but fat tears roll down his cheeks as he realizes there isn't a single person left in his corner.

This is the end, and I try to drag up sympathy, but all I feel is pity.

My gaze casts over my shoulder to Tyr, who also weeps as he clings to Hylene. Atlas stares at him, and I swear every single person standing in the square feels the accusation that moves between them.

Maybe, in the end, they both let one another down.

Tyr slowly lifts a hand, and I don't know if it's a signal for something because Atlas loses it then, thrashing, bucking, crying.

"You think he'd accept this with some dignity," Erevan says under his breath.

And I shake my head. I knew he wouldn't.

It takes two more warders to wrestle Atlas under control until finally they force his head onto the chopping block, his cheek pressed to the rough wood. He stares out at the crowd, and then his gaze falls on me again before an entire lifetime passes in that look.

He struggles with his restraints as the executioner walks up to the block, swinging his axe. It's then Atlas goes still, his gaze sweeping over the crowds chanting for his head. Slowly, he studies them all as another tear leaks from the corner of his eye and drips over the bridge of his nose. What does he understand in this moment?

The executioner waits for the signal, and I take another breath that does nothing to settle the churning in my gut.

As I give him a dip of my chin—the signal to proceed—I feel myself moving in slow motion, willing myself not to throw up.

In a few seconds, there will be no turning back.

Atlas's eyes move to me, and they stay there, watching me. Weighing me. Surprisingly, there is no accusation in his expression, only sadness.

Erevan shifts closer, his shoulder brushing mine.

"You don't have to watch," he murmurs.

"I know."

But I must.

To find closure in this chapter of my life.

I must.

The executioner lifts his axe as thunder booms overhead and the rain falls harder. I blink drops out of my eyes as they mingle with the tears that slide down my cheeks.

Around the courtyard are shaking shoulders and bent heads and so many more tears.

Despite everything, for a little while, he was their king.

The axe falls, and as much as I want to look away, I force myself to bear witness to it as it slices clean through Atlas's neck and then . . .

The false Sun King is gone, and there is only the sound of the rain.

CHAPTER 56

NADIR

THE AURORA KEEP

I make my way towards Amya's wing later that evening.

Lor is waiting in my room, where my people will keep her presence a secret. I don't like leaving her alone, but she can take care of herself. What I must do tonight, I must do without her at my side.

As I walk through the halls of the Keep, it feels strange and ominous that my father isn't here. We might be completely wrong about our theories, looking for explanations where there aren't any. But I also sense nothing amiss other than Father having descended into some kind of twisted madness. He abandoned this place to go searching for something.

Lord Herric of the Underworld.

Is that even possible? Were those the ravings of a madman too lost to the drink to see clearly?

Who was the "her" in his note?

I knock and Amya opens the door, blinking expectantly. Her dark hair is tied up, and she's dressed simply in a black tunic and leather pants. She looks like she's already been crying.

What I must do tonight, I must do with my sister.

"It's time to see Mother," I say, and she nods, understanding what that means.

Tomorrow, I will bond with Lor, and then we'll go after my father. I don't know what will happen, but if we succeed, then it is my every intention to end him. That has always been my goal, and no matter what complicated feelings I'm holding for the man who refused to be a father to me, that hasn't changed.

That means tonight might be the last time I see my mother unless we meet in the Evanescence again.

When my father dies, so will she. We never got the chance to fix things, but there's nothing I can do for her on this plane any longer. I'll never forget the day my father tossed her into her room and shut the door on her forever. If we succeed, then she'll finally be free, and that will have to be enough.

We skirt through the Keep and enter my mother's wing, finding her staring out the window. One of her caretakers bows at the sight of us and then leaves to offer us privacy.

I kneel in front of my mother and take her frail, cold hands. She continues to stare out the window.

Amya stands behind me with her arms folded, her body curving into itself. She's never been comfortable in this room.

"Mother," I say. I get stuck on the words. I don't know how to tell her this, but I have to. I don't know where to begin, so I share everything.

Starting from the very beginning, I tell her about Lor in Nostraza and the Sun Queen Trials. I tell her about my mate, about how much I love her, and how she makes me feel. I hold nothing back. I tell everything to my mother, including the fact that we might never see her again.

I lay out my heart, my hopes, and everything I've kept in. It's now or never.

When I'm done, I feel lighter. Like I can breathe. I drop my head in her lap. "I love you," I say. "I'm sorry I failed you."

Amya and I wait in silence as we prepare to say goodbye.

But a moment later, someone touches my hair, fingers softly running through it. I look up, and she's staring at me.

"Mother?" I ask. I can't remember the last time she moved or touched me or even noticed I was here. Her eyes. For the first time in decades, her eyes are awake. They fill with tears that remain suspended just on the edge of everything.

"You never failed me," she says so softly that I must strain to hear it. "It was I who failed you, Nadir. Over and over. If I had just been strong enough to stand up to him . . ."

Her hand falls from my head, her lips pressing together as a tear finally slips down her cheek, curving under her chin.

"No," I say, taking her hand in mine and pressing it to my face. "You did the best you could. He is a monster."

She closes her eyes and inhales deeply, her head shaking slightly as if disagreeing. Another tear streaks down her cheek. "You found your mate," she says, looking at me before her mouth curls into the ghost of a smile. "All I've ever wanted is for you to be happy."

She leans over and presses her nose to the top of my head, inhaling deeply like she's pulling me into her soul.

"Do whatever you need, my boy. Whatever you need to be free of him."

"But this is it," I say. "Your life here is over."

"It was over so many years ago. I'm ready. I only wanted what was best for you, to protect you, and I did such a poor job of that. All I can do is try to live with that guilt."

"Don't," I say. "When you get to the Evanescence, be free of this. Okay? I don't want you to feel guilty for anything." I squeeze her hand.

Another tear slides down her cheek, and then her gaze moves to Amya, who watches her with a mixture of fear and vulnerability on her face.

"I'm sorry," Mother says. "I'm sorry that I never had the chance to know you."

Amya's face pulls together, her lower lip trembling as she sniffs. She wipes an errant tear with the back of her wrist.

"And I'm sorry that I let him take you from me. I always wanted a daughter," she whispers, and there's so much heartbreak in it that my chest nearly cracks.

Amya chokes out a sob, and then she dives forward, wrapping her arms around Mother's neck and sobbing against her.

"I'm sorry," Amya says. "I should have come here more. I should have tried harder to understand, too."

Mother doesn't move at first, and I watch her face, something passing over her expression that speaks to every haunting memory that lives in her thoughts—every moment of pain caused by my father. Every tear and cry of anguish.

Slowly, her arms lift to wrap around Amya as if she's just taught herself how to hug someone. At that moment, I curse the short memories of our childhoods.

I remember her in flashes—her warm smile and snuggling up with her under the blankets. I remember soft touches and her singing as she helped me drift off to sleep, but they're distant, buried in the haze of so many passing years. What I wouldn't give to go back and have a record of it all. Of our lives rendered in relief or on an oil canvas to remember forever.

We were happy. With her, I was happy, even if it was so brief.

Amya sobs and another tear drifts down my mother's cheek.

"Thank you," my mother says. "I know . . . I know I haven't said much, but I've appreciated every day you've visited me. Neither of you had to do that. Neither of you owed me that. Not after how I let you down. But know that every time you've come to see me, I've been so proud that you both turned out the way you did."

My chest aches, a heavy knot tying up my ribs. I wrap my arms around both of them, and we hug for a long time. My eyes burn with so many unshed tears, and when I can't hold on any longer, one falls, landing on my mother's dress, where the fabric darkens. I stare at it, contemplating the entirety of my existence in that one spot.

We hang on a little longer, and then we pull apart.

Amya is hiccupping, her eyes bloodshot and makeup running

down her cheeks. She wipes at her tears, and my sister looks different. She, too, looks lighter.

"Mother, we're going after him tomorrow," I say.

"After you bond to your mate," she says, covering my hands with hers. "I understand. I hope she takes good care of you, Nadir. You deserve that after caring for me for all these years. You deserve everything."

I smile and tuck a lock of hair behind her ear.

"No one will take better care of me than Lor," I say. "No one would dare cross her."

"Then she sounds perfect for you."

I touch her cheek, running my thumb along the bone.

"I am ready to go," she says. "I've been ready for a long time."

"I'll miss you."

"I'll see you someday," she whispers. "I hope. And I'll miss you, too," she says. "More than you can ever know."

I press a kiss on her cheek and then pull away.

"Goodbye, Mother."

"Goodbye," she whispers, "my children."

Then Amya and I turn to leave.

As the door closes behind me, I feel so many things I can't begin to put into words. As children, we're taught to believe that good will win over evil. That there is always sun after the storm. But those are fairytales meant to keep us warm.

I couldn't free my mother from this pain while she lived. There will be no justice for her in this life, but I have to believe that once she crosses over, she will be at peace, and only my father will feel the retribution of his sins. Inside this Keep, evil has won out over and over, but this story isn't quite finished yet.

"I wish we could have had more time," Amya says, looking at me. "Why couldn't we have had her like that? Why did she talk to us now?"

Still holding the handle, I allow my head to drop against the door. Taking in a deep breath, I blow it out slowly before I look at Amya. "I don't think that was who she is anymore, and I suppose she understood this was the end, too."

Amya folds her arms and scrubs a hand across her cheek. "I guess."

"She found the strength she could never offer us and gave us that last moment at least. Now we can remember her this way."

"Yeah." She nods, and we share a look.

Then I reach out and take her hand before my sister and I walk away from our mother for the very last time.

CHAPTER 57

LOR

That night, I dream of Nadir in the Aurora Keep throne room. He sits with a sword, the point digging into the ground and his hand gripped around the hilt. He wears a pair of fitted black pants and nothing on top, the bright swirls of his tattoos illuminating the dark.

I tiptoe across the cold tiles, wearing the nightgown I fell asleep in. As I approach, I stop, contemplating the lines of his face. The arch of his brows and the curves of his lips. The inky pools of his eyes reflecting with flashes of violet and emerald. My gaze travels over the contours of his stomach and his chest, the aurora borealis from outside gilding him in bursts of color.

He lifts an eyebrow, and he leans back, spreading his legs.

"Hi," I say, and he tips his head.

"My queen," he answers with a growl that makes a needy pit in my stomach quiver.

"Are we dreaming?" I ask. "Or is this real?"

"I'm not sure."

"We were lying next to each other in bed. Is this the mate bond?"

"I think it might be. Do you remember when this happened in the manor?"

"Of course I remember," I say. "I remember everything."

With his mouth crooked, he taps his thigh while his eyes spark with mischief.

"Care to join me?"

I tip my head and continue tiptoeing over. He holds out a hand, and our fingers link as he helps me straddle his hips. He props the sword against the armrest before his hands land on my waist.

"Why do you think we're here?" I ask, looking around us. The Torch sits between the thrones, orange flames licking the darkness.

"I'm not sure," he says. "After saying goodbye to my mother this afternoon, maybe I'm here to say goodbye to this place too."

Melancholy laces his words as his gaze sweeps over the room.

"This will still be your home," I say. "No matter what."

"I know that. But it will be the last time I'm here as the future king of The Aurora."

My mouth opens, but he presses a finger to my lips.

"Before you say anything, I am not questioning my decision. I'm reflecting on almost three hundred years of my life and the future I expected. But I regret nothing. I thought I was on one path, but I now know that every step I was following was never leading me to this throne or that crown." He drags a finger down my cheek, pressing it to my lower lip. "It was all leading me to you."

My hands smooth over the curves of his rounded shoulders as I give him a soft smile. My fingertips continue to explore the ribbons of his tattoos, and I take my time, reveling in the warmth of his hips pressing between my thighs. They flex as a flame curls in my stomach.

"You've never told me what these are for," I say, and he shrugs.

"I got them after the war. I told you once that I've always tried to remember what I was fighting for, and these have always been a reminder."

"Tell me about it?" I ask. "The war. You always retreat inside of yourself every time you mention it. What happened?"

"It's a story I've been too afraid to share with you. I'm worried you'll look at me differently."

I shake my head. "I couldn't. I wouldn't. Anything you did was a result of the mess my grandmother caused."

He blows out a breath. "There are many things I'm not proud of, but the one that sits with me the most happened near the end. I'd been captured by Aphelion, where I languished for months. They kept us bound with thin chains of arcturite, rendering us powerless, in addition to providing almost no food or water."

My fingers dig into his shoulders. "Was this Atlas?"

Nadir's chin dips. "He oversaw this particular camp, yes. I don't think it was personal, but I do think he liked the idea of making a fellow prince suffer under his hand. Now I realize he was probably feeling the slight from your grandmother and trying to compensate."

"That sounds like him," I say wryly.

Nadir tips his head. "That was where I met Mael and Etienne, too. We were chained together, and there's nothing like suffering as one to form a bond. One day they brought in a new batch of prisoners, but they didn't have enough arcturite to chain us all, so they bound only those they believed to have magic. Of course, they knew I did, but they assumed otherwise of Mael because he let them believe he was a mere foot soldier.

"Well, that was a mistake on their part." He stops and winces as if the memory hurts and explains how Mael helped free them all using that deadly violet power I witnessed in Heart.

"I left Atlas alive," Nadir says, shaking his head. "I had him right there, but I just couldn't do it."

He bites his lip and looks at me. "It's funny, though, isn't it? If I'd killed him that day, then he would never have schemed to get you out of Nostraza, and you and I might never have met."

I nod. "Maybe. But none of this seems bad. You did what you had to."

"No," Nadir says. "It's what came after. I returned to my father, half-starving and weak. He blamed me for getting myself captured and, as punishment, sent me out to destroy a blockade that was preventing supplies from coming to our camp. I could barely move. I never slept. I was a wreck."

Nadir sucks in a sharp breath as his hands tighten against my hips.

"It was inside a village, and he promised that everyone had been evacuated. I took him at his word, and we set it on fire," he says, his voice rough. "By the time we realized there were innocent people—whole families—still living inside, it was too late."

He swallows, and his distant gaze returns to me.

"I spent a lot of years hating myself for that. I still do. The screams..." He shakes his head. "I still hear them."

With my hand against the back of his neck, I lean in and kiss his cheek, pressing my nose against it. I don't tell him it wasn't his fault because I know it will make no difference. Only he can decide that, but I want him to understand that it also changes nothing. We've both had to make choices against impossible circumstances. We've both been manipulated and abused by the Aurora King.

"I love you," I say. "I will never stop."

"Thank you," he says softly as he wraps his arms around me and holds tight. We stay like that for a while, feeling each other's heartbeat. Eventually, I pull away to study his face, tracing the contours of his cheek. I press my thumb into his bottom lip and lean in, our mouths hovering an inch apart.

His hand slides up my nightgown, his thumb digging into the crease of my hips.

"In one more day, this throne will no longer be mine," he says. "I think we're here because I needed to say goodbye."

He crooks up an eyebrow with a suggestion in his smile. *"And there's something I've always wanted to do."*

"And what's that, oh Prince of The Aurora?"

"Fuck the woman I love in this chair," he growls, and those words send a wave of liquid heat between my thighs. Thanks to the fact I'm wearing nothing under my nightgown, I immediately feel him growing under me, the fabric of his pants brushing my sensitive core.

"You're telling me you've never been with anyone in here before?"

"Never," he answers solemnly.

His hand slides up the back of my neck and into my hair, before he pulls me down for a kiss. Our bodies press together as I roll my hips, seeking the friction of his thickening cock. We moan into each other's mouths, and then he stands, lifting me up before he spins around and settles me back on the seat.

He drops to his knees, hooking my leg over his shoulder as he bites the corner of his mouth and peers up. "Since the day you threw yourself at me at the Ball, I've thought about the sounds you'd make when I ate you out on my throne."

I let out a breathless laugh as he dips down, running his nose through my wetness.

"Fuck," he breathes. "You break me every fucking time, Lor."

Then he drives his tongue into me, circling my clit as my head tips back with a moan. His hand slides up my body, under my nightgown, and over my stomach, leaving a trail of fire. He kneads my breast, pinching the tip hard enough to make me gasp. One of his fingers dips into me, curling as he sucks and nips, causing heat to build at the base of my spine.

"Oh gods," I groan as I clutch the back of his head with one hand, the other gripping the armrest. He pumps his hand in and out as his tongue caresses rough circles over me. It doesn't take long before I'm cresting, my limbs shaking and my stomach bottoming out.

"Beautiful queen," he says, and then I blow apart with a ragged moan, waves rolling through my limbs. He pulls away and then stands up, lifting me from the seat to wrap my legs around his waist.

My arms loop around his neck as we kiss, the taste of myself on his lips. Then he flips around and drops back into the seat. I waste no time, reaching between us, my hand dipping under his waistband as I take his cock in my hand.

I squeeze as he groans and pump for a few languid strokes before I position myself over him.

"Lor," he growls as I take him inside me, adjusting to his presence inch by inch, sliding down slowly. His hands grip my hips, and then, a moment later, he thrusts up into me, my back arching in response. We shudder together as my forehead tips against his.

"Ride me," he says as he shifts my hips back and forth, grinding me against him. I cling to his shoulders as he thrusts up, over and over. My hands move to the back of the throne, my body curving as our foreheads meet again.

We breathe into each other as we churn together in a wash of heat and heavy breaths. In this space where we exist, fighting for each other and everyone we love. Inside this nebulous future we're both clinging to with all of our hopes, I will see us through this no matter what it takes. Because if I can't have him like this every day of my life, then nothing else matters. Then nothing I've done will mean anything.

We continue moving, becoming two pieces that fit together perfectly because that's always what we were meant to be.

"Fuck," I moan when he finds my clit and presses, my release crashing over me, liquid, hot, and blazing with color. My magic sparks along my arms, but this time, I don't hold myself back. Protected inside this dream, I let my power unleash in a swirling storm of crimson lightning.

When we come together, magic spears from every direction, lightning mixing with his ribbons of light. Static raises the hairs on our heads and arms as every sensation ricochets through my bones and blood. The world around us flashes, and I come so hard my vision whites out, and my breath seizes.

We're a tangle of groans and gasps and that unmistakable wave of longing that rolls through my limbs.

My skin has grown warm and flushed, and I take a moment to catch my breath before I lean down to kiss him. He grabs the back of my neck, and we continue to move together, our bodies as one as we kiss and kiss, feeling every moment.

"I love you," he says into my mouth. "I love you, Lor. Tomorrow, I will lay down my life, my crown, and my heart, and I will be yours forever."

CHAPTER 58

"Hold still," Willow complains as she pins up the front of my hair, allowing long curls to trail down my back. We stand inside a small cabin deep in the mountains, surrounded by snow and stars and nothing but white and grey stretching on all sides. She's wearing a borrowed dress from Amya, constructed of black lace and silk, all edged with bright aurora colors. It looks amazing on her. Almost like she belongs here.

After Bronte located a cavern made of virulence to perform the ceremony, she also happened upon this small, dusty, but surprisingly cozy hunting cabin where we could get ready.

Between Anemone, Willow, and the queen of Tor, they did the best they could to make it presentable, and the irony of having this fearsome warrior queen scrambling about like a mother hen isn't lost on me. Morana and Khione wait patiently at the door, lying on their paws, watching us flit about the space.

Anemone and Bronte both wear the clothes they arrived in—Anemone in a blue dress covered with a cloak she borrowed from Amya and Bronte in her grey fighting leathers. She's clearly used to the cold and comfortable, even with her arms bare.

What a motley crew we make.

"You look beautiful," Willow whispers as she adds some finishing touches to my makeup. Without a mirror to use, I have to take her word for it. "He's going to lose his mind."

"Pretty sure he's about two seconds from that every time she walks in the room," Anemone jokes from the rickety table, flipping through the Book of Night.

"You sure we'll be okay?" I ask her, my constant worries about what happened with my grandparents ever at the forefront of my thoughts.

"Not entirely," she answers, offering me an uncertain look. "But mostly."

"Willow, maybe all of you should go somewhere else," I say. "Far away. Just in case . . ."

Just in case this causes another explosion and kills everyone within firing range.

"If you think I'm about to let you bond without me there, you're dreaming," Willow says.

"But—"

She flips a hand. "But nothing. Anemone will ensure we're all fine, and I will not let you do this alone. I wouldn't miss this for anything."

I give her a small smile. "I love you, Willow."

"I love you too. Now let's get going. They're waiting for us."

We gather our things and, with the dogs leading us, make our way down a short path to a cave entrance. We wind down a tunnel, deeper and deeper into the mountain. It takes us what feels like a long time to get there, and I try not to think about the weight of stone over our heads. As we descend, it starts to feel like the walls are closing in on me. My breath grows tight, and sweat breaks out on my forehead.

"Lor? Are you okay?" Willow asks as I come to a stop, pressing one hand along the wall and one to my chest as I try to draw a proper breath.

"She's claustrophobic," Bronte says, her voice distant and hollow in my ears. "It's normal for a lot of people when they go under the mountains."

Bronte gently touches my forehead with two fingers, and the tight feeling in my chest dissipates, the wooziness clearing from my head.

"Common enough that my magic can help," she says.

"Thank you," I whisper, grateful that I can breathe again.

"Come. We have a ways yet to go."

We continue to wind into the mountain, and though I continue to feel a bit like we're being buried alive, Bronte's magic makes the trip more bearable.

Finally, she takes a left and gestures us down another tunnel. "Through here."

We enter another short path where lanterns sit at the base, guiding our steps. Set into the wall is an opening that branches off.

"Lor," Willow says, turning to me, "Wait out here for a moment. We'll go in and make sure everything is ready."

Anemone brushes past me and enters the next cavern.

"I'll come get you," Willow says, stretching up to kiss me on the cheek before she disappears around the corner.

"Sure," I answer. Then I wait in the dimly lit tunnel, trying not to feel like a thousand eyes are watching me from the shadows. Thankfully, Morana and Khione wait with me, their ears pricked in alertness, which makes me feel less alone. I crouch down, pressing my nose into Morana's fur as I rub her head, inhaling her fresh, earthy scent.

A noise catches my attention, and I spin around, peering down the path, but beyond the row of lanterns, the black is as impenetrable as a thick, heavy sheet of velvet. I shake my head at my foolishness. What could possibly live all the way down here?

All kinds of horrible, wretched things, that's what.

I read Rion's notes about his experiments with the low fae that created the monsters in the Void. And that's probably only a taste of the ancient, long-forgotten creatures that might dwell in these mountains.

Anything could be down here. I shiver as a chill races down my spine. I keep staring into the dark, refusing to turn my back on it when something touches my shoulder. I screech, spinning around to find a surprised Willow with her hands up.

"It's only me," she says. "Are you okay?"

I blow out a long breath, willing my heart to settle.

"Sure. You startled me. I . . . don't like it down here."

"It is pretty creepy," she agrees. "Sorry. I should have thought of that."

I shake my head and smooth down the front of my dress as I square my shoulders and wave a hand at my face, trying to cool myself off. Though a chill seeps through the layers of rock, my anxiousness about a million things that could go wrong is making me too warm.

"I'm fine. Are we ready? The sooner we get out of here, the better." I try not to think too hard about our next step—following Rion's map to the Underworld and traveling even deeper than this. Add it to my list of problems.

"Come on," she says with a huge grin. Then she turns around, and I follow her around the corner with the dogs trotting behind me to find a large cavern.

The sight makes me still in my tracks. They've filled the entire space with hundreds of candles lined along the edges. Balls of colorful light hang suspended from the ceiling courtesy of, I assume, Amya and Nadir. In addition, there are roses *everywhere*. They cling to the walls, hang from the ceiling, and carpet the floor.

It's the most beautiful thing I've ever seen.

"Willow, what did you do?" I whisper, my voice raw with emotion.

"No crying yet," she says, taking me by the hand and pulling me down the center, where candles light our way. Nadir stands in the middle of the space wearing a tailored black suit and a bright smile that shifts the pieces of my heart. I take in the broadness of his shoulders and the way the fabric molds to the curves of his arms and thighs. His long dark hair shines in the dim light, as smooth as glass. He's not just beautiful, he's raw and wild, forged in the knifing chill of arctic winds and the sinuous glow of the northern lights.

He stares at me with the universe reflecting in his gaze, and I'm so overcome I can't make my feet move.

He tips his head, his smile crooking higher. "Not having second thoughts, are you, Lightning Bug?"

I shake my head, tears blurring my eyes. "Of course not."

His gaze drags down my body and then lifts as his eyes swirl with points of crimson and cobalt.

I'm wearing the red dress I bought in the Violet District with Amya when I told myself I'd never belong to Nadir.

It was still hanging in his room and felt like the perfect choice. The *only* choice.

Around my waist is a belt holding the dagger with the heart-shaped jewel he purchased for me in Aphelion.

"That dress," he says. "I thought I'd never get to see you in it."

A wave of tears threatens to drown me, but I push them back. Willow is right. No crying yet.

He reaches out a hand, and that's all I need to stir me into movement. I trip towards him, and he tugs me against him before I collapse into his arms.

"When I first tried this on, I swore you could never claim me," I say with my hands pressed to his chest and looking up. "That I would always be mine. That I was my own fucking castle."

He smiles and touches a curl lying against my cheek.

"You will always be your own castle, Lor. I never wanted to take that from you."

"I know. I see that now."

"But I *am* claiming you," he adds. "Never forget that you are mine."

"And I am yours for as long as you'll have me."

"You're stuck with me until the end, Lor . . ."

I blow out a shaky breath and notice everyone else watching us with soft smiles. Tristan and I exchange a look. Something changed in Heart when Nadir talked him down from his fears.

I remember my brother's shouted words in the Heart Castle.

All I ever wanted was for you both to be happy.

Tristan tips his head as though he can read my thoughts.

I am happy, big brother. Despite every challenge we have yet to face, I am happy.

"Shall we begin?" Anemone says softly. On a table behind her sit the Heart Crown and the Aurora Torch. She picks up the Torch and hands it to Nadir.

"First you must ask it to release you," she says.

"Will it speak with me? I'm not ascended."

Anemone nods. "As you've seen from your mate's experience, the Artefacts will speak to others when it's necessary. It's just simpler to let everyone believe they communicate only with their rulers, lest anyone gets it into their head to ask for favors."

"And then what?"

"While that is happening, I will begin reciting the necessary lines."

"What if it refuses?"

She tips her head. "It may. But I believe that if you explain the situation, it will see reason."

Nadir nods and accepts the Torch, clasping it in his hands. He turns to face me, and I watch as the flames reflect in his eyes.

Anemone then picks up the Crown and holds it out to me. "You will need this."

I place it on my head, feeling its weight settle.

"And this won't make me ascend?" I ask.

"No," Anemone asks. "You must be in Heart to ascend. You are as safe as you can be here."

Anemone opens the Book of Night, flipping through until she lands on the page she's looking for.

"Are you ready?" she asks.

"This could still go wrong," I say, looking around the cavern. "I'd still feel better if everyone moved away."

"I'm not going anywhere," Willow says, folding her arms and spreading her stance.

"Nor I," Tristan adds, mimicking Willow's position.

"We aren't leaving either," Cyan says, indicating him and Linden. She tosses him a scowl but remains quiet.

"Same here," Mael says. "You think I'd ever let our boy go through this without us?"

I look at Bronte and Cedar. "What about you?"

"I think I'll stick around," Cedar says, and Bronte nods her assent, all of their expressions resolute.

I blow out a breath and hope to the gods that this works.

Nadir and I hold hands as Anemone starts reading the incantation, repeating the words over and over. The Crown grows warm on my head while the Torch in Nadir's hand begins to flame and spark.

The world around us melts away until we're both standing together in another place. Around us is a mixture of roses woven with bands of colorful aurora light. My mouth parts on a gasp as we witness this melding of ourselves, this coming together.

Nadir squeezes my hand and then asks the Torch to release him from his duty. We both wait in the swirling nothingness of this space. Then I hear the voice I recognize from when I also spoke to the Torch. The voice of King Elias.

Aurora Prince. I have been expecting you.

"Have you?" Nadir asks into the void.

Indeed. I understand what your mate must do and what your role must be.

"Then you'll do it?"

I once told your mate that your love would lead only to heartbreak and ruin, Aurora Prince. I believed your connection would lead down the same path of destruction. I did not know if you would make this choice. But unlike your father, you are choosing love, not a crown.

Nadir gives me a puzzled look. "Unlike my father?"

He chose his power over love, and though it did not break the world, it did break him.

Our gazes meet as we both attempt to tease out that riddle without much luck.

"I'm not sure I understand."

No . . . but you may yet.

The Torch falls silent.

"Will you do it?" Nadir asks. "Release me?"

There's another long pause, but I know it will answer.

We will need another.

"My sister. It should have always been her."

Another pause.

It is done. Farewell, Aurora Prince. May your sacrifice not be in vain.

After the Torch goes silent, we remain suspended in the void. Somewhere in the distance, I hear Anemone continuing her chant, the syllables dancing around the cavern. I can practically feel the spell it weaves.

The walls around us begin to dissolve, transforming into crimson forks of lightning and beams of aurora power. Our magic's two halves twin together, the sharp edges of lightning meeting soft curves of light. We've always felt like two parts of a whole, one but separate, and now our magic will become that way too.

I feel the ground beneath us rumble as Anemone recites her lines while more magic moves around us. It fills me up. The magic of The Aurora grows in my veins, trickling in slowly, and then . . . the magic of Heart crashes in behind. It flows into me in rivers, filling my cells and my pores. I can feel it growing, swelling in my chest with such force that it feels like it might tear straight out of me.

I clasp Nadir's hand tighter, and the magic swirls as our surroundings continue to shake. I feel the sting of pebbles shearing from above.

Anemone's voice grows louder and louder, and then our magic twists around and engulfs us in a swelling wave. This looks so much like the vision in the Woodlands Staff before my grandparents ruined everything, and I wonder if we've made a mistake.

Fear seizes my chest, my ribs growing tight. I want to stop this, but it's too late, and then a white light flashes in my eyes before everything goes dark.

CHAPTER 59

It takes a few moments to realize that I'm here and still whole. I blink, clearing my vision, to find Nadir standing in front of me, healthy and whole. I choke out a sob.

The cavern is fine, and everyone is okay. Nadir is okay.

"Did it work?" I ask, but at the same moment, I realize that question is pointless because I feel it. I feel *him*. My pulse beats in its natural rhythm, but it echoes as though I have two hearts living inside me now.

"It worked," Anemone says. Sweat runs down her temples, and she wipes her forehead with the back of her hand.

"For a moment there, I thought—" I say.

"I know," she replies. "I admit I had my doubts, but we did it. Do you feel each other's magic?"

Nadir and I look at one another, and I hold out my hand as

I filter out a tendril of green light. I let out a squeak of delight as it twists around the cavern. Perhaps the best part is that I have complete control over it.

"What about you?" I ask Nadir. Red lightning dances between his fingertips as he also holds up his hand, and I shake my head at the sheer joy of this moment. I thread my fingers against his, and then we press our foreheads together.

"Now we are truly one," Nadir whispers, and my eyes close as a tear slips down my cheek. Some part of me thought we'd never get here.

"How do you feel?" I ask.

"Honestly? Lighter."

He looks at his sister and walks over, handing her the Torch. She accepts it warily as he drops to a knee and presses his forehead to the back of her hand. Then he peers up and says, "Hail to the future queen of The Aurora."

Amya laughs nervously. "Really?"

Nadir stands up and pulls her in for a hug. "You'll make such a wonderful queen."

A chorus of cheers circles around the room as everyone else offers their congratulations, including an extra-long hug from Willow. I hug my brother and sister and Amya and Mael, who are now officially my family, even though they've been that way for a while now.

Cyan and Cedar congratulate us with handshakes and hugs. "When you have the time, I'd love to host you both in my forest retreat," Cedar says. "It's beautiful, lost deep in the woods, and the perfect spot for some alone time."

"That would be lovely," I say. If we ever get that chance.

"Congratulations," Bronte says warmly, and even Linden gives us both a firm nod.

"Come on," Amya says. "Let's have a drink."

At the back of the cavern, they've set up another table with some bottles of wine and a bit of food. I'm overcome by the effort they all went to for the two of us.

We all gather, toasting the day and not thinking too hard about what comes next. The map that I found in Rion's room waits for us. We'll have tonight to celebrate, and then tomorrow, it will be time to confront what I suspect will be the final test. The moment that saves us or breaks us forever.

"Oh no, where's the Armata?" Willow frowns, peering at the table. "Elswyth sent it. She said it's an incredibly rare bottle and perfect for such an occasion. I must have left it with the boxes when we brought everything in."

She backs up. "I'll go grab it. Be right back."

She bounds away and disappears out of the cavern. I smile at her retreating form, feeling so lucky to have her.

Tristan comes over and wraps an arm around my shoulders. He looks at Nadir, and the two study one another. Finally, Tristan holds out a hand for Nadir, who pauses before he accepts it.

"I know you and I have had our differences, but I'm trying to move past them," Tristan says. "My sister has always been a good judge of character."

"Tris—" I say, and he waves me off. "I might have been too hard on you, Aurora Prince. Thank you for everything you've done to help Lor. I understand those were your father's actions, not yours. It wasn't fair to judge you so harshly against them."

Nadir's face briefly remains expressionless before he dips his head.

"Lor is fortunate to have you," he says. "Anyone would be honored to call you a brother."

They both smile, and I also try not to think about how perfect this all feels because an axe swings over us, ready to chop it all away. I shake my head, attempting to push away these maudlin thoughts. This is a happy occasion and there will be plenty of time for worrying soon enough.

We continue chatting, and a few minutes later, I realize Willow hasn't returned with the Armata. I cross the cavern to look for her. Rounding the corner, I enter the tunnel where the flickering candles struggle to illuminate the oppressive darkness.

A stack of boxes sits against the wall, barely visible beyond the perimeter of the lanterns. I pick one up and proceed down the tunnel.

"Willow?" I call. "Willow! Where did you go?"

Something crunches underfoot, and I realize it's glass from a shattered bottle lying on the floor, where liquor pools in the rock's many crevices. My chest seizes, and my heart stutters, the beats tripping over each other.

"Willow!" I scream into the echoing dark. "Willow is gone!" I shout in the other direction, and then I'm running, the light from the lantern bouncing against the walls, offering the barest glimpses into the surrounding blanket of night.

"Willow!" I scream as I twist through the tunnels. "Where are you!"

My voice cracks as I scream her name over and over, moving

deeper and deeper. I hear the others following behind me, but I keep running, crashing into corners, my shoes skidding on the rocks. "Willow! Where are you?"

A path angles into the darkness, and I don't hesitate to pick my way down. My toe catches on a rock, and I stumble, falling onto my hands and knees. The lantern tumbles from my grip, smashing into pieces and plunging me into night.

"Nadir!" I scream in the other direction as I lurch to my feet. My skirt is torn, and my knees ache. I wipe my bloodied palms on the fabric. "Tristan!"

The darkness is like a living thing, filling my ears and eyes and nose. I nearly choke on it, feeling blindly into nothing. Then I remember the new magic in my veins, and I draw on it, marveling at how smooth and easy it feels. I send out a tendril of bright violet light just as everyone comes running up.

"Lor, are you okay?" Nadir asks as he barrels down the path, wrapping an arm around my waist.

"We have to find her!" I choke out. I'm breathing so hard, I can barely speak.

"What happened?" Tristan asks.

I gulp down air as my vision spins. "I don't know. She's gone. Something took her."

I think again of the creatures Rion created using the virulence, dreading what foul nightmare might have my sister in its clutches. Suddenly, my legs feel like mist, and I cling to Nadir before I collapse.

"We have to find her," I repeat, gasping for breath.

"We will," he answers. "We *will* find her."

I nod and push up, wiping my eyes with the back of my

hand before Nadir grabs it. Amya is beside me now, and I take her hand on my other side, squeezing it firmly. Neither one of us says anything, but I understand how much Willow has come to mean to her.

"We'll get her back," I whisper. "I won't let there be any other outcome."

"I know you won't," she answers.

"Let's go," Nadir says as we continue through the tunnel with Morana and Khione on our heels. The others follow behind us until we reach a cavern with five branching pathways.

"Which one is it?" I ask, spinning around. "Willow! Willow!"

"Everyone be quiet for a moment," Mael orders, holding out his hands. I attempt to control the loud breaths sawing out of my chest as we all strain to hear anything over the thick silence. A high-pitched scream ricochets in the distance, turning the blood in my veins to ice.

"Willow!" Tristan shouts as he, too, spins around and around. "Which direction did it come from?"

"I can't tell," Amya says, half sobbing.

"We'll split up," Nadir says. "Mael and Tristan, you take that one. Amya, you and Linden go that way. Anemone and Cyan, you take that one. And Cedar and Bronte, that one. Lor and I will take this path."

"We meet back here in half an hour," Nadir says. "If you find her, bring her here immediately and wait for the rest of us."

We share a look around the circle before everyone nods and then turns towards their respective tunnels. My brother and I look at one another.

"Tris," I say before he grabs my shoulders.

"We will find her, Lor. I swear it. We didn't come this far to lose her now."

I nod as more tears fill my eyes.

Then everyone breaks off as Nadir takes my hand, and we plunge into the darkness of our tunnel with the ice hounds trailing behind us. The walls feel like they're closing in on me, and I inhale panicked breaths. If anything happens to her, I will destroy this entire mountain and everyone who's responsible for laying a single hand on her.

Using Aurora magic, we light our path through the twisting tunnel until we emerge at another cavern that splits into two directions.

"Which one?" I ask. We both pause. The silence is crushing, weighing us down like a blanket made of iron. My ears pop from the absence of sound, and I work my jaw at the uncomfortable sensation.

"I don't want to split up," I say, squeezing his hand tighter.

"We aren't," he says.

"Let's try the left one first before we double back."

Angling towards the opening, we enter yet another dark tunnel as it winds us further into the mountain. My breath starts to tighten as it grows narrower. I wish Bronte were here with her magic, but I can't lose control of myself. Willow needs me.

But as we continue walking, I'm starting to get worried we might become lost down here forever.

"Maybe we should try the other one," Nadir finally says. The sound of his voice is so loud that it makes me jump.

"Maybe," I say, peering into the darkness. I wish there was *something* to indicate if we're on the right track. And then I hear it—a scream, echoing so softly far, far in the distance.

"Did you hear that?" I ask, but I'm already running.

"Willow," I gasp. "Willow!"

I pick up my pace, my skirt twisting around my ankles. The shoes I'm wearing are useless, so I kick them off, ignoring the stabbing in my feet and their stinging slaps against the stone. Morana and Khione let out soft yips as they follow ahead, guiding my path.

"Willow!" I come to another branch and stop, checking over my shoulder for Nadir.

"Nadir?" I call up, but the tunnel remains empty.

Cold dread trickles through my chest, turning my toes and fingers numb. He must have just fallen behind.

"Nadir?" I call again. "Where are you?" My voice sounds even more hollow. The silence more dense. The hairs on my neck rise in apprehension.

When he still doesn't appear, I head back up the tunnel. Maybe he hurt himself, and I ran away from him like a jerk. *Please* let that be it.

"Nadir!" I call, winding up the pathway with the ice hounds trotting on my heels. The tightness in my chest eases when I finally see him standing in the middle of the tunnel, violet light filtering around his frame, obscuring his face in shadows. "Nadir, what are you doing?"

Morana and Khione start barking furiously as I trip up the path before a beam of emerald light falls over his face.

But it isn't Nadir.

The Aurora King stares down at me, his glittering eyes as dark as midnight pools.

A breath wheezes out of my chest as I grind to a stop.

"Rion," I whisper. "Where is he?"

He tips his head and arches a brow. A silent, weighted exchange passes between us. We are two opposing sides, pushing and pulling over the years. He tried to break me, but I survived, and now, only one of us will come out of this alive.

He advances a step as I shuffle back. Morana and Khione howl and bark, their panicked sounds vibrating through the enclosed space.

Rion sneers as he approaches. "This time, there is nowhere for you to run, girl. Finally, you are *mine*."

And then he blasts out a wave of pure, dark magic that fills my nose, mouth, and lungs before everything goes black.

CHAPTER 60

RION

The girl lay at his feet, her hair spilling over the tops of his shoes, her eyes closed, and her jaw slack. He noted her red dress. The heart-shaped jewel on the dagger strapped around her waist winked in the dim light.

The Heart Queen.

Finally. After months of frustration and losing her at every turn, he had her. This girl who he'd captured and tortured a decade ago on an ephemeral promise that failed to manifest would now become his salvation.

He bent down and hauled her up, tossing her over his shoulder before he spun around to face his son. Liquor flowed through his veins, and he blinked as everything around him tilted. He waited in a staggered stance until his vision returned to normal.

Nadir sat on the ground, tethered to the unconscious sister, both of them bound and gagged by the magic of virulence. He'd leashed those foul dogs to the stone floor, where they thrashed against their restraints, their teeth bared and their snarls filling the tight cavern.

Nadir struggled, too, shouting over the gag stuffed in his mouth, but the words were lost. Rion didn't need to hear them to understand his vitriol. The dark loathing in his son's eyes had been dragged from the deepest pits of the Underworld. Nadir had always hated him and with good reason. *This* hatred was borne from the most shadowed corners of the world.

Was Nadir in love with this girl? How deep did that love go? She was technically a Primary, and thanks to Cloris, Rion knew what had happened during that cursed bonding between Serce and Wolf, even if so few others did. Would Nadir give up a crown for love? Never, Rion decided. As much as Nadir might be loath to admit it, they were more alike than either wanted to admit. They were cut from the same cloth, and his son would never let anything get in the way of what he wanted.

Rion stared at Nadir and the sister, considering what to do as uncertainty stayed his hand. He could kill them both without a thought, but perhaps some weak, sentimental part of him lived in the deepest recesses of his withered heart. A father shouldn't kill his son, no matter the misery he'd caused.

"Say goodbye to her," Rion said instead. "I do hope you enjoyed whatever time you had together."

"Mmmmppfff," Nadir screamed against his bindings. He thrashed and bucked, but the restraints held on. They would dissipate in time—but by then, Rion would be long gone.

Not just gone but reunited with the woman that *he* loved.

Rion spun on his heel and continued deeper into the cavern until Nadir's muffled shouts receded into the distance. Down, down, down Rion carried her as their surroundings grew darker and darker. He'd left the map Herric had directed him to create in his library, but he'd already memorized every step. The moment he knew Rachel was waiting at the end of this journey, he didn't hesitate.

Rion used a ball of magic to light the way, but the oppressiveness of this place was enough to smother even his strongest magic. Whispers floated up from below, bouncing off stone walls and the inside of his skull. They were vacant and yet full of presence. They could only be souls of the Underworld calling him deeper. Deeper than he ever thought possible.

How had Rachel fallen so far? What desperation had steered her towards the sorts of people who'd condemned her to this fate? Rion wasn't sure how, but he would make it his mission to bring her back out. Herric had hinted it was possible, and he would use the girl as his bargaining chip.

Herric obviously couldn't reach her on his own, so Rion would withhold her and the ark until he'd extracted a promise to return Rachel to the surface. He knew negotiating with the Lord of the Underworld was a risky gamble, but it was the only thing he had left.

Rion stumbled over a rock and crashed into a wall, his head

spinning. He couldn't remember the last time he'd eaten, but the alcohol burned in his blood, making walking over the rough terrain challenging.

The girl moaned, and he sent out another tendril of virulence magic to keep her unconscious.

As he wove back and forth, the walk dragged on. Rion winced at the ache in his shoulder and back as he hoisted her up, trying to find a more comfortable position. Even with the benefit of his Fae strength, her body was starting to drag him down.

He shook his head and inhaled a deep breath, but without the freshness of a breeze, it just congealed in his lungs, making him even more lightheaded.

But he had to get to the Underworld before his son found him. Rion knew he would. Nadir had never liked anyone touching the things he believed belonged to him.

After what felt like hours, Rion was ready to collapse from exhaustion, his joints and muscles quivering from strain. Finally, he entered a dark cavern, the ceiling soaring so high that it disappeared into the shadows.

Peering up, he threw a ball of magic into the air and watched it dissipate into the gloom pressing in from all sides. A smooth wall of rock stood at the far end of the cavern, shimmering softly with its own source of dim light. His breath hitched. *This* was his destination.

Rion hoisted the girl higher on his shoulder before he crossed the cavern. Every footstep echoed like a lightning strike as he felt the air crowd in around him. It felt almost like walking through water as the weight on his lungs increased, trying to drown him. When he reached the wall, he placed his palm against it as Herric had instructed. The stone was warm to the touch despite the frigid air permeating these mountains.

Now he heard the whispers more clearly as they grew more distinct. Through the sounds he could make out the words and eventually the voice he'd come to know all too well.

You have her? Herric asked, and Rion nodded, relief expanding in his chest. Despite everything and the lengths he'd gone to find this place, a small part of him had wondered if any of this had been real. *And the ark?*

"I have it."

There was a long pause as Rion was left stewing in the bleak mire of uncertainty.

A click broke through the whispers, and then, the wall started to move. It ground open slowly, dust and debris raining down as though it hadn't been opened in a very long time.

Rion stepped back, his chest and shoulders expanding with deep breaths.

Then Rion, king of The Aurora, enter.

The door revealed another tunnel, glowing with purple light, its walls made of luminescent stone.

"Come," Herric said, his voice no longer a whisper in his mind but solid and corporeal, echoing off the walls like nails penetrating steel. Rion hesitated, suddenly wondering if this was madness. Some instinct told him he could still turn back if he chose. That it wasn't too late. But if he crossed over that threshold, he might be trapped here forever.

"She's waiting for you," Herric said, and that was all the

motivation he needed. It was a risk he would take willingly. There was nothing left for him on the surface, anyway.

Rion proceeded carefully down the tunnel as the colors shifted around him in a wash of glowing pinks and greens and blues. He'd always imagined the Underworld to be even darker than the mountains—not this riot of color. He wondered if this was all an homage to the aurora that Herric had lost sight of all those years ago. Perhaps deep down, every one of us was a bit sentimental.

Rion continued walking, his shoulders and back aching from carrying the girl for so many hours. The alcohol in his blood had finally worn off, and though his head pounded, he could at least manage a straight line.

Movements slithered in and out of Rion's periphery, and every time he turned, they would be gone. It was impossible to catch their source. He shook his head, deciding it didn't matter. He had one destination now, and it was the woman waiting for him.

He wound down, deeper and deeper, like the world was swallowing him up, until finally the path leveled off and he entered another long tunnel, this one lined with mirrors reflecting more of that eerie luminescent light. He continued walking, seeing his face reflected in the mirror over and over. He barely recognized himself, his eyes wild and his skin pale. He was no longer the king he once was. Maybe he hadn't been for a long time.

The ground vibrated beneath his feet, a thrumming swimming in his limbs. As he continued walking, the rhythm pulsed through his chest, throbbing into the marrow of his bones.

It felt like...music? Nothing about this place was what he'd expected.

He continued around a bend until a large archway appeared before him and beyond that, a massive, brightly lit room. The floor turned from rough stone to silver, white, and black tiles, each one as shiny and smooth as glass.

He entered the cavern, where hundreds of bodies danced and swayed to the sounds of thundering music. They were dressed in things Rion had never seen before. Shiny black leather layered with silver spikes that sprang from their shoulders. Helmets made of various colored metals, with more spikes and feathers. Their faces were painted with swirls and lace and all manner of intricate patterns. They laughed and chattered, their heads tipping back as they cackled, the sound like shattering glass.

If he didn't know better, he'd say this was a party.

He watched for several long seconds, marinating in the incomprehensible existence of his surroundings. *This* was the Underworld? Had he been tricked? Was any of this real?

Suddenly, the music cut off, and every eye in the room slowly turned his way.

Rion waited, holding completely still as though he might escape their scrutiny. He felt their naked examination as they eyed him up and down. After another moment, they began to shuffle towards either side of the cavern, clearing a wide path down the middle.

He regarded the crowd with suspicion as they studied him, their gazes vacant but also... curious and hungry.

"Approach," came a deep, slithering voice that rooted into the corners of his mind. He stared down the length of the path, swallowing hard as he gathered the slivers of his courage. Then he straightened his shoulders as best as he could with the girl weighing him down.

Slowly he placed one foot in front of the other, his boots ringing on the slick tiles as everyone held completely still. As he made his way down the path, he stared straight ahead, trying not to let their heavy, silent stares unnerve him.

A massive throne sat on a wide dais at the front. Made of shimmering black stone, its back rose many stories high, spreading out in tendrils like curling smoke. As Rion drew closer, a chorus of whispers and twitters filled his ears.

Rion kept his focus ahead, on the male High Fae with midnight-black hair and glittering dark eyes occupying the throne. He, too, wore the same strange garments, though his were more subdued, as though he had no need of ornaments to prove his worth. A snug leather top covered his neck and arms, and his pants showed off the curves and muscles in his powerful thighs. Rion saw the family resemblance immediately. Herric sat with his elbow resting on the arm of his chair as he studied Rion with cool detachment.

He exhaled a shaky breath, trying to maintain a sense of calm as Herric stared at him, his leg flung over the opposite arm of his throne, his foot swinging casually from side to side.

"So nice of you to join us," Herric said, sweeping out a hand. "As you can see, we've been celebrating your arrival."

Rion didn't respond. *Couldn't* respond. Sweat beaded on his forehead as his stomach twisted in knots. His tongue felt like paper glued to cardboard.

"Some of us more than others," Herric said as he then

gestured to the side. Rion followed the direction, noticing the woman who knelt beside the throne with her head down and her hands folded in her lap. A dark tumble of hair fell over her face, but Rion would have known her anywhere.

His breath solidified into lead, and he nearly dropped the girl, but he clung on, determined to barter Rachel's way out of here. After centuries of regretting his choices, Rion no longer cared about power or magic. All he wanted was her.

Herric smirked and leaned forward, placing a finger under Rachel's chin and tipping her face up. She stared at her master, unblinking.

Rion's heart felt like it turned to ash, burning with the ardent fury of his need. She was exactly as he remembered.

"Rachel," he choked out, and her eyes turned to him. They were endless. Dark pools of light reflecting off a still pond under a full moon.

He felt everything in that moment: the years he had spent missing her, the mistakes he'd carried in his chest, cracking his ribs. This was his chance to start over, to finally have the life he'd given up almost three hundred years ago.

Rion wanted to toss the girl down and wrap Rachel in his arms, but he resisted the urge to give in to his desires. He had to think clearly. He had to play this wisely.

Reluctantly, he dragged his gaze away to find Herric still smirking.

"Is this who you were after?" he asked, as though he didn't already know.

"I bring the girl," Rion said with a knot wedged in his throat, deflecting the question.

"I see you bring someone," Herric said. "Turn around. I want to be sure it's her."

Rion hesitated but then did what he asked, facing the hundreds of gawkers who continued to stare at him like he was a fresh steak tossed into a lion pit. After a pause, Rion heard the echoing click of footsteps. Before Herric could get too close, Rion swung around. He held up a hand and retreated a few paces, consciously aware of the crowd behind him inching closer.

"Stay back. I have some conditions before I release her to you."

Herric arched a brow and lifted his hands in surrender.

"I only want to see her face," he said. "Then you may tell me your *conditions.*"

Rion nodded as he waited for Herric to loop around before he lifted the girl's hair.

"So like Amara," he said softly. "Remarkable."

Herric circled to Rion's other side and returned to his dais, spinning around and falling onto his throne before crossing his legs with a flourish.

"So tell me then, what do you want?" He gestured to Rachel. "*Her*, I presume?"

"Yes. I ask that she be returned with me to the surface."

Herric threw his head back and laughed, the sound ricocheting off the cavernous ceiling until it sounded like a thousand Lords of the Underworld mocking his utter stupidity.

"The surface?" Herric asked with a gleeful spark in his eyes.

"Yes," Rion said, squirming under the girl's weight. He couldn't wait to get her off him, but he couldn't release her yet.

"But you realize she is dead."

"Surely someone as powerful as you can rectify that."

Herric laughed again, steepling his fingers together and studying Rion like he was a bug.

"You came to *bargain* with me? Are you . . . a fool?"

Rion didn't answer, and Herric stared at him for so long that the hairs on the back of his neck rose. Suddenly, he became aware of his position. He was alone, surrounded by the dead, as they gathered behind him, creeping forward, pressing into his space.

Herric chuckled as Rion's gaze swept around the room. He *was* a fool. What had he been thinking coming to the Under-world with his demands?

In his desperation, in his drunken haze, in the splinters of his broken mind, he had walked in here thinking he held any sort of power. He realized then how grievously wrong he'd played this. He'd become so *used* to power that he'd forgotten he would have none to speak of here.

"The ark," he croaked. "I left it in the Keep."

Herric's amused expression didn't waver.

"Is that right?"

"Yes," Rion said, once again hoisting the girl on his shoul-der. It was screaming now, his entire back aching, pain radi-ating down through his hips and thighs. But he refused to let her go, clinging to this last hand he had to play. "You'll release Rachel to me, and then I will send someone down to deliver it."

Herric narrowed his eyes. "You will leave the girl here."

Rion's jaw clenched, wishing he could defy the order, but

he heaved her up and set her on the ground. She lay at his feet, her eyes closed and her skin pale, her lips gently parted. Rion remembered the girl he'd tormented. The sound of her screams. That scar over her eye that he had been responsible for. He tried to drag up some sympathy for what he'd done, but the heirs of Heart had never meant anything to him. They had always been a means to an end.

"There," Rion said, looking up.

"There," Herric repeated as his eyes lit with a feral shine.

Before Rion could say anything else, he was consumed by a wall of black smoke. He hacked and coughed as it filled his lungs, choking off his air. His eyes watered, and he clutched at his throat, sure this was the end.

When the smoke cleared a minute later, he found himself in a black iron cage dangling next to Herric's throne. Across from him was a second cage with the girl's unconscious form crumpled at the bottom. Rion clutched the bars as it lurched from side to side.

"Let me out!" he cried as the entire room burst into vicious, taunting laughter.

Rion's gaze rolled over the room, searching for Rachel, who remained kneeling on the floor with her head down.

"Rachel!" he called, but she stayed inert as Herric rose from his throne and bounded down the dais. A cape of black smoke formed over his shoulders, and then, from his hand, he produced the ark of Heart, holding it high over his head.

Rion felt in his back pocket but already knew it was gone.

"Rachel!" Rion screamed, gripping the bars.

Herric threw his head back and laughed again, the dark

sound filtering into the fissuring cracks snaking through his bones. Herric grabbed Rachel by the hair and dragged her up. She didn't react, even when it was apparent she was hanging by nothing but her roots. She was like a hollow porcelain doll.

"You *fool*," Herric said with a snarl. "You thought you could trick me? Come into *my* kingdom with *conditions*?"

He shoved Rachel, and she tumbled down the stairs, rolling over until she landed on the floor in a limp heap, her arms and legs settling at awkward, unnatural angles. Rion screamed as he lunged for her, but he was trapped.

"This is *my* domain, king of The Aurora," Herric said with a wicked grin as he threw the ark into the air and then snatched it in a fist.

"Welcome to hell."

CHAPTER 61

NADIR

UNDER THE BELTZA MOUNTAINS

After what feels like a century, the magic pinning me down finally dissipates. "Lor!" I shout down the tunnel, but it's been at least twenty minutes, and I'm sure my father is long gone.

Willow's restraints disappear as she slumps against me. Though she's unconscious, she appears unharmed, her chest moving steadily up and down. Morana and Khione's restraints also melt away, and they pace back and forth, snarling into the darkness that swallowed my father and Lor.

I look up the tunnel at the way we came, and I have to make

a decision. I need to go after Lor, but I also know she would be furious if I left her sister lying here alone and helpless.

After scrambling to my feet, I heave Willow into my arms and start running up the path the way we came.

"Help!" I roar at the top of my lungs. "Help!"

Gods, someone else has to be close.

Finally, I see two figures moving in the dark and nearly collapse in relief when Mael and Tristan emerge from the shadows.

"What happened?" Tristan demands as I transfer Willow into his arms. I explain as quickly as I can.

"I need your sword," I say to Mael.

"What are you planning to do?"

I hold out my hand and shake my arm. "Go after her, of course! Give it to me."

"You can't do this alone," he says as he drags the weapon from its sheath.

"Get Willow checked out," I say to Tristan. "Lor will never forgive me if anything happens to her."

"I'm coming with you," Mael says, clutching his blade in his fist.

My lips thin as I face him. "No, you're not. It's too dangerous."

"Nadir—"

"No. You aren't coming. My father didn't kill me when he had the chance, but he *will* kill you to punish me, Mael. I'm not taking that risk."

I hold out my hand again, and he passes me the sword, his expression clouded with displeasure as my dogs trot over and stand next to me. His mouth opens, but before he can protest any further, I wave my hand, erecting bars of light across the tunnel, leaving them all trapped on the other side.

"Nadir!" Mael shouts, thrusting his shoulder against the shield, but it remains firm. "Don't do this! He will kill you too."

My throat tightens, and I reach through the barricade for Mael. We clasp forearms as I stare at my best friend. "Thank you for being the brother I never had," I say. "For being with me during some of the worst days of my life. And thank you for helping put me back together."

Mael's dark eyes shine in the glow of my magic as he shakes his head. "I should be the one thanking you. For everything."

I squeeze his hand as a ball of emotion presses the backs of my eyes and then dip my head. "It has been an *honor* to be your friend, Captain."

Mael runs a hand down his face. "Fuck. Don't do that. Don't get yourself killed."

"I can't promise that. Take care of Amya for me?"

"Of course," he answers after a long pause.

I nod and look at Tristan holding Willow in his arms.

"Please find her," he says to me in a raw voice as he clutches his sister closer.

"I will try until there is no breath left in my body."

Tristan stares at me and blinks. "I know that. I know you would do anything for her."

With one more glance at Mael, I dip my chin.

"Go and get your girl," he whispers as we release our hold. "I love you."

"I love you too."

Then I spin around and barrel down the tunnel with Morana and Khione at my side, praying that wasn't really our last goodbye.

Winding down into the mountain, the darkness closes in on me, my ice hounds keeping close at my heels. They prowl on silent paws, their hackles raised. I have the map we found in my father's study in my pocket, and I pull it out, banking on the fact that he took Lor this way.

It feels like it takes hours—I have no sense of the day or time buried under miles of stone—but eventually, I'm spit out into a cavern with a ceiling that soars high overhead. At the far end stands a wide opening and a tunnel beyond glowing with bright luminescent lights. I blink and shake my head because this seems *impossible*.

Is this really the Underworld? How could my father *do* this? My desire to kill him increases tenfold. I will not allow him to live after this. He has spent his entire life hating me, attempting to carve away every sliver of joy I might find. But taking Lor from me to be delivered to this devil? Some actions can be answered only with the end of a sword.

I approach slowly, and a deep-seated instinct tells me this is the end of everything. All the years and months of chasing this hazy future I've been imagining will come down to whatever lies beyond this doorway.

As I stand at the threshold, studying the luminescence beyond, I understand I'm about to go to a place from which I might never return. I once told Lor I'd follow her into the fires of the Underworld if that's what it took. I never expected to mean that literally.

But I *did* mean it, so I won't hesitate. This might truly be the end, but I have to try. I could never live with myself otherwise. I'd rather be dead than live in a world without her. I refuse to let her down.

"Wait here," I tell Morana and Khione. They whine in protest, but they obey the command as I take a step, crossing into the unknown. With my sword raised at the ready, I touch the walls, my fingers coming away coated with a layer of shimmering dust. My mind spins with the sheer impossibility of all of this, but it's here, and it's real.

"Lor," I whisper. "I'm coming. Hold on, my queen. My heart. My mate. I'm coming."

With one look back over my shoulder, I take a deep breath and plunge into the tunnel, hoping there's the slightest chance we're ever coming back out.

CHAPTER 62

LOR

When I wake up, the world is a bright flash of white. My head pounds to the drone of voices and the rhythmic thumping of . . . music? My hip aches from lying on the hard floor. It takes a moment to summon the strength to lift myself up. Still wearing my red dress, I shiver from a chill that skates down the back of my neck.

As my vision clears, the sight that greets me makes absolutely no sense. I'm in the biggest cavern I've ever seen. The rough stone walls shimmer with iridescence like they've been coated with fairy dust.

And the people—the *people*. Hundreds of them mill about on a field of shiny black, silver, and white tiles, drinking, eating, and chatting. They wear the most outlandish costumes, also in black and white and in patterns like stripes and checks, their heads and shoulders adorned with feathers and silver-plated armor and their faces painted with colorful makeup.

Some wear heads or masks that render them into animals like lions, elephants, or serpents. Dread pools in my stomach, burning like a puddle of acid. It's both beautiful and horrific. It's also a sign that wherever I am, I'm totally fucked.

As if the sight before me weren't alarming enough, the fact that I appear to be locked in some kind of swinging cage churns bile up the back of my throat. I try not to hyperventilate as it pitches back and forth, making the world spin.

Suddenly, the music cuts off, and everything below me grinds to an abrupt halt. The silence sends a shiver down my back as I cling to the bars, sucking in deep breaths, trying to prevent myself from passing out.

That's when I hear footsteps. *Click... Click... Click.*

A male High Fae approaches me. He wears fitted leather from head to toe, everything of the deepest black. His long dark hair falls past his shoulders, and his dark eyes are ringed with smudges of black.

He's familiar in a way that feels distant but also much too close.

Fucking fuck. This is *not* good. I lurch up onto my knees, causing my cage to sway and jerk with enough force that I nearly tip over. I peer down as the man draws closer. I note his pointed ears and his devious smile that has my blood running cold. I know that face.

"Welcome," he says as he comes to a stop below me. "I'm so glad you could join us in the Underworld Court."

I almost choke on my tongue at that announcement, but why should I be surprised by anything anymore? I've met Zerra, killed my mate, and been to the Evanescence, where I'm being groomed to become a god.

Why shouldn't I now find myself in the literal pits of hell?

"How did I get here?" I ask, trying to drag up the last thing I remember. The bonding with Nadir, searching for Willow, finding Rion in the tunnel, his dark magic, and then everything going black.

"Willow," I shout. "Where is my sister?"

Herric's face twists into disdain, and he gestures across the room. "You might have to ask him."

My hands tighten on the bars as I look across the space. Rion sits at the bottom of a cage matching mine, his legs up and his arms wrapped around them. That fucking bastard *took* Willow. He *brought* me here. Our gazes meet, and I don't understand what I read in his expression. If he did anything to my sister, there is no limit to the suffering I will visit upon him.

But I see no anger or hate.

None of that cold, brutal arrogance I remember every time I close my eyes.

There is nothing left as if he's become only a brittle shell of the Aurora King.

"Then *why* am I here?" I demand, turning back to Herric.

"Ah, *that* is the right question, isn't it?"

He strolls a few paces before he spins and walks back slowly, every step deliberate.

Heel. Toe. Heel. Toe.

"You're here because of this." He reaches into an invisible pocket and draws out the ark of Heart. Oh gods. *No.* I think back to the notes we found in Rion's study. I was right.

All this time, we've been so focused on Rion's plans when it was actually the Lord of Hell who we should have been worrying about.

He stops and faces me, twisting the object between his fingers.

"I want you to destroy it," he says.

"Why?" I ask, stalling for time because I know why.

He wants to kill Zerra and take her place.

His mouth twists up at the corner. "Because I've been trapped down here for thousands of years, and I'm tired of it. I have waited a very long time to take my rightful place as a god, and you're going to help me."

I blink, cursing my utter stupidity. In my desire to save myself, have I opened the door to something so much worse?

"How does that work? How will it free you?"

Herric grins and tosses the ark in the air before he catches it. He paces a few steps and then pivots around with his hands behind his back. "While everyone believes the Artefacts to be the most powerful objects in Ouranos, *this* ark is imbibed with years of Heart magic. Mined from the lowest pit of the mountains, it contains multitudes."

He spins the end on the tip of his finger, the sparkles flashing in the light.

"I've spent many years learning how I might break the tether that keeps me bound here, and this is the key. Zerra grows weaker and the barrier between this world and yours grows thinner with each passing century. That's how I managed to contact the perfect, gullible little pawn to aid in my schemes. The fact that he has absolutely *no* conscience ensured my plans went off without a hitch."

His attention drifts to Rion, whose face stirs into the slightest hint of emotion as his brows draw together. Herric tricked Rion into delivering both me and the ark. I had no idea the Aurora King was this big a fool. Clearly, I've been giving him way too much credit.

"After I earned his trust by explaining how to steal his father's crown, all I had to do was wait for the Primary of Heart to appear and the ark to be found. When it's destroyed, it will generate an immense amount of power," Herric continues. "It will last for only a few seconds, but it will be enough to harness and break myself out of this place." He tips his head and mock pouts. "As you see, we are both caged in our own way.

"And once Zerra is dead, I will be able to take her place, right where I have always belonged." He flips the ark again and smiles. "And you've been so generous in helping me with that, haven't you?"

"I don't know what you mean," I answer, hoping he can't detect my lie. Does he know all but two arks remain? Or has Tyr completed the task yet? Is the ark of Heart all that's left?

He smiles in a way that tells me he knows.

A thousand thoughts churn through my head.

He wants to free himself and, in the process, kill Zerra with the ark.

I *also* want to kill Zerra with the ark.

He wants to take over Zerra's position.

I do not want that, despite what the Empyrium want. Speaking of which, where the fuck are they? Do they not realize what's happening?

But I can't let *Herric* take over.

If I get the ark and destroy it, I can't do it in his presence.

I press a hand to my forehead, feeling a headache build behind my eyes.

Herric tips his head. "Is she not trying to kill you?" he asks.

"So let her kill me," I snarl. "It would be a better fate than allowing you to terrorize Ouranos. I'd rather die than help you."

The Empyrium refused him last time, claiming his heart was too dark. I carry little hope that he's changed during all his years trapped down here.

Heart might be lost if I fail, but *everyone* is lost if he escapes this world.

"I thought you might say that," Herric says. "So perhaps we can make this interesting."

I frown, knowing that whatever he's about to reveal will turn my world upside down.

"A test, perhaps?"

"Test?"

"Or maybe a trial? You're good at those, aren't you?"

The crowd behind Herric breaks out into a series of excited twitters, and I shake my head at the sick sense of déjà vu threatening to drown me.

"Trial." I keep repeating his words because I'm not sure what else to do. What is he asking of me?

"Yes. I've devised a challenge just for you. If you pass, I'll hand you the ark and let you walk out of here."

"And if I don't?"

"And if you don't, then you'll destroy this in my presence, and because I'm such a good sport, I'll still let you walk out of here. I'll even let you have your crown, and you can rule over your broken queendom, under my guidance of course."

His face stretches into a cat-like smile, and I clutch my stomach, about to throw up.

"How do I know you'll keep your word about any of this?"

"Good question, Heart Queen."

He stretches out his arm and opens his palm. A moment later, pain sears my hand. I clutch at my wrist, groaning as I sink to my knees. I writhe as my arm burns like I've been shot with flaming arrows. A few seconds later, the worst of it recedes, and I pull my hand away to find a glowing silver mark branded on the inside of my palm.

"A promise," Herric says. "Now I am bound to keep up my end of our bargain."

My vision swims before my eyes as I will myself not to pass out.

"How do you know I'll keep my word if I lose?"

"Oh," Herric says. "I know you will."

He waves a hand again, and a third cage materializes as my breath turns to rust in my lungs.

"Lor!" Nadir shouts, and we lurch towards each other, our cages swinging. We stretch through the bars, our fingertips an inch from touching, but we can't quite reach.

I whip around to face Herric, rage boiling in my blood.

"He just walked right in here," Herric says with a shrug. "I presume to save you? How very noble."

"You let him go," I scream, shaking the bars, and everyone

erupts into laughter. Gods, why does it feel like I'm right back in Aphelion? Herric ignores my outburst as he continues speaking.

"Should you double-cross me, then your little prince remains here with me," Herric says. "I'll toss you back into the world, where you'll have to live knowing he's down here suffering because you refused to keep up your end of our deal."

I snarl as I lurch at my bars, the cage pitching dangerously. "I'll kill you!"

"You cannot kill the Lord of the Underworld," he says, all confidence and swagger. "The good news is that I can't kill you, either, until I get what I want. So *your* life isn't on the line during the challenge…"

His gaze swings to Nadir. "But I can't say the same for his."

My hands grip the bars so tight that my knuckles turn white. "What does that mean?"

"I'll let him help you," he says as though he's being generous.

"If he dies, then I'll never help you," I snarl.

"I could kill him right now if you like. Shall I send our mutual friend here to retrieve another family member to motivate you, perhaps?" He gestures to Rion, who still sits in his cage, glaring at everyone.

Anger swells up my throat. "If you touch m—"

"Shh," he says, flinging a hand at me. My voice cuts off, and I try to speak, but no sound comes out. My jaw works uselessly, searching for the syllables. "Just for fun, let's say that if you want me to return the ark, then he must also survive. So … you know, good luck with that."

My mouth opens to silence when I scream, so I settle for uselessly rattling the bars.

"These are my conditions. Do we have an agreement? Nod to say yes."

I stare around the cavern as my magic sparks. I stare at thousands of faces of the dead, who sneer up at me with teeth and claws sharpened with malice. How far will we get if we try to fight our way out? Tears burn in my eyes.

"Lor!" Nadir shouts, and my gaze darts to him.

Herric rolls his eyes. "Not you too." With another flick of his hand, Nadir's voice slices off as he flies back, slamming into the wall of his cage, which swings with an ominous squeak. I try to leap for him, but of course it's no use.

"And just to show you what a truly fine gentleman I am, I'll even do this."

He waves his hand, and I'm engulfed in smoke. When it clears, I'm no longer wearing my tattered red dress but rather a leather suit much like Herric's, with a fitted jacket and pants that conform to my skin. The long sleeves go past my wrists, and the collar covers my throat. Black boots finish the ensemble. Nadir is now clothed in a similar fashion as well.

"That's better," Herric says. "I do like it when everyone looks the part when visiting my court."

Then he gives me a wicked smile before he spins around.

"Enjoy your stay in the Underworld, Heart Queen."

A black cape materializes on his back, and he runs across the dais before swinging around and tossing it with a flourish. Then he spreads his arms and declares, "Let the game begin!"

CHAPTER 63

GABRIEL

APHELION—THE SUN PALACE

I stand with my brothers, forming a circle in the throne room with Tyr at the center. We're all shirtless, our bodies honed from decades of training, the golden tattoos on our necks exposed to reveal the glittering sinuous lines curving over our collarbones.

The Mirror sits uncovered, reflecting sunlight streaming through the open ceiling. We cleaned up the dome's shattered glass but have yet to repair it. Add it to my endless list of shit to deal with. It isn't raining for the first time in what feels like forever, and I tip my face up, closing my eyes, basking in the rays of the sun.

Hylene and Erevan wait in the corner, but no one else was invited to witness this moment. It's too private. Too raw to expose to anyone but the people we trust the most.

The scuff of a boot draws my attention to Tyr, who clutches the ark in his hands. He's looking at me, scanning my body from head to toe. I can't decide what I read in his expression. It straddles so many lines—regret, sadness, conviction. What's going through his head?

"The Mirror will assist," Tyr says. "I have studied how to release you—"

His words cut off as he sucks in a breath that rattles in his chest, clutching the ark in his thin hands.

"I'm sorry," he says in a hoarse whisper. "I'm sorry for all the pain I caused and for ever tying you to my will in the first place. I was young and entitled, drunk on what I believed was my right to power, confident I had every right as your king. I regret that it was only through my brother's actions that I finally saw the light and the error of my ways. Had he not imprisoned me and used you against me, then we might have lived like this until the end of my days."

He studies each of us in turn, his gaze unwavering. He isn't asking for our forgiveness. He's looking each of us in the eye and admitting his mistakes.

I watch my brothers as Tyr seems to have a silent conversation with each of us, their expressions a mixture of acceptance and resolve. Tyr's gaze lingers on the scars that cover our arms and chests—the markings left by Atlas when he punished us for our defiance. I try not to look too hard. For so many years, I've tried not to look too hard. I also try not to notice that mine are the worst—that I paid this price so dearly in more ways than one.

"And even if I'd like to think I would never have done what my brother did, it is no excuse," Tyr continues before he swallows. "What *I* did is unforgivable. What every ruler of Aphelion has done to their warders is unforgivable and a stain that will live on in our history forever. I do not ask for your absolution, only that you hear how much I regret every single day, and I'd do anything to start at the beginning of my rule when I would make so many different choices."

When his gaze finds me again, tears shimmer in his eyes. As he says these words, I begin to understand what I should have known from the beginning. No matter what we might have felt for one another, he would always have been a king, and I would always have been his servant. We could never have been anything else.

There is too much pain and too much memory. Too much to overcome anyway.

Though he isn't asking for it, I *do* forgive him. If only for my own peace of mind. If only because I deserve it.

Slowly, Tyr lifts the ark above his head and closes his eyes. We wait in silence, sharing looks around the circle. I glance over my shoulder at Hylene and Erevan. She tips her chin, offering me her silent support.

As I turn back to the center, the Mirror begins to glow, and I assume Tyr must be speaking with it. His body trembles as he holds the ark over his head, his lips moving softly as his ashen hair falls around his face.

A soft yellow beam arches slowly from the surface of the

Mirror, hitting the ark. The object glows with gilded light before eight more beams spring from the ark and find their way to the centers of our hearts.

I tense as one hits me, bracing for the impact. But there is no pain, only warmth like a sunbeam through a window. Golden light spreads over my chest like I'm being dipped in bathwater before it ripples over my shoulders and down my arms, melts down my legs, and then rises up to my throat, where my skin tingles.

Tiny crackles spark against the lines of the marking that has kept me a prisoner for so many years. With my breath held, I feel it slowly burn away. I watch as the lines flare on my brothers' throats until, a few moments later, the light dissipates before the Mirror returns to its usual reflective surface.

We stare at each other, and tears burn my eyes. The sight of their smooth, unblemished skin is the most beautiful thing I've ever seen. Emotion swells in my chest and a sob cracks out of me. A tear leaks down the side of my face, and I wipe it with the back of my hand. It acts as a signal because then we all move, circling together in a tangle of arms and wings, embracing each other as we share in the collective grief of our trauma.

"It's over," Rhyle says, and I look up. He hooks a hand around the back of my head and presses his forehead to mine. "It's over, my friend."

"Captain," says Jareth, and we break apart as all seven of my living brothers stand in a line, pressing their hands to their chests and bowing their heads.

"Captain," they murmur in unison.

"Thank you for everything you did to protect us," Rhyle

says, and I can barely respond over the pressure squeezing my heart and my ribs as I nod.

"Any of you would have done the same," I answer when I can speak, knowing it's true. These are good men, and every last one of them might have done great things. Any of them still could. "I am honored to have served at your side, and I would not have survived this without any of you. But from now on, there will be no more captain. From now on, I will only be Gabriel."

Hylene and Erevan rush over, also wrapping me in their embrace. We hug for a minute before I feel Tyr's eyes on me. I pull away and turn to him, walking over and falling to a knee.

"No," Tyr says. "There will be no more of that either. For your service to Aphelion, you will all be granted anything you need or desire to live in comfort until the end of your days. I know it cannot make up for everything that happened, but you will never want for anything in this life again."

I stand up and nod, dragging Tyr towards me in a messy hug as he wraps his arms around me. It's been so many years since we've touched one another like this. I remember the strong man he used to be, but that man is gone.

I don't know what the future holds for any of us, but as I pull away, I know I will always care for him. We walked a path so dark that we nearly lost our way, but together, we stumbled into the light, and no matter what happens, I will always be there for him.

He seems to understand what I'm saying without words and nods before the first smile I've seen in so long barely creeps to his face.

"It's time to destroy it," he reminds me. "This will never happen again."

As my brothers and I dress in our tunics and shirts, Tyr places the ark on the floor. We all circle around him, staring at it. So much power and destruction are contained in that small object. If Herric had never gifted it to our first king, then all of this might have been avoided. It occurs to me how the tiniest acts can ripple over time, changing the entire course of our destinies. What might my life have been had I never been bound to Tyr?

Maybe now I'll get the chance to find out.

Tyr watches me, waiting for a signal to proceed, and I nod.

Another reason no others were invited is that we don't know what will happen when we destroy the ark. I was hoping Nadir would send more information, but no further letters have arrived, and I worry about what that might mean.

Erevan continues refusing his help, and I'm trying not to be angry with him. I understand his convictions, but sometimes I wish the bastard weren't so damn noble. Our gazes meet, and I'm sure he can read my thoughts. Neither one of us agrees with the other, but this isn't new for us.

"Everyone back away," Tyr says, and we do, but only by a few steps. I can't fight the instinct to protect him, that deep-rooted need to throw myself over the explosion if it would save his life.

Tyr shakes out his hands and then rolls his neck. He hasn't allowed anyone else around him while he's tried practicing his magic. I have no real sense of how much control he has. But he told me he was ready, and all I could do was trust that.

I'm almost shocked when Tyr lifts his hand and golden sparks dance at his fingertips. His shoulders lift with a deep breath, and he concentrates a beam of light into the ark. It sinks into the surface. My brow furrows when nothing seems to happen, but Tyr doesn't stop. After another second, the ark begins to glow.

I take a step back, my arm crossing over Hylene as I shuffle her behind me. Though she makes a sound of protest, she stays where she is, rising up on her tiptoes to peek over my shoulder. Her body presses against mine, and I wrap an arm back around her waist to keep her safe.

Tyr continues filtering magic into the ark as sweat beads on his brow, his mouth pursed in concentration. The ark jumps and twists, and then a plume of smoke billows from its surface, forming into the shape of a woman wearing a long flowing gown.

"Zerra," I breathe. I recognize her likeness carved into the ark. Tyr flinches in shock, nearly releasing the control on his magic. "Don't stop!" I shout. "Keep going!"

Gritting his teeth, Tyr hangs on as the ark glows brighter. Zerra turns around, and I almost choke when she faces me, her eyes filled with loathing and her expression twisted with pain. She doubles over, clutching her stomach before her back arches and her arms fling out. Her head tips back and to the side as her mouth opens wide in a soundless scream.

I press Hylene harder against me as black veins form across Zerra's skin, climbing up her neck and down her arms like a crystal vase cracking into pieces. She twists, her body bending like a blade of grass blowing in the breeze.

I'm so focused on Zerra that I almost don't notice Tyr clutching his chest, his body also curling inwards. "I can't..." he croaks out as his magic stutters and flashes.

"Tyr!" I shout. "Everyone get out! Hylene! Go!"

They begin to make their way towards the door as I run to Tyr, catching him as he stumbles. "Don't let go! You can't let go!"

Some instinct tells me that if Tyr releases his magic, Zerra will have the ability to hurt him. He shakes as I cling to him, trying to offer whatever inadequate strength I can. "Tyr! Hang on! You must hang on!"

But he isn't strong enough. He groans, the sound tearing out of him with a roar, as his magic flickers one last time, and then he falls against me and collapses.

Zerra's form solidifies, a grim smile twisting her face. She lifts an arm, white sparks gathering in her palm.

And then she hurls a ball of crackling silver light in our direction.

I'm clutching Tyr, waiting for the strike, when everything seems to reverse in slow motion as a beam of pure golden light spears into the center of Zerra's chest.

She bends back and screams before the sound cuts off, and she morphs back into her previous, barely there form. Gaping, I stare at her. It takes me a moment to realize it's Erevan, his jaw set as he holds out his hand, funneling magic into the ark, his light brighter and so much more vibrant than Tyr's.

He moves closer, the ark glowing brighter and brighter as Zerra continues her silent scream. More and more cracks form on her skin while she claws at her face and chest and arms.

Her hair rises from her head, fanning out as static streaks of lightning surround her in a flashing, throbbing column.

The ark explodes in a blinding flash, splinters arrowing through the air.

Again, I brace myself for the impact, but Erevan spins up his magic and encases us in a protective shield of golden light. I see the pieces crash against it in bright flashes before they fall to the floor.

A moment later, he releases it, leaving the three of us alone in the silent throne room.

We stare at each other.

Childhood friends. Boys drawn together by chance. Boys whose positions and responsibilities pulled them apart before fate forced them back together again.

A king. A prince. A slave. And a revolutionary.

A broken crown.

A traitor.

A free man.

And Erevan. The future of Aphelion.

He watches us with a wary look before he stares at his hands as if unable to believe what he's just done.

"You *fucking* asshole," I half growl, half choke out.

That breaks the tension in the room and then we both start laughing.

Erevan falls to his knees, throwing his arms around me and Tyr as the sky booms with the promise of another storm. We all look up to witness streaks of silver lightning flashing overhead, and a scream echoes in the distance.

We did it. Whatever Lor and Nadir are up to, they're on

their own now, but at least we helped with this. I say a silent prayer that they survive, and I see them again.

Erevan looks at me, and we both smile.

Finally, we can move forward.

Only three of us are left, and I hope we survive this too.

I think we all deserve that.

That's when the clouds roll in to the crash of thunder, and the sky opens up before the rain, once again, starts to fall.

CHAPTER 64

LOR

THE UNDERWORLD

With my hands gripped around the bars of my cage, I watch in horror as Herric paces back and forth, his cape streaming behind him while he riles up the crowd. He's like some evil court jester, but instead of making everyone laugh, he's tempting out the very worst parts of themselves.

"What do you think?" he shouts with an arm raised. "Should we start now? Or give them another moment to contemplate how absolutely *fucked* they are?"

A chorus of screaming mixes with frenzied chants of "nows" and "laters," and my head feels like it's been stuffed with cotton and lit on fire. My heart thrashes in my ribs, my breath coming in tight gasps. This shit can't be happening again.

Lor. Calm down.

The voice enters my head, and I look at Nadir.

Don't look at me.

What?

Lor. Look at Herric.

I shake my head, trying to form coherent thoughts while the Lord of the Underworld continues circling his arms as he stirs up the crowd. They're loving every moment of this.

He doesn't know we're mates. This is our advantage, Lor.

I grip the bars tighter, my fingers aching, and drop my head against my hand, inhaling deep breaths, trying to clear my head.

Keep looking at him, he says as I sneak a peek over my shoulder. Nadir watches Herric before he turns his gaze to Rion, who's regarding all of this with a strange sort of hollow detachment. Why has he done this to us? I wish I could walk over there and rip out his spine.

Did you find Willow? I ask. *Is she okay? Did he hurt her?*

She's fine. She's with your brother.

My breath eases with relief as Nadir exchanges a look with his father. In his expression, I see that any qualms he had about killing him have been wiped away, leaving only pure, seething rage churned from a lifetime of neglect and abuse.

Nadir, I'm freaking out.

His gaze swings to me. *Don't panic, Lor.*

Sure. I won't panic. Another fucking test, but this time it isn't my life on the line but Nadir's. That's assuming Herric keeps his word about anything.

How did we come full circle?

Herric continues performing for his minions, working them up into a frenzy that tells me they want action, and they want it now.

I study these . . . creatures—these souls of the dead. Even from here, I can sense their emptiness, their hearts and spirits given up to the earth. To whatever body they might find next. They snarl and shriek, and it's obvious there's nothing mortal left. They're mindless animals scenting blood. Were they always a bit like this? They found their resting place with the worst of Ouranos. Maybe here they enjoy free rein to cater to their basest instincts.

"I think," Herric screams, drawing my attention back to him. "It's time we begin!"

He lifts his arms and drops them down, and everything goes black. A second later, I remain cloaked in darkness, but the world no longer sways beneath my feet, suggesting I've moved from my cage. It's a small consolation because I have no doubt that whatever Herric has planned will be so much worse.

I'm surrounded by a disorienting mash of voices, whispers and chants, laughs and jeers. I look down at my wrists as they start to glow with the pulsing blue of arcturite. These cuffs are different from the ones Tyr wore—his were more like thick bracelets, but these are thin and smooth, more like vambraces. I wrap a hand around the left one, finding no seams or breaks in the material.

"Nadir?" I call tentatively into the heavy blackness, relieved to discover I once again have use of my voice.

"Lor!" My name punctuates the veil of darkness, and if I squint, I imagine I can see the faint glow of arcturite in the distance. It's difficult to gauge how far away he is.

Stand still. Don't move. I think we're on some kind of ledge or platform.

I think he's right. I can't explain why, but it feels like we're high up. When Herric granted us these outfits, he also braided my hair. A breeze tosses the few strands framing my face, tickling my cheeks. The idea of him clothing and manipulating us makes my skin crawl, but that's the least of my problems right now.

Are you also wearing cuffs? Nadir asks.

I look down at my hands again, twisting my wrists left and right. Herric doesn't know I'm immune. Along with our mate bond, maybe this is the edge we need.

I am. What's about to happen, Nadir?

I don't know.

I'm scared.

So am I.

The seconds pass as my heart beats in my throat. Slowly, I turn around, trying to orient myself. Without my sense of sight, I'm unbalanced, and I bend my knees, holding my hands out, attempting to find my equilibrium. Ready for whatever is coming. I hope.

The voices swoop higher, buzzing with anticipation, and I hold completely still, though everything in me wants to find something solid to touch.

A bright light sears across my vision, startling me, and I stumble back, shielding my eyes with my hand. My heel slips off an edge, and I scream as my arms windmill for several long seconds to the sound of delighted gasps and screams. I have just enough presence of mind to make out that I'm standing atop a platform suspended over a drop that disappears into the darkness. I continue to tip and lurch, trying to recover my balance. My foot slips and I pitch forward, my knee crashing against the sharp edge.

I cry out as my shin scrapes a rough corner before I collapse. Rolling over, I clutch my throbbing leg. "Fuck!" I shout, earning me a chorus of snide laughter.

Inhaling a deep breath and blowing it out of my mouth, I will my fury to settle. I can't believe I'm in this fucking place again, surrounded by monsters who delight in my suffering.

Flipping onto my hands and knees, I take in my surroundings. Everything is still dark except for two bright spotlights, one shining on me and the other on Nadir, who's also perched on top of a small platform.

Are you okay? Don't nod.

No, I'm not fucking okay.

Waiting on my hands and knees, I stare across the space, but I can barely make out his features.

We're going to get out of this.

Tears fill my eyes, and one rolls down my cheek, slipping off my chin. I drop my head, staring between my hands as I suck in a long breath.

He keeps saying that, but everything just gets worse and worse. Of all the endings I imagined for myself, this blows every notion I could have conjured out of the water.

Another light flares and my head snaps up to find Herric standing several feet away.

"Welcome to your challenge," he shouts from where he seems to hover in the air. "I hope you enjoy what I've put together for you."

A moment later, more lights spring to life, revealing a massive round stadium filled with thousands of spectators.

"Your task," Herric shouts, "is to reach the center and retrieve your gift, Heart Queen."

Instead of that empty blackness, a microcosm of jungle and forest, swamps, lakes, rivers, trees, and rocks sprawls below us. In the very center is a mountain with a single red rose suspended over its peak spinning slowly in the air.

I try to swallow, but my mouth feels like it's coated in wool. Panicked sweat breaks out over my forehead.

"You'll find a few surprises along the way," Herric continues. "But I'm sure you'll have no problem dealing with them. Or maybe you will. That's sort of the point, isn't it?"

I harden my jaw and push myself up into a fighting stance, my hands curled in tight fists.

Whatever is about to happen, I must get to Nadir.

My life is safe for now, but Herric will do everything to kill him.

"There are no rules in the arena. Do whatever you need to stay alive. Good luck, little queen."

I'm coming for you, I say to Nadir. I can feel him across the distance separating us. I almost lost him once, and I swore I would never let anyone take him again.

I love you, Lor.

My throat knots at the raw finality in his voice.

No, this isn't the end. Tell me that again when we get the fuck out of here.

Over the distance, our gazes meet, and I see him fall to a knee with his hand pressed over his chest. *Then let's fucking do this, Heart Queen.*

"Ready!" Herric shouts as I turn to look at him.

He drops his arms, and our platforms slowly start to lower when a disembodied voice floats over our heads, backdropped by thousands of breathless, vicious cheers.

I make a promise to myself.

I don't care what it takes.

This will not be goodbye.

3...

2...

1...

Go!

CHAPTER 65

For several seconds, the platform descends at a steady pace until a horn blasts through the white noise of the spectators, and it plummets. I scream, airborne for several long, stomach-lifting moments before I plunge into the prickly heart of a thick bush.

At first, I'm grateful it broke my fall, but then I realize it's a tangle of thorns. They cling to my hair and my clothes, pulling, scraping, and tearing as I struggle to extricate myself. I curse a blue streak, not only for the awkwardness of this position but for the fact that I've once again been forced into a contest that I never entered.

What kind of sick poetic justice is this?

I continue to struggle as warm blood trickles down my cheek and my hands sting from scratches. Finally, I heave myself over and roll off the bush before collapsing in a heap on the ground, finding a patch of short grass to cushion my landing.

Lor. Where are you?

I fell into a fucking nest of thorns.

Okay, well, I don't want to alarm you . . .

He drifts off, but I'm already on my feet, running, leaping over small plants and rocks, my arms pumping to gather speed.

I seem to have landed in quicksand.

Fuck.

I weave through a dense tangle of trees and plants while the crowd screams all around us. I try to tune them out, knowing they're here as a distraction. As I run, I catch the slither of movement in the corner of my eyes, but it's too fast to identify what's lurking out here.

Given the nature of our environment, I'm sure there will be deadly monsters or creatures, and who the fuck knows what else waiting for us.

Dry grass crunches under my feet, dust kicking up. I focus on the spot where I think Nadir was standing, hoping I'm headed in the right direction.

I chance a glimpse to my left and then to my right, checking for any signs of danger, when my gaze snags on a small pile deposited against a tree. A sword, a canvas pack, a bow, a quiver of arrows—and my dagger with the heart-shaped stone. I was still wearing it when Rion knocked me out. This is another part of Herric's sick game.

How much time will I lose if I go for them? I make a split-second decision.

They flicker in and out of focus as if in warning that they won't remain there for long.

Nadir needs me, but we need these. I swerve right, maintaining my pace as I scoop up the items with a triumphant whoop, when suddenly I'm hanging in the air, upside down, one ankle bound by a rope.

Lor? What happened? I heard you scream.

I'm coming. I'm fine.

I decide not to enlighten him. By some miracle, the dagger is still clutched in my hand while the pack, sword, and bow lie on the ground. Swinging up my top half, I use the dagger to saw at the rope. It's awkward and difficult, and it only takes a few seconds before my abdominal muscles are screaming. Releasing myself, I dangle upside down for a second before heaving myself up again. I flip up and down until only a few threads remain intact.

Lor!

I'm coming!

I swing around, trying to catch my breath for one more solid slice. Magic burns in my fingertips, and I wish I could use it, but I have to keep this wild card concealed until the right moment. This will be over once Herric realizes the cuffs don't work on me.

With a final heave, I swing up, slice the rope, and then fall. I hit the ground so hard the wind is knocked out of me, but I force myself to roll, grab the pack, and swing it over my shoulders as I scoop up the sword and the bow and quiver, and then I'm running again.

"Nadir!" I scream.

"Lor!" I hear him in the distance and alter my course, heading towards the sound.

A narrow bridge over a churning river crosses my path. From a distance, I can see it's barely held together by a wish and a few pieces of fraying rope. My stride doesn't waver. All I can do is hope I'm fast enough.

When I leap onto the bridge, it shudders ominously under my weight. Refusing to second-guess myself, I run as fast as I can when I feel a jerk behind me. Peering over my shoulder, I see it tear loose from its mooring.

Still running, I leap just as the entire thing collapses under me, and I hit the far edge. My legs dangle over the gap as I cling to my weapons before tossing them in the dirt and hauling myself up.

Then I'm running again. No doubts. No hesitation. Every moment I waste is another opportunity for Nadir to die.

I barrel down a path packed tightly with trees, obscuring anything beyond them. "Nadir!" I scream as my chest and thighs burn with adrenaline. Finally, I emerge to find a wide-open plain dotted with scrub and sparse, spindly trees.

Nadir stands chest high in a patch of sand. Herric must have dumped him right into it.

"Don't move," I scream, looking around for something to help. Trees, short grass, and rocks surround me, but not much else.

Rope. I need rope. The bridge. "I'll be right back."

I don't wait for him to answer as I drop everything but the dagger and sprint back the way I came. My surroundings melt into a blur. I feel nothing as a branch scrapes my cheek, and my chest aches with leaden breaths. I can't think. I can't stop. The crowd screams and cheers, their judgment and cruelty knocking around the inside of my skull.

Lor!

I'm coming! Hang on!

Returning to where half the bridge dangles from the ledge, I skid to my knees and heave up the rotting planks. With my teeth gritted, I let out a roar and pull with all of my strength, dragging them up, hand over hand. When I have a pile gathered at my feet, I hack away at one end and then unwind a length of rope, moving as fast as I can, my fingers trembling and numb.

I don't realize I'm crying until I taste salt on my lips.

"I'm coming!" I scream, even though I don't know if he can hear me. "I'm coming!"

When I think I have enough, I loop it around my arm, and I'm up again. My thighs hurt as I skim through the narrow pathways and emerge back on the other side, finding only the top of Nadir's head visible.

"Nadir!" I scream.

Quickly, I knot the rope onto the thickest nearby tree I can find. My fingers fumble with the knot and don't seem to work right. Soft sand slides out from under my feet, making it tricky to keep my balance. The crowd is getting louder and louder, but they become a wash of white noise as I focus on saving my mate.

Tying the other end around my waist, I stagger to the edge of the pool. A small divot in the surface indicates where Nadir disappeared. I take a few steps back and then leap, aiming for a spot just short of that.

My feet hit the sand, and I sink as the rope cinches around my waist, burning through the leather covering my torso. I wiggle to force my body lower, inhaling deep breaths. I don't think about being buried under the sand or the way it will suffocate me and crush me with its weight. Nadir is the only thing that matters.

I wiggle further up to my shoulders, using my hands to feel around for him. I sink lower and inhale a deep breath before sand covers my mouth and nose.

Nadir. Where are you?

My hands push through the wall of grains, and then I touch something solid and warm. I want to cry, but I focus on squeezing my eyes and mouth shut.

I'm here. I have a rope. But I need your help.

Despite my best efforts, sand fills my nose as I fumble for his hand and wrap it around the rope.

Can you lift us both out?

I feel him moving and shifting as his arms circle around me.

Hang on.

I cling to him as he hauls us up. Inch by inch, we drag through the sand until we break through the surface. We both inhale deep, gasping breaths, choking on the grit. Then we maneuver across the pit, collapsing onto the edge and lying side by side for several long seconds as the world spins overhead.

The crowd explodes into a deafening crescendo of screaming and cheers. I can't tell if they're happy for us or mad we succeeded.

Finally, Nadir rolls over and gathers me in his arms. I sob into the curve of his throat, my tears mixing with sand, making everything gritty and . . . just fucking horrible.

"Gods," I groan, trying to catch my breath.

When we were separated, all I could think about was how I lost him once. But now that he's here and solid and I can touch him, my mind arranges itself into something more coherent.

Both shaking, we hang on to one another for a few more seconds. The crowd tapers off until the arena is filled only with a soft murmur, probably wondering what we'll do next.

"We have to keep moving," he whispers before he kisses a tear away from my cheek. "I don't think we should stay out here in the open."

It takes every ounce of my willpower to nod. I just want to lie here, curling into a ball, pretending none of this is real. We roll apart and push up to stand.

Thankfully, the pack and weapons are still where I dropped them. I scan our surroundings, hoping for some clue about what's coming next. Another sword would be handy. Why is Herric offering us anything at all? Is this just for his amusement?

Nadir opens the pack and pulls out a canteen of water.

"Drink some and wash the sand from your mouth." He hands it to me while he also watches over our environment. I can practically see him strategizing. I clear my mouth, spitting out the grit, before I take a few long gulps and hand it back.

"Finish it," I tell him when he stares at it and then up at me with an uncertain expression. After crossing the river, I am reasonably sure we can find more water when needed.

Though it's probably poisoned or something. Or we won't be alive long enough for it to matter. I shake my head. One problem at a time.

Nadir slings the pack over his shoulders and hangs the quiver over his arm. He picks up the dagger and studies it before he looks over to where Herric watches us. The Lord of the Underworld's bright grin is visible even from this distance.

"Fucking bastard," Nadir growls as he hands me the dagger. "Use it to carve out his heart."

I tuck it into a strap around my thigh.

Nadir then picks up the bow and the sword before he wraps an arm around my waist and draws me in close.

"Keep an eye out," he says in a low voice. "I can't tell how long it will take to reach the mountain, but let's just head straight for it."

I stare at the mountain looming far in the distance. Without any roadblocks, reaching it might cost us most of the day. But I'm under no illusion we'll be able to march our way over without interruption. The crowd continues twittering while I scan their faces and their hungry eyes.

"Don't look at them, Lor," he says. "Pretend they're not here."

I nod and glance back at him, feeling tears well up.

"I don't want to do this," I whisper as I clutch the collar of his jacket. "I want to go home."

"What is home, Lor?" He tucks a strand of hair behind my ear.

The corner of my mouth lifts in a sad smile. "You. You are home."

"And I'm not going anywhere," he says. "If anyone can

survive this, it's you and me. You and I are forever. We are inevitable, Lor. I'm the Aurora Prince, and *you* are the fucking Heart Queen. This son of a bitch will not stop us."

He tips my head back and kisses me deeply. I feel the strength of his words and his conviction. The entire crowd breaks into another excited frenzy that's impossible to ignore, their voices swelling around us in a way that only makes me kiss him harder. Then he touches his forehead to mine, and we breathe in each other's space.

"Then let's do this," I whisper. "You and me. Forever. No matter what it takes."

"That's my girl," he says, sweeping a thumb over my cheek. "My fearless, brilliant, *astonishing* queen."

A second later, a rumbling chorus of low growls draws our attention up.

We pull apart and spin around, pressing back to back, when six of the largest bears I've ever seen emerge from the trees.

CHAPTER 66

NADIR

"What do we do?" Lor asks as we circle. I'm no stranger to grizzlies—plenty live in the Beltza Mountains—but these things are monstrous. They close in around us, their eyes hungry with longing. They pause as if giving us a chance to gather ourselves, probably so they can enjoy their victory more thoroughly.

"Normally, you're supposed to shout at them when you encounter bears in the wild," I say. "It usually scares them away."

Lor snorts. "Sounds like a great plan."

She peers over her shoulder at me. I see fear in her eyes but also determination. This queen, who was always a queen, is the bravest person I've ever met.

We look away, and I scan our surroundings to take stock of our assets. If I'm lucky, I could fire off at least two or maybe three arrows before they're on us. But it's been a while since I've used a bow, and my aim is rusty.

"Hide in the quicksand?" Lor jokes, and I toss her a rueful smile.

They'll go for me first.

Lor doesn't give any indication that she's heard me as she blows out a heavy breath.

So I'll just fight them off with my bare hands, then?

If anyone can do it, it's you, Lightning Bug.

Her shoulders jerk, and I can tell she wants to laugh, but her face remains expressionless. Our survival depends on keeping this connection a secret from Herric.

I'll fire arrows at the one in front of me. When the others charge, you fight them off with your dagger and the sword. Aim for their eyes and mouths.

We continue circling as I slowly pull out an arrow and notch it before peering over my shoulder. Lor holds up her weapons, gripping them in her fists.

"Ready?" I ask, and she nods.

"Let's end these fuckers."

And then I fire, aiming for the eye of the closest bear. It hits its mark, and its head rears back as it lets out a roar and stumbles to the left, its legs tangling together. I don't have time to savor the moment because the next bear is already charging, and I pull out another arrow, notching it and firing, somehow managing to keep my hands steady.

It goes wide and lodges into the side of its neck. The bear

roars and tosses its head, but it continues running as I reach for another arrow. I fire, and this one hits its front shoulder, causing its leg to buckle. It all happens in an instant, and my head spins as I try to maintain my balance. It feels like it's been days since we bonded inside the cavern, and it's impossible to gauge the timeline. I wonder if the minutes pass like they did in the Evanescence.

Behind me, I see the flash of Lor's sword as she uses two hands to slice a bear across the face. It roars and lurches away while another lunges from the other side. I call out to her as she pulls the blade from her thigh and arcs it overhead, plunging it into its muzzle. I note the surprise on her face as she stumbles into me. Catching her with my free arm, we both watch the injured bear bleat as blood sprays our clothing. It shakes its head and then swipes at her with a large paw.

I scuttle back, pulling her out of its reach before I set her back on her feet.

"You okay?" I ask, and she nods.

"I think so."

The bears left standing close in, forming a half circle as they prowl closer on their massive paws. Going on the offensive, I swing and crack a bear across the face with the bow. It leaves a gash but does little to deter it. I try again and the bow nearly snaps in half, then I duck when it hooks a massive paw at my head. Catching me in the shoulder, it tears the leather of my jacket.

Lor slashes and hacks, and I watch the bear open its mouth and close it over her arm out of the corner of my eye. She screams, and her knees buckle just as she thrusts the sword upwards and pierces through the top of its skull. The bear pauses and then collapses in a heap. Lor releases the hilt of the sword now lodged in its skull and, without missing a beat, picks up a rock and hurls it at the next bear as it paces back and forth. It strikes the bear's flank, earning us an ominous growl as it starts pacing faster.

Lor's arm and hand are bleeding, and I can't tell how badly injured she is, but at least she's still standing.

The bear that just attacked me is coming in for another round, and I duck again, dropping to the ground and rolling under the beast as I snatch a fallen arrow. It roars and shakes its head as it spins around, trying to dislodge me. Icy rage billows through my limbs, fury curdling in my chest. I'm so fucking *pissed* that Lor was dragged here by my father and that instead of saving herself, she's forced to protect *me*.

With a cry born of three centuries of anger, I thrust the arrow up, piercing the soft skin of the animal's belly. It slides into the flesh like a knife through butter before warm, thick blood coats my hands. The bear roars, lifting up on two legs, and I waste no time leaping up and driving my shoulder into its ruined stomach, tipping it off balance.

Lying on its back, it pedals in the air, screaming and roaring. This poor thing didn't deserve this either, I'm sure. That doesn't stop me from picking a large rock and smashing it into its face. The bear whimpers and then rolls onto its paws before it starts to drag itself away.

I watch it heave itself across the ground as ragged breaths saw out of my chest.

Only one animal is left, and Lor and I spin around to face

it as it charges, swiping a paw as she cries out and jogs back, lunging for her dagger where she dropped it. I pick up the bow and another arrow and fire at close range. The shot lands right between its eyes, and the bear roars, a paw swinging again and catching Lor across the stomach.

She screams as she goes flying, landing in the grass with a thud. I want to go to her, but the bear drops back onto all fours, its head swaying side to side as blood drips down its face. Again it charges for Lor, who's hunched over, clutching her stomach, but instinct takes over, and I throw myself on its back.

It swerves with the weight of my body, and we both careen to the side, back and forth, before it loses its footing and crashes to the ground. We both go rolling, and it feels like my organs are going to squeeze out of my body as it tumbles over me.

Somehow, we get turned around, and now the bear is on top, blood dripping down its face. I try to scramble away, but it pins me to the ground, and it opens its jaws wide as it dives.

A moment later, the bear jerks, and Lor appears on top of the beast, both hands clutched around the hilt of her dagger, the blade wedged into its skull.

After several heartbeats of silence, the bear starts to collapse. I scramble out, and Lor tips off its back as we stumble towards one another. She leans against me, breathing heavily.

"I . . ." she gasps.

The bear's claws tore straight through the leather over her stomach, and she's covered in blood. We both are. I look around frantically. Herric doesn't plan to kill her, but he clearly intends to let her suffer.

She clutches her stomach and sinks to her knees.

"Hold on," I say. "I'll be right back."

I run to retrieve the pack from where I dropped it, then pull the dagger from the fallen bear and tuck it into my belt. I consider the sword, but it's firmly stuck, as well as the bow, but all the arrows have been scattered. Deciding I don't have time to collect them, I scoop Lor into my arms and start running. We need to find somewhere to regroup and maybe wash this blood off.

Lor's eyes flutter open and closed as I crash through the brush, hoping no surprises find us. Finally, I spot a small stream and beyond that the opening to a cave. Perfect. Setting her gently on the bank, I reach into the cool water and scrub my hands, arms, and face. Then I do what I can for Lor, being careful as I clean away the worst of the blood from her arm and stomach. She grits her teeth as I maneuver her, clearly trying to be brave.

"Hold on," I whisper as she shivers. Then I scoop her up again and duck into the cave to discover it's shallow enough to ensure nothing is concealed in its shadows but deep enough to keep us hidden from anything passing by.

I lower Lor to the ground and then open the pack, praying there's something useful inside. I find some food—hard bread and strips of dried meat—and wonder why Herric has bothered. My only thought is that he wants a show and this is all just window dressing.

I find a thin blanket, some socks, and, by a miracle, some bandages, along with a tin of what smells like pine needles. I hope it's some kind of ointment. Carefully cutting away some of the leather on Lor's torso, I apply the salve to the jagged lines of torn flesh.

She groans as her chest expands.

"Is that okay?" I ask.

"Yeah," she says, gritting her teeth. "It's great. I'm just having the fucking time of my life."

I snort a dry laugh. Then I wrap the bandages around her to stave off the bleeding. Once she's patched up to my liking, I hand her some dried meat. I'm relieved to see some of the color is returning to her cheeks.

"Eat this."

As she chews, her eyes spread wide. "Nadir. Your shoulder!"

I look down at the exposed meat of my arm where the bear clawed me. I was so focused on Lor that I didn't feel anything, but the reminder makes my vision blur, my head swimming as my surroundings tilt.

She shuffles over and forces me to lean against the wall. It's her turn to tend my wounds, using the salve and the remaining bandages. Once she's done, she digs into the pack, but there isn't much else to find. A second canteen and a small hunk of cheese, along with a single apple. I could eat everything in a single bite right now. I try to recall the last time I ate—it was before the bonding ceremony, which might have been only a few hours ago, but it feels like it's been a century.

"Here, eat this," she says.

"We should save some," I say. "We don't know if there's more coming."

"We need to keep up our strength."

"Lor," I say.

"Just eat it. I don't think we're meant to be here long anyway."

We exchange a meaningful look, and I know she's right.

With a resigned nod, I tear into the apple's flesh. We eat everything, refilling our canteens in the stream as the light outside dims.

"Is it supposed to be night?" she asks. "Is this real?"

I shake my head. "I think he's just making it seem that way."

"Do you think this will be worse in the dark?" she asks.

"I don't know."

"Do you think he can see us right now?" she asks, looking around while I scan the cave.

"Fuck, I hope not."

"Herric?" Lor calls. "Can you see or hear us?"

Not surprisingly, there's no answer.

We exchange another wary look.

"We should try to sleep," I say. "Just for a few hours. I think we are better off waiting for daylight." I draw her in close, wrapping an arm around her shoulders.

"I'll keep the first watch."

When I see she's about to protest, I silence her with a kiss.

"Shh. I promise I'll sleep after you do."

She nods, and I can tell she's desperately trying not to cry.

"I'm scared," she whispers so softly that I barely hear it.

"I am, too," I say, and she nods. I've never been more scared in my life. I don't believe for one moment that Herric plans to allow either of us to walk out of here, nor will he allow her to leave without forcing her to destroy the ark, probably using me as leverage.

I take her hand and expose her palm and the silver marking Herric claimed would bind him to his promise. Sweeping it with my thumb, I assess it, not trusting him at all.

He will find a way to get what he wants and, in the process, get rid of us both.

Lor looks up at me, and I flip her hand over, touching her ring.

"Remember when I gave this to you? Do you remember what I said?" I ask, and she nods, her mouth pressing together.

I will follow you until the very end.

"I still mean every word."

"I know," she whispers. "I've never doubted you or your intentions for one moment."

Then I press a kiss to her forehead. I don't know what else to say. I wish this weren't happening. I wish I could take her away from this. All I've ever wanted is to protect her, and I feel like I've failed at every turn.

She seems to understand and nods.

"Get some rest," I say again.

Then she lays her head on my shoulder as we watch night descend inside our prison.

CHAPTER 67

LOR

Neither one of us really sleeps. As the light fades, the temperature drops, and Nadir and I cling to one another for warmth, making use of the threadbare blanket Herric provided. The wounds in my stomach start to heal, and the gash on Nadir's shoulder looks better after a few hours of rest. At least Herric can't stop our Fae healing.

Still, my stomach is empty and I'm exhausted from lack of sleep. In the hazy place between awake and asleep, I literally *dream* of sleep. Of a quiet room in a quiet cabin somewhere on top of a mountain, surrounded by miles of softly falling snow, where I can rest for days and wake up only to feed myself. I imagine Nadir next to me, his long dark hair spread over the pillow and the sheet tugged down to reveal his bare, chiseled torso.

I imagine curling up to him and basking in the warmth of his skin as sunlight falls over our bodies. I smell coffee and freshly baked bread that we share together under the covers before we make love until we fall asleep and then do it all over again.

I want it so much I can taste it.

"Lor," he whispers as his mouth presses to the curve of my throat and to the dip of my collarbone. To the soft place below my navel. I snuggle deeper into soft white sheets, sighing in contentment.

"Lor, wake up."

My eyes peel open, and reality crashes back in when my surroundings come back into focus.

"It's starting to grow light out," he says. I push myself up and rub my eyes as I roll my neck.

"Did you sleep at all?" I ask, noting the dark circles under his eyes and his pale cheeks.

"Not really. But I'm fine."

"You're not fine," I reply. Neither of us is fine.

"No, but what are we going to do about it?"

I press my mouth together and shake my head, trying to hold in my tears.

"Let's go. The sooner we get that rose, the sooner we can get the fuck out of here." I'm about to protest that we have no chance of finishing this when he silences me with a look and clasps my chin between his finger and thumb. "We are getting out of here. There is no other alternative."

"Okay," I reply, wishing I could believe it.

He stands and then draws me up, and we wrap our arms

around each other, holding one another for several long seconds.

"Come on."

We pack up our meager possessions. I tuck my dagger into the sheath around my leg, and we emerge into the sunny morning. Or whatever this is.

Instead of the crowded stands, a mirrored dome now spreads over our heads, reflecting everything trapped beneath. Are the crowds still there, sitting beyond it? I close my eyes and embrace the freedom from their screams and cheers, basking in the comfort of the forest's normal sounds: the rush of wind, the distant tumble of water, and the buzzing of insects.

"Where is everyone?" I whisper, and Nadir shakes his head.

"I suspect this is part of the game and intended to throw us off."

Sticking close to the trees, we weave our way towards the mountain, and I can't help the shiver that travels up the back of my neck. It feels like we're being watched by a thousand invisible eyes rooting for our downfall.

We continue our journey to the center, keeping our sights trained on the distance and awaiting potential threats. The forest is dense and lush, filled with flowers and mushrooms. Trees hang with shiny red berries, and my mouth waters at the sight.

"What are the odds that any of these are edible?" I pluck one from a branch and hold it up to the light as if a warning might be etched into the tender skin.

"Oh, I bet some are. That's the point. To taunt us."

"What if I try it?" I suggest. "I can't die."

"But you could get very sick. You were severely injured yesterday."

As if in a reminder, the wounds in my stomach pull with a twinge.

"But what's a little vomit?" I ask, only half joking.

"Lor, no," Nadir says. "You'll only weaken yourself further."

"But we need to eat something."

"I'm not letting you make yourself sick for me."

"I'm doing it for me," I say. That's not strictly true, but he can't really argue with that.

"Lor—" Well, he can try.

I pop the berry into my mouth before he can stop me. It bursts on my tongue, and I moan at the fresh, sweet, and slightly sour taste. The juice drips down my throat and I feel like I've been reborn.

"See?" I say. "Perfectly fi—"

Bile climbs up my throat and I bend in half, clutching my middle as I expel a stream of vomit. My stomach cramps and I drop to my knees before its entire contents find their way to the forest floor. Nadir crouches next to me, holding back my hair as I continue to retch.

When I think I'm done, I sob out a laugh.

"What is funny right now?" he asks.

"Remember when you held my hair back in The Aurora?" I ask, thinking of the night I got so drunk, I passed out on his bathroom floor.

"Of course I remember," he says fondly. "It felt like the first time you ever really needed me."

I look up at his serious expression. "I did need you."

"I needed you too. You have no idea how much." He tugs away a piece of hair pasted to my cheek.

"You told me I smelled."

He laughs. "You did a little, but I didn't mind."

I wipe my chin with the back of my trembling hand, tears forming in my eyes. He sweeps one away with the tip of his thumb, the corner of his mouth curling up softly. "I remember everything, Lor."

"Thank you for not saying I told you so," I answer. "About the berries."

Nadir wraps an arm around my neck and draws me in close, pressing his lips to my temple.

"Thank you for trying, Lightning Bug."

"You aren't going to tell me I'm an idiot?" I grumble as he helps me stand. I sway on my feet, lightheaded. That was so stupid. Now I've coughed up the little sustenance I had in my stomach.

"I'd never tell you that," he says with a wink. "I love your . . . impulsiveness."

I laugh in spite of myself.

"But how about no more experiments with the weird berries and mushrooms?"

I look mournfully around us—everything looks so bright and luscious, and surely something here is edible? But Nadir is right, and Herric has done this on purpose.

"Fine," I concede, and we continue picking our way through the quiet forest as the sun climbs before clouds start to roll in. I pray that doesn't mean rain. The only thing worse than being tired, hungry, and stuck inside this fucking bubble would be to be tired, hungry, stuck inside this fucking bubble, and wet.

I shake my head, admonishing myself for wallowing in worst-case scenarios, even in my imagination, because fate will find a way to prove me right.

As we keep walking, mist crawls along the ground while the grass gives way to rocky terrain. "I don't like this," I say. "It's too quiet."

"I agree," Nadir says. "Just go slowly."

I nod as my hand tightens around his while the fog thickens around us. We continue tripping blindly over scrub and wildflowers, and I've lost every sense of the direction we were going.

Where is the mountain? I ask.

He stops and looks around as if trying to orient himself. *I think we should keep going that way.*

With no other options, we keep walking, our eyes on our feet, lest anything materialize out of the fog. Nadir pulls out the canteen, and we share the water as the humidity climbs and sweat trickles down our backs.

As I'm swallowing the last drops, Nadir jerks to a stop. I crash into him, almost knocking him over, too focused on our surroundings to notice. He grabs me, yanking me around the waist against his front, and then I see what's caught his attention.

My foot rests on the edge of a steep drop. Another step and I would have fallen. It stretches before us, and whatever is across and below is lost to the mist. Sharp spears of rock jut up from the fog, all at various heights. I squint down at the swirling clouds.

"I suppose we have to figure out a way over this," I say wryly, and Nadir nods.

"I suppose." Dropping to my knees, I stretch flat onto the ground, hoping to discern something useful through the fog, but everything is by design and thus hopeless.

"I'm guessing those spikes are anchored to the bottom of this drop," I say, pushing myself back onto my knees, and Nadir nods. "But we have no idea how far down they go."

"Or if more are hiding," he adds.

Unless the drop is miles and miles, we should be able to survive it. But if one of those spires is disguised by the mist, not even Fae strength will help us.

"I'll go first," I say, staring into the swirling void, grinding my back teeth.

"Lor," Nadir says, dropping down next to me. "It's too dangerous."

"I was wrong about the berries, but this has to work."

I look at him and lay a hand against his cheek. "We *have* to get out of here. It's the only way."

His eyes darken, and he looks like he wants to argue. Like he wants to tear apart the sky.

I look down again, swallowing thickly. "Once I'm at the bottom, I'll find you a safe place to jump."

"I don't like this," he says.

"I know."

Pressing up to my feet, I inhale a deep breath that does nothing to settle my nerves. Herric won't kill me, I remind myself. But that thought offers little comfort. He obviously isn't above hurting me, but I can handle a little pain. Nadir watches me, and I offer him a watery smile. For him, a little pain is nothing.

I throw my arms around his neck and whisper, "I love you."

Trying to clear my mind of every negative thought holding me back, I hurl myself over the edge, bracing myself for impact. As I plummet, I graze the edge of something sharp, but I continue to fall and then land, rolling over stinging bits of gravel strewn across the ground.

As I come to a stop, I inhale several ragged breaths before I scramble to my feet, examining the long slice up my arm. Sure enough, I caught on something, but the wound only scratched the surface. Nothing I can't handle.

"Nadir!" I shout up through the mist. I can't see him or anything beyond a few feet around me. The feeling is claustrophobic and disorienting.

"Lor," he calls from somewhere above, a little bit to my right.

"Drop a stone," I say. "And I'll tell you if it's safe."

"Coming!" he calls. A second later, a small stone plunks through the mist. I stare at it, trusting nothing as I scan left to right, wishing I could see something.

"Okay, just drop down straight from there," I say. "The way is open."

I hope.

"Okay, on the count of five," he shouts. The fog muffles his voice, making him sound further away than the fall would suggest. I hate it. I hate how alone I feel down here, blanketed by this suffocating mist.

On the count of one, he says in my head, thinking one step ahead.

"One!" he shouts, and then suddenly, a dark shape appears above me. He plummets and lands, rolling to the side just as a spike spears up from the earth exactly where he just fell.

Herric, that fucking bastard.

"You said five," I say to cover our tracks, trying to keep the wobble out of my voice.

"I changed my mind," he answers, and our gazes lock. The only way to survive this is to think three steps ahead. But how much longer can we rely on that? This is Herric's playground, and we are less than the ants scrambling through the dirt.

We explore our space, determining we're at the bottom of a canyon. Everything looks the same: high stone walls on both sides interspersed with those deadly spires of rock. Gauging the slope of the far wall, we surmise we walked further than we realized, and it's actually the side of the mountain where that rose hovers at the peak. At least we traveled in the right direction. I examine the rock face. Smooth and almost featureless, it would be tough to climb even with equipment and impossible without it.

Hand in hand, we pick our way across the rocky surface. The mist slowly dissipates the longer we continue, but that offers no further clarity. The wall stretches on forever, curving ever so slightly, revealing an endless forest of stone spires. We keep circling, hoping something will present itself.

After we've been walking for a long time, I start to wonder if we've already made this loop more than once.

"Does this look familiar?" I ask Nadir, and his gaze meets

mine with an expression that suggests he was wondering the same. We continue walking, keeping our senses open for any signs of what's coming next.

It's then I notice a rumble at our feet. It's faint at first, but after another few seconds, I'm sure I'm not imagining it.

"Do you feel that?" I ask, and Nadir nods.

"Unfortunately."

We peer behind us, noting a cloud of dust gathering in the distance. Something is coming. Something big and heavy. Nadir's hand squeezes tighter against mine as we stand paralyzed in the face of uncertainty. We should run. We should do something, but I can't make my feet move.

A moment later, a horde of massive shapes appears through the dust. Hundreds of antlered creatures stampede towards us, closing the distance at an alarming rate.

"Run!" Nadir shouts. Finally, I stir myself into action and we both take off.

"What are they?" I scream as we dodge through the maze of stone spikes. They don't seem to slow the animals, which are simply trampling over them, rocks smashing into pieces under their enormous hooves.

"I don't know!"

Fuck. What does it matter? We keep running, weaving through obstacles, but it's clear we won't last long before they catch up. Desperately, I scan the mountainside, searching for some way we can climb up that I somehow missed the other fifty-three times I checked. One of the spikes? But these, too, are all smooth stone with nothing to hold.

Nadir's toe catches on a rock and he stumbles. I slow my

pace to ensure he's okay and then we're off running again. Checking behind me, my eyes widen at the beasts right on our heels. They kick up a cloud of dust that once again blinds me to everything.

Suddenly, Nadir grabs me, and we swerve to the right. He shields my body as we both fall, rolling over the ground, thudding against the back of a shallow cave cut into the side of the mountain.

Lying together, we both pant heavily as we watch the stream of animals thunder past our hiding place. They don't seem to see or care about us as they run.

After a minute, they finally pass, and Nadir's head collapses against me as we hug each other in relief.

"Are you okay?" Nadir asks.

"Yeah. Gods, you're fucking amazing, you know that, right?" I ask, framing his face with my hands and kissing him. He tips up an uncertain smile.

"Now what?" I ask. We sit up and I lean against the back of the cavern to catch my breath. "Was this cave here before? I swear I would have noticed it."

"I don't know," he says, peering out. "We need to find some way to scale this mountain."

"Any bright ideas, Aurora Prince? Can we go back out there? Do you think this is a circle and those animals are just looping back around?"

"Let's wait and see if they return. Then we'll find a way to scale the other side."

I pull my knees up and wrap my arms around them as Nadir scoots in next to me.

Our surroundings are deathly quiet. There's no evidence of the stampede at all, and I have a sick sense something even more awful is about to happen.

I look up at Nadir, and I see the same thing reflected in his eyes. I take his hand and squeeze it, understanding this has become a moment of reckoning for us both. Since the day I was taken from The Woodlands, I've been tested over and over, often without even realizing it. *This* moment is testing everything we are and everything we are yet to become. If we survive this, neither of us will ever be the same.

We huddle together and I think of Tristan and Willow. Of Amya and Mael. Of Gabriel and the others, hoping we'll see them again. I look at Nadir, aching for the chance to just *be* with him. To escape the sword that's been dangling over our heads since the day we met.

We both peer out into the canyon, listening to the stillness, inhaling the scent of a bitter, ominous wind.

That's when the back of the cavern drops away and we tumble back.

And then we're falling.

CHAPTER 68

RION

THE UNDERWORLD

Rion stood beside the Lord of the Underworld with his wrists bound in arcturite. Herric had allowed him out of his cage only so he could observe the spectacle happening below and bear witness to the fruits of his actions.

Rion seethed with indignant rage at Herric's trickery, though he was doing his best to conceal it. The ark was visible tucked into Herric's belt, and how he itched to take back his only bit of leverage.

He hadn't been thinking straight when he'd stormed down here believing he could order the lord to do anything. The drink had dulled his senses and scrambled his thoughts. If he got out of here alive, he'd never touch the stuff again.

Despite himself, Rion couldn't help but watch. He'd seen his son fight off a pack of bears standing back to back with the girl. Watched them comfort each other. Tend one another's wounds. They, too, wore arcturite cuffs, but Rion knew the truth about her. Had that been a one-time occurrence, or was she truly immune to their effects?

Rion *could* have shared this tidbit with Herric, but after the lord had tossed him into a cage and stolen the ark, he wasn't feeling all that amenable.

Despite Nadir's warnings, the girl swallowed a poisoned berry, and they all cringed as she vomited it back up. Then she threw herself into the canyon full of stone spikes with barely a moment of hesitation.

All to protect Nadir.

He wondered if the girl was addled in the head. Even if Herric technically wasn't trying to kill her, it still required overcoming a significant mental barrier to put yourself in harm's way. But she seemed fearless. Unstoppable. And the way she looked at his son . . . even from this distance, he could see how much she cared for him.

Rion dragged his gaze towards Rachel, who sat beside him, her hands folded on her lap, her expression devoid of emotion.

"How are you?" Rion asked, settling into his seat. She turned to him and blinked.

"I'm well. Thank you."

After Herric had freed Rion from his cage, he had also

released Rachel into his care. He'd tried to coax her into speaking and share what she'd been doing for all these years, but all he got were these insipid platitudes.

He took her hand, wrapping it with his. It was cold and thin. She'd lost weight since he'd last seen her. He'd always loved her curves and the way her hips sloped. When he got her out of here, he'd do everything he could to nurse her back to health. "Rachel, tell me what happened. Why did you turn to a life of crime? You had everything you needed from me," he pressed, and once again, she slowly turned to him.

"I don't remember," she said. The same answer he'd gotten numerous times already.

"Did you think of me?" he asked, verging on a flimsy line of desperation. He'd spent his life pining after her, and he needed to know he'd figured into her existence in some way.

She tipped her head, studying Rion from head to toe. "I remember the smell of butterscotch," she said, and a feeble hope flared in his chest. She *did* remember him.

"Yes. Do you recall that week we spent in the Cinta Wilds? My father had taken ill, and I'd finally pushed through the bill to conscript the low fae to the mines. We decided to get away for a short while." He continued talking, describing the cabin and the sound of the wind howling through the trees and the patter of rain. The feel of sunshine on their skin. He remembered every detail like it was yesterday.

When he stopped, he stared at her, willing her to react.

"That sounds lovely." She paused, her brow knitting in concentration. "What was your name again?"

Rion blew out a sharp breath like he'd been struck in the

chest and resisted the pressure swelling in the backs of his eyes. Turning away from her, he rubbed a hand over his mouth, scanning the vacant-eyed crowd that cheered and shouted at the arena. They were the dead. They were just bodies with damned souls. He dropped his face in his hands, understanding how foolish he'd been.

Rachel wasn't coming back to him. She was gone, and this shape sitting next to him was only flesh and bone. Only a memory.

He looked up and watched Herric perched over the edge of the platform, obviously reveling in his sick little game. Rion wondered where all of this had come from. Clearly, it was the magic of the virulence, and for the first time since he'd discovered Herric's journals, he didn't crave this power. He saw the edges of it blurred with tainted smoke. It felt wrong and like poison. Like something rotten dug from a rancid pit.

Suddenly, everything Herric had seemed like ash in Rion's fingers. What did the lord have but this place of death and darkness, ruling over a kingdom of barren souls? If Rion continued using the virulence, would this also become his fate? Maybe he deserved this place, though.

His gaze moved back to the sprawling arena below. Nadir and the girl were running through the canyon while a stampede of massive antlered creatures chased them. He watched as they wove through obstacles checking in on one another.

Nadir stumbled, and immediately the girl slowed down to wait as he recovered. They kept running, shouting to one another, working together. *Believing* together.

Rion shook his head.

All those months ago, he'd sent Nadir to look for the girl, and then Nadir had hidden her. His son had pretended he couldn't find her and then brought her to Rion's Keep. He'd been convinced it was part of Nadir's plan to steal his crown, but now he wasn't sure about anything anymore.

What had happened to bring about this . . . relationship?

Rion had killed her parents, and yet she still loved Nadir. That much was obvious, even to him.

Why did Rion care at all?

But something stirred in his chest as he watched her.

She was strong. That he had already known. She'd fought him when she was only a child. She'd resisted the violence of his torture and clung to her magic, surviving things that would have broken most grown men. She had been only a slip of a girl, a child with nothing left to her name, yet she'd held on.

She'd survived Atlas's Trials, and then his son had fallen in love with her. Rion saw the change in Nadir. He appeared . . . softer, but not in a weak way, rather in a way that only made him stronger. It reminded Rion of the way he'd once felt about Rachel and how he'd always felt towards the woman he remembered.

His gaze returned to her as he finally accepted that he'd never get her back. While this might be her physical body, she had died, and this place had nothing to do with reality.

Herric watched the girl and Nadir with a fevered light in his eyes, and that's when Rion realized how lonely the Lord of the Underworld must have been for all these years. He was of sound mind—for all intents and purposes a living man—but he'd been surrounded by only death and these vacant corpses for so long.

Rion's hand gripped the railing as he watched his son weave in and out, constantly checking in on the girl.

Lor.

A simple name. A strong name.

He didn't understand why he always refused to use it, but maybe a small, buried part of him felt shame for what he'd done. Maybe in his quest for power, he'd lost sight of everything. He'd never been a good man. He knew that. He'd never pretended to be anything but the black-hearted villain he was.

But something about Lor and Nadir cracked a tiny fissure in his chest.

His gaze slid to Rachel once again, and for the first time in centuries, he saw everything he'd lost. Instead of a life with a woman he loved, he'd chosen the hollow emptiness of his power. And then, when he'd made that decision, he'd regretted it. Instead of acknowledging that he'd made his own bed, he made his mistake everyone else's fault. Meora. Nadir. Amya.

What a monster he'd been.

Maybe if he'd tried, Rion could have found a version of happiness. Maybe if he'd looked beyond himself and his selfish desires, he could have been the partner and father his family had deserved. It had taken three hundred years, but finally, he recognized what he had done.

Watching Lor and Nadir together, he saw the love they felt for one another and that she had *chosen* to put herself in danger for him. She loved him enough to agree to this test, and she was doing everything she could to keep him alive.

She was noble. She was nothing like her grandmother had been, and if someone like that could love his son with such reckless abandon, then maybe Rion was the one who'd been wrong from the very beginning.

The strangest thing happened then. He wanted to cry. He wanted to say sorry to Nadir, Amya, and Meora for all the hurt he'd caused. He wanted to take it all back. He wanted to start again in that throne room all those years ago, when fate had bound him to his son and his partner, and chart a different path.

His gaze fell on Herric, who continued to watch while Nadir covered Lor's body as they tumbled together, seeking safety in a small cave carved into the side of the mountain.

"It's a shame," Herric mused, drawing Rion's attention.

"What?"

Herric smirked and leaned in. "Your son. He gave up his crown for her. What will happen to your legacy now?"

Rion blinked, once again recalling the tale Cloris shared with him. Two Primaries could never bond unless one of them gave up their position. His son had made the choice Rion hadn't been brave enough to face. Would Amya succeed him?

As he watched them comfort one another, Rion realized his son had been so much smarter than he could have ever hoped to be. That maybe none of this had been about taking his crown after all.

A moment later, Lor and Nadir fell through the back of the cave. The stadium blinked out, the entire dome darkening before they suddenly found themselves inside a cavern hewn from the center of the mountain, everything lit with a soft glow.

Rion could make out the edges of the space and the animated faces of the crowd.

A bright light flared, illuminating Lor and Nadir balanced on a tiny cliff at the edge.

They blinked in confusion, staring at their surroundings.

Herric spread his arms wide with a grin on his face, and Rion...noted the ark tucked into the Lord of the Underworld's belt before he turned to look at his son, silently rooting for him to win for the very first time.

Chapter 69

Nadir

We tumble out of the back of the cave and roll down a tunnel, bumping against its jagged surface. My hand smacks against the rock, and I grunt at the impact before we land in a heap.

"Gods, what now?" Lor grumbles as we both become aware of our new surroundings. We're inside a massive soaring cavern lit only by a few lights suspended over the crowd and a single hole cut into the top.

"You've done well so far!" booms a voice, echoing through the space. I exchange a look with Lor as we slowly climb to our feet.

"You're so close to your goal," Herric adds. "But not quite yet."

I scan our environment, noting we're once again surrounded by the dead. The sound of their laughter and chatter is hollow and cold. Herric stands inside a box adorned with swaths of black fabric and silver accents hovering in the air.

Next to him is my father, who stares at me with an enigmatic expression. What does he feel about doing this to Lor? About dragging us both down here for his own gain? Probably nothing. He's probably enjoying watching me scramble and suffer. After all, my suffering has always been one of his greatest pleasures.

Lor takes a few tentative steps as she peers into the darkness. Once my eyes adjust, I make out several more platforms floating in the air around us. At least, I think they're floating, but it's hard to be sure.

Another light flares, revealing a platform in the center of the cavern. It's a few feet across and dangling above it is a ladder that stretches up and up, disappearing into the opening far above our heads.

"We're under the mountain," Lor says, and I nod.

We're under the mountain, and all we have to do is climb that ladder to reach our goal. In theory.

Lor approaches me, and we whisper to one another.

"We have to run and jump, maybe?"

"Or there's another way," I say.

"Come now!" Herric shouts, interrupting us. "Don't keep secrets from everyone. That is so very rude."

I look up and glare. Gods, how I wish I could incinerate him to a crisp. If I ever get my hands on the bastard, I will beat him with my bare knuckles until he's nothing but a puddle of blood. He grins back, enjoying himself. I know he made a deal with Lor, but I don't trust for one moment that he plans to honor his promise. I'm just not sure *when* he plans to double-cross her.

Lor inhales an angry breath and blows it out slowly before she turns to face me, determination written into the fabric of her expression.

"Which is the closest one?"

We walk along the edges of our tiny perch, trying to gauge the distance.

"That one," she says. "I think if we take a running jump, we could make it."

"It looks big enough for only one of us."

She nods. "Then I'll go first before I move to that one." She gestures to the left and a platform that hovers nearby. "I can also ensure it's stable enough for you."

She gives me a preemptive look that dares me to argue, but I don't bother. I see the logic in allowing her to use herself as the test, but I hate it. I hate that she has to put herself in danger for my sake.

"When this is over, I will find a way to make this all up to you," I swear. "I'm supposed to be the one protecting you. I was supposed to save *you*."

"Nadir," she says softly. "You've protected me over and over. You did save me. But it's my turn to protect you. And this isn't your fault. We've both been the victims of everyone else's desires." She takes my hand and kisses my knuckles. "When this is over, we're going to spend the rest of our lives making all of this up to each other, not because either of us did anything wrong, but because we deserve happiness."

I nod, my throat too tight to speak as I marvel at this

woman who's chosen to love me. Who deserves so much better than the man that I am. But I'll take it and hope she doesn't realize it eventually.

Then she backs up and leaps. My stomach sinks to my feet, and I stop breathing. I swear everyone in the stands does the same.

She lands safely in a crouch, and I let out a whoosh of air. Then she prepares to leap to the next one, and I see her pause. But she runs anyway and jumps, sticking the landing.

"Come on!" she calls, and I follow after, clearing the first jump before I see what made her hesitate. The perspective from the previous platform is off, making this next landing further away than it looks.

I hate not having the use of my magic, and I hate that I'm so vulnerable right now. But the fierce look she gives me bolsters my confidence. She *wants* to protect me, and I . . . Gods, what a lucky asshole I am.

I run and leap to the next platform, and we continue in the same vein, drawing closer and closer to the center. There are a few near misses, backdropped by the crowd's oohs and aahs and screams. It's distracting, but I try to shut it out. I think of when Lor described her time on the gauntlet in the heart of Aphelion, and I watch her carefully for signs of distress. It can't be easy to be reliving the same shit yet again. But she is resolute. Nearly unshakable.

"That one," Lor says as she leaps for the next platform, where she waits a moment before I follow her. We make slow progress, the experience now bordering on tedious. I can tell even the crowd's interest is waning as their chatter dies to a muted hush.

But I remain on alert. I'm sure this is intended to lull us into a sense of complacency.

Be vigilant, I say to Lor. *Something is up.*

Her jaw hardens as she stares around the cavern, her gaze skirting over the spectators. She rubs her face with a hand and then uses the back of it to wipe away a bead of sweat. We exchange a look filled with so many things we can't say.

I take stock of myself. My limbs feel shaky and hollow from the lack of food and sleep, and I pray we're almost at the end. We continue leaping between the platforms, some of them further apart than others, as we wind our way towards the center. My aim feels off every time I jump, and what I wouldn't give for some water right now.

We stop on a larger spot to catch our breath, using each other for support.

"You okay?" I ask, holding her in my arms and murmuring into her hair.

"I guess," she answers, burying her face into my chest. I can feel her trembling, and again I slide into the simmering pit of my blood-soaked rage. Pulling her tighter, I listen to her heart as it beats in tandem with mine, using it to calm myself. I won't do us any favors if I lose my temper. A clear head is the only way we win this.

The sound of a loud crack has us jumping apart. We both spin around, scanning our environment.

In the distance, I see movement in the dark, and it takes me a moment to realize the platforms are starting to crumble.

"We need to move," I say, taking her hand.

This is the true test.

"Go!" I say, and she leaps onto the next platform and then the next as I follow.

More cracks and rumbles shake the cavern as everything around us starts to disintegrate.

Finally, we reach the middle, and Lor leaps onto the larger platform. The one under my feet starts to crumble, and I run before I've really gauged my distance. I fall short, my stomach hitting the edge of my target.

Lor leaps for me as I start to slide, snagging my wrist as I slip.

Our hands snap together just before I fall, so I'm dangling beneath her.

"Lor!"

"Swing your arm up!" she shouts. She grits her teeth, her face turning red as she hauls me up inch by inch. Slowly, she drags me up. Just as I'm about to reach the top, we both hear another loud crack. The far edge of our platform is starting to crumble.

"Come on!" she screams, and then she heaves on my arm, and my shoulder pops with the force. I ignore the pain that radiates down my limbs and lurch for the edge.

Lor keeps tugging on me and then grabs the back of my jacket, hauling me up.

"The ladder! Go!" The platform disintegrates around each edge, herding us into the middle.

I leap onto the ladder and start the climb. I peer down over my shoulder and watch as Lor grabs the bottom rung just as the platform disappears in a falling shower of dirt and stone.

"Go! I'm fine! Go!"

Keeping one eye over my shoulder, I watch her swing herself up and then start climbing.

"The ladder is disappearing!" she cries, and I pick up my pace.

Hand over hand, we scramble up the rungs as that same cracking and crumbling follow us. The crowd is awake now, screaming and shouting as I aim for the top. It seems like a hundred miles away as I keep climbing, my muscles and my aching shoulder protesting with the effort.

"Faster!" Lor shouts just as I clear the top and look back. The ladder melts out from under Lor, and she screams as she begins to plummet, but there's no fucking way I'm letting her go. I leap out and reach down to grab her, hauling her up by my good arm just as the ladder completely evaporates.

She collapses against me, our breath heavy and our hearts pounding. I'm shaking all over, and I can feel her trembling against me. A breeze cools my cheeks, and I look up, exhaling a choked breath.

The forest spreads in every direction below, and we're once again under the mirrored dome, although the screeching crowd is also under it this time. I shake my head, attempting to understand how any of this is happening.

Lor's gaze meets mine, her dark eyes pooling with uncertainty before we both look up.

We're on a rocky plateau with a single red rose spinning slowly above us.

We did it.

We're on top of the mountain.

Chapter 70

Cautiously, Lor and I rise to our feet with our hands clasped. Cheers greet us from every side, mingled with boos and hisses. Herric watches us from his box. Everything has shifted, so they're closer now, forming a circle around the mountaintop.

Is this all an illusion? How is any of this possible?

I don't really care. None of that matters. All that matters is Lor and getting us out of here. I capture her face between my hands and kiss her deeply as the crowd's chants swell to a crescendo, their feet stamping so hard I feel it vibrate where we stand.

Perhaps no one can resist a love story.

And if we survive this, ours will be one for the ages.

Lor pulls away and blows out a relieved breath.

"Are you okay?" she asks.

"I'm fine," I say with a wince as I attempt to rotate my shoulder. "Go and get the rose."

She nods and then runs across the plateau and leaps for the flower.

Suddenly, I'm seized from behind, my arms pinned behind my back as I grunt in pain.

I watch as the rose melts into the air, and Lor lands in a crouch.

"What the—" She spins around to face me, her eyes widening. I'm being held by two massive trolls wearing beaten leather armor. I've never seen one before, but I know they dwell in the deepest caves of the Beltza Mountains and are constructed of brute strength and vicious tempers. One wrenches on my bruised shoulder, and I fall to my knees with a cry.

"Let him go!" she shouts at Herric. "We made it! Let him go!"

Herric laughs, and my chest caves with the disappointment of knowing I was right about him all along.

"Perhaps I changed my mind," he says.

"We have a bargain!" Lor spits.

She lifts her arm, brandishing the silvery mark on her palm like a shield.

He shrugs and waves his fingers. There's a flash of light, and I see the silver dissolve from her skin. She stares at her hand, open-mouthed, while I fight uselessly against my captors.

She turns to look at me, her chest heaving with anger. Her

hair is wild, standing on end, and her eyes burn with the sum force of her rage.

I'm going to use my magic.

We need the ark first. We can't leave here without it.

She drops her hands and stamps her foot, screaming out a sound of frustration.

"So this was all for nothing?" she shouts at Herric. "Why did you do this?"

"It wasn't for nothing," Herric replies. "*I* had fun."

"You fucking asshole!" She cries so loud her voice cracks, her hands squeezed into fists.

He places a hand against his chest. "My dear. I'm the Lord of the Underworld. What were you expecting? I admit, I assumed you'd lose and make this easy, but you just *had* to go and be clever, didn't you?"

She takes a slow step towards him, her fists still clenched. "You can't make me destroy it."

"Then he dies," Herric says, gesturing to me.

"Then I won't do it! You know that."

He shrugs again. "I think . . . I'll call you on that bluff."

He licks the tip of his finger and holds it up as though he's testing for the direction of the wind. "The odds feel like they're blowing in my favor."

Lor snarls, and I can feel her magic responding to mine. It rises to the surface, threatening to burst from her fingers.

Lor, stay calm. You can't let him see your magic yet.

She rolls her neck and flexes her fingers, and I feel her power sink lower, simmering just under her skin instead of boiling over.

Good girl.

"Make him bleed," Herric says, and a dagger is placed against my throat.

"I'll destroy you!" Lor screams.

"How?" Herric gestures. "You're in my domain without your magic. You are *nothing* unless I decide to free you."

I hold my breath, feeling the edge of the blade bite into my neck. It's then that I notice my father inching towards Herric. He's looking not at me but at Lor. I'm so used to my father's mask of imperviousness, his cold stares, and his complete indifference, and what I see in his face makes me go still.

I notice a woman seated on his other side. She's stunning, with long dark hair, but with those same vacant eyes of the dead.

My father glances away from Lor and then at the woman, and something breaks in his expression. I can't puzzle out what I'm seeing. Who is she? I remember the scribbled phrases in his notes, but I don't think I've ever seen her before.

My father slides closer to the lord while he and Lor continue to argue, and my head fills with static as I watch.

His gaze flicks to me and then back to Lor before everything slows down.

The king of The Aurora—the man who has never once shown me an ounce of kindness—reaches for Herric, yanks the ark from his belt, and then . . . tosses it.

CHAPTER 71

LOR

"**L**or!"

Nadir's voice cuts through my argument with Herric, and that's when I notice several things at once. The Aurora King stands next to Herric with his arm overhead before he flicks his wrist, and an object comes hurtling towards me.

"The ark!" Nadir shouts, and I have just enough presence of mind to understand what's happening. I leap and snatch it out of the air, opening my hand to take in the gentle sparkle of virulence carved with Zerra's likeness, a relic of Herric's betrayal. I feel its power and its connection as my magic twitches under my skin.

The ark of Heart. Finally, I have it. And this time I won't lose it.

When I look up, Herric is alternately staring at me and the Aurora King, clearly not sure what to make of the situation.

Did *Rion* just throw us the ark?

I'm rewarded with a split second of surprise, but it's all I need.

Veins of crimson lightning circle my limbs as the arcturite cuffs crumble off my wrists. I watch the pieces tumble to the dirt, and then I look up to catch Herric's furrowed brow and the slight widening of his eyes as he realizes that he, too, has just been had.

The corner of my mouth tips up into a smug smile as I arch an eyebrow.

"Problem?" I ask, making a show of checking my wrists. "I think . . . you may have underestimated me. People are always doing that."

And then we both react, flinging out magic across the space that divides us, black smoke and red lightning crashing together like bleeding thunderclouds. I feel him push against me, and I dig deep into the recesses of my power as I throw it back. I unleash it all. That wild magic that followed me from the throne room in Aphelion, swelling with every step I took. That magic that lived locked inside my heart after a vicious king tried to take everything when I was a child.

Herric is strong. So powerful.

The force of his magic attempts to drag me under.

I cling to the ark, feeling its strength. It surges into me as we wrestle for dominance.

Without my bond to Nadir, none of it would be enough, but because of him, I *am* enough.

With a roar, I filter out a blast of power, shoving it into Herric. He goes flying as his power cuts off, and I spin around.

"Duck!" I shout at Nadir. His captors don't even know what hits them as I spear them with lightning, knocking them back. And though my magic flows through me in churning rivers, it's no longer an unrestrained torrent.

The bond didn't only give me more power, it also gave me something else.

Finally, I am in control.

"Hold this," I say, tossing Nadir the ark, worried about using too much power and accidentally destroying it before we get it as far away from Herric as possible.

Nadir catches it and then looks at it before his gaze flicks to his father, who's studying us as the crowd loses their shit. Nadir moves behind me and wraps an arm over my shoulder and across my body, as he kisses my cheek.

"Seize her!" Herric shouts, finally recovering from his shock. But I don't know who he's talking to because no one is listening.

With Nadir still behind me, I lift my arms and look into Herric's eyes. My cold smile causes his face to blanch.

"Everyone has always underestimated me," I repeat. "But Herric, Lord of the Underworld, that mistake is about to cost you everything because I. Am. The *fucking* Heart Queen."

Then I unleash hell.

Magic spears from my fingers, striking the massive cavern's walls and ceiling, shattering the bubble that surrounds us and raining down showers of glass. The stands erupt into a sea of panic as everyone scrambles over one another for cover.

The ceiling drips stones and screams fill the air as they crash down. I filter out more and more magic as the mountain rumbles beneath our feet and the entire cavern shakes loose.

"Lor!" Nadir shouts. "We need to run."

Herric stands on his platform watching us while his world falls apart. Our gazes catch for another second. He thought he had us. But we proved to be more formidable opponents than he could have possibly imagined. Nadir tugs on my hand, bringing me back to the present. We run to the edge and slide down the mountainside, the smooth surface making for a quick escape.

My feet slam into the floor, and the dome's walls fall away as we run, diving into the bowels of the Underworld and into a network of tunnels lit with a bioluminescent glow.

We run while the cavern shakes, more stones raining down on us. The whole world feels like it's splitting at the seams.

"Which way?" I ask.

"There was an entrance," Nadir shouts. "That's how I got in here."

"Where is it?"

"I don't know," he answers as we keep running. The ground shakes so hard I'm having trouble keeping my footing.

"Nadir, we'll be trapped here!"

He comes to a stop. "Do you hear that?" he asks.

I strain to listen, and a moment later, the sound of barking dogs echoes off the rock far in the distance. Nadir puts two fingers in his mouth and belts out a sharp whistle. We continue running in the direction of the sound when Morana and Khione come flying around the corner.

I've never been so happy to see these furry monsters in my entire life.

Without pausing, we toss ourselves onto each of their backs, and then they're off, streaking through the caverns as rock and debris rain over our heads.

I keep my head down and covered, trusting in the ice hounds, their feet sure and confident as they race through the rocky tunnels against the echoes of their howls. They duck around corners, weaving back and forth as more stones attempt to crush us. Their senses are preternatural, anticipating danger seconds before it finds us. With my hands clutched in her fur and my thighs pressed tight, I whisper to Morana to go faster. That she can do this.

"There!" Nadir shouts, and I look ahead to a wide opening and the cavern that lies beyond. "That's the exit!"

"Hurry!" I shout, and the ice hounds kick up their pace, digging into the recesses of their speed as piling rocks threaten to block our exit. Just as we approach the barrier, they leap smoothly over it, landing us inside another tall cavern.

Their pace never wavers as they sprint across the rocky floor.

"Stop!" I shout when we make it to the other side. I slide off Morana, feeling the deep rumble of the Underworld dissolving under our feet. "We should make sure it's sealed off!"

I prepare to aim for the high ceiling with a blast of magic when I notice Nadir has gone completely still.

He's staring at a figure standing in the opening.

The Aurora King watches us with the saddest, most defeated expression on his face. He's like an entirely different man from the one I know.

I look at Nadir, who still hasn't moved, frozen in shock.

The world shakes around us, and more rocks fall, blocking more of the doorway.

"Nadir, the whole thing is coming down!" I shout.

He looks at me, his mouth closing and then opening, clearly at a loss for words.

I wait as father and son stare at each other, and then the Aurora King does the last thing in the world I expect. Pressing a hand to his chest, he tips his head forward before looking back up and mouthing the words "I'm sorry."

Nadir steps back, shaking his head.

More rock falls, nearly obscuring our view of Rion, who continues to watch his son like he's become the only thing in the world that matters.

"Nadir!" I shout. "We have to go. Now."

He looks at me and nods, and then, with one more glance at his father, we both mount Morana and Khione before they race up the path.

Behind us, I hear the roar of the cavern collapsing in on itself, forever burying the Aurora King.

The dogs howl, and the sound echoes a mournful cry against layers of stone. They deliver us up and up through the mountain and its winding tunnels, ferrying us to safety.

Billowing clouds of dust chase our heels until we burst out of the mountain and race along a blanket of glittering snow under a canopy of stars and the rippling lights of an Aurora sky.

CHAPTER 72

The dogs slow to a stop, and I slide off Morana's back, falling onto the snow to press my forehead to the cool surface. My mind spins, struggling to comprehend the scale of what we just experienced. For several long seconds, I spiral into the tumbling void of my thoughts, trying to arrange the pieces back into place.

When I feel like I can breathe again, I drag myself over to Nadir and throw myself on top of him, thinking of the look on his face when his father tossed me the ark and that last moment before the Aurora King was lost to us forever. I spent so many years plotting his death, imagining the day I'd get my revenge. But now that he's gone, I don't feel the relief I expected. I just feel hollow.

"Are you okay?" I ask, framing his face with my hands. Nadir spent even longer than I did seeking retribution against Rion, and I wonder if he also feels this same yawning emptiness.

"He's gone," Nadir says as if he's testing the words for their truth. "I never thought I'd see the day."

He blinks and meets my gaze.

"It's okay to feel conflicted right now," I say. "He was still your father, no matter what happened."

He shakes his head. "He helped us in the end," he says, his brow furrowing. "Why did he do that?"

"I don't know. Maybe...he found a sliver of something redeemable in his heart."

His hands come to my waist, squeezing it.

"He said he was sorry," Nadir says, his tone edged with disbelief. "Do you think he meant that?"

I consider his question. I doubt Rion was sorry about the things he did to me and my family, but I'm finally okay with that. Not because I forgive him, but because it's time to let this go. He's gone, and he can never hurt us again.

Nadir got the apology he deserved, which is more important in the end.

"I think he did," I say. "Maybe he finally understood everything he missed when he abandoned you and your mother. Maybe even the worst of us can still find redemption when faced with the final seconds of our mortality."

"It still doesn't excuse anything he did," Nadir says, sweeping a piece of my hair back. "Everything he did to you."

"Of course it doesn't, but it's over now."

He runs a hand down his face and sighs.

"What are you thinking?" I ask.

"Why couldn't he have tried to become that person sooner? We could have tried to forgive each other. Maybe none of this would have happened."

"Often those moments come only when it's too late. But it did come. Maybe you can take comfort in that."

He wraps his arms around me and buries his face into the curve of my throat as we cling to one another on the wind-swept mountaintop.

"Did you see that woman he was talking to?" he asks, and I nod.

"Do you know who she was?"

He shakes his head. "I wondered if she was the woman he was in love with. The one he was trying to make jealous when he met my mother."

"Maybe she had something to do with it?"

He gives me a bemused look. "Maybe."

The wind gusts, tossing our hair as it knifes through our ripped clothing. Finally, I roll off him, and we sit up. Scanning our surroundings, I have no idea where we've ended up. We didn't exit the same path we entered. I wonder if the others are still looking for us below. We need to find them.

But first there is something I must do.

I pull the ark out of Nadir's pocket, holding it up. The stone catches the light, sparkling in the night. There's so much power and heartache contained in this object, but I have no choice.

"I have to destroy it," I say, tears filling my eyes. "But I don't want to leave you."

He rubs my cheek with his thumb, sweeping away a tear. "I don't know what to say," he replies. "I hate this."

"She'll try to kill me again. And we can't ever let Herric get his hands on it. You heard what he said: the weaker she gets, the closer he is to the surface."

He reaches towards me, and I take his hand, clutching it to my chest as I sob.

We didn't find another way to stop this. In my heart, I hoped, but a part of me knew I'd end up here.

"Lor." His voice is so soft that it feels on the edge of cracking apart into a million pieces. "I . . ." He trails off because what is there left to say?

I let go of his hand, and clutching the ark, I stand and walk a few paces away to lay it in the snow. I wonder if Tyr has also completed this task. Soon enough, I'll find out.

Then I back up. I can barely breathe.

I turn to Nadir and throw my arms around him as I cry harder than I ever have in my life. These last few months have been nothing but ups and downs. Heartbreak and joy. The highest highs and the lowest lows. I lost everything only to find *everything*, and now . . . I might lose it all for good.

"I love you," I gasp. "No matter what happens once that thing is gone, I love you. No matter where we end up, never forget that."

"I know," he says. "I love you too. In this life and the next one. Wherever you go, I'll find you. No matter what it takes. This *can't* be the end."

"I'm going to miss you so much." I'm sobbing so hard that my throat and my chest ache. I feel like my insides are spilling out and spreading across the snow in a crimson puddle of loss.

He doesn't have to say anything else as we cling to one

another. He kisses me deeply, and I kiss him back as we pour every shred of love and heartbreak into our embrace. I can't believe this is the choice I'm being forced to make.

Finally, I pull away, hiccupping on a sob.

"Hold my hand," I say, and he nods as our fingers weave together. "Don't let go."

I try to stop thinking about it. I have no choice. It's me or Herric. I've bought myself a bit of time, but he'll be back soon enough.

Magic surges to my fingertips as I open my hand and aim it towards the ark. It absorbs my lightning as I filter in a stream of magic so powerful it becomes a thick red beam.

It glows, and I feel the power that lives inside of it. My magic flows into the ark, more and more of it, and then I start to feel it crumbling. Hairline fissures shining from within spread along its surface.

A figure appears, and I knew Zerra would come. She flickers above the ark, but she's different now. Covered in cracks that snake over her skin. I swallow hard as she stares at me. But there is no rage left in her eyes, only defeat. I wonder what she's thinking. Does she also regret the things she did?

We watch one another as her head droops to one side and her shoulders curve. In her gaze I see the understanding that she knows her time is over. Neither of us wanted this.

My magic filters into the ark, and then Zerra starts to crumble into dust—first her head, then her shoulders, then her torso and legs. Slowly, she puffs apart, sparkling silver particles being carried off by the wind. Finally, the ark shatters, pieces of glowing virulence skidding across the snow.

A moment later, the sky fills with white lightning. It glows so brightly that I have to shield my eyes. Nadir clings to me as it flashes, crackling and popping across the horizon.

"She's dying," I say as we watch the light turn to every color of the rainbow, cycling through reds and blues and purples and greens and all the colors. I can't help but mourn the woman Zerra was before her life as a god twisted her into the thing she became.

When the sky returns to normal, darkness settles over us as the wind blows gently, whistling off the distant peaks.

"It's done," I whisper. "It's over."

The quiet is so loud that my ears ring. I wait, wondering what comes next as I look at Nadir. We both search around us and I'm not exactly sure what I'm waiting for, but I was expecting *something* to happen.

"What now?" I whisper, and Nadir shakes his head.

Suddenly, the world melts away, and we're both falling.

A moment later we land on hard marble somewhere with warm light beaming in through high windows. I look up, my breath stalling in my chest.

We're back in the Evanescence.

The Empyrium stands in the middle of the room, flickering with its many faces, their hands folded in front of them, watching us.

"Welcome back, Lor," they say. "Thank you."

CHAPTER 73

I stumble to my feet, using Nadir for support and scan our surroundings, noting we're in the same room I visited last time. Soft sunlight streams from the high windows, and the air is still with the nothingness of this place.

"Thank you for what?" I ask, wiping sticky, sweat-soaked strands of hair out of my eyes.

"For killing Zerra," the Empyrium says. I share a look with Nadir and then back.

"I don't . . . understand."

"We could not kill her ourselves," the Empyrium says. "You were the only one with the power to do so."

"I . . . What?"

"We're sorry to have put you through that, but we let it slip to Zerra that you were to be her replacement, knowing she would come for you."

I blink, unable to comprehend what I'm hearing. I'd wondered if they'd told her, but I couldn't begin to imagine *why* they would do this to me.

"You mean, you used me?"

"It was necessary," the Empyrium says.

"Why couldn't *you* kill her? I almost died. Nadir almost died!"

"That was beyond our powers," they say.

"But you're gods!"

"We can only create, not destroy. It was why we were forced to banish Herric."

"Banish? But you said *he* caused that."

"He did in his own way. We couldn't allow him to continue on his path of destruction and thus had to contain him. But we could only bind him to the Underworld, not kill him."

"But he almost got out!"

They nod. "Yes, we did not realize that Zerra's weakening meant he would be able to interact with those on the surface to that extent."

"To that *extent*? So you knew he was capable of this?"

"We did not imagine he would be able to get his hands on you. But you prevailed, nonetheless. Another thing for which we offer thanks. Zerra is gone and a new god will take her place, ensuring he is trapped once again."

My mouth opens in disbelief. "Where were you?" I scream. "You could have helped us."

"Once you were in his domain, you were beyond our reach. All we could do was wait."

"And you didn't think to tell me any of this?" I ask, getting angrier. They used me to do their dirty work? I clutch Nadir's arm as his hold tightens.

"Knowing would have changed nothing. It would have made no difference," they say.

"Bullshit. It would have made a difference to me!"

The Empyrium turns and walks away as though they are done with this conversation. I'm about to follow and demand... *something* when a ripple in the air catches my attention.

I watch as it stretches and morphs into a dark blot, and then...Amya, Mael, and Willow stand across the room, blinking at us. They're no longer dressed in the clothes they wore at the bonding ceremony, and it's the first time I've really had a chance to think about how long we've been gone.

"Amya?" Nadir asks, and she gives us a bewildered look.

"Willow?" I ask, taking a step towards her before another ripple turns into Cedar and Elswyth, and then Tristan.

"Tris!" I yell.

"Lor!"

We all converge and embrace in the center of the room. I truly thought I'd never see any of them again.

"What happened to you?" Amya asks. "We were so worried."

"You disappeared," Tristan says, looking us over.

"Lor, we thought you were dead," Willow says as we continue chattering.

"Why are you dressed like that?" Mael asks.

"Well—"

We're interrupted by the appearance of several others. D'Arcy, Bronte, and Cyan all materialize out of thin air, along with Anemone and Linden. With Bronte and her bonded partner, Yael, is a young girl with silver hair, and next to D'Arcy stands a teenage male High Fae with her same dark eyes and long white hair.

A moment later, Tyr, Gabriel, and Erevan also appear.

We all stare at each other across the space. It takes everyone another moment to notice the Empyrium. They've all heard the story of my previous encounter, and they all understand immediately.

"Welcome," the Empyrium says. "Zerra is dead, and the Third Age is upon us."

They sweep out a hand towards me. "Your new goddess awaits."

Every eye swings to me, and I shake my head.

"No. I don't want this. Please."

"Someone must control the magic of the Artefacts," they say.

"But why me?" I ask.

"You are the right choice. You defeated the greatest evil in Ouranos."

"No, I'm not. I have people I need to take care of, people who need me to restore the magic of Heart, and I don't *want* this."

I take Nadir's hand. "I have a mate and a family I want to grow old with. Please don't do this."

They give me a hard look. They weren't expecting me to refuse.

"You forced Zerra into this all those years ago, and look how that turned out," I say.

"You are not Zerra," they reply. "We chose better this time."

"No! I don't want this!" My voice pings around the room. "You won't make me abandon my mate. You can't make me!"

"But we can," they say. "You are the best choice. Only a Primary or an ascended king or queen will be strong enough to control the magic. And you are without a home to rule."

At that declaration, I feel everyone in the room go still.

"Lor?" Nadir asks. "Did you know that?"

I squeeze his hand. "I did, but I couldn't tell any of you. I couldn't ask any of you to shoulder this burden for me."

Nadir's jaw turns hard as he turns back to the Empyrium. "Take me," he says.

My head snaps up. "No! Absolutely not. This is why I didn't share this with you."

The Empyrium fold their hands together and dip their chin. "As we understand it, you are no longer a Primary, Aurora Prince."

Nadir huffs out an angry breath. I'm not sure if it's directed at me or at them.

My gaze shoots to my brother, who looks like he's about to speak.

"Don't even think about it," I snarl before he snaps his mouth shut.

Turning back to the Empyrium, I shake my head as tears coat my cheeks, panic swirling in my chest. "There must be another way. Please. I'm not the right choice. I just wanted to live the life I was born for. I want to be with my brother and sister. I want to be with Nadir. He just gave up everything for me so we could kill Zerra for *you*. I only want to be with him. The people of Heart need me."

"Ouranos needs you more," they say. "It will be the difference between some lives and all of them."

"There has to be another way!"

"There is not," they say.

"Then give me Nadir," I say, desperate now. "Allow him to come with me, but let him keep his spirit."

I shake my head. I've been talking a mile a minute and only now realize what I've just said.

"Sorry," I say. "I . . . shouldn't speak for you . . ."

"No," he answers. "If there's a way, then I accept it. I just want to be with her too."

The Empyrium tips their head, and for the first time, they seem a bit sorry about all of this.

"If we could, we would," they say, and that's when I break down.

My stomach cramps, and I bend double, dropping to my knees. The Aurora King is gone. I have the Crown. I'm finally free, and I'm about to lose it all.

"No," I sob. "Please. No."

Nadir drops to the floor, wrapping me into him as we both cling to one another.

"Lor," he whispers, his voice on the edge of cracking.

"I'm sorry," I whisper. "I tried. I tried so hard for us."

"I know you did. This isn't your fault."

More arms circle us as Tristan, Willow, and Amya join our wretched little huddle. We weep together as I feel my spirit draining out. Already I feel detached from reality, like I'm not really here.

"I'll do it," comes a soft voice that, at first, I think I imagine. It comes again, stronger this time. "Take me instead."

It takes a moment for us to pull apart. I hiccup as I wipe my nose with the back of my hand.

Tyr stands at the other side of the circle, his back straight and his eyes clear with purpose.

"I'll do it," he repeats, and the vice around my heart releases an inch.

"Tyr," Erevan says, coming up next to him. "What are you doing?"

"I'm doing something useful," he says, then turns to Gabriel. I notice the absence of the golden tattoo on his neck, and my throat knots at the sight. "I'm sorry. I'm never going to be the king I was. No matter how much I want to, I can't ever go back. It hurts too much. Those walls will always be a reminder of what I want to forget."

So many emotions cross Gabriel's face. Absently, he touches his throat where the golden lines of the Sun King once marked him as a prisoner.

Then his shoulders drop in resignation.

"I know," he says softly. They bend their heads together as they each wrap a hand around the back of the other's neck. They murmur soft words to one another I can't make out.

Then Tyr releases Gabriel and turns to face me. "I will take this burden from you," he says before looking to the Empyrium. "If you will have me."

The Empyrium says nothing for a moment, the various people of its form flickering in and out as if they're having a discussion. I watch in hope while Nadir clings to me tighter.

"But you'll be alone up here," Erevan says. "You'll have only this place. You already lived like that for a century."

"I've been alone for so long," Tyr replies. "When I sat in that tower, looking out over Aphelion, I could do nothing. But here, I can make a difference. I can be better than Zerra, and maybe everything that happened will have had a purpose."

Tyr's gaze meets mine, his eyes soft with conviction.

"Are you sure?" I ask.

He smiles and tips his head. "It's the first thing I've been sure of in a very long time, Heart Queen."

The Empyrium confer for another few seconds before they speak.

"The Sun King is pure of heart. If he chooses to relinquish his crown, then we accept his offer. Is the Primary ready to step into his place?"

Every eye turns to Erevan before he exchanges a long look with Gabriel. I hold my breath, waiting for my entire life to shift in one direction or the other.

Gabriel rests a hand on Erevan's shoulder.

"This was inevitable, Erevan. You've resisted for as long as you could, but you understand it's time," he says. "Besides, after everything Aphelion did to Lor, it's the least we can give her."

He gestures towards me, and my eyes fill with tears again as he gives me a small smile that feels like I've just won a war

I've been battling since the day he dragged me out of that hole in the Void.

Erevan lets out a long sigh. I watch as his shoulders droop like a giant weight has been set on top of them. He looks at me and then dips his chin.

"Very well," he says. "I will accept my place."

I expel a shaky breath as Nadir kisses my temple. I can hardly dare to believe this is real.

"Say your goodbyes," the Empyrium says to Tyr. "Your life changes today."

I watch as Tyr turns to Gabriel, and they stare at one another, both of them holding very still. I swear I can feel the moment they both accept that this is the end for them. The air around them seems to bend and then settle into another place, but maybe this is what they all need.

"I love you," Gabriel says, choking on the words. "I'm sorry that I let you down so many times."

Tyr shakes his head and then wraps his arms around Gabriel.

"You were the only light in my life during all those years. I would have died without you, Gabe. Never forget that. I love you too."

They cling to one another as their tears flow and their shoulders shake.

"He will be able to visit you," the Empyrium says gently. "From time to time."

"I'll come whenever I can," Gabriel says, and Tyr nods. They squeeze each other's hands, and Tyr kisses Gabriel's knuckles.

"Be happy," Tyr says. "Promise me you'll stop blaming yourself. None of it was ever your fault."

Gabriel blows out a long, slow breath. "I'll try," he says before Tyr then turns to Erevan. They exchange a few quiet words, and then Tyr faces the Empyrium. He straightens his posture and smooths down the front of his beige tunic. I've seen the Sun King only a few times, but already, he seems like a different person. Like someone who dragged himself back from the teetering edge.

"I'm ready," he says, looking at me.

"Wait," I call. I stand up, run across the room, and throw my arms around his neck. He stumbles from my weight but catches himself as he squeezes me back.

"Thank you," I say. "Thank you for offering yourself."

"It is not a burden," he answers, a gentle hand settling on my back. "It will be my honor to stand in this place and allow you this life, Heart Queen. It was over for me. Perhaps I can find peace in this next one."

I pull back and nod before he turns to the Empyrium. "Take me then."

"It is done," they say, and then in a flash of soft white light, our surroundings melt away.

A moment later, we all stand amongst the ruins of Heart, blinking at one another.

I sway on my feet, then fall to my knees and press my forehead to the hard stone, savoring the feel of solid ground and the unmistakable scent of roses.

Finally.

I am home.

Chapter 74

Lor

Queendom of Heart

When I've caught my breath, I look up. Nadir stands before me with a small smile on his face. Sunlight gilds his dark hair, and his eyes spark with emerald and violet. He's so beautiful it makes my throat ache. I remember the first time I saw him in Aphelion and how my world changed in that moment. I could never have imagined the journey we would travel.

And now he's mine forever.

"We did it," I say softly.

"*You* did it. And I'm so fucking proud of you."

I choke out a sob as he takes my hand and pulls me up.

"I couldn't have done any of it without you."

He clasps my chin in his hand. "We make a pretty good team."

"We really do," I say as I break down again. We embrace, clinging to one another as I cry against the curve of his throat. I let the tears begin to heal me. I let them find a place in my heart and allow the first wounds of my spirit to finally start closing over. I have so much trauma to overcome, but now I can finally face it, and I won't do it alone. I will never be alone again.

Finally, we pull apart to find everyone watching us.

"Thank you for your help," I say. "All of you. I don't know how I can ever thank you enough."

Cedar and Elswyth, hand in hand, are the first to approach and bow their heads. "Welcome home, Heart Queen," Cedar says. "I never thought I'd see the day."

That stirs everyone from their shock and the tension around the circle breaks. We all burst into laughter and smiles and hugs. It's a moment for celebration.

We didn't just save the magic.

We didn't just save Heart.

We saved Ouranos from Herric. It was a battle we didn't even know we were fighting until it was almost too late.

Gabriel strides over and wraps an arm around me, tugging me close.

"I'm happy for you, Final Tribute," he says.

I laugh and squeeze him tight.

"You *could* stop calling me that—I am literally a queen now."

"I still don't see a crown on your head," he says with a wry smile.

"Maybe it's time to fix that," Tristan says, opening the pack slung over his shoulder and pulling out a bundle of fabric. He unwraps the Heart Crown and holds it up to me. "I thought you might need this."

"Tris," I say as my throat knots again. After all the years of running towards this, it's nearly impossible to believe we finally found ourselves here.

"You ready for your ascension?" Nadir asks. "That's what all of this was for, right?"

"Should we do something?" Willow asks. "Like have a big ceremony or something?"

She looks around us at the crumbled buildings and the ruined city. The ghosts of what our grandparents left us.

"No," I say. "Let's do this now. We've waited long enough." I look towards the settlements in the distance. "*They've* waited long enough, and I don't need anything fancy. You're all here with me, and that is enough."

I turn to Nadir, pressing his hand to my chest. "I know you're no longer destined to become king of The Aurora, but how does the title of Heart King sound?"

He breaks into a smile that lights up every corner of my spirit. He pulls me in close. "It sounds really fucking perfect."

He leans down to kiss me, and we linger on it, savoring the feel of each other until Mael clears his throat very pointedly, and we pull apart.

"Sorry," I say, feeling my cheeks blush. But there are smiles all around the circle.

"How do I perform the ascension?" I ask.

Anemone steps out of the circle. "Place the Crown on your head, and it will take care of the rest."

"Thank you," I say to her. "For helping us too. I know what I did—"

She cuts me off. "You have freed me from Zerra. I am the one who can never thank you enough." She presses a hand to her chest and dips her head.

Cyan comes up behind Anemone, resting a hand on her lower back. "All is forgiven, Heart Queen."

"Thank you," I whisper.

Linden joins them and hesitates before she bows at the waist. "Thank you," she says curtly, and I can't help but laugh.

"Are you always going to hate me?"

She shrugs. "We'll see."

I'll take it.

Then I turn to my siblings.

"I guess it's time."

"Wait," Willow says. "Tristan and I got you something. Maybe it was silly, but we couldn't help ourselves."

Tristan reaches into his bag and pulls out a small box wrapped in shiny red paper and tied with a gold silk ribbon.

"What's this?" I ask, holding out my hand for it.

"Open it," Willow says, her eyes sparkling. My siblings exchange an amused look, and I narrow my eyes.

Nadir peers over my shoulder as I tug on the ribbon and then lift the lid. When I see what's inside, I burst out laughing.

"What is it?" Elswyth asks as I pull out the smooth bar of soap. She looks around the circle. "Soap? I don't understand."

"I'll tell you the story someday," I promise, and then I bring it to my nose, inhaling its soft floral scent.

"It's perfect," I say to my brother and sister. "Thank you."

"Make sure you keep it somewhere safe," Tristan says with a wink. "Wouldn't want anyone to steal it."

I laugh again and then look at my brother and sister.

"Should we do this?" I ask. Tristan takes my gift and exchanges it for the Crown.

"Willow, Tris," I say, placing it on my head and then holding out my hands. They each take one as Nadir stands before me, wrapping his hand around the nape of my neck, his forehead tipping against mine.

"Ready?" I ask him, and he nods.

I close my eyes, and something tugs in my chest as I spiral into nothingness before I feel solid ground at my feet. When I open my eyes, I'm standing in the same rose garden, the white stone path bordered by benches and hundreds of rose bushes. The air is warm and still, the sun a softly glowing orb.

This time Willow, Tristan, and Nadir are all here too. We all share confused looks as we scan our surroundings.

"Where are we?" Tris asks.

"This is where the Crown took me last time," I answer as I turn around and notice a figure standing at the end of the path.

"Mother," I breathe, sensing Willow and Tristan go still.

A moment later, another person steps out of the shadows, and our father, wearing a simple brown tunic and pants, loops his arm through our mother's. He looks exactly as I remember, with that rich chestnut hair curling over his shoulders. His emerald eyes sparkle above a thick beard that always tickled my cheeks whenever he'd give me a kiss. My heart ricochets in my chest as he smiles, and I hear Tristan and Willow's soft gasps.

Our mother holds out her free arm.

"Children," she says, tears filling her eyes.

"Mother." Tristan stumbles towards her, tears already streaming down his face. He throws himself against her before Willow does the same to our father. I watch as they all hug while I hold Nadir's hand. He squeezes it, and I look at him, my bottom lip quivering.

When Tristan and Willow move away, my parents turn to me. I release Nadir's hand and run to them, throwing an arm around their necks. They cling to me as we all shake.

"You did it," Mother says. "I knew you could."

"Why are you here?" I ask. "I thought you said only you and I could see each other."

"The Artefacts pulled some strings on our behalf," Father says.

"I've missed you so much," I say to him, and he smiles, his green eyes crinkling at the corners in a way that makes my chest hurt.

"I miss you too," he says. "Every day."

"I wish—"

"I know," he says. "I know."

We hug again and then I say, "I want you to meet someone."

I gesture to Nadir, and he approaches. I don't think I've ever seen him look this unsure of himself, and it almost makes me laugh.

"This is Nadir," I say. "My mate. My bonded partner and now the king of Heart." I take his hand and look up into his eyes. "The man who helped . . . make me."

Nadir smiles and holds out his free hand, but my parents will have none of that. They ignore it and wrap him in a long, tight hug from each side. His arms hang at his sides, and it's clear he doesn't quite know what to do with himself. My siblings and I burst out laughing. Finally, he figures it out and hugs them back.

After they finish, Nadir steps back and glances at me.

"I assure you that your daughter was the one who made herself. I just stood behind her."

"Thank you," my mother says, clutching her hands together. "Please take care of her."

He bends at the waist and presses his hand to his heart. "With my life."

We all hug and chatter a bit longer, describing everything that happened in the Underworld and in the Evanescence. Tristan and Willow tell them everything they can about their lives. Willow gushes about Amya, and Tristan shares his fears and hopes about being the Primary of The Woodlands.

Soon, the mood turns somber again.

"This is it, isn't it?" I ask. "This is all the time we have?"

"I'm afraid so," Mother says with her arm wrapped around Willow's shoulders. "But we'll keep an eye on you whenever we can."

"At least we had this," Willow says, brushing the tears from her cheeks. "I never ever thought we'd see you again."

We all stare at one another as I feel my heart breaking all over again. But I remind myself of all the things I've gained.

"What happens now? Is this the ascension?" I ask.

"It is," Mother says. "At least in your case. When you leave here, you will officially be the Heart Queen."

My parents both drop to their knees and bow their heads. My endless flow of tears won't stop as they look back up.

"This is all we ever wanted for the three of you. Take care of each other," Father says. "You will be a wonderful queen, Lor. I always knew you would be."

"Be happy, my children," Mother adds. "Never forget how much you were loved."

Then she presses her fingers to her mouth and blows us a kiss. Nadir, Willow, and Tristan, along with my parents, all melt away.

I spin around, wondering what I'm still doing here, to find Tyr standing at the end of the path. It feels like we just left him, but he looks entirely different. His golden hair shines in the sun, and color glows in his bronzed cheeks. He fills out a white tunic and pants, and his shoulders are relaxed. I imagine this is what he must have looked like before Atlas ruined his life.

"Tyr," I whisper as he smiles and then holds two fingers to his lips before dropping his chin.

"My first duty as the god of Ouranos is to see you crowned, Lor."

I nod and smile. "Thank you again. For everything."

He bends at the waist in a deep bow before he straightens. "Farewell, Heart Queen."

His words echo as the scene melts away, and I once again find myself standing amongst the ruins of Heart, surrounded by everyone I love.

"Did it work—" I start to ask, then my eyes widen.

The roses are blooming again, only they're everywhere now. Spreading over the entire city. The walls. The ground. Climbing over the rubble and what's left of the castle.

"I think it worked," Nadir says.

They continue climbing over everything, surrounding me, Nadir, and my siblings in a wreath of flowers, welcoming us home.

My gaze turns to the settlements in the distance. A thin plume of smoke curls in the air like a signal, reminding me of what all of this was really for.

"We should go tell them," I say. Not waiting for anyone to reply, I start running as vines of roses chase my heels. I hear everyone following as we pass the city walls.

My feet have wings as I fly over the ruined landscape until I come to a halt.

Nadir stops behind me, his hand finding my lower back. Everyone else falls into a line as we watch a mass of people approach.

The roses follow us. They spread out, climbing across the landscape, coating everything in a carpet of red and green. It's the most beautiful sight.

We wait as the crowd draws closer. Those at the front note the crown on my head, and they all start dropping to their knees.

"The magic!" someone cries. "It's back!"

"The queen! She lives!"

"We are saved!

"We can return home!"

Etienne and Rhiannon emerge out of the crowd with their hands linked.

They stop in front of me and also fall to their knees.

"Long live our queen," Rhiannon says before everyone else picks up the chant, repeating it over and over.

And if all of this weren't enough, the sky starts to fill with lightning bugs. They flit around us, tiny balls of glowing light dancing in the sky. I share a smile with Nadir, who stands to my left, and then one with Willow and Tristan, who stand on my other side.

I look at the three most important people in my life.

At the ruined queendom behind us and the devastation of the land that surrounds us.

I inhale the scent of a million roses on a shaky breath.

"So what do we do now?" I ask.

My brother wraps an arm around my shoulders and sweeps an arm out.

"We finally live," he says. "And then we build it all again."

CHAPTER 75

GABRIEL

E revan has finally taken his place as king. Though I understand his reservations, he also understood this was his
duty. If he truly believed in helping the people of Aphelion,
then he would have to take the crown destined for him.

We held the ascension shortly after our return, and it was
a spectacle worthy of the occasion. Everyone in the kingdom
clamored to see their new ruler and fall at his feet. He was
beloved by so many and yet had many bridges to cross.

But it was the celebration the people needed. After all the
lies and deceit, after the loss and heartache, we all needed
something to believe in. Aphelion's new golden Sun King is

just the thing. I know he will succeed where Tyr and Atlas failed. I've always known he would be great, even if he had to be convinced of it.

Today, I stand outside the Priestess of Payne flanked by my brothers Jareth and Rhyle. We wear plain clothing, simple tunics and pants, no longer forced to bear the golden armor that marked us as servants to our kingdom. While the wings will always make us stand out, at least we have this freedom.

Lor told me what happened when she tricked Cloris into revealing her knowledge about the mate bond. She said she left her alive, just barely, but I have it on good authority that Cloris succumbed to her injuries, leaving this plane once and for all.

It's certainly no loss, and I hope she's rotting in the Underworld, where she belongs.

"What are you planning to do with it?" Jareth asks.

"We're tearing it down," I answer. I want no more reminders of the priestess or of the horrors she brought to Aphelion. It was her scheming and lies that nearly duped Atlas into killing Tyr.

The only positive, I suppose, is that she also brought Lor into our lives.

A line of workers approaches the boulevard carrying shovels and pickaxes. Behind them rolls more equipment required for the demolition. Erevan was more than generous in providing whatever I'd need.

"Bring it down!" I yell at them. I've already relocated the staff to new and better establishments, and there's no reason left to keep this place standing. We watch as the workers swarm over the site as the sound of hammers and saws fills the air. I wanted it done quickly and employed everyone I could get my hands on.

"What are you doing next?" I ask my brothers. They both consider the question for a moment.

"I've always wanted to open a bookstore," Jareth says. "One with lots of rare editions and a coffee shop where people can come and read for hours."

I smile, remembering how often I'd find him with his nose buried in a book.

"What about you?" I ask Rhyle.

"I bought a very swish flat in the Twenty Fourth," he answers with a sparkle in his eyes. "I plan to do a lot of 'entertaining' with all that gold the king gave us." He grins, and we all laugh. It's amazing how easy it feels.

"Sounds perfect," I say as we all return to watching the workers for another moment. Then I clap them both on the shoulders.

"I better get back to the palace," I say. "The council meeting is starting soon."

"Are you staying?" Jareth asks. "With Erevan?"

"I don't think so," I say. "I just need to see him settled, and then I'll decide what to do next."

"I understand," he says.

"I'll see you both around."

"You've got an open invite to my flat," Rhyle calls as I start to leave.

I spin around to face him. "I'll remember that."

"What are you going to do with the empty space?" he asks, gesturing to the Priestess of Payne.

I cock my head and look at the building before I bow to them both.

"Build a rose garden."

Then I turn on my heel and walk away.

I arrive back at the palace and make my way to the council chambers, where I find everyone gathered. Erevan stands at the head of the table with his hands behind his back and gives me a quick nod as I enter. His blond hair is tied back, and he wears a simple but well-made brown jacket and breeches. His posture is straight and sure, and he already looks like a king. The Mirror chose well this time. I knew it from the very start.

Though I don't strictly belong here, Erevan asked if I'd support him since I did spend a few weeks acting as Aphelion's ruler. I'm so glad he's finally accepted the role. I would have had to dig myself a grave and hide in it if I'd had to keep it up much longer.

As everyone settles in, Erevan clears his throat and launches into the speech he prepared. He implores them to return the rights of the low fae, and he speaks with such passion and such determination that I watch as the council members' eyes clear and their expressions open. He literally changes their minds on the spot. Erevan might have thought he'd have little power as Aphelion's king, but I think what it gave him was the confidence to approach his changes in a way that would work with the council and not against them.

When he's done, he's breathing heavily, but I don't know how anyone could look at him and not believe he was always the best person for this role. If they continue to harbor any animosity towards him and his actions to help the low fae, then they're all fools.

"Time for the vote?" he asks tentatively.

Several looks are shared around the table as his gaze flicks to me.

I wait with my breath held as the first hand rises in agreement. It belongs to none other than General Cornelius Heulfryn, head of the Twenty-Fourth District. He informed me that after he insisted his daughter start volunteering in the hopes of turning her into a better person, she found her passion for helping the needy children of The Umbra. Apparently, she's working on a proposal for Erevan to build a new school and orphanage. I have no doubt he'll approve it as soon as it crosses his desk.

Erevan and Cornelius exchange a look, and it's then I know Erevan will do just fine.

I watch as more hands lift around the circle.

Erevan needs eighteen votes to amend the laws.

In the end, all twenty-four hands rise and stay there.

Erevan looks at me, and we both breathe a sigh of relief. What a road we traveled to get here.

The next day, we gather outside the palace where I first exposed Atlas and his lies. I recall the faces of everyone around us and the way Tyr looked when everyone turned his way, realizing the truth. I rub my chest, feeling that ache that bound me to my king and nearly killed me.

I stand next to Erevan on a raised platform as he holds up a paper reading out the rules that will govern a new and better

Aphelion than the one we knew. After the vote to free the low fae, he took the opportunity to make a few more changes.

Low fae will be free to live like all citizens. Free to use their magic. To live in any district and pursue any passion they desire. Or if they prefer, to return to the forests and lakes and mountains from which they came. Everyone will be referred to as simply Fae from now on. No more class distinctions. He's hoping it will catch on across the continent, and I have faith it won't take long.

He appoints ten new warders. A mix of Fae of all types, each of them free to make this choice and leave their positions should they ever desire. They won't have the wings or the tattoo, but when I look at them all standing proudly in their golden armor, I don't think they mind. In fact, I'd argue it's a vast improvement.

They are a reminder of what we all let ourselves normalize for far too long.

And finally, Erevan abolishes the Sun Queen Trials, denouncing them as inhumane and barbaric. He promises to honor every person who lost their life competing for a crown.

After Erevan shares the news to a roar of cheers, it's time for the unveiling of a new addition to the courtyard. He sweeps an arm out to a chorus of 'oohs' and 'aahs.'

A giant structure covered in shimmering cloth stands in the center, and at Erevan's gesture, it's hauled off, revealing a gold statue of Tyr, our god. He stands proudly with his chin up and his gaze to the sky. He looks like the man I remember.

The man who gave up this life to give Lor hers.

The man who gave up this life, hoping to find purpose in another.

I've gone to visit Tyr once already, and finally, I think he's content.

Two months later, I'm standing on a balcony overlooking the sea as I inhale a deep breath, contemplating my next move. I've been helping Erevan establish his rule, and now that he's comfortable, I think I'm ready for a break. I'm ready for some distance from this place and a chance to just exist. I don't want any responsibilities or weight on my shoulders. I want to just breathe.

Aphelion is better than ever. We cleaned up the effects of the quake and other disasters and word is everything is back to normal across Ouranos. Fae of every kind are thriving, and the populace is finally at peace.

We tore down the tower where Tyr spent so many years. In fact, we closed off the entire wing of the palace. Maybe someday it will become something useful again, but for now, I think we're all content to forget its existence.

The new garden in the Sixteenth District is blooming, perfuming the air with hundreds of roses. People come in droves to visit, especially at night, thanks to the inexplicable presence of thousands of lightning bugs that flit between the petals.

Lor's friends and former Tributes, Halo and Marici, have taken on the task of caring for it. Though I said I'd hire someone, they categorically refused and can be found there lovingly tending the gardens almost every day.

Lor promises to come and see it when she arrives for their bonding ceremony in a few weeks.

I'm leaning on my elbows when a sound draws my attention to where Hylene watches me. She's been living with

Nerissa in the Eighth District, helping where she can. We haven't had much time to spend together as I've been so busy with Erevan. But I dream of her. I think about her all the time.

She's as breathtaking as always, wearing a simple yellow gown that sets off her fiery hair.

"Hi," she says, tipping her head with a soft smile.

"Hey," I say, turning around to face her.

"What are you doing?"

I shrug. "Just wondering what I do next."

"Any ideas?"

She stops in front of me and peers up.

"I was thinking I'd find a quiet place to live for a while. Cedar offered me a cabin in his forest right on the shore so I don't have to miss the sound of the ocean."

"That sounds perfect," she says.

"Almost," I agree, and she blinks in question.

"It might be nice to have some company."

"Oh?" She moves closer until she's nearly pressed against me, and I lift a hand to her face, trailing my fingers along her jawbone. I tip her face up, and I stare at her, taking in the soft slope of her nose and the freckles dusting the bridge. Her bright green eyes spark, and I note the gold ring surrounding her pupils.

"Care to join me?" I ask.

She smiles. "I wouldn't be interrupting your quiet brooding?"

I tip my head back and laugh. "I think it could use a few interruptions."

She stretches up onto her tiptoes and kisses me. "Well then . . . that sounds like something I could do."

I smile at her, and then I, too, am finally content.

CHAPTER 76

NADIR

THE AURORA

I stand outside the gates of Nostraza, staring up at the forbidding entrance that was the beginning of the end for so many people. I regret everything about this place. Even if Lor hadn't found her way into my life, I'd still regret everything. I'm just grateful she helped open my eyes before any more found their way into the jaws of this beast.

"Nadir," Amya says, and my attention moves to her. She gestures me to the opening, where Mael, Willow, and Tristan wait with her. "Come on."

I inhale a deep breath and enter, thinking about the last time I was here when I'd been sent to investigate Lor's disappearance. I remember dropping into that hole where they'd left her and picking up her scent. I hadn't met her yet, but she was already a memory I couldn't touch. Though I can't say why, I think I knew even then that everything was about to change. I had no idea just how much.

Willow and Amya clasp hands and walk ahead of us. The rest of us follow behind as our footsteps echo in the hollow silence.

When we returned to The Aurora, we announced my father's death. The reaction was mixed, but he didn't have many friends, and it felt more like a sigh of relief than one of mourning. I went straight to my mother's wing in the Keep, and as I expected, she was gone. Only a memory left. I stood in the silence of her room, staring out across the view that was her only companion for so many years. With my forehead pressed to the cool glass, I allowed myself a moment to grieve. To remember that final conversation we had when she found the strength to talk to us for the last time.

Our relationship was far from ideal, but I refuse to blame her for any of it. I'm now an ascended king and one day, I will see her again. Anemone suspects that because my father was lost to the Underworld, there's a good chance he did not make it to the Evanescence, and I like the idea of her being free of him forever.

That moment when he helped us might have been his lowest point. Something drove him to dig into the recesses of his compassion, and I'll have to live with never knowing what. But despite that, he never deserved the Evanescence. He never deserved any of us.

I stop in the middle of the large foyer where prisoners were admitted into Nostraza's walls. I see the hall where I was taken to search the records for prisoner 3342. My gaze meets my sister's, and we hold it before we look away.

Also on our return, Amya ascended, and I couldn't have been prouder as I watched her hold the Torch while it welcomed her as the new queen. Wearing a long black dress, the skirt slashed with bright colors to mimic the streaks in her hair, she looked exactly the part.

After it was official, Amya's first order of business was to close down Nostraza. The cells were cleared out of every inmate, and they were moved to housing in the districts where they're being set up with programs to help them rehabilitate and start new lives. Never again will we abandon our people when they need us.

Each of the guards that worked here has been sequestered and will be tried for their actions. Those found guilty of inhumane conduct will be executed without mercy. I'll never forgive myself for what they did to Lor, her siblings, or anyone else they hurt. I think of the warden who showed me the prison records and the way I took his life. I refuse to feel bad about that either.

We continue walking, surrounded by dark stone, the drip of water echoing in the distance. I remember the screams and the torment that used to fill these halls.

Lor had planned to be here too before we tore it down but claimed her duties in Heart were keeping her there for an extra few days. Thanks to a generous infusion of gold from The Aurora, as well as the other realms, we've been hard at work putting the pieces of our queendom back together.

Even though she didn't come out and say it, I think she didn't really want to see it again.

She's told me enough times that she *never* wants to see this place again.

"You okay?" Amya gently asks Willow, who looks around the empty space.

"I . . . think so," she answers, and Amya draws her closer as Willow's head rests on her shoulder.

After discovering she has a powerful vein of healing magic, Willow has also been charting her own path, setting up sites inside Heart and throughout the rest of Ouranos where anyone can come for healing whenever they need. Her goal is to make sure every person on the continent can access help. She's also very close to discovering a cure for the Withering.

Tristan and I share a look. After the events with Herric and the Empyrium, he forgave me for everything that happened. I've gained a second brother alongside Mael, and I couldn't be happier about it.

"I wondered how I'd feel seeing it again," Tristan says as Amya and Willow look back at him. He stares around us, his expression contemplative.

"And?" Willow asks.

He pulls his gaze away from the high stone ceiling.

"I feel strangely at peace," he says. "The man responsible is gone. We saw our parents one more time, and I forgave them for everything. Plus, all of us are destined for so much more. I never thought we were ever getting out of here."

Willow nods. "I feel the same."

"This place will no longer define who we are, and I think we can leave it behind once and for all."

"I wish Lor were here," Willow says. "But I understand why

she isn't. I know we all lived in misery, but I think it nearly broke her the most."

She looks at me, and I nod in understanding. Lor is a force that was never meant to be contained.

"Then let's leave it behind," Amya says. "They'll start the demolition immediately, and we'll allow the forest to reclaim this land."

Over the past few months, Amya has made other changes, including closing down the Savahell Mine. She freed every low fae from conscription with outrageous amounts of gold in compensation. She also ordered new protections for every worker, including restrictions on hours, proper healthcare, and increased pay. The Aurora will continue to rely on its remaining mines for trade, but our security will not come at the cost of blood.

The virulence caves are currently being sealed up and hopefully forgotten forever. Beyond the trouble it caused, we also need to protect Tyr from its effects. We owe him so much.

We also cleared out the forest of my father's unnatural creations. It didn't take long to realize these creatures could still remember who they had been, all of them living in misery in their mutilated bodies. Though we tried, we couldn't turn them back, and in the end, their deaths were the only mercy we could offer.

"Then let's go," Amya says.

My sister, the queen, who should have been the one from the very start.

We all walk out of Nostraza for the last time, vowing never to make the same mistakes again.

*   *   *

Two days later, we sit at a pub in the Violet District. It's the same one where we all gathered when Lor and I were trying to find the Heart Crown. Tristan is telling us a story about the Heart siblings' childhood when someone covers my eyes with their hands.

"Lor," I say, immediately recognizing her scent, my magic reacting to her presence. She loops her arms around my neck and kisses me on the cheek. "Miss me?"

"Every moment," I say, looking up at her, and she smiles. Gods, she takes my breath away every fucking time. Sometimes I lay awake at night thinking of how close I came to losing her. But then I open my eyes and reach for her, feeling her soft skin and hearing her soft breaths, reminding myself that she's mine forever.

Etienne and Rhiannon are with her, having all just arrived from Heart. They settle around the table, and we chat for hours, toasting every single thing we can think of until we're finally kicked out.

We trek back to the Keep with the lights dancing overhead and Lor's arm looped through mine. We pass the square where we danced that night during Frostfire, and we both stop, staring at the space still bustling with people out for an evening of drinks and dancing.

"I think that was the moment everything changed for me," she says. "When I realized you weren't the villain." I look down at her and smile. "Even if it took me a little while to accept that."

I lean over and kiss her on the cheek before we follow the others.

Once we arrive back at the Keep, we all say goodbye to Tristan, who's leaving tomorrow for The Woodlands to get to know Cedar and Elswyth and to prepare for his inevitable future.

Rhiannon and Etienne are staying for a few days before returning to Heart to help continue with the rebuilding. They've been invaluable assets to Lor and me, and we've been dreaming up ways to thank them.

We also say goodnight to Mael, who's taking some time off to be with his family.

Willow and Amya bid us all farewell, and I watch them disappear around the corner. Amya has been hinting at a bonding, and I'm sure it's only a matter of time.

When they're all gone, Lor and I stand together in the hall of the Keep.

"I have a surprise for you," I say, and she breaks into a smile.

"What is it?"

"We'll have to fly there."

"I'm ready whenever you are." Her expression is open and full of trust. I worked so hard to earn it, and I'll never take it for granted.

We head back outside, and then I fly us across the frozen tundra. She wraps her arms around my neck and buries her face against me.

I had the cabin where she prepared for our bonding ceremony cleaned up and renovated so we have somewhere to stay when we visit The Aurora. We still have the manor house, but this place will be only for the two of us.

We land gently in the snow, and her eyes widen in delight.

"What did you do?" she asks as I take her hand and lead her inside.

She looks around the space, and I have to admit, I'm pretty impressed with myself. It's small, just one room with a kitchen and bathroom, but three whole sides are floor-to-ceiling windows, offering a view of snow-capped mountains and the wide Aurora sky. Tonight the lights ripple with their full brightness, dancing overhead.

Most of the room is taken up by a massive bed covered in crisp white sheets and a mountain of furs. My plan for the next several days is for us to never leave it unless absolutely necessary.

Lor expels a soft breath and walks over to the window, laying her hand against it. I watch her stare up at the sky, the lights gilding her nose and mouth in a rainbow of color. I hang my coat on a hook and lean against the wall with my hands in my pockets, just enjoying the sight of her. My mate. My heart. The woman I went to hell and back for.

"What are you doing over there?" she asks, looking over at me with an eyebrow raised.

Walking over, I circle my arms around her waist, resting my chin on her shoulder as we stare out the window. Staring at the vast mountains and the endless stretch of snow, it's easy to feel like a tiny speck in an infinite cosmos, but with Lor, I never feel that way.

After a moment, she turns around and kisses me. "So, is our plan to never leave that bed?" she asks, and I grin.

"Well, we *do* have to get started on making that heir."

She laughs, and then we kiss again. My hands slide into her hair, and I devour her mouth, our tongues slicking together. The kiss is slow and decadent, a luxury to be cherished now that we finally have the time.

Slowly, I undo the button on her black wool coat, and it falls to the floor with a thump. Her hands slide under my shirt, her fingers tracing over the lines of my chest and stomach. She tugs at the hem and pulls it over my head before she stands back to admire me, her gaze traveling over me in a way that makes my dick stir.

She bites her lip and then carefully undresses, peeling off her clinging black sweater and leather pants, leaving her in a pair of lacy red underwear that makes my heart stop for five entire seconds.

Her breasts swell above the fabric, her dark nipples visible through the lace. She slides a hand down the smooth plane of her stomach, stopping just short of the apex of her thighs. Gods, I can't wait to get my tongue inside her.

"Fuck," I growl as she prowls over and presses me against the wall.

"Turn around," she orders, and I do as she says as she flattens herself against me, the feel of her breasts and her soft curves making me shiver with want. I grip the wall as she stretches onto her tiptoes and pushes my hair to the side before licking the back of my neck. My entire body exhales at the contact of her warm, wet mouth.

She gently bites my shoulder as her hands explore my torso and slide lower, palming my already hard cock through my pants.

"Hold still, Heart King," she whispers in my ear before she nips my earlobe with her teeth. "I'm going to ruin you."

CHAPTER 77

LOR

I press myself against Nadir, savoring every inch of him. He's warm and solid, my rock and my home. He sighs as my hand slips below his waistband, where I find him hard and ready.

"Ruin me?" he asks, as I wrap my hand around him and stroke his cock, pulling out a ragged moan, his hips thrusting into my hand.

"Isn't that what you said to me that night in The Woodlands?"

He gasps as I stroke him firmly again. "Fuck," he hisses, his forehead dropping against the wall. "I did."

"You did ruin me," I whisper before blowing over the back of his neck. "In all the best possible ways."

He chuckles just before he moans again. "It was my pleasure."

I laugh and then kiss his neck again before I back away and take his hand, leading him towards the bed.

"Now it's my turn. Lie down."

He arches an eyebrow. "For what?"

"It's payback time."

His face breaks into a grin, and he crawls onto the bed before flipping over. Tucking his hands behind his head, he spreads out his legs and lies back with a cocky smile and a brow arched in challenge.

"Hold out your arms," I say, and he spreads his hands wide.

"Show me what you've got," he taunts. "Ruin me, Heart Queen."

"You're going to be so sorry," I reply as I send out a sparkling line of crimson lightning. I circle it around one wrist and then the other before I pull his arms over his head and secure them to the headboard.

He looks up and then back at me, still sporting a huge grin, and then lets out a breathless laugh.

"Oh, I sincerely doubt that."

I climb onto the bed and unbutton his pants before tugging them over his hips. His erect cock springs up, and I lick my lips before I peer up at him.

"I like this," I say. "Having you helpless and naked under me."

"Can't say I mind it either," he answers as I slip my bra strap down on one side and then the other. He watches me with a hungry look as I unhook it and then toss it away. Backing off the bed, I stand up and slowly peel off my underwear as his eyes never leave me.

"Lor," he growls.

When I'm naked, I crawl over him and lean down to kiss him, driving my tongue into his mouth. He sucks on it, bucking against his restraints as I press my body to his, relishing the feel of his warmth and the hard lines of his chest and thighs.

Pulling up, I tap my bottom lip. "What *shall* I do with you like this?"

He tugs on the restraints, sitting up as much as he can.

"Sit on my face, Lor," he growls. "Smother me with your pussy."

My mouth opens with a gasp of surprise, liquid heat pooling in my stomach. I was supposed to be the one in control here, but I like the sound of that.

I drag my hand down his chest and then I move up, positioning my knees on either side of his head. With one hand on the headboard, I look down and he stretches up, but I hover just out of reach.

"Lor," he snarls. "Stop fucking with me."

I gasp and then lower myself with a whimper as his tongue sweeps out to lap my center. "Oh gods," I whisper as my head tips back, and I grind myself against him. He feasts on me as I grip his hair with my other hand. My hips writhe back and forth as I seek friction while he sucks and nips. It doesn't take long before I feel my release curling deep in my stomach.

"Give me my hands," he begs, coming up for air. I release my magic with a snap before he wraps his arms around my thighs and then *devours* me.

We spend the next few hours exploring one another under the light of the stars and the aurora lights, finding each other over and over.

But he could never truly ruin me.

I think back to that night in the Aurora throne room when the Torch said we were destined for heartbreak and ruin.

At one point, I believed it. At one point, I vowed never to let him have my heart. But it's his now, every last piece of it.

And he was never my ruin.

He was always my salvation.

Our footsteps crunch over the snow, the night so still and quiet, I can hear my heartbeat. Nadir squeezes my hand as we crest a ridge that offers us a view of The Aurora's snowy peaks stretching out for miles.

A soft breeze tugs at our hair, but our Aurora magic keeps us warm. We've spent the last three days doing nothing but lying in bed and enjoying each other, just like I dreamed during that night in the cave in Herric's arena. It's been even more perfect than I imagined.

But it's a clear night, and Nadir decided we needed to get some air.

I stare up into the sky at the aurora lights rippling overhead. They seem even more brilliant than usual, their colors so vibrant it's hard to believe they're real. I remember those nights I sat in the Hollow when this sight was the only thing keeping me together.

How far we've all come since.

I look at Nadir and smile, the edges soft.

He takes my breath away every single time.

"This was a good suggestion," I admit.

"I'm full of them," he replies with a smirk.

We continue walking a bit further until we ascend to another high ridge. The snow sparkles like a million diamonds, and the breeze tugs at the strands of my hair. I inhale a deep breath, filling my lungs with the crisp scent of this place that is now one half of my home. I stare up at the stars, thinking of Tyr watching over us, so grateful he gave me this life.

Nadir wraps his arms around me, and we stand together, two people who almost lost everything and then found the world.

"I love you, Lor," he says, and I nod as my throat swells with the threat of tears. It feels like they're always at the surface lately. I used to hide them and stuff them away. I spent so many years pretending they didn't exist, knowing they would only be used to hurt me, but now I understand how much they've helped me heal.

These are tears of joy, not sorrow. These are tears that prove how strong I had to be.

These tears remind me that I finally learned how to trust. The lies and the secrets are no more. Finally, I can be everything I've wanted without the burdens of my past defining me.

And now I am free.

"Every time I think of how close we came to losing everything . . ." I say, looking up, and he nods.

"I know. But we're here. And we're together."

"Forever," I add.

He captures my chin in his fingers. "If I have to follow you into the very depths of the Underworld."

I laugh. "Let's hope we never have to do that again."

We both turn to look at the sky and watch the lights. My eyes flutter closed as peace spreads over me, slipping between my ribs and settling into my heart with a steady, constant beat that will carry me anywhere.

"Do you remember that night in the Aurora Keep when we went on the balcony? It was a night just like this," he says as I open my eyes to peer at him. "You rocked my entire fucking world that night."

"You did a number on mine, too," I say with a laugh. He draws me close and kisses my temple. Then I look up and pull his head towards mine, staring into the endless depths of his eyes.

"I remember," I whisper softly against his lips.

"I remember everything."

Want to relive Lor and Nadir's reunion? Sign up for my newsletter at nishajtuli.com and gain access to exclusive art featuring this emotional scene!

Acknowledgments

Why is this the hardest part? They say it takes a village and there are few places where that's more true than when it's time to publish a book.

A big thank-you to Madeleine Colavita, my editor at Forever. I think this almost killed us both, but we did it. Somehow, we did. I can't wait to continue this journey and dive into what comes next. I'm not sure how you aren't sick of me yet.

To my agent, Lauren Spieller, you are truly the best. Thank you for supporting me. For seeing the big picture. For understanding all of my goals and dreams. It was SO fun finally meeting you in person in DC, and I felt like I could have talked to you for four more hours and still not run out of things to say.

Thank you to Estelle Hallick and Dana Cuadrado, my publicists at Forever. Your kindness and enthusiasm don't go unnoticed, and I can't believe all the exciting things I get to do this year thanks to you.

To Nadia Saward, my UK editor at Orbit, thank you for being so lovely and supportive. I'm so excited to see your own debut out in the world! It was amazing. People are going to love it.

A massive shout-out to Soneela Nankani, Corvin King, and Shane East for bringing Lor, Nadir, and Gabriel to life on the audiobooks. You all were absolute perfection in these roles. You were exactly as I pictured them.

Also, thank you to Miblart for all these fantastic covers. When I first commissioned them, I truly didn't think they'd end up in bookstores all over the world. The fact that everyone has kept them for each edition is a testament to your fantastic work.

A thank-you to the whole teams at Forever and Folio Lit, especially the foreign rights team, for all your expertise and guidance.

And of course, to my readers—none of this would be possible without you. I'm so glad that Lor and Nadir and the others have found a place in your hearts.

To those who've become friends and those who scream about my books constantly, I can't thank you enough. It was so exciting to be able to meet so many of you at Apollycon this year too. You know how to make an author feel loved. A massive thank-you to Shaylin Gandhi for coming as my assistant, as well. I would have not survived without you. (I also can't wait for your debut to come out soon too!)

And finally, to my husband Matt, who didn't even blink when I asked him to take over literally everything in our household—meals, kids, bedtimes, etc.—when I had to do major edits on a time crunch. You are the real book boyfriend.

Also by Nisha J. Tuli

Artefacts of Ouranos
Trial of the Sun Queen
Rule of the Aurora King
Fate of the Sun King

Night Fire Quartet
Heart of Night and Fire
Dance of Stars and Ashes
Storm of Ink and Blood

Cursed Captors
Wicked Is the Reaper
Feral Is the Beast

About the Author

Nisha is a Canadian fantasy romance author whose books feature kick-ass heroines, swoony love interests, and slow burns with plenty of heat. When she's not writing or reading, Nisha can be found enjoying travel, food, and camping with her partner, two kids, and their fluffy Samoyed.

Follow Along for More

Website and newsletter: https://nishajtuli.com